Chilling Characters in a Terrifying
Setting—You won't want to put it down
- Book Review

SEEKERS AND DECEIVERS

Which One Are You? It Is Time to Join the Fight!

Kevin Hoyer

SEEKERS AND DECEIVERS

Which One are You? It Is Time to Join the Fight!

Kevin Hoyer

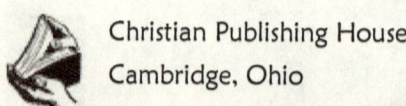

Christian Publishing House
Cambridge, Ohio

Christian Publishing House
Professional Conservative Christian
Publishing of the Good News!

Unless otherwise indicated, Scripture quotations are from the Updated American Standard Version of the Holy Scriptures, 2016 edition (UASV).

SEEKERS AND DECEIVERS: Which One are You? It Is Time to Join the Fight!

Authored by Kevin Hoyer

ISBN-13: **978-1-945757-24-2**

ISBN-10: **1-945757-24-8**

Table of Contents

PART ONE

CHAPTER 1

Startled, Ezra gasped for air suddenly awake. His eyes adjusted as he wiped the sweat from his face. He sensed someone there and quickly glanced around the room. His hands were shaking. He desperately clenched them into fists, slowly sat up.

It was that same dream again. Was it a dream? It seemed so real! Something had brushed against him, and a chill consumed his body. It whispered, "You must find the *Book of Prophesies*. It will show you the Light of the Word."

"Who's there?" His voice was harsh in the silent room. He scanned the darkest corners of his room and listened for someone lurking. Nothing. Ezra saw no one and pushed aside his covers. He quietly slid out of bed.

The room was pitch black and cold. All he could hear was the howling of the wind, and the creaking of the damp, wooden floor. Sliding his feet across the cold wooden floor, he crept toward the dresser next to the open closet. It was too dark to see into it.

What if someone is there, ready to grab me? He groped for the dresser that had the oil lamp he needed, but the closet was between him and the dresser.

Warily, Ezra approached the open closet ready to fight off the attacker. His heart pounded. He quickly moved past the closet to the dresser. No one attacked. Feeling the dresser top, he found the oil lamp and matches.

Soon, the lamp's glow illuminated all the dark corners in the room especially the closet. No one was there. He knew no one opened the bedroom door because it always stuck and that rattling noise would wake the dead. No, the door would have wakened him instead of the whisper.

What could have brushed against me, thought Ezra, *and where did the whispering sound come from?*' It must have been a dream, but it seemed so real. He convinced himself it was only a dream and went back to bed. Leaving the light on, he eventually fell back to sleep.

The whisper came again, more urgent and strident. "You must find the *Book of Prophesies*. It will show you the Light of the Word," the words sent chills over him.

Ezra was wide-awake now. The words still lingered like cold fingers running down his spine. He sensed there was something beyond this world in the room. The lamp's flame, still flickering, cast ghostly shadows on the wall. Heart pounding, Ezra searched the room. He found nothing.

"You must find the *Book of Prophesies*. It will show you the Light of the Word?" He repeated the words softly. Ezra wondered, *But what did it mean?*

His heart stirred. There was no going back to sleep. He felt the whisper compelling him to find the *Book of Prophesies*. Instinctively, he knew something was present in the room, but not physically. The words kept echoing in his mind.

Ezra decided to watch and wait until morning. Then he would ask his father or grandfather what it meant. Maybe they would know where to find this book.

CHAPTER 2

The valley of Thanoton was always overcast, foggy, and most days had a light mist. It was never sunny or clear enough to see the sky. The valley held a thick, wet fog during the day, the night was black as pitch. There hadn't been sunshine for a thousand years in Thanoton. When the valley was a beautiful, sunny place, the people loved living there. Everyone was happy. They all lived their lives ruled by the Light of the Word found in the *Book of Prophesies*.

Darkness pervaded the valley now. An element of people in the valley did not want to be ruled by the Light of the Word. Over time, this rebellious group convinced others to reject it. As they refused the Light, the valley grew dim. The fog rolled in. The people pulled the cloak of darkness over their evil doings. They did not embrace the Light of the Word because it exposed their wickedness. They rejected it, and ruled themselves. The valley of Thanoton soon resembled the peoples' hearts. The clear sky was gone, overcast with a thick fog by day and pitch black at night. One could not see for great distances because of the fog. At night, with a good torch, you might see twenty feet. The evil lovers killed those few who embraced the Light of the Word and hated the darkness. All who tried to pursue, talk, or teach others about the Light were arrested and sentenced to death by stoning. Their dead bodies left on the pole erected in the center of town for all to see as an example and warning. It had been centuries now since the pole was used. All the Children of the Light were dead or in hiding, or so believed the Children of Darkness.

Descendants of the Children of Light lived among the Children of Darkness in secret, not mentioning the Light for fear of death. Generations passed, father left son ignorant of the Light of the Word. No one ever mentioned or dared even to talk about the Light, until now.

CHAPTER 3

"Father, what does the Light of the Word mean?" Ezra asked.

"Who told you that? Where did you learn about the Light of the Word?" demanded Asa, his father, his face red with anger. "Don't ever mention that again!"

"What did I say that made you so upset?" Confused, Ezra watched his father head toward the kitchen.

Asa whipped around. "You must never talk about the Light!"

"But Father," Ezra followed him, "In a dream, something brushed against me and whispered."

"Whispered, whispered," Asa waved a dismissive hand. He grabbed the teapot off the wood stove and poured a cup of black tea then turned toward Ezra. "You must never talk about this—or mention it again!"

"Father, the whisperer told me I must find the *Book of Prophesies*. It will show me the Light of the Word."

Asa slammed the tin cup down on the thick, wooden kitchen table, and tea splashed everywhere. Oblivious, he grabbed Ezra by the shoulders. "You must stop, or you will get us all killed! For the sake of your grandfather and me, you must stop. Now go open up the blacksmith shop! I don't want to hear another word of this foolishness." He sighed and watched Ezra run out the kitchen door toward the blacksmith shop.

"Asa, what's wrong?" asked Labin, Ezra's grandfather, coming into the kitchen.

"Nothing. Nothing that concerns you," Asa said. He finished cleaning the mess he made then used a rag to grab the hot teapot from the wood burning stove to refill his cup. "Would you like some tea?"

"Please," Labin said, choosing a cup from one of the shelves lining the kitchen. He held it steady as Asa poured. "Let's sit in the living room, and drink our tea by the fireplace. The temperature is quite cool this morning."

"Good idea," Asa answered. He followed Labin out of the kitchen to the fireplace. "Work can wait." Asa sat by the fireplace stroking his thick black beard like he always did when he was in deep thought. He had a scared look on his face.

"Asa, are you all right?" Labin questioned. He was bothered by the fact he didn't know what was going on.

"This is between Ezra and me," Asa said. "It does not concern you."

"You are my son and Ezra is my grandson. Of course, it concerns me. What were you both discussing?"

"Ezra had a dream last night is all," said Asa trying to downplay the situation.

"Tell me! Tell me! What kind of dream?" Labin insisted. He walked up behind Asa and set his hand on his shoulder. "If it was just any old dream you wouldn't be so upset."

"He said something brushed against him and whispered, 'You must find the *Book of Prophesies*. It will show you the Light of the Word.'"

When Labin heard this, his countenance changed. Bewildered, he sank down on the leather couch with a log frame. Both men mused quietly for a few minutes, watching and listening to the fire crackle.

Suddenly Labin said, "Impossible! How would Ezra know about the *Book of Prophesies* or the Light of the Word? Did you tell him?"

"Of course not!" said Asa.

"I told you," Labin said, "we would not pass this information on to the next generation. It stops with us!"

"I did not tell him," said Asa. "For all we know, it's a myth."

"It's not a myth," said Labin as he stood. "Nevertheless, talking about the *Book of Prophesies* will get us killed. We must be careful. Supreme Commander Javan has spies everywhere. We can't even trust those in our own family. Ezra must never know we are descendants of the Children of Light."

"There must be others," Asa said. He watched his father take off his thick, wool sweater.

"I don't know of any others," Labin said. Agitated with Asa, he started to pace around the room.

Asa watched his father fume. Even though Labin was looking older this year with gray hair and large bushy beard, he was as fiery and intimidating as he was thirty years ago. When angry, his blue eyes seemed to pierce and punish.

Avoiding Labin's eyes, Asa asked, "What if there are others like us?"

"Stop this foolishness!" Labin sneered. He turned his wiry body towards Asa. "Why does this intrigue you so much? Did you tell him? Tell me the truth!"

"I told you I did not tell him," loudly Asa insisted. He stood up and moved away from Labin's accusative stare. "He must have found out from someone else. Possibly the dream he had, or whatever happened, was real."

"Asa, sit back down," Labin said. "We must keep our voices down. We don't want Ezra or one of the workers to hear us."

"Wasn't there a prophecy concerning a Whisperer?" Asa asked. He opened a shutter to look out the window toward the blacksmith shop.

Labin thought deeply for a few minutes and said, "There have been many interpretations of that prophecy. We don't have the *Book of Prophesies*. We don't know what was actually written. All we know is what has been passed down for a thousand years—by the Children of Light."

"And, what did it say?"

"Mind you," Labin said, choosing his words carefully, "No one has seen this prophecy written down. It was passed down verbally through the generations. The prophet spoke it before he was stoned to death. He was the last martyr before the Children of Darkness dispelled the Light."

"What did it say?"

CHAPTER 4

The kitchen door opened and closed. Asa pressed his finger to his lips for Labin to be quiet. "Ezra, is that you?" asked Asa getting up from the couch.

"Yes, I just came in to get an apple and a slice of cheese," Ezra answered. He came out of the kitchen feeling he was interrupting something. "I didn't eat breakfast, yet."

Asa walked toward his son Ezra, "How are things going in the shop?"

"Good," Ezra shrugged. "The workers are wondering where you both are."

Labin stood up from the couch. "Ezra why don't you run along to work, and tell them we will be there soon."

"Okay," Ezra said, as he stuffed the rest of the cheese in his mouth and headed out the door.

Ezra hated when his grandfather talked down to him. *Telling me, to run along, like I'm a little kid,* Ezra huffed. *I wonder if they're talking about the conversation I had with father this morning.* Ezra entered the blacksmith shop still munching the cheese.

Asa looked at Labin and said, "Are you satisfied now? No one is here; it's safe to talk."

"What about Ezra?" Labin asked.

Asa raised his hands. "What about him? Listen to that pounding in the shop. There is no way he can hear us."

Labin, choosing his words carefully said, "This is the prophecy my father passed down to me. It was passed down to him just as it has been for a thousand years. The Children of Light have been waiting for its fulfillment. The prophet had spoken this before he was martyred. The Children of Darkness also heard this prophecy. They stand ready to kill anyone who tries to fulfill it."

"So what is the prophecy?" asked Asa, sitting closer to Labin. "What did it say?"

"'The Children of Darkness were eager to kill the prophet. He read the *Book of Prophesies* and knew the Light of the Word. They figured if they killed him, like the others before him, the Light of the Word, or should I say the Truth of the Word, would die with him. Just before he died he said, *'The Whisperer will come and empower three witnesses that will make manifest the works of darkness and destroy it, and deliver my people from the grip of darkness to the freedom found in the light.'"*

When Asa heard this prophecy, he began pacing the room. He was furious with Labin. "Why have you waited so long to tell me this prophecy? Why have you kept this from me?" He glared at his father, "Answer me!"

"I didn't want to give you false hope—that's why," said Labin, watching Asa rub his fingers like a comb through his thick, black, shoulder-length hair.

Sensing Asa's frustration, Labin continued, "My father held on to this prophecy. He looked daily for it to be fulfilled, as did his father before him. They never made the best of the present, always living for some future spoken of a thousand years ago. They believed they would be delivered soon. I didn't want you to live your life centered on this prophecy and be disappointed."

"What else haven't you told me?" Asa questioned. He stared down at his father. "You must tell me everything you know about this Light."

"Why?"Labin questioned. He looked away from Asa's gaze and stared into the fire. "I don't want to keep this false hope going."

"Father, you said yourself this was not a myth!"

"The Children of Light, the *Book of Prophesies* and Light of the Word are not myths," Labin answered. "But about this prophecy? I think it's a myth! Where is the fulfillment? It was spoken forever ago. No one remembers how it was when the Children of Light controlled the valley. Regardless, this information will get us killed."

"My son's life is in danger!" said Asa, his anger directed toward Labin.

"We must not tell him anything about this!" Labin said. He pointed at Asa and walked over to check the kitchen. "Tell him it is only his imagination. He must keep his dreams to himself, and then he won't be in danger."

"But what if Ezra is one of the witnesses?"

"Don't be ridiculous," said Labin, holding up his hands. "He's only a youth!"

"Why do you always underestimate him? He is seventeen now. It sounds to me like the Whisperer talked to him last night."

"You can't connect what happened in a dream last night to what a prophet said a thousand years ago."

"Why not?" Asa asked. "How else would he know about the *Book of Prophesies?*"

"Someone must have told him about the Light of the Word," Labin answered.

"Who?" Asa asked. He did not believe Labin. "You don't know of any other descendants of the Children of Light."

"That's true, I don't know of anyone," Labin answered.

"It's time you tell me everything you were taught about the Children of Light, the *Book of Prophesies*, and whatever else I am supposed to know," Asa said. "You need to level with me, and tell me the truth!"

CHAPTER 5

"Jared, didn't Ezra say he was meeting us down by the creek behind his house today?" questioned Dara.

"Maybe he had to work late," answered Jared, taking a drink from his canteen. "Their blacksmith shop has been quite busy. I can't see if they're still working in there," joked Jared.

"Of course not—his house is three hundred feet away," she rolled her eyes.

Jared, ignoring Dara, said, "He might be coming this way. The fog is so thick I can only see forty or fifty feet."

"I've been thinking more about what might be outside the valley of Thanoton," said Dara, pushing back the hood of her shawl revealing her long, blond hair.

"Not that again!" shouted Jared looking up at Dara. He hated that she was a few inches taller. He always tried to stand as straight as possible, especially around Dara. "Why are you so obsessed with what's beyond the valley?"

"Because no one ever gives me a straight answer," she said, smoothing out the wrinkles in her long skirt.

"That's because no one really knows," said Jared. "Or, I should say, no one has ever come back to tell us what's out there."

"Jared, there's something inside me that really wants to know. I feel compelled to find out."

"Why don't you accept what we were taught in school?" he said as he sat down on a log. "They taught us the only thing outside the valley is a wasteland with creatures ready to devour anyone that enters."

"Doesn't it bother you," asked Dara, that there is no one alive who has ever been outside of the valley, or witnessed these creatures?" She wiped the dirt off the log and sat down.

"Don't you remember?" Jared said, scraping the mud off the bottom of his knee-high leather boots. "They showed us drawings back in school of the dragon-like creatures living in the wasteland."

"Come on!" Dara her hands slashed the air. "They are the same lame pictures they've shown everyone for hundreds of years. Answer me: Why do the border guards never see these creatures? If these creatures want to devour us so badly, you would think they would come into our valley. I believe that this is another tactic by Javan and his men to control us."

"Keep your voice down," said Jared, adjusting his glasses. "Quit mentioning his name. You are going to get us in trouble. You know how popular he is."

"People are so deceived!"

"How do you know?" questioned Jared.

Dara glanced at Jared with her bright, blue eyes and contagious smile and said, "A girl just knows, that's all!"

Jared shook his head. "Oh, that explains it then!"

"Ezra, there you are!" cried Dara. "Where have you been?"

"Hello, Dara and Jared," said Ezra, breathing heavy. "Sorry, I'm late. We had a lot of work to do today. My father and grandfather spent most of the morning talking privately, so they didn't start work until much later."

"What were they talking about?" Jared asked. He felt even shorter around Ezra.

"I can't tell you here, but I want to talk to both of you about it," Ezra said, as he swiped brown, wavy hair from his eyes.

"Where then?" questioned Jared.

"Let's meet tomorrow—same time, at our secret spot," said Ezra all excited.

"At the rock between the rocks?" asked Dara.

"Yes, at the rock between the rocks," Ezra answered. "We need to go to the rock separately. Make sure no one sees you going into the swamp."

Dara's eyes brightened. "I can't wait to hear what you have to say. It must be important."

"It is," agreed Ezra, smiling at Dara. "It'll be like old times."

"I don't think it's a good idea to go separately," Jared added, sounding very worried.

"We have to go separately," Ezra said. "If we went as a group, it might raise suspicion. From now on, it would be better if we went separately. If one of us was caught, it wouldn't give the others away."

Jared studied Ezra and asked, "Why are you so worried about being caught?"

"After what I tell you tomorrow, it'll be clear why I am taking precautions." Ezra unscrewed the cap of his leather canteen and sat down on the log.

Dara asked, "Which one of the three routes do we take?"

"We each need to take a different route," said Ezra, using a stick to draw on the ground. Almost two years had passed since they walked those three routes leading to the rock in the middle of the rocks.

Jared peered at the drawing. "We haven't been there since we reached the age to start working for our families after school and on weekends."

"We just didn't want to go," Dara said.

"That's why," Ezra continued, "we need to confirm that our routes are still good."

"I'm not sure I want to go alone!" Jared said as he studied Ezra's map. "I don't know if I remember the routes."

"Come on, Jared," Dara said. "I had to start working before you two. You went several times without me, and I still remember the routes. You're just scared to go by yourself, as always."

"I'm not afraid," Jared said, "It's—it's just been a long time since we took the routes."

"It might have been years ago," Dara responded, "but we walked those routes hundreds of times. We became so familiar with them that we could get there fast if we had to."

"You'll be fine," Ezra said, slapping Jared on the shoulder. "You can have the easy route, Green Lake. I will take Snake Pit, and Dara will take Silver Rock."

"I have an idea," said Dara, jumping up from the log. "If someone stops us and asks what we're doing, we can tell them we are picking mushrooms. They're in season."

"Good idea," agreed Ezra. "We should collect mushrooms while we're in the swamp tomorrow. It will give us a good alibi, especially when our parents ask us where we've been. Plus," he grinned at them, "they taste good."

"They do," said Jared, standing up. "I feel better about the trip already."

"Good!" Ezra erased the map he had made. "I will see you both tomorrow."

"I can't wait," Dara said.

The three friends said their goodbyes and went home unaware a Watcher was watching, and heard everything.

CHAPTER 6

Jared arrived at the northwest side of the swamp and surveyed the area surrounding the start of the Green Lake route. Checking for footprints, he saw none. Listening, he heard nothing. Jared really didn't want to go through the swamp by himself. He stopped at the start of the trail.

Why did I agree to another one of Ezra's made-up adventures? Jared grumped. *I should've told Ezra, no.*

They hadn't used these trails for years, and now, Ezra wanted to start again. Either what he had to tell them was really good, or it was another one of his theories about Javan and his men watching them. Ezra always said they needed to be prepared to escape. Jared thought his theory was ridiculous. Even if Javan's men never found their secret spot, where would they go? A rock cliff extended straight up on the other side of the swamp, and no one knew how high it was. Steep mountains and cliffs surrounded the valley. Javan would eventually find them. Jared wondered if Ezra made this stuff up just to add some adventure to their lives.

Jared glanced at his pocket watch, and let out a big sigh. He had arrived too early. If he started down the trail now, he would arrive before Ezra and Dara. Jared decided to wait another five minutes before he started walking. The rock in the middle of the rocks was a spooky place, and he did not want to be there alone.

Finding a log, Jared sat down and thought about Thanoton and Dara's infatuation for what was outside the valley. *I have to admit Thanoton is boring, or at least, there is never any excitement. Everyone works, owns a house, and is afraid of Javan, so they keep to themselves. The only unusual thing that ever happens is people somehow go permanently missing.*

Jared looked off into the distance and fidgeted, his anxiety seemed to expand. *The people that live in the valley are paranoid and superstitious. I'm becoming like them.* He checked his pocket watch again. *There have been so many secrets, riddles, and stories passed down throughout Thanoton's existence. People believe anything. That's probably why Ezra talks about this stuff so much. Everyone was warned. Never talk about life before a thousand years ago. And definitely, no one is allowed to talk about what might be outside the valley. But Dara does, in fact, she did it all the time.* He got up from the log and stretched.

He really did not want to walk through the swamp. He thought he could tell them his farm chores took too long. That would save him from getting all muddy, and mosquito bit. *But if I don't, mused Jared, I know Dara will give me a hard time. She loves to call me chicken. I am not a chicken—just cautious. It's obvious Dara's just trying to impress Ezra. I've noticed how they look and smile at each other.*

Jared marveled at what a beauty Dara turned out to be. *After growing up with Dara being such a tomboy, too,* he smiled. His thoughts took a different tack, *Of course, all the girls like Ezra,* thought Jared, a little jealous. *He's tall, strong, and good-looking with his wavy, brown hair. Ezra's always the leader of whatever group he's in.*

Jared remembered the last time they were at the community center playing four's, a favorite card game. Dara was sitting across from Ezra. She looked so beautiful.

Of course, I would never admit that to her. He thought about how the lamplight illuminated her bright, blue eyes and long, blond hair that night. *She does have a contagious smile with perfect white teeth and beautiful lips. It's funny; we, both just stared because she was so beautiful, even if it was Dara,* reflected Jared.

I had better start walking. If I remember right, this trip should only take me twenty minutes. This route is the quickest. Of course, it's harder to see in the swamp—the gray fog is incredibly thick. He looked around and entered the swamp, not knowing a Watcher was watching, and someone followed.

The Watcher did not to follow Jared. He did not want to compromise his position. He heard the rustle of vegetation as someone started along the Green Lake trail behind Jared. The Watcher remained for another ten minutes in his observation post overlooking the start of the route, watching and listening for others. When he was satisfied there were no others around, he slipped out and went the other way, wondering who had followed Jared.

Jared rehearsed the route in his head as he started to walk. *I need to go counter-clockwise around the lake until I hit a fast-moving stream that feeds into the lake. I'll hear the stream long before I get there. Then, I need to skirt along the right side of the stream, going uphill, the whole way until the stream forks. Once at the fork in the stream, I need to keep skirting and go up the steep hill. When the hill comes to a peak and starts to go down, I'll look closely along the stream-edge for our rock path to cross the river.*

I hope our rock path is still there. I'm starting to get muddy, and I sure don't want to get wet. But once I cross the rock path, I'll head downhill until I run into what looks like a rock cliff—but isn't, he pictured what he remembered in his mind.

Jared gained a little more confidence as the stream became louder and louder. Finally, he could see it and stood next to it. At the steam's edge, he admired the clear, fast-moving water, it's babbling soothed his soul.

A branch snapped. The crack seemed to echo against the fog.

Jared paused in mid-stride. Even though the river was loud, he had a keen sense of hearing just as did everyone in Thanoton. Because it was difficult to see during the day and impossible at night, powerful hearing was essential.

Jared's heart pounded. Someone was out there. It clearly sounded like a branch snapped under someone's foot. He immediately moved away from the sound and the river. Jared found a hiding place behind a thick, fallen tree. He waited for a minute. *What was that? Was someone moving?* He froze, shaking, unsure what to do next.

Thoughts churned in his head. *Why am I being followed? No one knows I'm out here but Ezra and Dara. What if Ezra tells us something dangerous?* He took a deep breath. *This is ridiculous. It's probably Ezra and Dara playing a joke on me.*

Jared shouted fear warped the timbre of his voice, "Ezra, come on out! I hear you moving around out there. Joke's over—I know you're out there!"

Underbrush rustled, and feet pounded down the trail. Jared stiffened scrunching deeper under the fallen log. "Hey! Who are you?" Jared yelled.

It wasn't Ezra. He would've said something. If they were going to play a joke on him, they would have done it together. It would be more enjoyable that way. They could laugh together for months afterward. No. This had been only one person. *Then who was that person?*

Jared's breath was ragged, his heart raced, his hands shook. He wanted so badly to go back home, but he couldn't. The person that followed him ran back that way. Jared didn't know what to do. Suddenly, the threat from the Children of Darkness became very real. Were they waiting out there to kill him? Worse yet, torture him for information he didn't even have? Jared felt all alone. He got up and ran as fast as he could for the secret spot. He needed to see his friends.

CHAPTER 7

Asa reluctantly walked into Labin's office in the back of the blacksmith shop. "All the fire pits are out, the workers gone, and the shop is locked up," Asa said and turned to leave.

"Wait a second! Where did Ezra say he was going?" asked Labin. "He sure took off in a hurry."

"He didn't," Asa answered as he turned back around. "He was meeting up with some friends."

"Who was he going to see?"

"I don't know."

"You didn't ask?" Labin questioned.

"Don't give me that look! No, I didn't ask him," Asa leaned against the doorway. "He probably met up with Jared and Dara as always. If I had kept him back from seeing his friends, he would become even more suspicious."

"Not any more suspicious than you already made him."

"What do you mean by that?" Asa retorted.

Labin closed the accounting ledger he had been working on, and scooted his wooden chair out from the desk. "If you wouldn't have gotten angry this morning, when Ezra mentioned the Light of the Word and the *Book of Prophesies*, he probably wouldn't be as suspicious."

"What else was I supposed to do?" Asa watched his father spin the dial and open the safe next to him. "Ezra caught me off guard with what he said. It still doesn't make sense how he knows."

"You should've played it off like another one of his far-fetched theories when he started to tell you what he'd heard," Labin lowered his voice trying to calm things down. "Then, maybe he wouldn't think it was all that serious. The boy has quite an active imagination."

"Father, what do you want me to do or say to him? I personally don't think it will matter much what I say to him. If he is one of the witnesses, and the Whisperer is leading him, nothing's going to stop him from pursuing the *Book of Prophesies*."

"There you go again!" Labin slammed the door of the safe and spun the dials to lock it. "You're reading too much into this whole situation. I will tell you who will stop him from pursuing the Light of the Word—Javan and his men."

Asa leaned over Labin's desk. "Why couldn't it be Ezra? He's smart, fearless, and he never gives up. Didn't you tell me all the prophecies will eventually be fulfilled?"

"Yes, if it's a true prophesy, it'll be fulfilled," Labin said. He motioned for Asa to sit down. "Calm down. I told you before; we don't have the *Book of Prophesies*, and we have nothing written. The only truth we have is what has been passed down verbally through the Children of Light." Labin straightened himself back in front of his desk. He continued, "In the Valley of Thanoton, we are so bombarded and blinded with lies. I don't think we even have a clue what is real or even true."

"Tell me what the prophecy said again," Asa said. He sat across from his father and looked directly into his piercing, blue eyes. "I want to hear it."

"Like I said this morning," Labin answered, "this prophecy was passed down verbally for a thousand years. My father told me to memorize it and pass it down." Labin saw a look in his son he had never seen before. There was a fierceness radiating from his brown eyes that was unnerving.

"So, why didn't you pass the prophecy down to me?"

"I didn't want to pass down this foolishness," Labin added.

"What if the prophecy is true? I need to know. Tell it to me again!"

When Labin spoke the prophecy, something rang true in Asa's heart.

"*The whisperer will come and empower three witnesses that will make manifest the works of darkness and destroy it, and deliver my people from the grip of darkness to the freedom found in the light.*"

"What if what was passed down and memorized was actually what the Whisperer spoke through the prophet?" Asa said.

"That seems impossible," Labin said, as he glanced out the window and doorway of his office into the shop, "How could something spoken keep its integrity after a thousand years? I've heard there were different variations of it."

"You heard different variations from your family or from others?" Asa pressed. He could tell he caught his father off-guard.

"Well, I heard from my family there were different variations. I didn't actually hear any," Labin said. He tried not to sound too defensive.

19

Asa shook his head. "That means the Children of Darkness also heard the prophet."

"They did. That's why it's forbidden to talk about anything that happened before a thousand years ago. Instead, they have spread lies. They took the Truth and mixed it with lies, giving it a completely different meaning. The Children of Darkness did that with everything. They made it look like the Children of Light were the ones oppressing the people. They accused them of taking away everyone's freedom by having them follow a life dictated by the Light of the Word. In reality, true freedom is only found in living a life given over to the Light of the Word."

"If the Whisperer, the *Book of Prophesies*, and the Light of the Word are all true," Asa said, "Isn't the Whisperer powerful enough to keep the prophecy pure?"

Labin contemplated what Asa had said. "This valley's foundation was built on deception and the blood of those that tried to hold on to the Light. Because of that, it is hard to differentiate what is truth and what is error."

Asa and Labin sat quietly looking at each other, contemplating everything said. Finally, Asa spoke, "When I hear the prophecy, something about the words rings true in my heart. Does it with you?"

"It does," Labin said. He leaned back in his chair and stared up at the ceiling, "I guess we should leave Ezra alone and see where this all leads. I'm just worried for his safety."

CHAPTER 8

The Watcher, Abia, was so glad to be out of his observation post for the day. He clutched his dagger tightly, moving as quickly as he could to distance himself from the damp, cramped, and cold post. He had to admit, his observation post was perfect. There was no way someone could stumble upon it. They could be sitting right next to the base of the tree, and never have a clue. A small dugout room was underneath it with several peepholes in between the roots to watch in all different directions—especially the route.

The Watcher thought over what just happened. *Who was it that followed Jared into the swamp? Why? Does that person know something we don't? Impossible. We are the Watchers and have been watching for a thousand years.*

Abia was instructed to follow whoever of the three witnesses used Green Lake route, to watch for any followers or if the witness met anyone before the rock was reached. Once the creek split, he was to peel away, and another Watcher would pick up where he left off. Abia knew someone was following Jared, so he followed orders and did not pursue. The risk of compromise was too great.

The Watchers never took unnecessary risks. Highly trained, they planned every mission to be flawless. No one would ever find them. They remained hidden for a thousand years, and still, they watch. Abia was excited. His heart was pounding so hard he could not hear himself breathe. Now, at last, the hourglass would begin.

Abia remembered back five years before when he watched them plan the three routes. They loved going to the rock because they thought they were alone. It was somewhat entertaining, listening to their conversations discussing all kinds of forbidden theories about the valley of Thanoton. It was during this time that he and his fellow Watchers built several secret observation posts using the natural elements like the rocks, trees, and mud, so they could watch when the hourglass started. He marveled that the three had no clue they were the chosen, and led by the Whisperer.

Abia cut through the forest, walking as fast as he could. He had finally reached the outskirts of the city of Thanoton. Abia sometimes wished he could ride his horse, but he understood it would attract too much attention. His horse required roads or wide paths instead of the dense thickets and steep gorges that would confuse anyone that followed.

Abia would also have to hide the horse before he entered one of the secret passages that led to the inner chamber. A horse tied up somewhere without the owner would lead to undue suspicion.

Abia entered one of the secret passages in the maze that led to the inner chamber. There were many passages, but only one was open at a time. Each passage had false corridors that led nowhere to corner anyone following. The Watchers had to know each passage flawlessly. The passageways changed daily, and every other one was blocked.

Each day a certain bucket placed on a vegetable stand in the market square revealed the open passageway. When a Watcher came to the inner chamber, or was summoned, the Watchers looked for the telltale bucket. To the untrained eye, they all looked the same. To the Watchers, the bucket was easy to find.

Abia entered secret passage L2, the lower-level stairwell that led to an aqueduct under the city. Instead of going into the aqueduct, he quickly turned and went to the space underneath the stairwell. He removed a grate and went in. For fifty feet, he had to crawl in pitch-black until he got to a larger tunnel where he could stand up and walk.

Abia finally arrived at the door of the inner chamber. He stopped for a moment to settle his breathing. He was excited to tell Shobal, their leader, what had just happened. He wished he had more information, but at least he actually had something to share. It had been several years since there had been any significant activity with the three. He thought, *At last what we have been watching for: Clear signs that the hourglass had started*.

Abia knocked on the inner chamber door. A peephole opened. He nodded at the eyeball that appeared in the hole, and the door opened. Abia was surprised when he walked into the inner chamber where there were a number of Watchers present. The storekeeper he recognized, but didn't know he was a Watcher. That was not surprising, though. Watchers had infiltrated every area and organization in Thanoton, and had remained hidden—even among their own. Usually, he would be there alone with Shobal or with one of his fellow Watchers that were assigned to the three.

He came there for training, and it was always one-on-one instruction. He became proficient in hand-to-hand combat, quick kill, sword fighting, archery, surveillance, counter-surveillance, camouflage and concealment, first-aid, secret communications and signals, counter-interrogation and cover stories, land navigation, escape, and evasion. The inner chamber always brought back good memories of his training.

As soon as Abia walked into the room, it suddenly became quiet. All eyes were on him.

"What are you doing here?" someone asked from the round table where the group of Watchers was seated.

Before Abia could answer, Shobal came from another room and told the men, "This does not concern you. Get back to work. Abia come with me." Shobal cautioned Abia not to say a word until they had reached his office. As he closed the thick, wooden door behind them, he asked, "Why are you back so early?"

"Someone followed Jared on the Green Lake route," Abia responded. He watched as Shobal took off his wire-rim glasses, and held them up to the kerosene lamp to see how dirty they were.

"Who was it?" Shobal carefully wiped the glasses with his handkerchief.

"I don't know. I couldn't recognize him. It was too foggy."

"Then how do you know for sure it was Jared who took the Green Lake route?" Shobal put his glasses back on, shoving the handkerchief back into his jacket pocket.

"Jared stood five feet from my position," Abia answered. "I saw him clearly—just not who had followed him."

"You didn't recognize anything distinct about this other person?" asked Shobal. His somber gaze held a gleam of admiration for Abia. He had watched Abia grow up into the young man that stood before him.

"No I didn't. He ran past my position." Abia concisely described what he saw, "He was wearing a face mask and a hood over his head."

"Ah." Shobal studied Abia and saw no inconsistencies in his story. "What was Jared doing?"

"It almost looked like he was trying to talk himself out of going."

"You're probably right. He is the timid one," Shobal said smiling at Abia.

"And, since I was ordered not to pursue if he was followed, I came back to report it," said Abia, gently reminding him of the instructions.

Shobal's wrinkles deepened, as did his gaze in intensity. "Are you sure no one else might have seen you leave your surveillance position?"

"No one saw!" responded Abia, sounding confident. "I waited for awhile then slipped away taking the counter surveillance route. No one followed."

23

Shobal placed his hand on Abia's shoulder. "Good job! I trained you well. We'll hear from the rest of your team assigned to the chosen. They will explain what the chosen talked about at the rock, and who might have been following."

Shobal squeezed his shoulder then motioned to a chair, "Have a seat and some water. You look thirsty. It will be a couple of hours before nightfall. The chosen and the rest of your team will want to be out of the swamp before it gets dark. I want you to stay here. When they arrive, we can discuss everything that went on tonight. Things are starting to happen fast, and I have other things I would like to discuss with you and your team."

"What's the meeting about in the next room?" Abia asked.

"Their operation does not concern you."

"Are they the Watchers assigned to the border?"

"I told you; it's none of your business," Shobal said. "You need to stay focused on your own mission."

With that, Shobal left to resume his meeting in the other room.

CHAPTER 9

Ezra felt good. He was finally out of the muddiest part. He'd forgotten how muddy the Snake Pit route got as it wound through the swamp. It was their least favorite. All he had to do was head uphill to the stream, and find the rock path if it was still there. He hoped it was, although he didn't care if he got all wet at this point. He wondered how Dara and Jared were doing on their routes.

As Ezra approached the stream, he suddenly heard someone running straight toward him on his left. He barely saw a figure coming at him through the fog. Ezra reacted from pure instinct, grabbing the right wrist of the attacker with his right hand and twisting it behind him. He drove his left palm into the attacker's right shoulder blade and took him to the ground. Quickly, Ezra put his left arm around the attacker's throat, and into a chokehold. Ezra froze. It was Jared!

"Jared, what are you doing running up on me like that?"

"Me? What are you doing, trying to kill me? Get off me!" Jared insisted as he pushed himself away.

"Why did you come at me like that, and why are you running so fast?" Ezra asked. "You're making unnecessary noise."

"I wouldn't be making unnecessary noise if you hadn't followed me back at the lake and scared me," Jared said. "I knew I shouldn't have come. This was one of your jokes, wasn't it?"

"Followed? You were followed?"

"Yes, I was. Why don't admit it was you?"

"I did not follow you," Ezra said. "Are you sure someone was following, and it wasn't just some noises you heard in the woods?"

"Come on, Ezra, I know the difference."

"Why would someone follow you?"

"I don't know," Jared's voice may have been a bit shaky.

"It doesn't make sense. No one else knew we were coming here," Ezra pointed out. "You were either followed from home or you told somebody."

"Look Ezra, I was not followed until I went into the swamp. Of course, I didn't tell anyone where I was going. Wouldn't that completely defeat the purpose of going to the secret spot? You think I am that stupid? I am sick of you assuming I do something wrong all the time."

"I'm sorry, Jared. I'm just getting a little paranoid."

"Little? You were born paranoid."

"How's your arm feeling?"

"It's feeling better. I can move my fingers now."

Startled, Ezra and Jared jerked around when Dara called out, "Hey, guys."

"What? Why are you sneaking up on us like that?" Ezra questioned.

"Yeah, and keep your voice down," Jared added.

Dara rolled her eyes. "How can I be sneaking up with a raised voice? What is wrong between you two? I didn't have to sneak up, anyway. I could hear you a mile away. What are you arguing about?"

"Dara, we'll have to fill you in later at the rock," Ezra responded. "We really need to get moving. We've been too noisy, and stayed too long at this spot."

"We need to look for the rock path," Jared said. He stretched out his sore right arm.

"It looks like you guys have been wrestling," Dara said. She tried hard not to laugh. "You both are covered head-to-toe with mud."

"Just look for the rock path!" Jared exclaimed.

~*~

Joab was to take over following Jared at the creek split and waited for the signal from Abia, his fellow Watcher. All he saw was someone running right past his position. According to the plan, if he never received the signal he'd wait two minutes then proceed to his next position. But moments after that person had run past his position, a loud commotion broke out. It sounded like a fight at the crest of the hill close to the rock path.

Joab didn't hear anyone following. Quietly, he moved to his other position overlooking the rock path to get a closer look. *What was this ruckus? Could it be one of Javan's spies had discovered what the three were up to? What could it be?* He seriously doubted Abia had been caught circling around trying to get a better position. He was too good for that. The fog was dense today in the swamp. It was hard to see past fifteen feet.

When Joab eased into his over-watch position, he could hear Jared and Ezra arguing. Obviously, they had scared each other when they accidently met. Moments later, he also heard Dara's voice. She was enjoying the situation by making fun of them.

Joab heard the three find the rock path. He was to stay in position overlooking the rock path watching for anyone that might follow the three. Although he could not see the path, he must wait until they came back through to leave. Then, he would follow them back out of the swamp, listening to their conversation. Seth, the third Watcher for the three, was already ready to listen in position at the rock in the middle of the rocks.

As Joab listened to the three witnesses, or "The Chosen," like Shobal liked to call them, cross the rock path, he wondered what happened to Abia. He liked having Abia as the leader of their little group. He knew Abia loved being in charge and took his job very seriously. *His job is fairly easy,* thought Joab. *He's only in charge of Seth and me.*

Joab agreed with Abia. They needed more Watchers assigned to the three witnesses. Today they could have used more help. The three witnesses split up. Therefore, Abia decided to follow whoever took the Green Lake route. Then, Joab would pick them up at the rock path, and Seth would take over at the rock in the middle of the rocks. So far, everything had gone as planned. Except Joab wondered what happened to Abia.

Joab remembered what Shobal had taught them in their initial training. "Less is always better," he would say. "We Watchers live by the philosophy: 'the fewer Watchers around, the less chance of compromise.'"

Joab listened until the three witnesses' voices grew faint. He doubted the three would ever know the Watchers were watching and aiding their every move.

CHAPTER 10

Javan looked out from the balcony of his palace and marveled at how thick the fog had become. He thought it seemed like the fog was getting worse. His agitation grew as he waited for the last few members of his twelve-man council to arrive. Burdened by the border problem, he called this last minute meeting. He used to enjoy watching the market square from the balcony, but now, he could not even see the square. The fog had blanketed it with suffocating moisture like a soaked woolen coat.

Tuval, Javan's second-in-command and leader of the twelve-man council, studied his leader. Tuval admired Javan. He had known Javan his whole life and had been his second for the last forty years. Still, he intimidated Tuval. Javan was a large man, standing head and shoulders taller than most. His flaming red hair and beard stood out in the crowd while Tuval's shorter stature and dark coloring blended in. He was an old, frail, and wizened looking man. Tuval always had an uneasy feeling when Javan looked at him with his dark green, piercing eyes that didn't reflect light but sucked it in like deep wells. Sometimes, Tuval wondered if Javan could look right into his soul. It was always uncomfortable being around Javan; his life radiated evil.

"Commander, the council, is assembled," Tuval said.

Javan came in from the balcony and stared at Tuval. "Good. Let's get started."

"All rise," Tuval commanded.

The twelve council members stood up at attention. Their left hand gripped the handle of their sword, strapped to their waist. It was a tradition that even annoyed Javan. He seemed to like it more informal. Javan liked action, not meetings.

"Take your seats. Sit down," Javan said. He motioned with his hands. "I have some important information concerning our border. Things have gotten worse. I have asked Hyrum, the head of the border guards, to give you the report he gave me less than two hours ago. We need a viable solution this time!"

Hyrum sat quietly and listened while Javan talked to the council. He could not wait to get back to the border. It had been a long time since he had been at one of Javan's meetings. He hated to come out of the mountains and into the valley to the city of Thanoton. The border was a different world than the city of Thanoton and the rest of the valley.

Hyrum had been a border guard his whole life, as his father was before him. He loved living in the mountains, seeing the sunny, plush landscapes and valleys beyond their fog-ridden home. In Hyrum's career as a border guard, he had never seen any fierce, cannibalistic people or man-eating dragons. The valleys on the other side of the mountains were always sunny and peaceful. The meadows were plush with flowers, birds, and herds of deer grazing. He had never seen anything that looked dangerous outside the valley of Thanoton.

Supreme Commander Javan's chest swelled as he spied his portrait among all the supreme commanders for the last thousand years. He liked the portraits hanging opposite his seat. He grabbed his coat lapels, drew a deep breath, and expounded at length on Thanoton's history, the border, and all their enemies as he strode down the gallery of portraits. He stopped only for a moment to admire his own portrait in the middle of the others.

How arrogant, thought Hyrum, not listening but reflecting on what his father had taught him when he was a boy. He thought back to when he had asked his father why the valley of Thanoton was always foggy, wet, and miserable.

"Why did the surrounding valleys look so beautiful?" he asked.

His father warned him, "It's a trap the cannibals use to lure us out, to capture us." He would also frequently warn his son, "You must never believe that it's safe to leave Thanoton. You must trust those that did your job before you. They fought to keep the dragons out. You owe it to them to trust what you heard and keep the border secure."

Hyrum switched his thoughts from his father to what he was going to say. He was baffled by the recent activity. Throughout his years as a border guard, they had seen human tracks leaving the mountains surrounding Thanoton. Once, they also saw some tracks coming into their border. But lately, they had seen more tracks going both ways, not to mention more missing people reported.

"Hyrum, Hyrum!" Javan snapped. He awakened Hyrum out of his thoughts.

"Y—Y—Yes commander," Hyrum responded. He quickly got out of his seat and stood up.

"What's wrong with you?" Tuval added. "We're waiting for your brief."

Hyrum cleared his throat. "Gentleman, as you know, we have had more foot traffic coming from the eastern cut." He walked over to the large area map on the wall in the command center.

"How much more?" asked one of the council members.

"In the last two months, at least five people have not returned," Hyrum said. "And—"

"Why haven't you seen them?" interrupted the captain of the palace guards. "Are you guys sleeping on duty up there?"

"That's enough from all of you," Javan commanded. "Let's hold all our questions till after Hyrum's brief."

Hyrum fought back the urge to jump across the table and slay the captain of the palace guards with his sword. The man always was a source of trouble. It was no secret he wanted Hyrum's job. Hyrum refocused, not willing to give up his position yet. He pointed to the map and said, "The eastern cut is not just one trail, as it sounds, but a series of lower rock peaks. There are many rock formations, peaks, trails, and narrow passages through to Cannibal Land. It's hard to cover every avenue around the valley with the amount of personnel I have."

"Quit making excuses, and go on with your brief," Javan scolded.

"In the course of our investigation, we have also noticed the same tracks, from the same individual, going back-and-forth on a regular basis. At first, he would only come at night, but now that the fog has gotten worse, he sneaks in at different times."

"How many times has he come over?" interrupted Tuval, the second-in-command under Javan.

"At least four times a week for the last two months," Hyrum answered.

"Go on," Javan said.

"In the mountains, it has been harder for us to see lately due to the fog. I think we've all been noticing the fog getting worse. Because we are unable to see Cannibal Land from our normal over watch positions, we have had to move to higher ground. We are not just on the eastern cut but on the north crest as well."

Hyrum pointed at the north crest mountain range. "The north crest mountain range is about a thousand feet higher than all four points around the valley of Thanoton. At the eastern cut, we send all information to the north crest to pass on to the other positions. They are high points in the mountains, above the fog. We send coded information from the sun's reflected light off pieces of metal. The north crest is our highest position. We use it to relay all our information to the other regions from our border command center in the eastern cut. The north crest passes this information on to the western point, and in turn, they relay the message to the southern point. If the southern or western points need to send information to the eastern cut, they send it back through to the north crest and onto us."

Hyrum turned from the map and looked at the others around the table. "That's why we needed to go as high as we could on the north crest."

Hyrum relaxed a bit; relieved he had finally gotten to his point. He pulled out a piece of paper. "Yesterday, we received a series of coded flashes from north crest stating: 'We see a large city off in the distance with houses. We know they are occupied. Their houses are lit up with fires at night, and their smoke stacks are working. The city is too far away to judge how many cannibals live there. Captain Hyrum, you need to see this for yourself.'"

Hyrum looked up from reading the message. "I am headed back to the eastern cut station right after this meeting. Tomorrow, at first light, I will go to the north crest observation point to see for myself."

Loud discussion erupted in the conference room as the council members talked angrily.

"How long will it take to get to the north crest?" someone asked.

"It takes about a day and a half, taking the ridgeline trail that goes around the valley of Thanoton. It's too steep to go any other way," said Hyrum.

"I'm going with you," Javan responded. His eyes were bright with excitement.

Expecting that Hyrum said, "Yes, sir."

"Can I go with you Commander Javan?" asked the captain of the palace guards. It was obvious to everyone he wanted to be with Javan every chance possible.

Javan sensed what everyone around the table was thinking. He commanded, "No. You need to stay here and help the rest come up with a plan to catch this intruder."

CHAPTER 11

"Wow, I can't believe this rock path is still good," Dara said. She held up her skirt and stepped off the last rock that crossed the river.

"I know," Jared agreed. He stepped off behind her. "It's amazing considering how strong the current is."

"Hold up you guys," Ezra said. He still was at the edge of the river. "I'm going to clean some of this mud off my boots on this side of the river."

Jared laughed. "You're probably lifting a few extra pounds with all that mud on your feet."

Ezra looked up at his two friends. He could tell even Dara was trying to contain her laughter. "The Snake Pit route was super muddy," Ezra said. "I thought I was going to leave my boots stuck in the mud a couple of times."

Dara started laughing, then Jared. Ezra, seeing them laugh, started to laugh too even though he didn't understand what was so funny. *Just like old times*, he thought.

"All right," Ezra said. He got up and dried his hands on his shirt. "We need to get moving. We have totally compromised our security by being so noisy."

They headed straight down the hill from the river and arrived at a rock wall.

Dara was always amazed how it looked like a rock wall but actually wasn't. A row of rock pieces stuck out of the ground and rose about twenty feet high. The tops of the rock pieces were not visible because of the fog, so it looked like a cliff. The rock wall was a half-moon that protruded from the actual cliff wall. The cliff was part of the eastern cut that continues straight up for thousands of feet.

The offset rock pieces left a squeezable gap. Ezra squeezed through first. All three stopped on the other side, amazed at the plush, green grass inside the semi-circular shaped rock wall. In the middle was a large flat rock. It was a four-foot square platform, three feet off the ground with a smooth flat top providing an excellent seat.

"I wonder what this place was used for," Jared said. He stood on top of the rock, impressed at how well sound traveled in this place. "It's amazing. You can stand here on the rock, talking normally, and be heard fifty feet away standing next to the surrounding rocks."

"That's why we need to keep our voices down," Ezra whispered. "This place is probably not a good place to talk in secret."

Dara studied the area around her and whispered, "It probably was a secret meeting place for some group."

"Sit close, so I can whisper what I need to tell you and the reason you're here," Ezra said. "We must hurry. The fog is getting thicker, and it will be night soon." Ezra told them everything.

Seth could not believe what he was hearing. Shobal was right. They truly were the three witnesses. He marveled at how well he could hear them talk even though they were whispering. Seth wrote everything they said in a notebook, so he wouldn't miss a thing. He held the notebook close to see it, for it was getting darker. He could not wait to tell the others, the Whisperer talked to Ezra.

Seth heard Dara question Ezra. "What did the Whisperer say to you again?"

The Whisperer told me, "You must find the *Book of Prophesies*. It will show you the Light of the Word."

Seth was excited. It was the confirmation they waited to hear. The hourglass had truly started. Soon, the people of Thanoton would be free from the grip of Javan's evil empire. The prophecy was being fulfilled. He repeated the words of the last prophet in his head, as he had done a million times over. This was what they were waiting and watching for.

"'*The whisperer will come and empower three witnesses that will make manifest the works of darkness and destroy it, and deliver my people from the grip of darkness to the freedom found in the light*.'" Seth listened and watched as the three stood up and got ready to leave.

"We cannot discuss this information with anyone," Ezra said to Dara and Jared. "I think Jared is right about waiting."

"That would be a first," Dara said. She gave Jared a shove off the rock.

"Ha, ha—very funny," Jared said. He stumbled to keep his balance.

"We should wait on the Whisperer to talk to me again," said Ezra. "Maybe I can talk to him, to see what I should do next."

Her blue eyes wide, Dara said, "It sounds a little spooky to me."

"Now who's scared?" Jared said. He wanted to shove Dara, but he was taught never to push girls, even if they deserved it.

Dara gave Jared a mean, squinty-eyed look and turned back to Ezra. "Why don't you ask Labin, your grandfather? He seems to be very wise."

"I don't know," answered Ezra as he shook his head. "We were always told to trust no one. We never know who will turn on us. I don't want to come up missing like my mom."

"Think about it Ezra." Dara gestured with her hands. "If your father knows so much about the Light of the Word and does not want to talk, it's obvious your grandfather passed it down. That's how it works in Thanoton."

"It's true," Jared agreed. "If he didn't know anything about the Light of the Word or the Whisperer, he wouldn't have gotten so angry. He would have just thought it was foolishness."

"Maybe you're both right," Ezra said. "I'll wait for the right opportunity to talk to him. Let's get out of here."

CHAPTER 12

Javan walked out of the command center with Hyrum, the captain of the border guards. He stopped and said to the council, "I want you to capture this intruder alive! I want to personally interrogate him."

"Yes, Commander," a number of voices said in unison.

Javan said to Hyrum, "Get the horses ready. I will be right out." Javan stopped in the hallway outside the command center. He whispered to Tuval who walked out with them. "Use every resource available to catch this intruder."

"I will, Commander," Tuval whispered. He glanced around to see if anyone was close enough to hear. "I think you should take some extra men with you for security. Who knows what's really going on at the border?"

"I was thinking the same thing," Javan said. He was pleased with Tuval. "Those border guards act and think differently than us."

"Exactly," Tuval agreed. "I have a hard time believing no one has ever seen this intruder."

Javan nodded in agreement. "We might have a breech in our organization."

"Maybe you should stay back," Tuval said. He could already hear the council members arguing in the command center. "This could be a trap to weaken our organization by killing you."

"I'm going," Javan said. He placed his hand on Tuval's shoulder. "It's been a long time since I've been to the border. I really need to see what's going on." Javan saw the worried look on Tuval's face. "I will take an extra security detail with me. One more thing, find out exactly where this intruder has been crossing. I want to know which border guards were on duty at that time. Maybe there is a connection."

"I'll find out."

Shaking Tuval's hand, Javan said, "Do not tell the others of our distrust of the border guards. This is just between us." With that, Javan left.

Inside the command center, the captain of the palace guard said, "Well, you heard Javan. We better come up with a good plan and have it implemented before he gets back from the north crest."

"What would the intruder want in our valley?" questioned the captain of the market square police.

"Maybe he's linked to the missing people," responded the captain of the palace guards.

"What do you mean?" said the chief investigator of Thanoton. He was already defensive.

"He's probably coming here to snatch people," chimed in one of the council members.

"I'm sure he is," agreed the captain of the market square police. "He is from Cannibal Land."

The chief investigator stood up to quiet and redirect the council members. They were debating back-and-forth on different theories concerning the missing people. "Hold on," he said. "Even if that were true, we have no proof. As chief investigator here in Thanoton, I have seen no link or signs that the missing people were abducted. There have been no signs of any struggle at all. They just disappear. We have informants everywhere, and they have never reported anything that verifies what has happened to the missing. Any new faces seen in Thanoton, we verify their citizenship and the town they're from in the valley. This intruder is obviously very stealthy and uses the cover of darkness."

"It's obvious we need to cordon off the eastern cut!" the captain of the palace guards shouted.

"I agree," responded the captain of the army. He had waited until now to speak. "Like I've said before a million times, to catch this intruder we need to form a sizeable force to block the eastern cut."

"Who's going to command this?" the chief investigator asked. He sat back down. He knew this would cause another stir.

"I will! I am the captain of the army."

"Your judgment is clouded," responded the captain of the palace guards.

"We know you're itching to attack Cannibal Land, even more, now that you heard there's a city out there. I'll be in charge of this operation."

"No, you will not," Tuval's deep voice held a steely tone as he strode back into the room. He gestured for everyone to sit back down. "I will be in charge."

The committee relaxed. They were relieved that Tuval would be in charge of this operation. He was well liked and trusted by them. Tuval was realistic and smart, and he had the ability to keep Javan from overreacting. He balanced Javan. The captain of the palace guards and the captain of the army were just like Javan. All they wanted was power, no matter what they had to do to get it.

"Like the captain of the army said, we need to lock the eastern cut down. This way no one can possibly cross over without us knowing." Tuval walked up and pointed to the area of interest on the map. "So we can capture him, we don't want to deter the intruder from crossing over."

"Where are we going to get all the people to cover this whole area?" said the captain of the market square police. He was crowding around the map where the other council members had gathered.

"We will have to run our respective sections with the bare minimum. I want all of you leaders to assign one of your subordinates to run your sections in your absence," Tuval said as he made eye contact with each of the council members. "The rest of your people will be sent to apprehend this intruder. We will split the eastern cut area into sections, and each one of you will be assigned a section to lead. I leave it up to all of you, to look at the terrain in your sector, and see the best way to set a trap. You are all capable leaders. I trust you will get the job done."

CHAPTER 13

Shobal left Abia in his office and headed back to the meeting. His mind anticipated what the other two Watchers assigned to the three would tell him. He was eager to hear what The Chosen had talked about at the rock.

"Okay. Let's get this meeting started," Shobal said. He took a seat at the head of the conference table. "Sorry for the interruptions." He scooted his chair closer, scraping the solid rock floor, an uncomfortable sound.

"Where is Abia assigned?" the storekeeper questioned.

"Like I said before, it does not concern you what everyone else is doing," Shobal said. "Stick with your assigned task."

Shobal looked around the table at the other Watchers present. "Don't give me that look. I know everyone wants to know all the details, now that there are clear signs that the hourglass has started. But it's best and safer if we only know our own operation. If Javan's men catch and torture us, we can only share what we know, and the rest will stay hidden. Storekeeper, you and the market square Watchers, were brought into this meeting to be briefed by Jotham, the head Watcher of the border guards," Shobal said. He smiled at the athletically built man. "Go ahead, Jotham."

"I will get straight to the point," Jotham said. "Like Shobal said, I'm head of the Watchers assigned to the border guards. We've had significant activity lately that concerns everyone in this room."

The storekeeper took a deep breath and said, "How can what happens at the border have anything to do with the market square?"

"For one," Jotham lithely rose as he responded, "we have been tracking a single intruder coming through the eastern cut on a regular basis. He seems to always elude us."

"Again, what does this have to do with us?" Storekeeper said. He shifted his fat body in the small, rigid, thick, wooden chair, not finding a comfortable position between its arms.

"Have you seen any people you don't recognize hanging around town?" Jotham questioned. He leaned over the table and got in Storekeeper's face.

"Of course not!" Storekeeper leaned away from him as much as he could in his chair. "If we had, we would have reported it." The other market square Watchers also voiced their agreement with the storekeeper.

Shobal sensed Jotham's growing frustration with Storekeeper. "Jotham, why don't you go on to your next point? Tell them about what was reported at the north crest."

Jotham went to the map and started talking about what was discovered when the north crest position was moved to higher ground. Shobal was in deep thought about the storekeeper. He was tired of his complacency. Storekeeper used to be very motivated, but over the years, he grew tired of persevering, and now was just going through the motions. He was the leader of the market square Watchers, and his attitude was rubbing off on them. He looked worn-out with big bags under his eyes and unkempt hair. His eyes were always red and irritated. He was out of shape and now supported a large belly. He had disregarded any urgings from his fellow Watchers to get back in shape. It was obvious to everyone his heart was no longer in it. This complacent attitude had started to grow within the Watcher community. That worried Shobal. *The recent activity is exactly what we needed to motivate everyone. Everything looks as if the prophecy is being fulfilled*, thought Shobal.

"We did see Javan leave with Hyrum today with two platoons of guards," said one of the Watchers.

Simultaneously, Shobal and Jotham spoke. "What! Why? Why didn't you report that?" finished Shobal.

"He leaves the castle every day," said the storekeeper. "You want us to report everything?"

Shobal stood up and yelled at Storekeeper. "Javan leaving with the head of the border guards and two platoons of guards is not normal. Aren't you the least bit concerned about what they're doing?"

"Wa-Well—"

Shobal interrupted Storekeeper and leaned over the table. "Listen, all of you. I want you to keep your eyes and ears open! Report anything unusual! That means anything out of the ordinary, and anything you hear about missing people! Do I make myself clear?" He stared directly at the storekeeper.

Storekeeper sat up straighter; his eyes bulging, "Ya-Yes."

Jotham also jumped in to drill the storekeeper. "Have you heard anything about what happened to the missing people? Is Javan snatching them?"

Storekeeper got defensive and regained his composure. "I have heard nothing. I don't think Javan has them or took them. You said yourself that multiple footprints were found heading out of the valley."

"I agree," Shobal said. He relaxed a bit to ease the tension in the room. "I don't think Javan has all these people who have come up missing over the years. At first, we all thought so, but he would have to secretly kill then hide the bodies. On the other hand, Javan would need to keep them hidden in a secret prison somewhere. There is no way he could do either of those things without us knowing. We're aware of everyone in the army's prison, and none of those are the ones missing."

"You're probably right," Jotham said. "We never used to be focused on peoples' tracks before. Now that people've started to disappear in small groups, we've noticed and studied them."

"In the past, it has been only individuals that have sporadically come up missing," the storekeeper said, trying to redeem himself. "No one ever thought they might be going over the border."

One of the other market square watchers chimed in and said, "The people of Thanoton still think Javan is responsible."

"To spread fear," Shobal nodded. "He certainly uses that to his advantage."

"That's why you are starting to see the footprints," Storekeeper said. "One set is hard to notice, but multiple footprints are more obvious."

"Yes, we are actively looking for footprints now," Jotham said. "That is how we discovered this intruder."

"I think this is all somehow related to what we are seeking," Shobal said. He stroked his gray beard in deep thought, and murmured, "The Light of the Word." With that, Shobal dismissed the group and sat down at the conference table.

He thought about all that had happened that day. He was still waiting for two more Watchers to brief him on what the three witnesses talked about at the rock in the middle of the rocks. He called out to the inner chamber guards, "I want you to change the secret passage to R4. Too many watchers have used L2 today."

CHAPTER 14

"If it wasn't for the lights of the city," Ezra said, "I don't think I would know which direction to take, coming out of the swamp from the Silver Rock route."

"Next time, let's not wait until the last minute to leave the swamp," Dara huffed. She tried to catch her breath while holding on to Ezra for support.

"I'm surprised we found our way out," Jared remarked. He wiped the sweat from his face with his shirt.

"My mistake. I forgot how dark it gets in the swamp," Ezra chuckled. The fear had left, now that he knew where he was. "We won't meet this late again."

Dara breathed normal and said, "I'm so relieved and glad I can see more than three inches in front of me."

All three started to laugh.

Ezra tried to get serious for a moment. "Let's meet in two days in the morning."

"On the first day of the week?" Dara questioned.

"Yes, on the first day of the week," Ezra repeated, "at the rock again."

"Oh great," Jared sighed. "Which routes? The Green Lake route has been compromised."

Ezra looked at Jared and was about to say something when Dara interrupted.

"Let's stick together," she said. "I think it's safer that way."

"We certainly can't use the Green Lake route," Jared said. He was in obvious agreement with Dara. "Someone followed me on that route."

"Okay," Ezra answered. "How about we all meet at the first stream crossing on the Silver Rock route? It's about halfway to the rock, and we can go together."

"Perfect," Dara said. She smiled and was back to her chipper self.

"Good. I will see you there," Jared said. He tucked in his shirt. "I better get home; my parents are probably wondering where I am."

~*~

The Watchers waited patiently, a good distance away. They listened as the Three Witnesses said their goodbyes and went home. As soon as the three were a safe distance away, the two Watchers came out of the swamp. They each wondered what the other knew, but it was not a good time for them to talk. They were curious what had happened to Abia. However, they didn't have time to discuss that either. They had to complete their mission for the night and get back to report what they had learned. They could talk freely about the mission in the inner chamber.

Hearing Seth's footsteps behind him, Joab walked as fast as possible through the forest. He thought this night would never end. The three had taken forever to work their way out of the swamp. *It was painful following them*, thought Joab. He wanted so badly to take charge and lead them out of the swamp. For a Watcher, that was an easy movement. Joab was glad that the three witnesses decided to stick together next time. *Still*, he thought, *it will probably be too dark for them*. He was frustrated by their slow, tentative movements.

Joab and Seth came into the city and entered the market square. It was dark and hard for them to see the vegetable stand, signaling which route to take to the inner chamber. Torches illuminated parts of the market square, and the vegetable stand had a kerosene lamp. Still, they had to stand next to the vegetable stand with noses practically touching the buckets to find the signal.

Seth saw the bucket on the vegetable stand first. He whispered to Joab, "R4."

The Palace had a rock wall twelve feet high that surrounded it. Except for the open market square to the front of the palace, the city's businesses and houses were built right up against the rock wall.

They veered right and on to the fourth entrance to the secret passage. There were grates ground level on the bottom sides of the buildings that drained rainwater from the streets. They were just wide enough for the Watchers to slip down into the tunnels. The specific one they needed this night was hidden around a corner—a blind spot. No one saw them.

Joab felt his way down the ladder as he headed toward the bottom. It opened into a large tunnel. He couldn't see anything; it was too dark. He knelt down and waited for Seth to come. Joab heard Seth get closer, and he marveled how the inner chamber was built under the palace, right under a clueless Javan.

"Joab, are you there?" Seth whispered as he reached out for him.

"Right here," Joab said grabbing Seth's arm. "Hold on to the back of my belt, so we don't get separated moving down this tunnel."

"It's been a long time since I've been down R4," Seth said griping the belt.

"Me too," Joab agreed. "If I remember right, it's pitch-black like this for two hundred feet. Then we enter a lit room, and we take the first hallway to the right. This takes us to the inner chamber's back door."

Seth laughed quietly. "Last time I came this way, I walked right past the back door."

"I always have trouble finding it myself," Joab agreed. He held out his arms and felt his way through the tunnel. "Abia never has trouble finding the back door. Of course, he comes here all the time to get our orders."

"Here's the wall. The door has to be here somewhere," Seth said. He felt around for a loose rock in the wall.

"I found it," Joab said. He pulled the rock out, revealing a wooden latch. Joab knocked hard on the latch. It opened.

"Who is it?"

"Seth and Joab." They stood back and watched as the rock wall opened. There was no way anyone else could know there was a door there.

"Come on in," Shobal said. He gave them both a hug. "It's so good to see you." Shobal stepped back. *How different the three were*, he thought. Joab was tall and lanky, Seth was husky, Abia although short, his muscular build and aggressive personality made him appear much taller.

"It has been a long time," Seth agreed. He noticed Shobal looked a lot older since the last time he had seen him. His hair was now white with gray, and his face tracked with more wrinkles.

"It has," Shobal said. He motioned for them to follow. "Abia has kept me up to date on all the good work you both have been doing. He is waiting in my office for us."

"Abia there you are! We were worried," Joab said. "We didn't know what happened to you."

"Someone followed Jared into the swamp on the Green Lake route," Abia answered.

"We know," Joab said. "The Three Witnesses know too."

"What?" Abia said. "How did they find out?"

Jared and Seth started talking at the same time.

Shobal interrupted, "Stop. Stop. Why don't you three have a seat and start from the beginning? Tell me what you learned tonight, one at a time, starting with Abia, so we don't miss a thing."

CHAPTER 15

"I can't believe Ezra's not home yet," Labin said, pacing back and forth.

"He's much later than usual," Asa answered. He raked his hand through his dark hair and glanced at the wall clock. "It's going to look suspicious if we're both waiting for him to come back."

"I know, I know," Labin peered out the window into the dark fog and sighed. "I'm just worried, I guess. I will head off to bed."

"Good night."

Labin stopped and turned back before he left the room. "Listen, Asa, don't mention anything about the earlier conversation with him. Maybe he won't mention it again."

"I hope you're right."

Asa watched Labin leave the room and wished Eva, his wife, was there. She would know exactly how to deal with Ezra. Asa had been very lonely since she went missing. The house and Ezra had not been the same since. Asa added firewood to the fire and kept thinking about his wife. He wondered if maybe she told Ezra about the *Book of Prophesies* and the Light of the Word.

Asa remembered the one time he did catch her praying. She seemed to be glowing. She wouldn't tell him how she learned. Asa forbade her from praying ever again, and their relationship changed after that. She became more secretive. Asa never told any of this to Labin for he would have made her life miserable.

"Hi father," Ezra startled Asa as he entered the room, "You're still up."

"You didn't come home at your usual time, so I stayed up to make sure you were all right."

"I'm fine," Ezra said, trying to act normal. "Time just slipped away from us."

"Where were you," Asa asked, "the community center with Dara and Jared?"

"No, we didn't go to the community center," he said, just in case his father had checked. He sensed his father wanted an answer, so he continued, "We just walked around."

"For a couple of hours?" questioned Asa.

"Yeah, I told you the time just slipped away," Ezra answered. He tried not to sound defensive.

Asa sensed Ezra's avoidance. "Why don't we sit down and talk for awhile?"

"I'm really tired," Ezra said. He really did not want a conversation with his father.

"Just a few minutes. Sit."

Ezra walked over to the couch and sat down. He noticed his father studying him. Determined not to mention anything related to the Light of the Word, he planned to downplay it as nothing if confronted. He knew he needed to play it safe from here on out.

"I really miss your mom," Asa said. "I know you miss her too."

"I do," Ezra agreed. He watched the fire crackle, and his throat tightened. "It's been almost two years since ... Since mom went missing," he choked up.

They both sat there awhile and watched the fire. Finally, Ezra said, "What do you think happened to Mom? I'm sick of rumors."

"I don't know. No one knows. It's a mystery where people go when they disappear."

"Someone has to know," Ezra added. He stopped before he said too much.

Asa faced sideways on the couch to look at Ezra. "Did Mom tell you stories about the past?" Asa inquired. "The stories that are unlawful to talk about?"

"She didn't," Ezra shook his head.

"If she did, you need to tell me," probed Asa, staring Ezra down. "You won't get in trouble if she did. We will keep it between you and me."

"She never talked to me about anything unlawful," Ezra said. He got up from the couch. "Father, I'm really tired. I need some sleep."

"Good night, then."

As Ezra walked up the stairs to his room, he sensed his father didn't believe him. But it was the truth. His mother had never said anything to him about this stuff. The only way Ezra knew anything was because the

Whisperer told him. It was obvious the Whisperer would have to show him what he needed to know and lead him to the Light of the Word.

Ezra thought about the way his father was acting. His mom must have known about the *Book of Prophesies* and the Light of the Word. He wondered why she never told him and why his father was keeping all this information from him. Ezra said he wasn't going to ask them, but he was getting really angry not knowing all the family secrets. He was tired of talking around stuff. Tomorrow, I need to confront my grandfather and get some answers.

Ezra lay down in bed. He was anxious and a little scared. Last night when the Whisperer came, it was unnatural and spooky. A part of him didn't want the Whisperer to come because he was scared, but he also wanted to hear the Whisperer again. Ever since the Whisperer spoke to him, he had a hunger to know the Truth and a longing in his heart to hear more. The Whisperer's voice had provoked a drive to pursue and learn the truth. Somehow, Ezra sensed that only the Whisperer could lead him to the Truth. He had to be brave and talk to the Whisperer tonight.

Ezra sat quietly in the dark and listened for the Whisperer. Ezra fought to stay awake, for he was exhausted. He kept drifting off to sleep, and then be jolted awake by every little creaking noise. The wind outside howled, and the windows rattled. It spooked him every time. He sat there, quietly listening to the trees brushing against the side of their old house. Ezra decided to call out to the Whisperer to see if he would answer.

"Whisperer, whisperer, are you there?" Ezra listened. "Whisperer, where do I find the *Book of Prophesies* that will show me the Light of the Word?" No answer. Nothing. Ezra eventually succumbed to his exhaustion, falling into a deep sleep.

It was light outside, the brightest Ezra had ever seen. He was with a crowd of people standing around the rock in the middle of the rocks. He felt such joy and supernatural energy as he looked around. He didn't recognize anyone—wait, his mother was bidding him to come. Mother! Suddenly, the chatter from the crowd ceased, and everyone gave their attention to a man standing on the rock.

Ezra felt the anticipation and hunger that everyone in the crowd showed.

The man standing on the rock wore a thick, rough robe with a wide leather belt. His hair was gray with a long, gray beard that went past his belt. His eyes radiated like flashes of light. They looked like they were on fire. He opened a book in his hands.

Ezra asked the person next to him, "What book does the man have in his hand?"

"Be quiet. He has the *Book of Prophesies*; he's talking about the Light of the Word."

Mesmerized Ezra listened to the words the old man was reading from the book.

"It is written, 'I am the light of the world: He that follows me shall not walk in darkness, but shall have the light of life.' He is life, the creator of all," said the old man. "If we follow the light, we will have the light of life. This light is the truth." The old man read some more. "The Word said, 'I am the way, the truth, and the life. No man cometh unto the father but by me.'" The old man turned some pages and read, "'For with thee is the fountain of life: in thy light shall we see light.'"

Ezra was so taken by the words the old man was reading that he glanced at his mother to see her response to the words, but he couldn't see her. Frantic, he moved quickly searching for her. He squeezed and pushed his way through the packed crowd. He didn't see her anywhere. Panic set in—searching, needing to find her, "Mother." Scared he couldn't find her—turning, looking, "Mother."

Ezra woke up suddenly; there was a pounding at the door. Catching his breath, he called out, "Who is it?"

"It's your father," he said, as he opened the door. "Is everything all right?"

"Yes, I'm fine," Ezra said. He cleared his throat. "I must have been dreaming."

"You must have been dreaming. I heard you call out, 'Mother.'"

"Mother, was in my dream."

"What was the dream about?" Asa probed.

"I don't remember," he lied. "All I remember is Mom was in it."

"You don't remember anything else?" Asa inquired. His eyes searched the room.

He doesn't believe me. "No, I don't. Good night, Father."

"Good night," Asa said. He closed the door behind him.

Ezra did remember every detail of the dream. It seemed so real to him. Lying to his father made him feel bad. But who could he trust? His father had warned him to stop talking about the *Book of Prophesies* and the Light of the Word, and he practically went crazy when he mentioned the Whisperer.

Ezra knew he couldn't stop. So many questions. He wondered what all this had to do with his mom, and he had this inward drive to know the Truth no matter what the cost. He just had to be cautious and wait for the right opportunity to find out the Truth. He needed to wait on the Whisperer.

CHAPTER 16

Shobal grinned ear to ear. "I have been waiting for this moment my whole life. I still can't believe the Whisperer visited Ezra in the night and talked to him—not just talked to him but commissioned him."

"Another confirmation among many," Abia said. "They are definitely the three witnesses."

"Without a doubt they are," Shobal said.

"Agreed," Joab responded. He stood up, almost hitting his head on the ceiling. He was taller than the rest with a lanky build. Rubbing his short-cropped hair, he asked, "Why would the Whisperer pick them? You should have seen them tonight, navigating through the swamp. They were pitiful."

"They were bad," Seth agreed.

"I am surprised this group can find their way home," continued Joab sarcastically. "And they're supposed to find the book."

"Haven't you been listening to what I've been telling you all these years?" Shobal questioned, frustrated at Joab. "It's the Whisperer that has the power. He is the one that will lead and empower them to accomplish the Light of the Word's purpose. All he needs are willing vessels that will take his direction. He empowers. He made Ezra, Dara, and Jared willing to fulfill his purpose. He has prepared us to help and facilitate their success. I don't know why you're surprised anyway. They're a bright group of kids and most of all they are a good team. Only through good teamwork will they be successful."

"I just thought the three witnesses would be different," Joab said, "and not so ordinary."

"The Whisperer uses ordinary people to accomplish his purpose," Shobal assured them.

"Yeah! Case in point—look at us!" Abia chuckled. Finding it funny, Seth and Joab also laughed.

"I'm very disappointed with Labin and Asa," Shobal said. He scratched his chin thatched with a scraggly, gray beard.

"So am I," agreed Abia. "They are descendants of the Children of Light, and none of this information has been passed down to Ezra. I wonder if it's been passed down to his father. I'm totally frustrated at the complacency of the Children of Light."

"I know it's been passed down to Labin," Shobal answered. "Go ahead, and take a seat. That information has been verified on our genealogy charts that track the Children of Light."

"That will make our job harder," Seth said. He reached for the water pitcher.

"How?" Joab asked seated next to Shobal.

"He doesn't know the history of the Children of Light," Seth said. "If he knew the history, all this would make more sense. He would also have heard of the Whisperer before this."

"You're right," Shobal agreed. "We don't know how much he knows, but he's unaware of the last prophecy spoken by the prophet before he was martyred."

"I hope Labin will tell him," Seth said.

Abia, deep in thought, said, "We need a way the three witnesses will find out the prophecy. They need to know everything that was supposed to be passed down."

"There's got to be a way," Seth said.

They were all silent, thinking of the different possibilities.

"Let's think on that a while," Shobal broke the silence then stood. "Now, let's talk about this intruder."

"Not much to talk about," Abia said. "I don't know anything about him, other than he followed Jared on the Green Lake route."

"Did you see or hear anything, Joab?" Shobal asked.

"No, I didn't," Joab said, "not clearly anyway. I heard someone yelling at a distance, but I couldn't make out what they were saying or who it was. I know now, it was Jared. I didn't find out he was followed, till he ran past my position and into Ezra," Joab laughed. "After Jared and Ezra got done wrestling in the mud, Jared told Ezra he was followed."

"Did he give a description?" Abia asked.

"No," Joab said. "At first, Jared thought Ezra was the one that followed and played a joke on him. He only heard the intruder; he didn't see anything."

"I wasn't going to bring up what the Watchers assigned to the border found out," Shobal said, "but, I feel I must because it directly affects you. Why don't we all move to the big conference room? I can show you on the area map."

Shobal filled in the three Watchers on everything that had happened on the border, the footprints the border guards had found, and the newly discovered city in Cannibal Land. He described how the intruder had frequently been going back and forth across the border.

Abia listened to Shobal talk about the border. He was amazed how everything seemed to tie together. The intruder, who had eluded everyone, came into the valley to follow the three witnesses. He wondered how the intruder knew to follow them. Abia thought they were the only ones that knew. At first, he reasoned, Javan's man followed Jared, but everything pointed to someone else.

"So, Javan and his two platoons of guards should be at the eastern cut by now," continued Shobal. "Sometime tomorrow, or the day after, they should be at the north crest mountain range."

"When will you receive more information from the border Watchers?" Abia asked.

"By the afternoon of the first day of the week," Shobal answered.

"So, after we're done with the three at the rock that morning," Seth inquired. "Can we come to hear what Jotham the head of the border Watchers has to report?"

"No. it's too risky. Too many Watchers would draw attention," Shobal said. "Today was an exception. I only want Abia to come that night and report what you learned." Shobal sensed Joab's and Seth's disappointment. "I will brief Abia on everything you might need to know concerning the border."

"What do you want us to do if the intruder follows one of the three again?" Abia questioned.

Shobal took a deep breath. "Let me think about this a bit." He started to pace around the room.

"We should catch him before Javan and his men do," Joab suggested.

"Or at least follow him," Seth interjected.

"Joab is right," Abia said. "We should catch him and interrogate him. We are too close now to have an intruder mess things up."

"Agreed. But we have to work smart." Shobal sighed, as he poured himself a drink of water. He looked at the three watchers, and took a long drink, wiping some of the water off his shirt that dripped from his beard. "The hourglass has started, so we must change our tactics. I want Seth to be at the rock to overhear the three witnesses' conversation.

Then, I want Abia and Joab to catch the intruder. Keep him quiet and hidden in the swamp until nightfall. After Seth follows the three witnesses out of the swamp, I want him to go tell the storekeeper that we caught the intruder. The storekeeper will bring me word. He's a Watcher too. Then, I want Abia and Joab to wait until nightfall then bring the intruder to the back of the storekeeper's store. Knock on the door. Give the intruder to the person that answers and leave. If the storekeeper doesn't give me word, then I know you didn't catch him." Shobal looked at Abia. "I still want you to come that night and brief me, regardless."

CHAPTER 17

Dara liked shopping at the market square. She always ran into old friends, cousins, and even met new people. She wished she could work in the market square because there was activity, people, and many things to see as well as experience. However, her mom was a dressmaker, and Dara had to help her when she was not in school. So, she cherished the times her mom sent her out to do the shopping.

Dara was a little tired, considering how late she got home the night before. It was by pure luck her mom was asleep when she got home. Otherwise, she would've been in trouble for being late.

She couldn't wait to go to the rock in the middle of the rocks again. It was always adventurous and fun, even though it was scary. The night movement in the swamp was grueling and horrible. A few times she thought she would never make it home. Every day she wished she could spend more time with Ezra. At first, she thought Ezra was making everything up, but now, it appeared to be true.

Dara pulled out the grocery list her mom had given her. She looked around the market square for one of her friends. As Dara walked around the market place, she had no idea a Watcher was observing her.

Myka scrutinized Dara, waiting for the right time to put a note in Dara's pocket without her knowing. She was excited the storekeeper gave her a real mission. Her usual job was watching the market square for something unusual. Whatever that means, she didn't actually know. The storekeeper gave Myka the mission because she knew Dara from school. She waited for the perfect time to slip Dara the note. She wondered what it said. The note was folded so tightly she couldn't tell. Besides, he warned her not to peek. They weren't sure where Dara would be today, so Myka waited at the store until another Watcher gave word Dara entered the square. Myka was relieved. It was much easier to pass information off at the market square. With so many people bumping into each other, Dara wouldn't notice another bump.

Myka thought Dara was so lucky. She was beautiful, with her long, blond hair, and her tall, sleek body. She seemed always to attract attention. Her good looks didn't go to her head though. Dara was genuinely nice and fun. Everyone at school had noticed how she and Ezra liked each other. They always looked at each other every chance they had and would try to sit together in class. Myka had to admit that Ezra was very handsome. However, the reason she thought Dara was lucky was because she was close friends with Jared, Ezra's best friend.

Myka thought Jared was so cute, in a geeky kind of way. It was funny. Whenever she tried to talk to Jared, he would start to fidget and get nervous. Myka never knew what fidget meant until she met Jared. Jared was self-conscious of his freckles, and the fact he wore glasses. But Myka thought they made him look cute. He wasn't all that athletic, but he was super smart. He was, well—perfect. She only wished Jared would notice her more. If only she was tall with blond hair, instead of short with wavy brown hair that sometimes frizzed. She was known as a tomboy, and she had a hard time breaking away from that label. She hated it! Myka was growing up. Would Jared ever notice?

Encountering a glare from another Watcher, she controlled her wandering thoughts. She thought, *Don't they trust I'll get the job done? This is ridiculous. There are more Watchers on me than Dara.*

"Oh sorry," Myka said, as she bumped into Dara from behind.

"Myka?"

"I'm sorry. I wasn't paying attention to where I was going."

Dara laughed, "It's okay." She sensed Myka's embarrassment. "It's no big deal, really. I'm glad you bumped into me."

"Doing some shopping too?" Myka asked. She looked up at Dara and felt every inch of her shortness.

"Yeah, I'm glad," Dara responded. She smiled at Myka, happy to see her. "It gets me out of the house. Are you enjoying summer break from school?"

"Mostly," Myka said. "I don't miss school, but I miss seeing everyone."

"We should spend some time together."

"I would love that," Myka grinned hoping she didn't sound too needy.

"How about next Monday night? We could meet at the community center," Dara continued. "I'll get Ezra and Jared to come too."

Myka tried not to sound overly excited. "Great," she said and realized how excited she sounded. *Oh, well,* she thought, *so what if Dara knows I have a crush on Jared.* She had nothing to lose at this point. "Is Jared here today?"

Dara smiled. "No, I haven't seen him today."

"Well, I'll see you later. Monday night, for sure," Myka said. "I'm late for work at the store."

"It was good to see you, Myka," Dara said. "I can't wait till Monday night."

They gave each other a hug and departed.

Okay, thought Myka. *I actually accomplished the mission. You Watchers can stop watching me now.* She wanted to rub it in their face. *Girls made excellent Watchers, too!*

The storekeeper sent a messenger to Shobal. *The note was passed.*

CHAPTER 18

As Captain Hyrum, the head of the border guards climbed the last five hundred feet to the north crest lookout, he could hear Commander Javan's heavy breathing behind him. Clearly, Javan wasn't as used to the high altitudes as the border guards. Hyrum had to stop to let him and the others catch up. He looked out away from the valley breathing in the clear air. He loved being on the top of the mountains. It was a breathtaking view.

Captain Hyrum liked his position. Working and living on the border was truly a different world. It was always sunny, bright, and beautiful on the mountains surrounding the valley of Thanoton, and the guards were certainly healthier than the valley residents were. It was obvious. The border people had the advantage of eating better. The sunlight made it possible to grow more varieties of vegetables that were better for them, and hunting was better, too. The people living in the valley were pale and depressed all the time.

They left most of the men with the horses when the horses could no longer navigate the terrain. Hyrum instructed Commander Javan to take only ten men with him the rest of the way. He was glad Javan listened. Hyrum was tired of waiting on them. He couldn't wait to see the city himself.

"Only ten more feet Commander Javan," said Hyrum from the top of the ridge. "Then it's all flat the rest of the way."

Javan huffed as he reached the top. "Good," he said. He took a deep breath and struggled to talk. "Hurry up, the rest of you," yelled Javan down to the ten men that were still climbing.

"Welcome, Captain Hyrum and Commander Javan," said a north crest border guard.

"Is it just you?" Javan questioned. He looked at the young border guard that stood before him.

"No, sir. The other border guard is out hunting for dinner. Will you be joining us?"

Hyrum jumped in and said, "We won't spend the night here. After you show us everything you know about this newly-discovered city, we will head down and camp at the foot of this ridge line. The rest of Commander Javan's men are there."

Javan looked at Hyrum with a surprised look, and questioned, "You only have two border guards up here?"

"Yes, we work in pairs," Hyrum answered. He stated what he thought Javan already knew. "We have a lot of border to cover and only so many men, so we are spread out."

"I knew you worked in pairs, but I didn't realize how spread out it really was." Javan stroked his red beard while he looked around and said, "We are hours away from another position."

"That's right," Hyrum said. He slipped on his fur-lined hood. The sweat from the climb gave him a chill on the cold mountain top.

"I guess that's why—" Javan stopped. He did not want the others to hear what he was about to say to Hyrum. "Show me this city!"

"Commander Javan, if you stand over here, you'll see the city in between those two peaks," said the young border guard, as he pointed in the direction of the city. He handed him a scope to look through.

Javan adjusted the scope and said, "There, I see it now." He took a step to the right. "It's a big city, bigger than I thought it would be!"

"It is!" Hyrum said as he looked through his scope. "It only looks about twenty miles away."

"Do the inhabitants of that city ever travel this direction," Hyrum asked, "close to our position?"

"No," answered the young border guard. "The closest we've ever seen people is near the lower level mountains." He pointed in that direction.

"What were they doing?" Javan asked as he scanned the lower level mountains with the scope.

"Hunting," responded the young border guard.

Javan was amused the way the border guard had said "hunting." Javan could almost hear the guard's thoughts, *Of course, they were hunting. What else would they be doing?* It was truly a different world out here.

"At night you can see the city really well," said the young border guard. "It glows from all the lights and fireplaces in the houses."

"What else have you noticed about them?" Hyrum inquired. He was still looking through his scope.

"They spend their days working in the fields surrounding their city. They're farmers with a lot of horses to work the fields. They also have a lot of sheep and cattle. They seem to work as a community, sharing everything. We have never seen them eat each other."

Javan said nothing, seeming to think about what the young border guard had just said.

"Have you seen other people's footprints coming or going across the border?" Hyrum asked.

"No, it's just us up here."

Again, Javan saw what the border guard was thinking in his expression, *What a weird question!* Javan turned and studied the city some more.

Hyrum was worried. He wondered if Javan was thinking the same thing he was. It was possible some of the border guards at the eastern cut, had allowed the intruder to come in and out by looking the other way. Most of the border guards had never lived in Thanoton. They also dressed differently than the valley residents. Border guards wore brown leather fur lined jackets and caps to insulate from the high altitude temperatures as well as blend in to the terrain. They were equipped with body armor in case of emergencies but never wore it. The body armor would get in the way of squeezing through tight spaces and climbing. They lived on the border with their families. The north crest was the only location where having a family was not practical.

Back at the eastern cut, Jotham sat to take a break. He rubbed his blue eyes, and stretched then removed his leather, fur-lined cap, and scratched his scalp; his blond hair was tousled. Jotham was a border guard, but more importantly, he was secretly the head of the border Watchers. He was a messenger in the border guards delivering messages all around the border. He knew the ridgeline trail, better than anyone did. His job as a messenger was a perfect cover.

As he sat there thinking, he had this nagging feeling something else was going on. Where the border guards had seen the footprints, the intruder could have only come through area guarded by Caleb and Neptali—his fellow Watchers.

He thought about the conversation he had with them earlier that day. They had said, "We have not seen anyone or any footprints come through this area. All the foot traffic was found in a different location." Jotham didn't question them any further. He wondered if he should have. *Who knows? Maybe there are other ways the foot traffic could have funneled*, he thought. Jotham did not want to sound like he was questioning them. He did think they acted suspiciously. He hated suspecting them. *No Watcher would help the enemy. There would be no reason for them to help people leave the valley to go to their certain death. They definitely would not let an intruder enter. They were too skilled for that.* Still, he wondered.

Jotham was not satisfied, so he decided to go out a second time to track the intruder's footprints. He needed to find out exactly where he crossed the border. This time, he went without Caleb and Neptali, so they couldn't influence where he went. He ventured past the border with his sword drawn, ready to strike if needed. Jotham turned around to look at the eastern cut for the best way to enter. *How would the intruder enter?*

After careful scrutiny, he determined the best way and followed it. His suspicions were quickly confirmed when he saw multiple human tracks going the same direction. He followed the tracks up to the border. Jotham saw what looked like a small crevice in the massive rocks that naturally lined the border. The path led straight through the crevice. Just before he reached the crevice, he noticed a symbol etched into the rock at the start of the crevice. A symbol he had not seen before.

"Hey! What are you doing here?" Caleb stopped Jotham from following the path any farther.

"I, I was looking for tracks," Jotham answered. He was caught off guard with the suddenness of Caleb's shout. He noticed Caleb was not surprised to see him. Caleb must have tracked him the whole way and stopped him before he went any farther. *This area must be important,* thought Jotham.

"Did you find any tracks?" Caleb questioned. He had his hands on his hips and showed no signs of concern that he was outside the valley of Thanoton.

"I didn't see any tracks," Jotham answered. He lied because he sensed something was wrong, and felt uneasy around Caleb. He hoped he wouldn't be asked if he saw the symbol etched into the rock. "I wanted to take one last look around before I went home."

"We got this area covered," Caleb said. "We will let you know if we find out anything."

Jotham waved his hand trying to act casually, "See you later." He headed out a different direction to climb over the rocks to get into the valley of Thanoton. It was obvious Caleb did not want him to follow the trail into the crevice.

Jotham climbed through the rocks. He stopped to take a break once he was on the other side. He decided not to say anything to Shobal until he was confident Caleb and Neptali were helping the intruder. Jotham determined to keep an eye on them to find out the truth. He opened his notebook and drew the symbol he had seen etched in the rock, and then, he left for his home near the eastern cut.

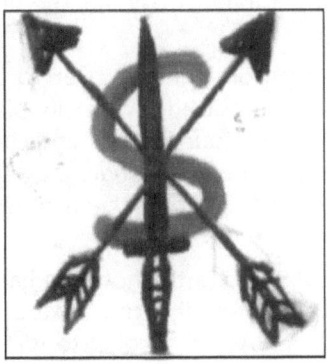

CHAPTER 19

"Dara, what a pleasant surprise," greeted Asa. "What brings you to our blacksmith's shop?"

"I came to see Ezra. Is he here?"

"He's out back getting a load of coal for the fire pits. He should be back soon."

Dara was still sweating from running over to the blacksmith shop. She couldn't stand being in that hot, musty, smelly blacksmith shop. It was truly like an oven, with at least four fire pits and the sound of hammers pounding and forging steel. *Noisy! I wonder how Ezra stands working here all day. I guess he adjusted to it, as I have with sewing,* Dara smiled. *It certainly makes him strong.*

She couldn't wait to show Ezra the note she had discovered late last night. She had tossed and turned all night, anxious for the morning to come, so she could tell Ezra. "Asa, I'm going to wait out back for Ezra," Dara said. She pointed at the back door. "It's too hot in here."

"Go ahead and cut through," Asa responded. He motioned for the other workers to get out of her way.

Dara walked through the shop around the fire pits and piles of scrap metal, and she couldn't help notice how Labin stared at her from the back office. She wondered what was on his mind that he stared so. Ezra was right. They certainly couldn't trust anyone if the note was true. Dara was getting paranoid like everyone else in Thanoton. They had good reason to be paranoid. Javan had left with two platoons of guards, and his soldiers were out in full force patrolling the market square, neighborhoods, and roads. There was even talk of searching people's houses again.

Dara got excited as soon as she saw Ezra. He came around the back of the shop, with a wagonload of coal. She looked at Ezra and started laughing. "You look as black as the pair of horses pulling the wagon," she chuckled. "You're supposed to scoop it, not roll in it."

"Ha, ha!" Ezra mocked then started laughing because she was laughing. "What are you doing here?" Ezra asked. He noticed, along with Dara, that Labin and Asa were watching them through an open window.

Dara turned away from the window and stood close to Ezra. She whispered, "I need to talk to you alone."

Ezra saw how serious she was, unlike her usual playful self. "Father, we're going for a walk. I'll be right back." He almost grabbed Dara by the arm but stopped himself, not wanting to get coal dust on her. "Let's go down to the creek."

"That would be perfect," she said. She glanced back and noticed Ezra's grandfather was still watching her. "Your father and grandfather are suspicious of me. They've never been before."

"They have been acting this way ever since I started to ask questions about what we talked about at the rock," Ezra whispered.

Ezra was happy Dara stopped by. He couldn't stand being away from her for even one day. He wasn't sure what all this stuff was about, but one good thing was coming out of it. They had an excuse to be with each other more. She smelled so good all the time. He backed a little away from her knowing that he probably smelled from sweat and coal smoke.

"Here we are; let's sit," Ezra said. He motioned toward a big tree lying on its side. "We'll be safe from prying eyes and ears here." He looked intently at Dara. "Still, we should keep our voices down."

She looked like she was ready to explode with information, and got right to the point. "Yesterday, someone slipped me a folded-up message with our names on it. I found it last night."

"What did it say?"

"Here, I'll let you read it." She handed it to him.

Ezra unfolded it and read.

Ezra, Jared, Dara:

You three are the descendants of the Children of Light, a group of people that lived serving the Light of the Word. This truth about the Light of the Word is found in the Book of Prophesies. *The Children of Light lived their lives ruled by this book.*

Over a thousand years ago, there grew an element in the valley of Thanoton that did not want to be ruled by the Light of the Word. Over time, they convinced the majority of people to reject the Truth found in the Book of Prophesies. *As they started to reject this light, the valley grew dim and the fog rolled in. This happened because the people craved the darkness rather than the light. They were evil. They did not want to embrace the Light of the Word because it exposed their wickedness. So, they rejected the Light of the Word and ruled themselves.*

Those few who embraced the Light of the Word and hated the darkness were killed. Since that time, anyone that tried to embrace the Light of the Word or pursue it, talk, or teach others about it, were arrested. Those arrested were sentenced to death by stoning. The Children of Darkness made an example of those who embraced the Light. They erected the pole, tied them to the martyr's pole in the town square, and stoned them to death.

This prophesy that has been passed down was given by the last prophet before he was martyred. He spoke it just before he was stoned to death. The Children of Darkness heard this prophecy and killed anyone who tries to fulfill it. The Children of Darkness were eager to kill the prophet because he had read the Book of the Prophesies, and knew the Light of the Word. They figured if they killed him, as the others before him, the Light of the Word, the Truth, would die with him. Just before he died, he said,

"The whisperer will come and empower three witnesses that will make manifest the works of darkness and destroy it, and deliver my people from the grip of darkness to the freedom found in the light."

All the Children of the Light went into hiding passing down this prophesy and waiting for its fulfillment. They have been waiting for the time they would be delivered from this darkness.

You are the Three Witnesses!

After you read this, destroy it! Having this paper is a guaranteed death sentence if caught.

Follow the Whisperer. Seek, and you will find.

You are not alone.

As Ezra reread the note, he felt Dara squeeze closer to him to read it again.

He slid away a little and said, "How come this was never passed down to us? Have you heard any of this before?"

"No, I haven't." She sensed she was making Ezra uncomfortable by sitting so close.

"I'm fairly confident Jared has never heard any of this either," Ezra said. He got angrier the more he thought about it.

"This information should've been passed down to us," Dara was also frustrated. "It says we're the descendants of the Children of Light."

"Our parents never passed this information on to us, as they should have," Ezra said. "Indeed, my father and grandfather are trying to stop me from finding out. I've decided I'm not going to ask Labin about any of this. Do you have any idea who might have passed this to you?"

"I have no idea," Dara answered. She took a deep breath. "I thought a lot about it, and it could have been anyone. I went to the market square yesterday, and it was crowded, everyone bumping into each other. I talked to some friends from school. That's about it."

"Someone knows who we are," Ezra continued. "Why would they slip us a note, and not speak to us in person?"

Dara wiped a tear from her eye. "Ezra, I'm scared. It says we are the witnesses. Why us? There must be a mistake."

"I don't know why we were chosen," Ezra answered. "I had a dream last night. The Whisperer was showing me the prophet, and it goes along with all of this. I will tell you and Jared about it tomorrow when we're at the rock."

"Maybe we should meet someplace closer. There are other places we can talk quietly."

"I just love going to the rock. It's fun."

"Is it because you've had several dreams about that place?" Dara inquired.

"I think the rock in the middle of the rocks is an important part of all this. I just don't know how. Remember you told me yourself how exciting it is to go there," Ezra said. "Anyway, we better get back, so we don't cause any more suspicion."

"Okay. But we should destroy the note. I don't want to carry it anymore. I'm too scared."

"I will destroy it," Ezra said. He wanted to comfort her. "We'll tell Jared what it said at the rock tomorrow. I don't want to take a chance of getting caught with it on our way to the rock, considering Jared was followed the last time. I will see you tomorrow at the creek split on the Silver Rock route." He stood up, helped her up, too.

"I can't wait," Dara said. She walked back to the shop with him. "What will you say if they ask you what we talked about?"

"I will just tell them it's boyfriend, girlfriend things," Ezra answered. He imagined their looks. "That should throw them off." He glanced at Dara and saw her expression. "Oh, is that all right?"

Dara wiped a tear. "That would be perfect," she said. Happily, she tried to control her tears. She smiled, and her blue eyes held a tender expression. She touched Ezra on the arm then ran off.

Ezra watched Dara as she ran off and thought, *I never saw her look or smile at me like that before.*

He walked back into the shop and went straight to his work area. He ignored his father and grandfather. He could tell they were curious to know what they had talked about. *If they want to know, they can ask,* thought Ezra. He watched his father and grandfather walk out back. He threw the note into the fire.

Ezra hated the fact he had to lie and keep all this stuff from his father and grandfather, but he had to. He justified it in his mind because they had lied and kept stuff from him. He knew his mother would've never let him make an excuse like that. However, it was for their own good, to protect them until he figured all this out. Until he could deliver everyone. *Deliver from what?* That's what Ezra didn't know.

"Go ask him," whispered Labin angrily.

"Ask him what?" Asa said. He knew what Labin meant.

"What do you mean, 'ask him what?' What they talked about."

"I'm not going to ask Ezra what he and Dara talked about," Asa answered.

"Why not?" Labin said, throwing up his hands.

"For one, he's not a little kid anymore. He has grown up into a young man. Two, he would be suspicious."

"At this point, who cares if he's suspicious," Labin responded. "We need to make sure he is not pursuing the Light of the Word."

"I thought the other day you said we should leave him alone and see what he does. You said we shouldn't bring it up again unless he does. He has not given us any indication he is pursuing any of this further," Asa said. He wanted to distance Labin from the situation.

It was true Ezra had not given any further evidence he was pursuing the Light. Nevertheless, if Asa was going to help his son, he needed to earn his trust, and that meant keeping Labin out of it. His plan was to stand back and wait until Ezra needed him.

"Well, you can at least ask him why Dara was wiping tears from her eyes," Labin said. He tried to sound sincere. "See if everything is all right with her." Disgusted Labin went inside the shop.

Ezra glanced out the window and saw his father scooping coal from the wagon into a wheelbarrow. He quickly went out back to help.

"Sorry, Father," Ezra said. "I forgot about the coal. I got sidetracked." He grabbed a shovel. "Here, I'll do this. It's my job to bring the coal in today."

"That's all right. I figured you had a lot on your mind with Dara's visit. Is everything okay? I noticed Dara was crying," Asa asked. Immediately, he was mad at himself, because he didn't resist asking. He was glad Labin wasn't there to hear.

"Oh, just boyfriend, girlfriend stuff," answered Ezra casually. "You know how girls can get."

"Yes, I do," he chuckled and slapped Ezra on the back. "Well, I better start bringing some of this coal inside."

Ezra smiled and watched his father take a load of coal inside the shop. He noticed his father was satisfied with his answer. He loved his father and hated that this situation had come between them.

CHAPTER 20

Myka was very anxious as she watched the storefront. She rearranged the pots, pans, and other cookware, trying to look busy. She wondered why Lot was so late. She was worried something might have happened to him. If he didn't come soon, she worried the storekeeper and two other Watchers would be back. Myka was the only Watcher at the store, so it was the best time to pass the message to Lot so no one would see her do it.

Of course, Myka thought, *I passed information to Lot before I was a Watcher. Now, I never get to go to the storekeeper's meetings with Shobal. Only his handpicked contacts go with him since everyone can't go. If Shobal only knew how stupid and lazy the storekeeper really was, he'd be replaced.* The storekeeper thought she should not be a Watcher because she was a girl. If he really knew the truth, he would probably keel over in unbelief.

Myka saw Lot coming her way. She marveled at the man that came toward her. No one suspected Lot. She guessed that was the whole point. Just look at how no one suspected her. The Watchers all thought she was the least of the least, little did they know.

Lot was a friendly man and greeted everyone. He never seemed in a hurry or rushed. He was not only friendly, but he looked friendly, too. Lot was short, about her height. His build resembled a tree trunk and looked huge compared to Myka with her petite body. His eyes always put her at ease, as if they were saying, "Everything will be all right," He was a pleasant bundle of peacefulness. People always relaxed around him because he genuinely cared for them.

Myka smiled, happy to see him. "Hello, Lot."

"Well, hello! How's my favorite girl?" Lot responded, loud enough for everyone to hear. He gave her a big hug. Oblivious to anyone around, two messages were passed.

"You say that to all the girls," Myka said, not able to contain her laughter.

"Well, you're my favorite of favorites." He said as he laughed with her.

"How may I help you today?" Myka asked. She enjoyed talking to Lot.

"I need to buy some supplies to deliver to the border guards. They ordered a cooking pot, spices, and two more scopes if you have them."

"We do have them," Myka said. She gathered the supplies for Lot. "They have been making more scopes lately because of the demand."

"Great," Lot said. He pulled a couple of gold coins from his pocket handing them to Myka.

"When do you think you will be back?" She asked casually while making change. She carefully watched for signs in his answer. Verbal and non-verbal signals were normal in their conversations. It was like code, or a conversation within a conversation.

"I will probably be back the third day of the week. It depends upon what supplies the border guards and their families need. I will be back the fourth day for sure."

Myka saw Lot wink when he said the fourth day, signaling he would be back the fourth day. Similarly, Lot would ask Myka "What are you up to?" "Nothing," meant, "I have no message to pass." If she said anything else, it meant she did have a message to pass.

Myka helped Lot load the supplies onto his wagon. "Have a safe trip. I will see you later this week."

"Goodbye, my favorite of favorites," Lot chuckled. He climbed onto the wagon and grabbed the reins to the horses. As Lot started to drive the horses away, the storekeeper was crossing the street on his way back to the store.

"Hello, Storekeeper," Lot roared jovially.

Myka couldn't help but laugh after seeing the startled storekeeper's reaction.

"Hello, Lot," said the storekeeper. He was obviously startled but happy to see Lot, as everyone always was. "Did you find everything you needed?"

"Oh yes. My favorite of favorites took good care of me. Thank you." Then Lot headed for the eastern cut.

The storekeeper, still smiling, walked up and put his arm around Myka. "I need to talk to you. Let's go to the back room."

"Okay."

The storekeeper sat down on a crate next to Myka. He whispered, "I don't have to tell you how important tomorrow night will be for us. This is probably the most important mission we've ever done."

"I'll be ready," Myka said. She was always full of energy.

"I know you will be." He smiled and wished he had never been caught up in this mess. "That is why we are going to add a few extra precautions along with the original plan. You will no longer be in charge of the backdoor, and you will not help bring the intruder in after the Watchers drop him off."

"Why?"

"Don't worry. I have another job for you." The storekeeper could tell she was disappointed. "You'll be able to help with the intruder later. Javan's heightened security around the city and Shobal is worried that Javan has sensed something is going on. He wants us to make sure we don't bring the intruder into the city if there is even the slightest chance of being compromised. So, you will be on lookout up in the loft that overlooks the market square tomorrow night. They will bring the intruder much later than we talked about. If you see any activity at all, or anything suspicious, I want you to light a candle and stick it in the window. The Watchers will look for a candle before they come in. If it's lit, they will leave and go to the cave."

"The cave?" Myka made a face. "That's so far away down south."

"Where else can we hide him?" the storekeeper said. He wondered why he was justifying it to her. "They will ride all night and get there before morning. Then, they will wait to hear from us for what to do next. If there is no candle, they will come in, and we will proceed as planned. I want you to be up there early and have enough candles to burn all night in the window. We must make sure they do not miss the warning. We don't know what time of night they might come in. They may run into problems. Do you have any questions about tomorrow night?"

"No, not at all," Myka answered. She was not looking forward to the cramped loft all night.

"Good. You can go home for the rest of the day. Come back tomorrow afternoon."

Myka always waited until she was outside the city before she would read her message. She took the dirt path that led to her aunt's farm. Myka enjoyed living with her aunt's family. She was tired of living in the valley of Thanoton and couldn't wait for her time to leave, but she knew it was very important for her to be there. She must do her part for the higher cause. The only comfort was her time spent alone, seeking the Light of the Word. She was definitely and defiantly a Seeker. She cherished those times the Whisperer would enable her to feel the Light of the Word's presence.

She longed to be around other believers and to worship openly. *Someday*, she thought.

Myka turned on to the dirt path and reached into her pocket. She unfolded the message and read:

M,

I received your last message concerning the Watchers' plan to catch our intruder in the swamp tomorrow. We will continue the mission, with a few changes. Tomorrow, we will not make contact with the Three Witnesses, as was originally planned. Instead, we will take the opportunity to draw the Watchers out and snatch them, as they try to catch us. We will scare them, threaten them, and warn them they are being watched.

Up to this point, they have thought they were the only element out there. We have relied heavily on their ability to collect information. But, they are starting to get in the way. So, our goal is to throw them off enough to be able to conduct our mission. Our hope, of course, is to enlighten them in the future.

We don't want you to reveal information to the Three Witnesses. It's great that you are friends with them and meeting them Monday night at the community center. Just keep alert for any important information. Win their trust. You are more valuable to us, and to them, to stay behind the scenes.

If you are compromised, your escape-and-evasion route is no longer through the eastern cut. Javan's men and the border guards have cordoned off the eastern cut. They are on heightened alert, as are the Watchers. Everyone is looking for an intruder. It's still easy to penetrate, but we don't want to take the chance with you. We want them to focus on the eastern cut so we will step up activities there. Myka, if you are compromised, we want you to take the way of the north as you learned in training to the cache site. You are to wait there until a rescue team arrives to lead you out of the northern route. It's the longest way, but it's the safest.

We understand you want out. You are in the perfect spot to get the information needed. You're vital for our mission. Hang in there! We're praying for you daily. Just think how many people you have helped escape the grip of darkness and come to the marvelous Light. Take comfort in that.

Run the race set before you!

L

Myka lit a match and burned the message, and then she headed home.

~*~

Lot pulled off the road to let the horses rest. He took out the message he received from Myka and read.

L,

I was recently given a message to secretly pass to Dara. They watched me like a hawk till I passed it, but I found a way to glance at it. It had a brief history of the Children of Light. It told the three Witnesses they were descendants. It also contained the last prophets prophecy, concerning the three Witnesses. The letter told them they were the three Witnesses.

Apparently, that information never was passed down as it should've been. We had assumed they knew; they know now. I overheard a Watcher tell the storekeeper that Dara showed the message to Ezra today. They probably will talk about it tomorrow at the rock in the middle of the rocks. It's quite obvious, at this point; they have been led by the Whisperer.

M

Lot folded up the message. He slid it in a tiny incision in the seam of his coat. One would have to work hard to find it. Then, he drove his horses to the eastern cut.

CHAPTER 21

Ezra woke up from a restful sleep. He was in no hurry to get out of bed, as he contemplated everything that had happened so far. Before he had fallen asleep, he wanted to spend some time talking to the Whisperer or the Light of the Word. He wasn't really sure who he was supposed to talk to. He must have been deeply exhausted, for he fell right to sleep, and slept the whole night. No dreams. He had also hoped for another dream where he could see his mother again. She looked so happy. *Next time, I'm going to talk to her*, he thought.

Ezra stretched and sighed then thought of his friends. He could not wait to talk to Jared and Dara at the rock in the middle of the rocks. He always loved the first day of the week. It was called, "the day of rest." No one in Thanoton worked this day. No one knew exactly how that tradition got started. However, everyone certainly loved having this day off.

As Ezra laced up his boots, he decided to start carrying his bow and large sheaf knife. He wondered why he did not carry his knife more often. He had made it in his shop and spent a lot of time perfecting it. The knife was beautiful. Actually, it was more like a small sword, with a twelve-inch metal blade. It had a wooden handle wrapped in leather strips to make a non-slip grip.

In Thanoton about half the men carried bows and arrows on a regular basis. It was a habit for the men that lived out in the country, mostly for hunting. Of course, all of Javan's men carried swords, bows, and spears. They wore body armor with metal chest plates, and helmets. Sometimes, the blacksmith shop got orders from the army to make, or repair, some of the equipment they used if their own blacksmiths were too busy.

Last time he had carried his bow, was when he and Jared went out hunting. It had been a while. They used to go out in the woods and target practice on a regular basis. He wanted to start practicing again. The way things looked, they might need those skills.

"Good morning, Ezra," Asa greeted his son as he was coming downstairs. He looked well rested.

"Good morning, Father." He searched the room to see if Labin lurked. He wasn't.

"What are you up to today?" Asa inquired. He looked like something was on his mind. "Maybe we could do something together."

"I can't," Ezra answered. "I've already made plans with Jared and Dara. We're going to do some target practice," said Ezra. He was glad he had brought the bow and arrows down.

Asa looked at Ezra's bow and arrows by the front door and asked, "Dara is going?"

"She wanted to go along to watch."

"She must really like you," Asa said with a smirk on his face.

"She does," Ezra laughed at his father's look.

"Well, have a good time."

"I will," Ezra said. He headed for the kitchen.

Telling my father that Dara and I like each other has made him less suspicious, thought Ezra. Frankly, he really did like Dara, so it was close to the truth. Ezra grabbed some bread, cheese, and an apple out of the kitchen to eat on his way to the swamp. He had slept in too late and was cutting it close to get to the creek split early enough to watch for any followers.

His plan was to catch whoever followed them and hold him with his bow and arrow. When he brought him to the creek split, Jared could tie him up then they could bring him deeper into the swamp to interrogate him.

~*~

The two Watchers, Abia and Joab, were already in a hidden position near the creek split. They had spent the day before concealing the position, using the natural terrain. They explored the whole area for possible paths the intruder might use to follow the three witnesses. They readied a place deeper in the swamp where they would hold the intruder. They decided it was best for two of them to stay together to catch the intruder. Only Seth would be alone at the rock waiting to overhear the three witnesses' conversation.

~*~

"What perfect timing," Jared said. He was glad he wouldn't have to walk alone to the creek split.

"Yeah, we can walk together," Dara responded. "Have you seen Ezra yet?"

"No," Jared said as he looked around. "Knowing him, he's probably already there."

"I got a surprise for you, Jared," Dara said with a sly smile.

"Okay. What is it?" He waited for one of her wise cracks.

"I invited your girlfriend, cute Myka, to go with us to the community center tomorrow night." Dara smiled as she noticed Jared's face turn bright red. "You know she'll want to sit right next to you," she said, while she jokingly elbowed him.

"Why do you always do this to me?" Jared said. He was mad. "She's not my girlfriend. I might not go now." Actually, he was scared to go, but secretly, he wanted to go. Jared hated that Dara always put him on the spot like this.

"You have to go," Dara said. She rolled her eyes because she did not believe a word Jared said. "It'll be fun. Be-sides," she dragged the word out in a teasing tone, "she asked about you. You don't want to disappoint her, do you?" She did not feel the least bit guilty for putting him on the spot. She grinned to herself; shy people had to be pushed.

"Let's go," Jared asserted. He changed the subject and didn't want to talk to Dara anymore.

~*~

Abia looked through his scope and said to Joab, "No, that's not the intruder. It's Ezra hiding behind a stump close to the creek split."

"It's just him?" Joab asked. He looked through his scope and tried to find what Abia had seen.

"He's lying down, behind the stump," Abia said.

"I see him now." Joab adjusted his scope. "He has a bow with an arrow, ready to pull back and shoot. I wonder who he's waiting for."

"I suspect the same person we are—the intruder," answered Abia. "Shhh! Someone is coming down the trail."

"It's more than one person," Joab said. "It's Jared and Dara."

~*~

"Here we are," Jared whispered. "I thought for sure Ezra would be here."

"I wonder where he is," Dara said as she looked around. "I guess we'll just have to wait."

Ezra watched as Dara and Jared sat quietly on the creek bank. He waited another ten minutes and didn't hear anyone. He was surprised how quiet Jared and Dara were. They didn't utter a word after they sat down.

"There you are," Jared said. He stood up and slapped Ezra on the shoulder.

"Hi Ezra," Dara said.

Ezra smiled back at Dara and looked around, still scanning for someone following.

"Did you take another route?" Jared asked.

"No, I came early," Ezra answered. "I hid to see if you two were followed."

"So we were bait, huh?" Dara said. Her hands were on her hips, giving him that look.

"Something like that," Ezra whispered. "We better get going. We're already too loud."

CHAPTER 22

Ian couldn't believe his whole purpose that day was to get caught by the Watchers. It was a lot of risk just to humble the Watchers, and show them there was another group more skilled and secretive than they. The elders were right. It was the best way for the Seekers to introduce themselves. This way, the Watchers would be prepared when they enlightened them to the way of Truth. The Seekers would eventually have to win the Watchers over to their side. What the Seekers had planned today, would spark the Watchers curiosity about them. Most importantly, it would distract the Watchers from following the Three Witnesses. The Seekers had to make this count. They had to make the Watchers paranoid about being watched.

Ian had hoped to make contact with the Three Witnesses at the rock today. He wanted to sit down and talk with them, thinking they were ready to hear the Truth. But with all the recent activities at the border and the Watchers always watching when the Three Witnesses were together, he had to wait for the perfect time to approach them.

His plan was to wait until the Three Witnesses crossed the river using the rock path, and were at the rock in the middle of the rocks. Then he would expose himself when he was about to cross the rock path. Fairly predictable, the Watchers would probably nab him there. There was no need for the Watchers to cross the rock path. They already had one Watcher hidden down at the rock in the middle of the rocks. Ian knew the Watchers' sole purpose today was to catch him, the intruder. He wanted to make sure they accomplished their mission.

Ian wasn't worried. He knew Caleb and Neptali, two of the best Seekers, were lurking ready to grab the two Watchers after they nabbed him. The two Watchers were no match for the Seekers ready to capture them. Not only were Caleb and Naptali Seekers, but they were also Watchers. The Seekers had infiltrated the Watchers' organization.

Ian's expression was sad as he thought about how the border guards, Javan's men, and even the Watchers were clueless. Ian was amazed they were so worried about something coming in or going out of their valley. They feared things that didn't exist. They were unable to recognize their bondage. Their solution was to kill all those threatening their way of life.

The Whisperer had strengthened the Seekers and prepared them to deliver this valley. At first, one by one, they had delivered people from the valley. More recently, they had delivered larger groups. Someday, they would win this whole valley for the Light of the Word.

Ian watched as the Three Witnesses crossed the river. He was nervous. It was time for them to catch him. He waited until the Three Witnesses were out of sight. Then, he started to rustle and make noise so they could locate him. He got up and listened intently as he walked toward the rock path that crossed the river.

Shew—wap—wap—wap. He ducked, out of instinct, as the arrows slammed into the tree next to him, only inches away from his head. He went down on one knee, not exactly sure which way to move. He braced himself as more arrows stuck in the trees around him. He heard footsteps and readied himself to be tackled as they came near.

Abia grabbed the intruder by the back of the neck and slammed him to the ground. Joab covered him with an arrow, ready to shoot.

"Keep your face down," Joab commanded. He didn't want the intruder to look at them, even though their faces were covered.

Abia put his knee on the intruder's back and bound his hands. "Give me the hood," Abia demanded. He pulled the intruder back onto his knees, ready to move. Abia placed the hood over the intruder's head and secured it. "Let's go!"

"Hey, who are you guys?" asked Ian, purposefully loud.

"Shut up! No talking!" they said in unison. Abia slammed the intruder to the ground. He pressed the edge of his knife to Ians's throat for him to feel.

"Keep your voice down," Abia warned in an angry, whisper.

The two Watchers took the intruder to the predestined place, deep in the swamp. They pushed their way through the thick brush, the water coming up to their knees, until they finally came to higher ground. They sat the intruder down and tied him to a tree. Abia and Joab distanced themselves from Ian, so they could talk.

"We've got a long wait till nightfall," Joab whispered. He already itched from multiple mosquito bites.

"Yeah, we do," Abia said. "It went smoother than I thought, quite easy."

"I'm surprised how easy it was," Joab agreed as he slapped a mosquito on his neck. "Getting him to the storekeeper's place will be easy. The waiting till the middle of the night won't be."

"We have to stay alert," Abia said. He wanted to keep Joab vigilant. He thought how pleased Shobal would be with him. After they dropped the intruder off, he would meet up with Seth and find out what the Three Witnesses talked about at the rock. Then, he would go brief Shobal. He didn't care how many mosquitoes there were. Their success eclipsed that.

Ian smiled under his hood as he listened to their conversation, even though they were whispering. *Noise did travel farther in the swamp*, he thought. He just hoped the Seekers would rescue him right away and not make him suffer the rest of the day.

One hundred feet away, deeper in the swamp, a couple of branches broke. Abia and Joab froze. They listened. Abia thought it might be a wild animal, as he held his finger up to his mouth.

Ian was smiling under his hood. He felt tension emanating from his captors. He knew the Seekers were coming to rescue him.

Abia and Joab sat quietly and waited. At fifty feet, they heard the cracking of branches, and then, it stopped. Abia peered where the sound came from, and saw nothing except fog and thick brush. All he heard was his own heart pounding. Then there was another crack and a pebble rattled down the path. Then silence. The tension was bunching their muscles as they could sense more than hear something draw closer and closer. Abia pointed in the direction of a slight noise, but neither one could see anything. They became fixated on the sounds, unaware that someone was sneaking up behind them with a club in his hand.

Abia woke up first with his head throbbing barely able to open his eyes. Paralyzed by pain, he lay there for a few minutes. Slowly, his senses returned. "What happened?" he murmured. He scanned the area and saw Joab leaning up against a tree across from him. He tried to move and realized he was trussed to a tree trunk. He studied the situation as much as his throbbing head would allow, and realized Joab was tied to the same tree they had tied the intruder to earlier. Abia had a warm sick feeling wash over him, as he looked at Joab, motionless. "Joab! Joab! Hey, get up!" He still did not move. He stretched out and kicked Joab on his foot.

Joab coughed then moaned. His eyes slit open. "What happened? Oh, my head," Then, he passed out and lay motionless again.

Abia waited a couple of minutes than gave Joab another kick. "It looks like we were ambushed."

Joab moaned, "The intruder!"

"Gone," Abia said, as he felt his blood-stained shirt sticking to his skin. He realized the blood had come from the side of his head. He looked over to Joab, whose head was still bleeding.

"Can you get loose?" Joab asked. He tried to wiggle out of the ropes.

"No, I can't," Abia answered. He was worried. "No one knows our location. They only know we're in the swamp."

"They won't send someone to look for us until early tomorrow morning," Joab added. "They're waiting for us to come sometime in the night. How did Javan's men know we were here?"

"They weren't Javan's men," Abia responded. "If they were, they would've arrested us, not left us. Javan's men certainly wouldn't have left us here to die. They would have tortured and interrogated. They would've made a public example of us so that others would fear."

"Who were they then?" Joab questioned. He didn't expect an answer.

"I have no idea," Abia answered. He took a deep breath and stopped trying to wiggle out of the ropes for a minute. "They certainly knew our every move. We need to try to get loose." He looked straight up and saw his knife he had threatened to cut the intruders throat with, stuck into the tree just out of reach. *What a cruel joke*, thought Abia. "Whoever did this, was sending us a message."

CHAPTER 23

Lot steered the horses onto the long driveway that led to his house near the eastern cut. He saw the signal as he came in, a branch lying in the middle of the driveway. It meant he had some visitors waiting for him in the barn behind the house. *I need to change the visual signal*, thought Lot. He couldn't remember the last time he had changed it.

"Whoa! Whoa!" Lot commanded as he neared the barn. He pulled the reins to slow his two draft horses down. Lot had good horses. They would go all day, every day, picking up and delivering supplies. Yet at the end of the day when they knew they were headed home, they seemed to get a second wind. The horses loved to get back home so they could eat some grain and be brushed down. It was only mid-morning, but they were acting like they'd worked all day. Lot laughed at them.

He was sure his visitors were the boys. He was eager to hear how it went. *We have to work fast*, he thought.

Caleb laughed. "Hello Lot, about time you showed up."

"Yeah, where have you been?" Neptali added. He gave Lot a big bear hug. They both loved joking and giving Lot a hard time.

"Working, as usual," Lot said. He laughed and gave Caleb a hug. Whenever he saw the young brothers, it always brought him joy. Lot knew they were ready for anything. Caleb and Neptali's blue eyes radiated fiery intensity. It was contagious.

"Did everything go as planned?" Lot questioned. He knew the answer before he asked.

"Of course," Caleb answered. "Everything went perfect, no problems."

"It was too easy," Neptali added.

"Where is Ian?" questioned Lot. He looked around.

"He's in the back room writing down the exact location where we tied up Abia and Joab," Caleb answered. "This will help when you write the message for Myka to find them."

"Good, good. I need you both to stay here while I talk to Ian and draft a message for him to deliver right away. Time is critical. We need to get the message to Myka's pickup sight before she heads into work. Once I send Ian on his way, I will come back and draft another message for one of you to deliver tonight to Sanctuary. That message will go on to the elders in Alethia."

Caleb watched Lot walk quickly to the back of the barn. He turned to Neptali and said, "We really need to tell Lot about Jotham snooping around."

Neptali shrugged. He did not want to disappoint Lot. "Maybe we should wait and try to take care of it ourselves first," he said.

"I think Jotham is on to us. He's been checking on us more and more lately. He snooped around the restricted area outside of the valley. I'm sure he saw the Seeker symbol."

"Lot might close it down if he thinks it's compromised," Neptali whispered. "We still have to get the Three Witnesses out. That's the fastest way in and out of the valley of Thanoton. It will ruin everything if it's shut down."

"We might not have a choice," Caleb responded. "I know Jotham was looking for the best possible way to cross the border. He discovered our secret shortcut through the rocks. Like I said, I'm positive he saw our Seeker symbol, marking the route."

"We should have removed the symbol after everyone learned the short-cut." Neptali said. "We don't need it to mark the route anymore."

Caleb agreed.

"Hey, what are you boys whispering about?" Lot said. He was joking, but he soon realized they acted as if they were caught doing something wrong. "What's wrong? What's going on?"

"There is something we have to tell you," Caleb said. He ignored his younger brother's glare. "It affects everything."

Neptali listened as his brother told Lot about Jotham. He was embarrassed and afraid they had disappointed Lot. He thought about how much Lot had helped his mom raise them without a father. Lot became their surrogate father and taught them everything they knew. He taught them how to hunt, work hard, and help those in need. Most of all, he taught them to live their lives for the Light of the Word. Neptali wanted to live his life to the fullest, like Lot did—all for the Light of the Word.

Neptali treasured those weekly studies about the Light of the Word taught by Lot and his wife from the *Book of Prophesies*. Lot had a copy of the *Book of Prophesies* and made sure both Caleb and Neptali memorized as much as they could. Both the brothers knew many passages.

Lot leaned back and took a deep breath. "Jotham hasn't told anyone yet, so I think he's not quite sure what you guys are up to. I do believe though, he has tied all this in some way to the missing people and the intruder. The fact he's a Watcher like you two, works to our advantage. He won't be so quick to tell Captain Hyrum what he finds out. Jotham will go tell Shobal, the head of the Watchers first, to see what he should do. This will buy us enough time to get the Three Witnesses out as planned. Then, we will destroy the passageway, and never use the eastern cut again. All that attention at the eastern border will be used to our advantage. It will distract Javan and his men, while we prepare for the next phase."

"Are you talking about when the Sanctuary Command Center moves inside the valley to the small town of Pistio out west?" Caleb asked.

"That's right, but" Lot held up his hand and stopped both the brothers from dwelling any more on the next phase, "we need to stick to the task at hand. I need you to do a couple of things before we bring the Three Witnesses out. It goes without saying, don't let Jotham see you. Scrape the Seeker symbol off the rock that marks the start of the rock path. Tonight block the entrances to the passageway after you come back from delivering the message to Sanctuary. Stay away from the passageway until the night you take the Three Witnesses through the cut. After that, block it permanently and never go around it again. Last of all, you boys know what to do if you are compromised."

"We do," Caleb nodded and glanced at Neptali.

"Good," Lot said. He scooted in closer and made direct eye contact. "Listen, the Three Witnesses have to make it out safely no matter what. Do whatever you have to do to make sure it happens."

CHAPTER 24

Myka had enjoyed the morning helping her aunt bake bread. She hated she had to keep so many secrets from her. It was for her aunt's own safety, Myka reasoned. Unless the Whisperer revealed the Truth in a person's heart, they wouldn't believe. Therefore, they waited on the Whisperer, to guide them to those ready to forsake all.

Myka knew that people had to love the Light of the Word more than anything else, even their very lives, in order to follow Him. It was easier for most people to stay in bondage to all the lies and false security than to embrace the way of Truth. Myka knew it wasn't easy to forsake all, but it was necessary. Then those who answered the call must leave the valley and grow up in this new-found Truth. They must learn who the Light of the Word is by following him.

She was in no hurry to sit all night in the loft. She took her time, thinking and praying, as she walked along the dirt path that led from the farm. She wished she could come later that night instead of in the afternoon. It was going to be a long night. She already knew they wouldn't bring in the intruder. Responsibilities of being a Watcher and a Seeker sometimes weighed heavily. She couldn't wait till tomorrow night to go to the community center with Jared, Dara, and Ezra. She wanted to be with kids her own age. She had been praying a long time the Light of the Word would reveal himself to them.

She reached the end of the dirt path that connected to one of the main roads, leading to Thanoton. Myka looked at the corner fence post to see if there was a signal. There was! The corner fence post had a stick leaning against it. That meant there was a message for her.

Myka went over to the fence post and kicked the stick flat on the ground. She then walked down the road fifty feet to a large tree on the side. When satisfied no one was around, she went into the woods another twenty feet, kneeled down, and picked up a certain small rock in the midst of many.

She knew exactly which rock to pick. It would have been impossible for anyone else that did not know what to look for. This special rock had a hollowed-out slot on the bottom holding a tiny rolled-up message. She read in silence.

M,

The trap was successful, and everything went as planned. The two Watchers are tied up and in the swamp awaiting rescue. You need to get on the search team when the time comes. Let them bring it up, not you. Do not act like you are eager to search. The Watchers will give you an updated map of possible routes and locations. If they don't, press them for it, so we can see how accurate our current information is. Follow the map to the rock path that crosses the river. Then, face 180 degrees away from the rock path. Start walking straight into the swamp for two hundred feet. You will start seeing our signs, which will lead you the rest of the way. Act natural, like you just stumbled upon them.

Seek Him!

L

Myka set the rock down in its usual spot and distanced herself from that location. Deeper in the woods, she took out a match and burned the message. She walked out to the road and headed toward Thanoton. She braced herself for what was going to be a busy twenty-four hours. She hoped none of this would get in the way of her going to the community center tomorrow night.

~*~

Back at the rock in the middle of the rocks, the three were still there. They had spent most of the day talking about everything that had happened so far.

"No, I've never been told any of this," Jared answered. "Nothing was passed down to me concerning the Children of Light."

"We were never told either," Ezra added. "Indeed, my father and grandfather are purposefully keeping this information from me."

"You don't have any idea who passed this note to you?" Jared questioned Dara.

"No. Like I said so many times before to you and Ezra, I have no idea who could've passed it to me," she said, a little too loudly.

"Keep your voice down," Ezra whispered.

Dara continued, "That day in the marketplace was packed. You know how it gets there, everyone bumping into each other. I talked to several people and of course, Myka."

Ezra laughed at the way Dara was teasing Jared.

"Maybe it was Myka?" she said jokingly.

Both Jared and Ezra laughed.

"That would be ridiculous," Ezra said. "There is no way she could keep a secret."

"Whoever it is knows who we are and is watching us," Dara said.

"I wish we had more from the *Book of Prophesies*," Jared added. "This stuff sounds so true."

"It does," Ezra agreed. "I'm eager to know more."

"Ezra, do you remember the first time the Whisperer spoke to you?" Dara asked. "Didn't it say for you to find the *Book of Prophesies*?"

"Yes, the Whisperer said, 'You must find the *Book of Prophesies*. It will show you the Light of the Word.'"

"I wonder where we can find this *Book of Prophesies*," Jared asked.

"I have no idea what we're supposed to do next," Ezra responded. "The prophesy said we are to deliver the people in this valley. We just don't know how."

Jared mused on the words for a moment then said, "'Deliver my people from the grip of darkness.' What does that mean?"

Dara brightened like a lit torch, "I think the Whisperer is the one who leads and empowers us to accomplish everything the Light of the Word wants. Isn't that what is implied at the beginning of this prophesy?"

"That's exactly how it's been so far," Ezra agreed. "We are definitely being led. If we need to know something, it's revealed to us, either in a whisper or a dream."

"Or by a note passed by a phantom messenger," Jared added.

"That's why I think we shouldn't stress so much over all this," Dara said. "I know this is going to be hard for you Ezra because you want to take charge and do something. That is not the way it looks like the Whisperer works. We need to wait for the Whisperer to show us the next step. We must let Him lead us to do or learn what we need to accomplish His purpose.

"We have no choice anyway," Jared agreed.

"You're both right," Ezra said as he stood up. "We've been here too long. Let's go home."

"The time sure slipped away today," Jared said. He stood up and stretched.

Ezra took the lead on the way back, and the others followed. "I told my father this morning we were going to target practice today. On the way home, I'm going to shoot some arrows so I won't feel guilty for not telling him what we actually did. I'm getting tired of lies—my lies and their lies."

"And the lies we don't even know about," Dara added, as she followed.

CHAPTER 25

"Myka, you can come down from the loft now," the storekeeper yelled angrily from the bottom of the stairs. "We're going to have a team meeting in the back room."

Myka was relieved. "Okay. I'll be right down!" It had been a long, grueling night. She was trying to stay awake while lying still in the loft staring out a window. Myka didn't think she would make it; then, the sun finally rose. She had dozed off a couple of times and hit her head on the floor.

"Listen up, all of you," the storekeeper said. He had drawn some final terrain features on an elaborate map on the blackboard.

Myka marveled at how detailed the map was that the storekeeper had made. She also noticed the storekeeper had gotten all this information from a little booklet he had. Myka wondered if he got it from Shobal. She knew the storekeeper had never been to the swamp. It was not part of their team's mission. *He must have gotten it from Shobal*, she thought.

"As you know, the intruder was not brought in last night by the team of Watchers assigned to the Three Witnesses. Two of the Watchers have not come back who were supposed to catch the intruder. Their names are Abia and Joab, for those that don't know them. The third member of their team, who stayed with the Three Witnesses, came back early yesterday with information on what the three had talked about at the rock in the middle of the rocks."

"Seth waited all night, as we did, for the rest of his team to show up. When they didn't, we figured something was wrong. About an hour before the sun came up, Seth and I went to talk to Shobal. He does not want Seth searching in the swamp for them."

"Why?" cried one of the marketplace Watchers. "He knows the swamp like the back of his hand."

The storekeeper held up his hand and stopped everyone else in the room from chiming in. "I know, I know. I had the same argument with Shobal. He said Seth needs to go to work and not vary from his normal routine so as not to raise any suspicion among Javan's men. So, he sent him home."

"Great, the one guy who can tell us about the swamp, he sent home," said a Watcher.

"That is why I've drawn this elaborate map and given each of you a sheet of paper to copy it down. Make sure you make your drawing as detailed as mine. I'll also give you each a compass to stay orientated."

"Will other Watchers be searching besides our team?" Myka asked.

"No," the storekeeper answered. He noticed the bags under her eyes and the frizzy hair. "It will be just our team, the marketplace Watchers that will search." He saw their looks and said, "Myka, and the rest of you, I know you are really tired. But we have two Watchers out there that could be dead or captured. I need all of you to reach down deep and give it everything you've got today."

The storekeeper pointed to the map. "These are the three main trails that the Three Witnesses use. These are all the other trails and hideouts the Watchers use. Here is the rock bridge. We do not want anyone to cross the rock bridge in the search."

"What if they're down there," someone asked.

"They're not," the storekeeper said. He quickly changed the subject. "If you get lost or disorientated use your compass and head west. West will take you out of the swamp. You will know you are headed west because the ground will gradually go up. Go east, and you run into this river where the rock path is. If you go north, you will hit Green Lake. If you go too far south, you'll bump into Silver Rock Ridgeline that juts out from the mountains. You shouldn't get lost. We don't have that many people, so all of you will have to split up. The faster you find them, the faster you can go home."

Myka raised her hand with a question.

"What is it, Myka?"

"What if one of us finds them? How do we signal everyone else to stop searching?" Myka knew she was going to find them as fast as she could. She wanted to get home and get some sleep before the community center that night.

"I didn't think of that," added the storekeeper.

One of the other Watchers said, "We could use our bird signal we make with our whistle. When we find them, blow it two times. Everyone that hears the whistle will blow their whistle two times. That way, the birdcall will be passed around the swamp, and everyone will hear. From the closest to the farthest, it should be heard all over."

"Good idea," the storekeeper responded. "And if you need help for some reason, keep making the bird sound until someone comes to help you."

The same Watcher asked, "What if we don't find them? When do we call off the search?"

The storekeeper paused for a minute. "I want you to keep searching until mid-afternoon." His look dared anyone to complain about it. "Here is food, water, and medical supplies you can put into your backpacks. Don't let anyone see you. Take the back way through the woods. The fog is unusually thick today, so no one should notice unless you run right into them. I don't want all of you leaving in a group either. Leave the back of the store in intervals. Spread yourselves out."

"If we find them, do we bring them here?" Myka interrupted. She was getting ready to leave.

"Yes, bring them here, to the back," answered the storekeeper.

Myka slipped out of the store and navigated her way around the back of the buildings that surrounded the market square. As soon as she was in the woods, she started to jog at a slow pace, to get there as fast as she could. She decided to just go and find them right away. She thought about waiting to make it less suspicious. *But, what's the difference?* she thought. *They'll never be suspicious of me. They will assume it was just blind luck, not incredible skill.* Myka smiled because she knew that was what made her so good; she was the least likely suspect. Besides, the Watchers weren't too smart, so it made it quite easy for her. *Javan's men are even worse*, she thought.

Myka laughed. She knew exactly who the Light of the Word uses. He uses the least to accomplish the most. The least have to depend on Him, and when they do, great things happen.

Myka arrived at the swamp on the Green Lake side and quickly took out the map she had copied from the blackboard. She knew from the map, if she kept Green Lake to her left, she would run into a river. At the river, she would turn right and keep the river on the left, walking up hill. Then, she would continue until she got to the crest of the hill where a rock path should be. Myka would start her search from there.

Myka arrived at the rock path. She kneeled down, reached out, and felt the cool water. She thought about how refreshing it would be if she jumped in. It would wake her up. At least it would get the mud, grime, and sweat accumulated from the swamp off her. What a relief from mosquito bites.

Turning her back on that temptation, she studied the rock path. She was sorely tempted to go across to see the rock in the middle of the rocks for herself. So much history surrounded it because it was a historical sight for the Children of Light.

Myka resolutely decided to stick to the mission, as always. She turned around and headed west into the thickest part of the swamp. Her boots quickly filled with water as she went deeper into it. She adjusted the scarf around her face. The less exposed, the better, to keep the swarms of mosquitoes away. Around two hundred feet later, she started to look for the Seekers' signs.

Myka saw the one right away. It was an eagle feather stuck in a branch on a tree. She walked to the tree and looked around for—*There it is*, thought Myka. She knelt beside two sticks lying on the ground forming an arrow. She headed the direction of the arrow and came up out of the water. There they were. Scared at first, because they were not moving, she rushed over and started to shake them. "Are you all right? Abia, Joab, talk to me!"

"Who are you?" Abia asked, barely audible.

"I'm a Watcher searching for you." She helped them take a drink of water from her canteen.

"I'm so glad you're here," Joab said. "I gave up hope of being rescued."

"Just pure luck I found you," Myka agreed. "I thought I was lost." She wove her decoy story well. "I better call for some help." Myka blew her whistle. Right away she heard other whistles around her. She took a quick break from her whistle, and asked," Did you see the person that did this or hear anything? Names?"

"No, we didn't. Nothing," Abia answered. "Whoever it was snuck up on us. We didn't know what happened until we woke up. They must have taken the intruder."

Myka was satisfied that the Seekers' operation was not compromised, so she continued to blow her whistle. She heard other Watchers headed in their direction to help.

CHAPTER 26

Javan stood in front of the area map in the Command Center of the palace. He had just finished telling Tuval, his second-in-command, all about his trip to the border.

Tuval surveyed the area map and asked, "So, you think the border guards are allowing people to come in and out of the valley?"

"That is exactly what I think," Javan agreed. "They are incredibly lax out there. None of their positions look like defensive positions."

"What are they then?" asked Tuval, while he updated the new information on the area map given to him by Javan.

"They are simple observation posts. The border guards seem to be more concerned with hunting than they are with securing."

Tuval felt the penetrating eyes of Javan on the back of his neck as he continued updating the map.

Javan continued, "Their families live all around them. They come and bring food or come up just to visit them, while they're at their post." Disgust laced his tone. "We even found posts that were unoccupied as we came back from the north crest to the eastern cut. They gave the excuse that they were out looking around." I got the impression they were at home or out hunting, but I didn't press Hyrum about it. We definitely need to make some changes. Who knows what's going on out west or south? We'll have to check that out some time."

"What about Hyrum? Do you think he's in on it?" Tuval asked. He sat down at the conference table across from Javan.

"No, I don't think so. There were times on the trip where I thought he was thinking as I was—that some of these border guards may be traitors. I could tell he couldn't wait for me to leave to ruffle some feathers and conduct an investigation."

"We should find out from our informants if he actually does investigate," Tuval said. He jotted down some notes.

"He better!" Javan slammed his fist on the table. "If he doesn't fix the problem, I'm going to make him a public example. I'll execute him in front of all the border guards and put someone else in charge. I will assemble every border guard from all around our valley so everyone sees it. They're not on guard at their posts anyway. Leaving to see an execution won't hurt a thing."

"That's a good idea," Tuval agreed. "It's been a while since we have made a public example of someone."

"Too long obviously. We need to tighten things up."

"Do you have an idea who would replace Hyrum?" Tuval questioned.

"No, not yet, I don't."

"Hopefully, we'll get some information soon." Tuval sounded a little frustrated. "We have every available man out cordoning off the eastern cut and the rest, working double time patrolling the city and the roads."

They both heard the sound of boots outside the conference room coming their way. A palace guard entered the room and stood at attention.

"What is it?" Javan said.

"Asaph, is here and would like to speak with you."

"Send him in," Javan gestured for him to come in.

"Commander Javan," Asaph said at attention, his hand on his sword.

"What is it?"

"I think I might have some information that will help us," Asaph said. He noticed that Javan and Tuval sat up a little straighter.

"Go on. We're listening," Javan leaned forward and watched Tuval close the door.

"Since we learned about the intruder, I decided to set up a few clandestine observation posts around the market square." He took a deep breath and continued, "I surmised the intruder must be helped by someone. Last night one of my guards reported significant activity in one of the main stores around the market square."

"What kind of significant activity?" Tuval inquired.

"After hours activity. The storekeepers' store had people coming in and out of it all night. They were sneaking in the back. We also spotted someone in the loft window of the store all night."

"All night?" Javan said. He stood up with excitement.

"Yes, all night."

"What were they doing?" Tuval asked.

"We have no idea," Asaph answered. "We did have one of our police sneak up and look through a crack in one of the closed shutters covering a window. He said it looked like six to eight men sitting around. They were fidgeting and anxious looking as if they were waiting for something."

"How come you didn't arrest them this morning?" Tuval said. "We could've interrogated them for this information."

"We were about to storm the house and bring them in for interrogation. Then, early this morning, they started to leave in intervals. Seven men left with packs on their backs."

"Did you recognize any of them?" Javan questioned.

"No, it was too foggy to see details in the person's features."

"It would've been easy to recognize the storekeeper," Javan said.

"None of the men that left were fat."

Tuval laughed and asked. "Did you follow?"

"Yes, we did," Asaph answered. "We waited till we knew no one else was coming out. Then, we picked up the trail of the last man that came out the back. He took great care, like the others, not to cut through the main areas of the market square. He skirted around the back and entered into the woods staying off the main roads."

Asaph walked over to the area map. He was pleased that he had their complete attention. This was a great moment for him. He pointed to the map and traced the route with a pointer as he spoke. "We followed him straight to the swamp, and this is where it gets very interesting."

As Asaph continued to talk, Javan and Tuval went to the map and studied the places where he pointed. "As soon as we got to the swamp, we started to hear bird calls all over. It was obvious they were manmade calls by the sheer volume and pattern of calls. We decided to split up and wait at the different locations they would most likely come out of the swamp.

"Why didn't you follow them to see what they were up to?" Javan snapped. He startled Asaph.

"B-Because," stuttered Asaph. "There was too much noise already in the swamp with bird calls, people breaking brush and voices. I don't think they realized how sound travels in the swamp."

"What's that have to do with you?" Tuval pointed out already frustrated. "Continue."

"It sounded like they were all around. It was more likely we would bump into one than to sneak up on one of them."

"Excuses," Javan snapped. "Well, did they come out?"

"Yes, they came out in one whole group, carrying two younger men—teens. From what we could tell, they were hurt."

"How could you tell they were teens?" Tuval questioned.

"We couldn't differentiate anyone," Asaph continued. "We heard their names, Abia and Joab, several times as they were cared for. We know who these two are, and they looked badly hurt. The group that found them bandaged their heads, gave them food and water, and were trying to find out what happened. Then, the group split up. Four took Abia and Joab to the store, and the other three left for elsewhere."

"You didn't follow the three that split off?" Tuval inquired.

Asaph quickly answered. "No, the three went all different directions. We decided to follow the main group."

"You didn't hear any other names or recognize any one?" asked Tuval. He walked back to the conference table to jot down some notes.

"No."

"Are they in the store now?" Javan asked as he continued to study the area map.

"Yes, they are," Asaph answered. "The problem we have now is the store is open. Many workers have shown up for work. It's a big store, and they are also in the storehouse out back. We have no idea who was in that group last night."

"They're probably not the workers of that store," Tuval pointed out.

"The storekeeper has to be a part of it," Asaph put the pointer down and crossed his arms over his broad chest. "It's his store, and he lives there." He thought for a moment, scratching his scruffy-bearded jaw. "Although, as lazy as he is, I'm surprised he's part of whatever this is."

Javan raised an eyebrow and inquired, "Do Abia and Joab work there?"

"No, they don't. Do you want me to arrest the storekeeper and the two teens? We know they're a part of this for sure.

Tuval raised his fingers and made eye contact with Javan. "Might I suggest that we wait? We don't want to tip the group off that we're on to them. We'll be able to find out more about them through their movements and associations. Let us follow the storekeeper, Abia, and Joab and see what they're actually up to. Right now, we have no idea what they are doing. We should keep surveillance on the store until we figure all this out."

"Good idea," Javan said. He was always pleased with Tuval's keen insight.

"Asaph, you have done a great job. I want you to concentrate all your efforts on this. Report every little detail to me personally. I also want you to brief Zesha, the chief investigator, on all that we talked about today. I am assigning Zesha and his section to help you gather intelligence on this situation. Tuval is right. Let's get as much information as we can on this conspiracy before we go in. We want to catch them all. I also want you to send word to Dakar, the captain of the army, to send a squad to search the swamp and let you know what they find. I will also relay that to him. I know how stubborn he can get."

Asaph tried not to explode with joy. "May I have that army squad permanently assigned to me? We could use the extra men."

Javan glanced at Tuval to see what he thought. Javan read Tuval's head bob to the side as *If you agree, I agree,* and said, "Yes, we'll assign that squad to you for this operation."

"Thank you Commander Javan," Asaph said. He looked like a horse ready to race, tense and excited.

Javan waved him away, "Go ahead, and get started."

Asaph rushed from the room.

CHAPTER 27

Oh, that felt so good, thought Myka as she stretched and yawned. *I needed the rest.* She glanced out the window and noticed the sun was starting to go down. "Oh," she said. Myka stretched and got out of bed, excited about going to the community center. She felt good. Much better than she thought she would, for being up all night, and not falling asleep until noon. She decided to skip shooting today.

Myka loved her normal routine in the morning. After she got out of bed, she would go outside, walk around the fields, and pray. Then practice shooting her crossbow. She especially enjoyed the time spent every day shooting when no one was around. Her crossbow, purposely designed to be concealed in her backpack, went everywhere with her.

Missing one day of shooting shouldn't hurt me, she thought, even though she knew consistency and discipline were why she was an excellent shot.

Myka thought about what she might need and started to organize her equipment. First, she needed to pack her backpack again with everything she might need. The problem was she never knew what she might need or what she would have to do next. She dumped out her backpack to see what she had and what she needed to pack. Myka would bring her crossbow with twice as many arrows as she usually took. She needed the first-aid kit, enough food rations for a week just in case, her scope, the notebook, two pencils, and two canteens full of water. She would also take an extra knife, flint and steel to start a fire, and a face-scarf for concealment and warmth. The heavy, hooded cape for the rain and cold, she would strap on top of the backpack. She always wore her eight-inch dagger concealed under her clothes. She grabbed her two canteens to fill up.

Myka was dressed and packed. She went outside to the water pump to wash her face and fill up the canteens. She closed her backpack and decided she had better go if she wanted to get there on time. Along the way, she ate an apple. She thought about stopping by the store but decided not to. Myka didn't want anything to mess up this evening.

Myka knew if they wanted her, they would find her. She didn't even want to look over at the fence post for fear there would be a message for her, but she did anyway. *Oh, no! Not tonight. Not a message,* she screamed inside her head. She walked over to the fence post and kicked the stick that leaned against it. She started to cry and wiped angry tears from her eyes.

"Not tonight," she said aloud. "I am so lonely. Can't I just spend one night having some fun with my friends?" She reached out, picked up a rock in the rock bed, and removed the message. She sat down and took a deep breath. Myka knew she had to pull herself together. Myka remembered she was doing all this for a higher purpose, not for personal gain.

She lit a candle and read the message.

M,

"Part of our plan to divert the Watchers attention from the Three Witnesses has been compromised. Javan and his men have the store under surveillance and followed you to the swamp. They know it was Abia and Joab you rescued. All of you made the mistake of mentioning their names aloud.

You're safe! They don't know names of the others. They believe the storekeeper is involved. They have put a task force together to follow Abia, Joab, and the storekeeper to find out what they're up to. We cannot allow that to happen, so they have been slotted for a _GHOST RIDE_, along with Seth.

This is what we need you to do. The storekeeper has numerous horse-drawn wagons that come into his storehouse in the back. Tomorrow at noon there will be a wagon drawn by two horses—one black, and one white. The driver's name is Kern. To authenticate the driver ask, "Are you here to pick up?" He will respond with, "Yes, I'm here to pick up four."

You need a way to get the storekeeper, Abia, Joab, and Seth to hide undetected in the back of the wagon with the supplies. Cover it all with a tarp and send it on its way. They will head out of town on the western route. At some point in time, the Ghost Team will intercept and take them to their final destination.

We don't care how you do it. As usual, no one else can know or see this happen. You need to continue to show up to work, as usual, playing ignorant with the Watchers' and Javan's men. They'll never suspect you. Use this opportunity to get closer to the Three Witnesses by taking the missing Watchers' spots.

The swamp is compromised, and they have commissioned an army squad to search every inch of it for clues. We need you to casually warn the Three Witnesses tonight at the community center to stay away from the swamp and never go back.

Be careful! Be alert! Be vigilant!"

L

After burning the message, Myka got up and headed into town.

~*~

"Hi, Ezra," Dara said. She entered the main room of the community center. "I thought, for once I would beat you here and be earlier than you."

"I got here about five minutes ago," Ezra said, always happy to see Dara.

"I should have known," Dara laughed. "No matter how early I think I'm going to be, you're always earlier."

"Hi, you guys," Jared greeted. He entered the room and already looked nervous.

"Hi, Jared," responded Ezra. He slapped his best friend on the shoulder.

"We're just waiting on Myka," Dara giggled.

"Don't start that tonight," Jared groaned. He turned, and in walked Myka. She was smiling and full of energy. Jared thought she was so pretty. She always seemed to glow.

"Hi, everyone," she gave Jared a special smile.

"It's good to see you," Dara said. "Now I don't feel outnumbered." She wondered if she had ever seen Myka without her backpack.

"Thanks for inviting me," Myka said. She made eye contact with Jared. "I've been looking forward to this."

Jared mustered up every bit of strength he could. "Me, too." His face turned beat red. He could tell by the look on Ezra and Dara's faces, they were surprised he said it. Facing the truth, so was he. He did notice that Myka didn't get embarrassed at all. Nothing seemed to faze her.

"Do you like playing cards?" Ezra asked.

"I love to play cards," Myka answered. She wished she didn't sound so overly excited all the time.

Dara dealt out the cards for the game of four's. "Hey, how about we play teams, me and Ezra, and you and Jared?"

"That would be fun. I'll keep score," Myka added. She pulled out a notebook and pencil from her backpack.

Jared cleared his throat, "H-H-How was work today at the store?"

"Good," Myka answered, as she gave him a grin. "There have been a lot of people in the marketplace lately, especially soldiers."

"Yeah, we've noticed more guards and soldiers patrolling the roads," Ezra said. "My grandfather said there is a checkpoint where they are searching everyone that comes out of Thanoton headed east."

"Really? I wonder why?" Myka asked. She was busy writing down everyone's score.

"Who knows?" Jared answered. He started to feel more comfortable.

Myka looked like she was concentrating on her cards and said, "In the store, I overheard some soldiers talking about how they're searching every inch of the swamp." She noticed the looks the three gave each other, while she put down a card. "Apparently, something is happening in the swamp, and Javan and his men want to find out what it is. Personally, I don't know why anyone would want to hang out in the swamp anyway."

"Me either," Dara agreed. "Nothing but bugs."

Mission completed, thought Myka. *They got the warning to stay out of the swamp. Now, I can relax and enjoy the rest of the night with my friends.*

She felt close to the Three Witnesses even though she did not spend that much time with them. Her closeness was no doubt because she prayed for them all the time.

CHAPTER 28

The next morning, Myka quickly walked into the store. She wanted to set the mood. "Storekeeper, I need to talk to you right away. It's urgent." She made sure she sounded scared.

"Settle down," said the storekeeper as he looked around. "Let's go to the back."

Myka took a deep breath, looked like she was about to cry, and said, "Okay." She noticed that her act had worked. The storekeeper actually looked scared too.

"You did a great job yesterday," the storekeeper said. He unlocked the door and closed it behind them.

Myka got straight to the point. "On the way to work today, before I got to the city, one of Shobal's inner chamber Watchers approached me. He had an urgent message for me to tell you. He said they can't pass it directly because everything has been compromised." She paused to wipe her nose.

"W-What's the message?"

"The store and the secret entrances to the inner chamber are covertly watched by Javan's men. Shobal wants to have a secret meeting with you, Abia, Joab, and Seth. He has a secure alternate location out west to have this meeting. Shobal has arranged for a wagon pulled by two horses, one black and the other white, to come to the storehouse at noon. The driver's name is Kern. To authenticate the driver ask, 'Are you here to pick up?' He will respond with, 'Yes, I'm here to pick up four.' Hide in the back with all the supplies and cover yourself with a tarp. Kern will take you to Shobal and bring you back when you're done. No one, not even any other Watchers, is to know about this other than me. Shobal thinks there might be a traitor in our group."

The storekeeper walked around in deep thought and said, "Help me make arrangements, so all the workers will be working in the store. You and I will work out back in the storehouse the rest of the day. You can control what wagon comes in and out, and you can clear it out when we come back."

"What about getting Abia, Joab, and Seth here?" Myka asked.

"I will send a Watcher to tell them to come as soon as possible."

Myka and the storekeeper went to implement their plan.

Three hours later Abia went around back into the storehouse to look for the storekeeper.

"Hello, Abia," the storekeeper said. He felt the thick, moist fog that came through the storehouse's double doors.

"What's going on?" Abia asked, not greeting the storekeeper. "The Watcher that came and got me sounded like it was an emergency."

"It is an emergency," said the storekeeper.

"I should be talking to Shobal, not to you," Abia pointed out. He manifested the tension that always existed between the two. It was no secret they didn't get along—about anything.

"We're waiting for Seth to show up, and then I will brief everyone," the storekeeper said. He purposely did not answer Abia's question.

"I'm taking off to talk to Shobal in the inner chamber right now."

"No! Absolutely not!" yelled the storekeeper. He got in Abia's face. "Wait till everyone is here, and then you will find out everything. Go and wait in the front room of the storehouse with Joab, until Seth shows up."

Seth walked through the double doors at the rear of the storehouse just about the time Myka came through the front door.

"Perfect timing," said the storekeeper. He smiled for the first time that morning. He couldn't wait for this day to end, and he secretly wished Shobal would just leave him alone. "Let's all go to the front room, so I can brief everyone."

Myka entered the room and felt the piercing glare of Abia, Joab, and Seth. *If they only knew how deceived they really were,* Myka smoothed any expression from her face. *They'll know soon enough.*

"What's she doing here?" Seth asked pointing at Myka. "Why is an outsider in this meeting?"

"She's not an outsider," the storekeeper assured him. "She rescued Abia and Joab. She's a Watcher."

"She's a Watcher? No way," Seth responded. He laughed, as he looked at Abia. "You're kidding me."

"No, she's a Watcher," Abia said, all embarrassed.

"Yes, she is. Now quiet!" said the storekeeper. His look convinced everyone in the room. "Myka, you don't need to be in here for this meeting. You already know what's going on. We shouldn't leave the storehouse unattended."

"Okay," she said, happy to leave the room. Myka knew the joke was on them as she walked to the back. She surveyed the area and made sure Javan's men couldn't see her through the windows or the double doors. Another thirty minutes and the wagon should be here.

At the thirty minute mark, she heard a wagon as it pulled up. "Whoa," said Kern to the horses, as he stopped them. Kern got down and walked through the double doors.

The storekeeper, who noticed one black and one white horse, asked, "Are you here to pick up?"

"Yes, I'm here to pick up four," Kern said. He reached out his hand to shake. "My name is Kern. I'm from a farming village out west," he said, quickly gaining his trust.

"Go ahead and back in," said the storekeeper. He slid the double doors open wide for the wagon to fit in. Then, he motioned with his hand, and said: "Myka go tell the others."

Kern climbed back on to his wagon and grabbed the lines to control his horses. He snapped the lines and snicked to the horses to move forward. He swung the horses out. Their ears perked up and turned toward him, ready for the next command. Kern loved how obedient his horses were. They lined up perfectly to back straight into the storehouse. He looked over his right shoulder and saw a young girl in the middle of the storehouse directing him back. He pulled back on the reins and followed her directions.

"Hurry up. Get in," Kern said. "Time's a-wasting." He heard other wagons pull up outside waiting on him to finish his business, horses stomping and snorting as he watched the four passengers hide in the back.

"I'll see you when I come back," said the storekeeper, as Myka pulled the tarp over him. "Make sure you're here when we arrive," he said. The storekeeper realized he only said it because he was nervous. "You know what to do."

Myka heard Abia and Joab making fun of her under the tarp as she tied it down.

"Are we ready to go, young lady?" Kern asked. He wondered if this was the legendary girl he had heard so much about.

"You're loaded, mister, you can go," Myka called.

Kern pulled out of the storehouse and looked over his shoulder one last time He watched the teenage girl direct another wagon to back in. He prayed to the Light of the Word thanking Him for her sacrifice. It truly was inspiring to know there were people willing to risk their lives for the Light of the Word's glory and the advancement of His Kingdom.

Kern knew everything was going according to the plan so far. The market square filled with supply wagons and the storehouse had wagon's coming and going all day. The cover was good, and no way could anyone have seen what just happened. The Seekers were getting better and better at ghost riding. That is why they started to remove larger groups of people.

With the city of Thanoton now in the background, Kern relaxed a little. One more hour, and he could get rid of his passengers and head back to his home on the western border. The fog was gradually getting worse in the valley of Thanoton. Frustrated, Kern grabbed a rag from under his seat and wiped his face. His clothes were soaked from the moisture in the dense fog.

Kern said in a low voice, "We should be there in less than an hour."

"One hour?" Seth questioned. "No one said anything about one hour."

"I thought the meeting was a short distance out of town?" Abia asked.

"Do we have to stay cooped up back here?" asked the storekeeper. He shifted around to try to find a comfortable position.

"Yes, you have to stay back there, and be quiet," Kern answered. "Just make the best of it. Take a nap. I'll stop in fifteen minutes to water my horses. I need all of you to be still and quiet while I do that. Sometimes, others are there watering their horses."

He worked to find the dirt road that veered off from the main road. Minutes later, he pulled into a clump of trees where six men stood feet apart and swords drawn. One man was holding the reins of Kern's horse. He knew the other men on the Ghost Team were hidden with their bows drawn forming a tight perimeter.

Kern stepped down from the wagon and walked over to the leader. He whispered in his ear, "Everything went perfectly. They're all yours." Kern grabbed the reins of his horse and walked him a bit then mounted and rode away.

The leader looked around at his men. He held up one hand and motioned, "one—two—three." They cut the tarp ropes on three then a small group of men jumped onto the back of the wagon. They wrestled the four on to their stomachs and twisted their arms behind their backs.

"Quit resisting," said one of the team members to Abia. He gave him a kidney punch. This allowed another team member to tie Abia's hands and put a gag on him.

"Who are you?" Joab yelled. He tried to fight off the gag.

"You led us into a trap, you idiot," Seth said to the storekeeper before he was gagged.

The storekeeper laid there, unable to speak or move. Both his hands and feet were tied. He had known this day would come. That's why he hated being a Watcher.

"Sit them up, facing me," said the leader. A scarf, like the others on his team, covered his face. "I'm going to have my men take the gags out of your mouths, so we can talk quietly. If we can't talk quietly and civilly, the gags will go back on, and you will not know a thing until we reach our final destination in a month or so. If you are willing to cooperate, then I will tell you everything I can this side of the valley. I want you to nod your head if you're willing to cooperate, and we will take the gags out."

The storekeeper was the first one to nod his head. He made a sound that sounded like, "Yes."

Abia, Joab, and Seth nodded too.

"Good. Take the gags off," said the leader.

Eyes wide, the four Watchers sat against the side of the wagon and said nothing, wondering what was coming.

"First, I'm going to talk," said Gabriel, the leader. He walked closer and put his sword back into its sheath. "Then I will allow you to ask some questions, as long as it does not compromise the mission."

He leaned his arms on the edge of the wagon, directly across from the four prisoners. "You four have gotten in the way of our mission on several occasions. Because of what you did on your last mission, your life is in danger, and you almost compromised our mission. We have a person that follows the Three Witnesses on special occasions, just like you three Watchers do." The captain, Gabriel, noticed the surprised look on their faces. "When we found out about your plan to catch him, the person you call the intruder, we set a trap, allowing you to catch him. The trap worked, and we easily caught you two. Our purpose was to intimidate and slow you down a few days until we could accomplish some things. Unfortunately, we did not anticipate how sloppy you Watchers really are. Your rescue team was followed by Javan's men."

"What? How did they know?" Abia interrupted. He noticed the way the leader looked at him, and said, "Sorry."

Joab took a risk, and asked, "You're not Javan's men?"

Gabriel laughed and said, "No, we are actually on the same side; although, you guys are too deceived to see it."

"Same side?" Abia asked. "Then why are you—."

Gabriel held up his hand for Abia to stop, and continued, "Not only did Javan's men follow your rescue team, but they also overheard the names of the two rescued. "Abia and Joab." They followed you back to the store." Gabriel looked around at his men and walked to the back of the wagon. "We found out Javan implemented a plan to keep you three under surveillance, to see what you were up to. Then, he had plans to capture and interrogate you to find out everyone involved. We knew we had to act quickly, once we found out what Javan's plans were."

"You don't understand any of this now," said Gabriel. "But, we did this for your safety, and to protect the Three Witnesses, who are about to start their next phase. Therefore, we are taking you out of the valley to a safe place. It's a very long trip with two parts. The first leg, we take you out of the valley of Thanoton to the mountain range out west. During this leg, we will blindfold you at certain points along the route because it's classified."

"When we get to the mountain range we will hand you off to another team, taking you the rest of the way. From that point, off come your blindfolds, and possibly, we will release your bonds. It depends on what the Whisperer impresses on our hearts." The leader saw how they reacted to what he had said. He continued, "Don't be shocked; you will be told more about who we are, and what we do outside of this valley."

"Now, you can ask a few questions. However, to save us some time, there are certain things we will not tell you, just in case we are caught. The less you know the better. We don't want to compromise the mission. We will not tell you who we are or what our mission is. That, you will find out at your final destination."

"Are you cannibals?" asked the storekeeper. He immediately noticed the Ghost Team members tried not to laugh. "You are taking us into Cannibal Land."

Gabriel noticed how serious all four considered the question. He couldn't believe how deceived they really were. "We are not cannibals, nor are there cannibals outside of this Valley. That's all a myth." They did not look convinced. He continued, "It's a lie that has been perpetuated to keep you from leaving the valley. I know you don't believe us now, but you will later."

"Did you say this trip will take one month?" Seth asked.

"Our portion of the trip will take one month," Gabriel answered. "The second leg will take another month to arrive at the final destination. There will be some towns along the way for us to rest the horses and pick up more supplies. The final destination is a city."

"What's the name of the city we are going to?" asked Abia. "What can you tell us about it?"

"I can't tell you the name of the city," said Gabriel, while he motioned for his men to get ready. "But I will tell you, it's a city like you have never seen or experienced. It hasn't even entered your hearts or minds how great it will be to live there. After you have been at this city, mark my words, all this will have been well worth it." Gabriel whipped his index finger overhead to signal his men to mount up. He said quietly, "Let's go. We can talk later."

With his final word, they felt the hoods placed back over their heads. They were pushed to the floor so the tarp could go over them.

One of the men said, "Be quiet. No talking. Or else, we put the gags back on."

As Abia bounced up and down on the wagon floor because of the rough road, he couldn't help but think how he had let Shobal down. Abia wondered what Shobal would do without them there? How would he continue the mission? He leaned over and whispered in Joab's ear, "We need to play along with these guys until we have an opportunity to escape.

Joab nodded in agreement. He knew he would do anything to escape.

CHAPTER 29

"Myka, there you are," Lot said, as he walked in from the front of the storehouse. "You're working in the back today, eh?" He winked and gave Myka a big hug, while he passed her a message.

Still, in a hug, she whispered in Lot's ear, "Everything went as planned." She released the hug and said in a normal voice, "It's good to see you, Lot."

"I didn't see my favorite of favorites up front, so they told me you were back here today. I couldn't leave without saying, hi."

"I'm glad. You made my day," Myka said. She squeezed his arm showing him she really meant it, even though their conversation was more for those working around them listening.

"Well, I better get going," Lot said. He hoped someday they would be able to have a normal, fun talk, instead of the usual cryptic, mission-oriented conversation.

"When will I see you next?"

"I will be back tomorrow, late afternoon."

"Goodbye," Myka smiled. She immediately felt lonely as she watched Lot walk toward the front.

"Myka, have you seen the storekeeper?" Samuel asked. He was the storekeeper's assistant manager and a Watcher.

"I saw him this morning, but I haven't seen him the rest of the day." Myka shrugged. "I don't know where he went."

"This is strange; he hardly ever leaves," Samuel added. "I wanted to tell him the good news from my trip. I got one of the sawmills down south to let us sell all their wood."

"That is good news!" Myka smiled enjoying his success.

Samuel drew closer to Myka and whispered, "Did Shobal call for him?"

"I don't think so; he usually tells us stuff like that." Myka quickly changed the subject. "May I finish the rest of the day in the storefront? I've been stuck in the storehouse all morning."

"Yes, you can. I'll rotate someone else back here."

Myka stopped in the front room on her way out to grab her backpack and closed the door behind her. She pulled out the message from Lot and read.

M,

"The Three Witnesses are meeting tonight to discuss what they should do since their secret spot is compromised. They will be at the community center because it's usually dead this night of the week, so they can talk privately.

We need you to show up unexpectedly and join them. In a few days, Ian is going to speak to them and prepare them to depart. He has a tough job because he must convince them to go to the city and learn who the Light of the Word is first before they can accomplish their mission. Then, by His abiding presence, deliver this valley of death.

Whatever opportunity presents itself for you to prepare their minds to leave, without compromising your position, bring it up. We know you are friends with the Three. We know you would like to go with them. We do not want you to reveal who you are or give them any warning about what is to happen. This will not be a ghost ride. We believe they are ready to come out on their own, like the others, even though we're moving more quickly.

Ian will give Ezra a note from his mother, Eva. She tells him to leave the valley and come to the city. She has revealed information in the letter that only she and Ezra would know, so that should authenticate she is alive and in the city. This should motivate Ezra to want to leave. The timeline has moved up. The Elders think it is best if we move now.

When it comes time for them to leave, nothing or no one can get in the way of their leaving. Do whatever you have to do to accomplish the mission.

May His Kingdom Come!"

L

Myka quickly folded up the message and stuffed it in an inner tear, on the inside of her coat. She planned to destroy it later, when no one was around.

~*~

Ezra pounded away on a hot piece of glowing red metal. He heard his name called. He glanced over his shoulder and saw his father and grandfather, standing outside the office door. *Oh, no,* thought Ezra. *They have been in that office all morning talking.* Ezra had an idea what it was. He ignored them and kept to his work.

"Ezra, Ezra!" roared his father, as he walked toward him.

Ezra shook his head and set the hammer down, along with the prongs holding the piece of metal he was forging. He took off his gloves and turned around. "What?"

"We would like to talk to you in the office," Asa answered.

Ezra followed his father into the office and asked, "What's this all about?" He heard his grandfather close the door behind them.

Labin walked to the front of his desk, while he motioned to a chair. "Have a seat."

Ezra reluctantly sat down, almost at the same time as they did. He noticed the looks they gave each other.

Ezra read their minds. "Well, one of you will have to start."

"Go ahead, Labin," Asa responded. He really didn't want to be a part of this, but he was tired of being pestered by his father.

"I will just get to the point," Labin said. He stood back up. "There have been rumors that there are some individuals who think they have been commissioned to find the *Book of Prophesies*." He made eye contact with Ezra, hoping to see a reaction but saw none.

Ezra already suspected this and said, "Really? I have not heard any rumor like that. Who'd you hear it from?" Ezra tried to put him on the spot.

"Oh, I've just heard it around," Labin answered. He realized he did not sound too convincing.

Ezra glanced over at his father, who looked a little embarrassed. "Is this why you interrupted my work because of a rumor?"

The meeting was not going the way Labin had hoped it would. He said, "We just wanted to make sure you didn't believe that myth. It's just mere fables and lies."

"If it is mere fables, then who cares?" Ezra responded. He shrugged his shoulders.

Asa finally forced himself to say something because he didn't want Ezra to get in trouble. "The only problem is, even though it's a myth," he paused to make eye contact with Labin, "Javan and his men do not think it's a myth. They will kill anyone that has anything to do with it. We just don't want you to come up missing." *Like your mom* thought Asa.

Ezra thought about his mom and said, "Don't worry. The only thing I'm pursuing is a game of four's at the community center tonight."

Asa wanted to end this charade, so he changed the subject. "With Dara and Jared?" he asked. Asa smiled at Ezra and set his hand on Ezra shoulder, ignoring Labin.

"Yes," Ezra answered. He made sure he avoided eye contact with Labin. "Can I go finish my work now?"

"I think—" Labin started to say.

Asa interrupted Labin. "You can go now."

Ezra walked out and heard his father say to Labin, "There. Are you satisfied? Now, leave him alone!"

Later on that day, as Ezra crossed the market square to go to the community center, he reflected on the conversation with his father and grandfather. The more he thought about it the more he had an inner urge to talk to the Whisperer for them. Not knowing exactly how to pray, he said softly, "Light of the Word, open my father and grandfather's hearts to see the Truth. I want them to act upon the Truth they have been given. Most of all, I ask that you would use me to open their eyes, and all the people here to see the Truth. Please show me what has happened to my mom. If she is alive, please let me see her again."

"Boo!"

"Ahhh!" Ezra cried, so startled he almost fell over.

"Gotcha. Payback," Jared laughed. He enjoyed his little victory.

"You scared me," Ezra gasped. "I didn't see anyone around. You really snuck up well."

"You must have been daydreaming," Jared said. He reached for the community center door and motioned Ezra to go in.

"Surprise! I beat you both here," Dara said, doing a victory dance that got them both laughing. "I already picked out a table in the back, and got a deck of cards out." She continued to beam with excitement.

Ezra smiled at Dara. He thought she looked more beautiful by the day. "You're right. This place is abandoned tonight."

"Yeah," agreed Jared, as he looked around. "We have the place to ourselves."

"Let's go play some cards, while we talk," Dara said. She did not want to waste a good opportunity. "I saw you, Jared," she said, giving him a light punch on the arm.

"What?"

"You rolling your eyes," Dara responded. She gave Jared a mischievous look. "You know what we're missing tonight, Jared?"

"I'm not even going to answer that question," Jared said. He ignored Ezra, who busted out laughing. "Not tonight, Dara! Let me deal out the cards."

"Pretty Myka with her brown, wavy, shoulder-length hair and her hazel eyes," Dara said leaning against Jared to tease him.

Jared changed the subject, and asked, "Where are we going to meet from now on if we can't meet in the swamp?" "I don't know," Ezra answered.

"This is a good place," Dara said. "I caught you rolling your eyes again, Jared," She scolded him with her index finger.

"I don't even know what we have to talk about," Ezra said. He looked perplexed. "I have no idea where to search for this *Book of Prophesies*."

"We don't have to search," Jared responded. "You even said last week that we need to wait on the Whisperer to show us what to do next. So we wait."

"He's right," Dara agreed. "We wait, as you said. It's your turn."

The Three Witnesses heard the door open and saw Myka carrying her backpack.

"Hi, Myka," said everyone, almost in unison.

"Hello," Myka answered. She ran her fingers through her hair and smiled at Jared. "I didn't expect all of you here."

"Uh—We decided to play cards at the last minute," Ezra answered. He wished it didn't sound like a lame alibi.

"Scoot over, Jared," Dara commanded. "Myka, sit down and play a few hands."

"That would be fun," Myka said, as she sat down next to Jared.

"This place is dead tonight," Jared added. He felt a little uncomfortable so close to Myka.

"It is dead," Myka agreed. "It's so weird. I was on my way home and on a whim, I decided to stop here to see what was going on. I'm glad I did." She glanced at Jared.

"We are too. Aren't we, Jared," Dara said, putting him on the spot.

Jared gave Dara a mean look, while he pushed up his glasses, and said, "I'm glad you stopped by, Myka."

Ezra was glad Myka had showed up also. He believed she was harmless, so he asked, "Have you heard any more about the soldiers searching the swamp?" He knew the latest news always floated around the market square first.

"All I have heard is that they're still searching," Myka answered. She laid down a card excited she was close to winning the hand. Myka intently studied her cards while biting her top lip. She said in her best off-hand tone, "I don't think they have found anything, though."

Dara picked up where Ezra left off and questioned, "What do you think they are searching for?"

"For people going back and forth across the border," Myka answered like it was a matter of public knowledge. She noticed she caught everyone off guard, so she asked, "What do you guys think?"

"Who knows?" Ezra answered. He shrugged his shoulders.

"Why would anyone want to come to this place?" asked Jared in disgust.

He caused Myka and Dara to laugh at the way he said it. They never expected him to say something like that.

"Why would anyone want to go to Cannibal Land and get eaten up?" Ezra asked. He started to deal out the next hand.

"I think that's all a myth," Dara answered. She picked up and arranged her cards.

"It is a myth," Myka agreed. "The border guards who live on the border say they have never seen any cannibals or dragons. Matter of fact, they say it's quite peaceful and sunny all the time. They actually live with their families where the sun shines, and never get attacked." After she saw the look on Ezra's face, she stopped, not wanting to say too much.

"You're right," Dara said. "I asked a border guard one time, and he started to laugh. He said he hasn't seen anything and thinks there is nothing out there but wildlife."

"What about all the missing people?" Jared said. He noticed Ezra seemed to be daydreaming again.

"I have no idea," Myka responded. She was busy writing down everyone's score. "Jared you're ahead."

"I wonder where all the missing people go?" Ezra pondered. He was thinking about his mom.

Myka could tell Dara and Jared sympathized, for they knew what Ezra was thinking. She pointed out, "There's got to be a city out there where people live."

Ezra snapped out of his thoughts, and said, "Why do you think that?"

"People have to come from somewhere," Myka answered. She tried to make it sound innocent and logical.

"They have to go somewhere too," Jared agreed.

"And people live in cities," Dara laughed.

"So, there has to be a city," Ezra said. He also laughed.

Mission accomplished, thought Myka. *I'm truly going to miss them.*

CHAPTER 30

"Good, you're early," Samuel, the storekeeper's assistant, said out of breath.

"Not really," Myka said. "This is the time I usually come to work in the morning." She noticed Samuel was sweating even though it was cool outside.

Samuel grabbed Myka by the arm and motioned for her to come with him, away from everyone else. Have you seen Storekeeper?" he asked.

"No, I haven't," Myka answered. "He's not back yet?"

"No, he hasn't come back," Samuel answered. He shook his head and said, "It gets even worse. Abia, Joab, and Seth are missing."

"No way!" Myka had a good shocked tone in her voice.

"I've been summoned to the inner chamber. What do I tell Shobal about all this?"

"Tell him the truth," Myka responded. She tried to boost his confidence. "Tell him they came up missing, and no one knows anything."

"What do I say if he asks what I am doing about it?" Samuel asked. He sounded like he was scared.

"Tell him we're searching for them," Myka answered. Myka tried to sound logical to calm him down. *He always was a nervous wreck*, thought Myka. *Now without the guiding force of the storekeeper, he's falling apart.*

"You want me to go to the inner chamber instead?" Myka suggested. "I will just tell them that you were caught up following a lead." She wanted to go to look at the area map to collect more information for the Seekers. She had only been there one time before. Myka thought Shobal didn't value her enough to give her a real assignment because she was a girl. "Your job is just to watch, listen, and occasionally pass messages," Shobal had told her.

"No," Samuel patted her shoulder. "No, he asked for me by name."

Myka's eyes got big, as she looked at Samuel. "You know what?" She sounded like an idea had just popped into her head.

"What?" Samuel said, all excited too.

"You could tell Shobal you have a plan to keep monitoring the Three Witnesses until you find out where Abia, Joab, and Seth are. He will love that you have a temporary solution to keep the mission going."

"I don't have a plan," Samuel agonized.

"Yes, you do," Myka continued. She glanced over the shelves in the store to see if anyone was looking their direction. "I could watch them easily because I'm friends with them. Last night I played cards with the Three at the community center. Or—" Myka looked like another idea popped into her head. "You could tell Shobal I found out last night they are going to start meeting at the community center since the swamp area is compromised. Yes, and I know Jared has a crush on me."

"Good idea. That should satisfy Shobal that we're doing something. Thanks, Myka."

"No problem."

"There is one other thing," Samuel said. "I am not supposed to tell anyone else." He glanced around and continued, "But you have been so helpful, so maybe you can help me with this, too."

"Anything."

Samuel waited for a shopper to walk by and said, "Shobal found out the storekeeper kept a book with a lot of sensitive information that he was supposed to commit to memory. You might have seen it when he was drawing the routes on the board."

"Yes, I remember," Myka said. "I did see the book."

"Do you know where the storekeeper kept the book? I have searched all morning and have not found it. Shobal wants it, so he can look at it and destroy it."

"I have no idea where the book is," Myka said. She looked like she was in deep thought wondering where the storekeeper might have hidden it.

"It could jeopardize everything," Samuel continued. "We have to find it."

"I'll look for it," Myka said, to reassure Samuel.

"Well, I better go," Samuel said. "I hate going to the inner chamber." He walked away and wished he had never been cursed with being a Watcher.

Myka watched as Zesha, Thanoton's chief investigator, approached the store. She was working in her usual spot in the front, straightening up pots and pans that were moved around by customers. Myka wondered how long it had been since one of the council members had shopped at their store. Although, she didn't think he looked like he was here to buy anything.

Zesha was a small, wiry man that had inquisitive eyes. His balding head with a small pointed beard gave him a mysterious look. Myka watched him as he came directly to her.

Myka smiled, and said, "May I help you?"

Zesha returned her smile. "I'm Zesha, the chief investigator, and who are you?"

"I'm Myka. I work here." She purposefully sounded like a teenager.

"I see that," Zesha said. He let out a little chuckle. "I'm here to investigate a few missing people, the storekeeper, Abia," he paused to look at his notebook, "Joab, and Seth. I want to talk to everyone here to see if they know anything about their disappearance."

"Feel free," Myka said. She motioned with her hands and marveled as he walked away, not asking her a single question.

Zesha walked away from the famous girl he had heard so much about. He was glad he had met her.

Myka worked to straighten up the shelves and restock everything. She noticed how the store seemed to run fine without the storekeeper there. She stopped to watch the investigator leave the store and work his way around the free stands in the market square asking questions. *I wonder* thought Myka.

"There's my favorite of favorites," Lot said. "I'm sorry for interrupting your thoughts." Lot had noticed her as she watched Zesha, but said nothing about that.

"Hi, Lot," Myka chuckled. "You snuck up on me."

They gave each other a long hug. No one noticed messages were passed, and Lot received the storekeeper's notebook.

"Why did you come through the back of the store?" Myka questioned.

"My wagon is being loaded in the storehouse," Lot answered. "My requests for supplies have gotten bigger with the additional troops at the border."

"Good for business," Myka added.

"As always, I couldn't stop by without seeing my favorite of favorites."

"I'm glad you stopped by," Myka said. She put her arm through Lot's, and she walked with him to the back. "When will I see you again?"

"You will probably see me before I see you," Lot said. He gave her a wink and left.

Myka wondered what Lot meant by that. He had her curiosity up. Lot would gently squeeze her arm when he gave her a hug if it was a message Myka should read right away. There was less chance of compromise that way. He didn't squeeze. She couldn't wait to read the message on the way home. Myka knew Lot would be pleased with the message she had given him to pass on to Ian. She didn't think the Three Witnesses would have a problem believing there are people living outside this valley and that cannibals and dragons are a myth. Myka had prayed the Light of the Word would give them truth.

Later that afternoon on her way home, Myka turned into the woods just before the dirt path that led to her aunt's farm and sat down. Throwing her apple core away, she pulled out the message and started to read.

M,

Received the go-ahead signal from you, and look forward to reading your message to get the details. Upon your go-ahead, we dispatched Ian to make contact with Ezra. Ian will talk to Ezra to convince the others to be ready to go in two nights. He has a large task ahead of him. We are all praying that Ian easily convinces Ezra, and in turn, Ezra can do the same with the others.

The Elders decided it would be best for the Three Witnesses to make their escape out of the eastern cut. It is the closest and fastest way out of the border. In three to four hours, they will be across the border and in the town of Sanctuary, awaiting transport to the city. We need them out quickly to move on with our next phase.

We missed the window to send them west like everyone suggested. If we send them west now, they will not be able to cross the mountains until spring because it takes a month to get there. By the time they get there, it will be too cold, and the snow will be too deep to cross. They can't go the way of the north for the same reasons. It takes much longer to get there because most of the journey has to be done on foot because of the terrain.

Our two Seekers at the border assured us that we can easily get through the eastern cut using the Seekers trail. The fog is thicker, and the soldiers have become more complacent by the day. They must be through the border before the sun comes up, so they can cross the first valley in darkness. The first valley is visible at sunrise to the border guards. They will be safe once they reach the second valley, which is hidden from view.

In two nights, Ian is going to have the Three, meet him under Thorn Creek Bridge. From there, they will follow the creek and cut through the woods, avoiding all the checkpoints to the Seekers trail. We want you to follow them secretly to provide security. Ian and the other two Seekers know you will be out there in the background. When they are safely in the first valley, we want you to go to L's house for the night. That is your cover if you get stopped. You are there to visit him.

You do whatever it takes to make sure they safely get out. Cross the border only if compromised. The two Seekers will deliver them, and come back. Ian will go all the way to the city with the Three Witnesses.

The whole city is praying for a safe escape out of the eastern cut.

Hang in there. Your labor is not in vain!"

L

Myka lit a match and watched the message burn. She was sad, even though this important mission would launch them into the next phase. She had finally made good friends, and now they had to leave.

Myka knew it would be more than a year before she saw them again. She was worried that Jared would find another girl he liked better in the city. She almost wished she would be compromised, so she could leave with them. Immediately, she felt guilty and said, "I'm sorry. It's not my will, but the Light of the Word's will be done."

Exhausted, Myka wearily rose and went home.

CHAPTER 31

Ian was running out of time. He looked around, and pondered, *Light of the Word, what am I going to do?* He'd been trying for a day-and-a-half to catch Ezra alone so he could talk to him. He was never alone. Now, Ezra had met up with Jared and Dara down by the creek near his house, and they were headed for town to go to the community center. Ian had no choice but to talk to them right then before it was too late. Tomorrow night, they would leave. He asked, *Light of the Word, please give me favor with them.*

Ian quickly circled around jumping over logs and moving tree branches to catch them before they hit the main road. He popped out of the woods onto a dirt path about thirty feet in front of them and stopped. He waited for them to come to him.

Ezra slowed down and said, "Who is that?" He barely noticed a tall skinny man who looked like he was waiting for them twenty feet away. The man looked like he lived in the woods. His clothes matched the vegetation around him, and he had the right amount of dirt on his face to blend in.

"I'm a friend," Ian said. He showed the Three his hands. "I've been sent to talk to you."

"I don't recognize you," Ezra said.

"Me, neither," Dara agreed, as she took a step back.

"I'm not from here," Ian said. He slowly moved closer to them, holding up both hands to show them he was unarmed.

As the man came closer, Ezra noticed he was probably younger than he looked, because he was quite dirty. He seemed like he could easily blend into the woods; no one would ever see him.

"What is it you want to talk about?" Ezra asked.

"Let us go into the woods, sit down, and I will explain everything."

"No way!" Jared exclaimed. He frantically looked around. "This could be a trap."

"You can tell us here," Dara added.

"Look, I know all about you three," Ian whispered. "I've been sent to help you fulfill the prophecy."

"What prophecy?" Ezra said. He did not want to admit to anything if it was a trap. He knew if they got caught, they would be killed for talking about it.

"You are the Three Witnesses," Ian whispered, while cautiously surveying the area. "I have been sent to talk to you to prepare you for your next phase. It's really important that no one hears what we talk about. You know how dangerous it is. Can we go into the woods? I have a campsite that is a five-minute hike from here."

Ezra felt this man was sincere with his gentle, blue eyes, so he finally said, "Okay. We'll follow you."

The Three Witnesses followed Ian in the woods. They all marveled how easily and quietly he moved around. He seemed in tune and touch with nature.

Ian looked over his right shoulder and said, "We're almost there."

Dara walked up to the campsite immediately impressed. She noticed an elaborate lean-to, made out of sticks and leaves that looked like it could withstand heavy rains. Located next to a creek, was a bucket to fetch water and a net to catch fish hung up to dry. The fire pit in the middle of the campsite was still smoldering. She watched as Ian grabbed some logs from off a pile and placed them on the smoldering coals.

"How long have you been living here?" Dara questioned. The campsite looked permanent.

"I live here off and on throughout the year," Ian answered. He put some more logs on the fire and motioned for everyone to sit.

"Have you been following us?" Jared asked. He watched Ian pull a letter out of his bag.

"Yes, I have. Others have followed you as well." He noticed the fear on their faces and said. "Let me explain what you need to know, and then you'll understand. I come from a city outside of the valley of Thanoton. I cannot tell you the name of the city until we are outside of this valley."

"What do you mean? Outside this valley?" Ezra said. He looked over at Jared and Dara.

"Keep your voices down," Ian whispered. "Let me explain. The Three of you have been chosen by the Light of the Word to deliver this valley. The people of this valley are deceived and living so far from the Truth. The only way you will accomplish this task is to know the Light of the Word, and to be empowered by the Whisperer. You cannot do this in your own strength. You three need to come with me to the city, to learn who the Light of the Word is by studying the *Book of Prophesies*. There you will learn to recognize and follow His voice. You will learn to talk to Him and be reliant on Him. Then, when the Elders feel you are ready, they will commission you to accomplish what you have been chosen to do."

Ian took a drink from his canteen and then held it out. "Would you like some water?"

"No, thanks," Ezra said. Jared and Dara shook their heads no.

"You have the *Book of Prophesies* there?" Ezra asked. "In that city, you're talking about?"

"Oh, yes," Ian answered. "Everyone that lives there has a copy." He noticed their expressions and said, "In the city, everyone worships the Light of the Word."

"So, I guess that's what the Whisperer meant," Dara added, "when it said to, 'find the *Book of Prophesies*. It will show you the Light of the Word.' It meant for us to go to this city and learn who He is."

"Yes," Ian responded with a surprised look. "*The Book of Prophesies* and explanations await you there. Do not believe all those lies and myths. They are untrue. Outside this valley, it's beautiful and safe."

Ian stopped for a second and intensely studied Ezra. "Ezra, I have a letter for you from your mother. She lives in the city." He handed it to him.

"From my mom?" Ezra exclaimed. He stood up and quickly opened it. As he read, streams of tears rolled from his eyes and a deep groan escaped from his inner being.

"Are you all right?" Dara asked. She had never seen Ezra cry.

"She's alive in the city, and she can't wait to see me. She is a follower of the Light of the Word and tells me to leave the valley. She also told me one other thing," he said smiling, "our little secret."

Jared put his arm around his friend. "Great news. I'm so happy for you."

"I wonder why she didn't tell you she was going to leave," Dara asked.

"I can't explain everything right now," Ian replied. "But we have a network of people in this valley. They make contact with and protect those that come to believe in the Light of the Word. We have found it's safer for them, and their families, if they leave the valley and go to the city. Once in the city, they can pray the Whisperer would open their family members' hearts to the Truth.

"There are also networks set on destroying or distracting people from believing in the Light of the Word. Just like in your mom's case, it was best for her to leave when she started to believe than to put her family in danger. Your mom, like all the others that have left this valley, is praying for the day there will be complete deliverance. Meanwhile, we've taken people out in small groups. While you three are away preparing, we will have people here to prepare and get everything ready for your return.

"So, when do we leave?" Ezra asked.

"Tomorrow night. We will meet under the Thorn Creek Bridge an hour after complete darkness. Only bring what you can carry in one backpack. It should be as light as possible; we'll move fast. The city has everything you need, so you don't need to bring much. You do need two canteens of water, food for three days, a change of clothes and a waterproof cold weather jacket or cape. Be sure to bring plenty of arrows for your bows. We must prepare for the worst. We will have others helping us escape. We might see them, but we might not. I use this route, and know it very well. I am aware of the checkpoints, and how to get around them. Do not tell anyone what we are doing. Tell your family you are going to the community center. It will be hard, but it is for their own safety. Once we cross the border, we have to quickly cross the next valley and enter the third, before the sun comes up. In the third valley, we have a small, hidden town called Sanctuary. There, we will spend the day and one night, so your eyes can adjust to the light." A broad smile split Ian's face, "At night, with the moon and clear skies, you will see better than you have ever seen during the day in Thanoton." Ian laughed, and said, "It will take you a week or so to totally adjust to the sunlight during the day. From Sanctuary, it is a three day trip to the city." Ian noticed that something bothered Jared. "What's wrong?"

"Well, I have this friend. I know she would go with us if we explained all this to her."

"Myka definitely would," Dara said. She read Jared's mind. "We could tell her about it tonight!"

"Or my father—" added Ezra.

"You can't tell anyone," Ian interrupted. "You can't worry about them for now. The best thing you can do is prepare yourselves for the time you will come back to deliver them." Ian turned a deeply concerned gaze on Ezra, "You especially cannot let your grandfather suspect anything." He leaned forward to explain earnestly, "Sometimes, those that know who the Light of the Word is, or have grown up hearing about it, but don't seek Him or encourage others to know Him, are our greatest threat. They are the ones trying to suppress us. They don't want to be ruled by the Light of the Word because they want to rule themselves. So, when someone starts to seek and actually live for Him, they deem it a threat. They'll do anything to water down the Truth and discourage others to live by it. We don't want that kind of a believer in the city. Those people only believe when it's convenient, popular, or safe to do so. We only want those that have a true belief in the Light of the Word, evident in their commitment to follow him."

"My mom did warn me about Labin in the letter," Ezra agreed. "She said she's praying hard for the Whisperer to open my father and grandfather's hearts to the Truth."

"Well, that's all I have," Ian said. He relaxed a bit. "I will see you all tomorrow night, right?"

"I'll be there," Ezra answered. He stood up and shook Ian's hand.

"Me too," Dara agreed, already excited.

Jared noticed everyone was staring at him. He shrugged his shoulders and said, "I always go where you guys go." He stared down at the ground and wished Myka could go with him. Jared realized he needed to start thinking of the higher purpose and not his own will.

"Good, let's ask the Light of the Word for help on our trip," Ian said. He held out his hands and motioned to make a circle.

The Three were in deep thought about what Ian had said, and how he talked to the Light of the Word. "I've never heard anyone talk to the Light of the Word before," Dara marveled. "It was absolutely beautiful."

"I didn't know what praying was until I heard Ian. He prayed like he knew the Light of the Word personally," Jared said. He stepped onto the main road headed to the community center.

"All I know is, I want to know the Light of the Word like he does." Ezra said.

"Me too," Dara agreed.

"That's why we're leaving for the city tomorrow night," Jared said. His heart raced as he approached the community center. He walked through the front door, held by Ezra, and noticed the look of compassion on his face. *What a good friend* thought Jared.

"Hey, Jared, Dara, and Ezra! I already got us a table," Myka said. She smiled at Jared and caused his face to turn all red.

"Sorry, we're late," Dara said. She looked at the clock. "An hour-and-a-half late to be exact."

"Yeah, sorry," Ezra said. He wondered what else he should say.

"That's all right," Myka said. "I was late myself." She didn't share she had watched them leave the woods a few minutes before.

"Boy, your backpack seems bigger tonight," Jared laughed. He caused everyone else including Myka, to laugh.

"You know me. I'm a pack rat," Myka said. She enjoyed the fun.

"Well, let's play cards!" Dara commanded. She realized everyone was going to make the best of this night, the last night with Myka.

CHAPTER 32

"All right, we've got everyone here," Ian whispered. He watched Dara duck down under the bridge and get down on one knee next to them.

"Hi Dara," Ezra said. He helped her take her backpack off.

"Your backpack is stuffed." Jared laughed, more because he was nervous than because of her backpack.

"I've got a Myka-backpack," Dara answered. She realized what she had said, and after she saw Jared's reaction, she reached to squeeze his shoulder.

"I want everyone to stay close as we move to the eastern cut." Shifting his weight, Ian continued, "Our biggest threats are running into someone by accident. It's extremely hard to see. Walk quietly, and stay quiet. Javan's men are out patrolling, so we need to be careful. When we arrive close to the eastern cut, one of our team members will take us over the border. We also have one more team member meeting us in the middle of the eastern cut to help provide security. All of us will cross the first valley, and then the team members will go back to the border unless compromised. We will go on to Sanctuary. Any questions?" Ian whispered. He was so close, he could hear all three of them breathe.

"Is there anyone else that will provide security, or is it just the two at the border?" Ezra asked.

"There is one other person that will follow behind us to the border to provide security," Ian answered. "We'll never see that person unless it's an extreme emergency. Listen, we can't rely on the others to keep us safe. We are a small group compared to the army that's out patrolling. They have the ability to surround us in minutes. The only advantage we have is speed and the cover of darkness. If trouble arises, we have to take care of it ourselves. If you wait for someone else to engage the enemy, it will be too late. If you hesitate, you will get us all killed."

"What do we do if we run into someone?" Jared asked.

"We have to be ready to kill or subdue anyone that attempts to stop us," Ian said. He grabbed Ezra and Jared's arm. "We can't allow anything to stop us, do you understand?"

Both Ezra and Jared nodded their heads and said, "Yes." Both of them hoped it would never come to that.

"Let's move out," Ian commanded. He put on his rucksack and helped the others with theirs. "Have your swords out, ready to use. I will go first. Then Dara, Jared, and Ezra, you bring up the rear."

"Okay," Ezra stood up and pulled out his sword.

Ian grabbed Ezra by the arm and pulled him close to whisper in his ear. "You might hear someone following from behind. Don't worry. That's one of us. If someone tries to stop us, kill him. Javan's men have been ordered to kill us if found."

~*~

Myka crept up. She held her crossbow ready to shoot anyone that got in the way. She followed Ezra as he left from under the bridge, moving down the dry creek bed. Only the sound of their footsteps on the rocky ground guided her.

The fog had made it impossible to see in the pitch-black night. Myka was amazed at how well Ian maneuvered. She felt her way under some protruding trees, glad when they came out of the creek bed. The solid ground would be quicker, but much harder for Myka to hear their footsteps. Everyone froze. They heard voices echo in the distance. It was hard to tell how far away.

"Hey! Who are you?"

Myka heard shouts and fighting up ahead. She quickly closed the gap enough to see Ezra throw down a soldier that lunged at him with a knife. She took aim and fired an arrow right under the soldier's arm into the heart, killing him instantly. She watched Ian pull his sword out of another soldier.

Myka slipped back into the fog and heard Ian command, "Let's get moving."

The sound of voices drifted toward Myka, as she quickly pulled the bodies off the trail. She hoped they wouldn't find them right away. She ran to catch up and stayed closer this time. The soldiers were closing in all around them.

Myka stopped immediately, almost running into Ezra. She backed away, so she was not seen. Ian and the Three Witnesses were stopped. Soldiers were headed their way. Myka decided to circle around and ambush them from the side.

Ian motioned with his hands for all three to be ready with their bows to ambush the group coming their way. He signaled that it sounded like four or five soldiers.

Myka heard, "Ahhh!" Then soldiers' bodies hit the ground, and one soldier staggered away. She quickly followed the soldier to hunt him down. She took aim and shot him between the shoulder blades. She watched as he collapsed on the ground, dead. Myka heard footsteps from behind and knew it must be Ian chasing after the wounded soldier. She whispered, "Seeker, Seeker, Seeker," to let him know it was a friendly. Ian saw Myka. He smiled and slapped her on the shoulder after he saw the dead soldier at her feet. He immediately left, went back to the group, and moved out.

Myka didn't worry about the bodies this time. She continued to follow Ian and the Three and was amazed at how well they did. *Ezra's a real warrior*, thought Myka.

"There you are," Caleb whispered. He was angry at Ian. "What did you do? The whole valley is after you."

"We accidently ran into some soldiers, and it went downhill from there," Ian answered. He noticed the dead soldier lying to the side with his throat slit.

"Let's go," Caleb said. "The Seekers' trail is compromised. Neptali is waiting for us on top."

The group cautiously approached the eastern cut. They squeezed and maneuvered through the jagged rocks, working their way over the ridgeline. Arrows struck the rocks all around them. Once they arrived at the top, they could see the clear valley off in the distance. Neptali was at the top waiting for them.

"Let's hurry up!" Neptali said. "They're all around us." He continued to fire arrows randomly at the voices below.

"Stop right there," Jotham shouted. "That's far enough." He startled everyone and had a knife against Caleb's throat, ready to draw blood.

Myka suddenly came out of nowhere and jammed an arrow right under Jotham's chin, waiting to shoot. Directly behind her, a soldier lunged out of the thick fog to strike Myka in the neck. Just before the soldier connected with his sword, Ezra blocked his arm. He shoved his sword all the way into the soldier's lower belly. He held it, as he watched the soldier slowly collapse and die.

Blood dripped from Jotham's neck. "Drop it, or I'll shoot!" Myka said. She applied pressure to his neck until he dropped it. Then Caleb turned around and helped Ezra throw Jotham to the ground.

"Thanks, Ezra," Ian said. He stood guard with Myka, while Ezra and Caleb finished tying Jotham up.

"You saved my life, Ezra. Thank you," Myka said.

"Myka, is that you?" Dara gasped. She noticed Myka's backpack, as did Jared and Ezra.

"You won't get away with this," Jotham yelled. He struggled to get out of the restraints.

"Traitors! Neptali, Caleb, Myka. Traitors!" Jotham screamed.

"Gag him," someone said.

Ezra and Caleb quickly gagged him.

"Myka and Caleb, we're compromised," Neptali said.

They heard voices nearby, all around them. Arrows now bombarded the rocks right next to them.

"There is no way we will make it over the top without getting killed!" Neptali said, while he and the others fired arrows.

"I will get them to follow me and divert them away from you," Myka said.

"You can't go back," Ian said. "You're compromised."

"I know," Myka said. "I will go the way of the north, my escape and evasion route. Let the elders know I will be at the cache sight." Myka pulled down her mask and gave Jared a hug. "I will see you in the city next spring." Like a vapor, she vanished in the fog before Jared could say a word.

Taking Jotham, prisoner, they went down the other side and headed out of the valley of Thanoton. They heard the soldiers going the opposite way. They were following Myka's diversion. She had saved them.

They moved as fast as they could through the valley with no one pursuing. The Three Witnesses only heard shouts and voices in the distance.

Jared was worried, and said aloud, "I hope Myka doesn't get caught." His voice trembled.

"You don't have to worry about her," Ian said.

"She's the best there is," Caleb said as he pushed Jotham. "Her diversion totally saved us."

"She is amazing," Jared agreed. "Who would have thought?"

Dara put her arm around Jared. "She is amazing. I can't wait to see her next spring," Dara said. In her heart, she asked the Light of the Word to protect Myka.

"It's astonishing how clearly we can see," Ezra whispered to Dara and Jared.

"Yes. The moon is so bright and beautiful," Dara said. She pointed toward some deer grazing in the distance.

~*~

Myka ran and made a lot of noise. She headed right toward the soldiers that were headed her direction. As soon as she saw them, she fired a volley of arrows, killing at least three. She gained their attention and got them to follow her away from the eastern cut and her friends. She headed north.

With her heart pounding, she ran as fast as she could down the north ridge trail. She took up a defensive position behind a rock, just off the trail. She waited while getting her arrows ready, to ambush the group coming her way. As soon as she started to see them, she fired, quickly loading another arrow and firing again until four soldiers were dead in front of her. She hurried up, grabbing the dead soldier's arrows for extra ammunition and ran up the mountain. She quickly disappeared, running and climbing as fast as she could. Her lungs burned. She pressed on and distanced herself from the soldiers. She heard their voices further away as she kept moving. Finally, when she could no longer hear their voices, she slowed down to catch her breath. Her hands shook from the fear she felt.

Myka knelt down and prayed. "Thank you, Light of the Word, for bringing my friends to safety. Help me to endure this long trip to the cache site up north and the long winter I will spend there." She couldn't wait for spring to come, so she could go to the city to be with her friends. She got up and started to run again, to get as far away from the soldiers as she could.

I've been praying the Light of the Word would allow me to go back to the city. I didn't think it would happen this way. I will take it any way I can get it. Smiling, she kept moving.

PART TWO

CHAPTER 33

A few months later on a very cold and even for Thanoton unusually dreary day, everyone in Thanoton was assembled. There was an eerie silence in the crowd summoned by Javan, the Supreme Commander of the valley of Thanoton, to witness an execution. It was unusual for a crowd this size to be so quiet. Some were whispering to each other, wondering and speculating whom it was being executed today. Javan ruled with an iron fist, and the people feared him, so they came. He and his commanders were notorious for killing those that rebelled against their authority. This was his valley. Everything and everyone in the valley of Thanoton belonged to him.

What made today's execution different from the others was its public nature. The whole city of Thanoton was there, along with the surrounding towns and villages. All the soldiers, usually guarding the borders that surrounded the valley of Thanoton, were there along with their families. The only people not there to witness the execution were Dakar, the captain of the army, along with two platoons of his most trusted soldiers. They secured the border, so the regular border guards could be at the execution. Nothing like this had been done since the last prophet was killed on the martyr's pole one thousand years ago.

The martyr's pole was a square, wooden beam measuring six-by-six inches that stuck straight out of the ground. It was eight feet tall, with metal restraints, stretching the arms overhead of the one being executed. Today, there was a set of new restraints attached to the pole. The old restraints had rusted shut over the years from lack of use. The martyr's pole stood on a raised platform in the middle of the market square, located in front of Javan's palace.

The brick platform stood six feet tall and ten feet wide with brick steps on all four sides. Usually, the market square was filled with people trading goods from baskets, wagons, and carts. Today, it was standing room only in the square. All the stores were closed, and no carts or wagons were allowed. Market square police made sure no space was left unoccupied. The border guards and their families had priority. They were up front, surrounding the platform.

Maximus felt a slight nudge. He looked behind to see who it was. No one was there. Maximus fought hard to stay in the very back of the crowd.

He felt a push this time, like a gust of wind. It pushed him forward. He looked behind—no one. The people that stood next to him didn't seem to notice. Maximus was pushed again by something. This time, he stumbled forward, being nudged and shoved by an unforeseen hand. It pushed him through the crowd.

"Watch out boy," said a man in the crowd, bumped by Maximus.

Maximus hated to be called "boy," even if he was young, so he ignored him. He finally realized it was the hand of the Whisperer pushing him forward for some reason. He maneuvered his way through the crowd. Maximus didn't want to go up front, but he couldn't resist. He loved when the Whisperer led him.

With his freckles and short brown hair, Maximus looked young. He remembered the first time he felt the Whisperer's nudge. In Pistio, they were asking for a volunteer to work undercover in Javan's palace to deliver messages back-and-forth for the Seekers. They needed to communicate more, now that the Children of Light were close to establishing the kingdom for the Light of the Word.

Maximus had felt a nudge in his heart to volunteer. He ignored it at first. When he felt it get stronger and a quiet voice from within say "go," he volunteered. After much prayer, he was chosen out of all the volunteers. He was the youngest, thirteen years old, and least qualified. He knew he wasn't chosen because of his qualifications. The Light of the Word wanted him—chose him.

Maximus was grateful and glad to help establish the Kingdom of Light in this final hour. He would do whatever it took to prepare for the safe return of the Three Witnesses and to establish Ezra as King.

Maximus no longer felt pushed, so he stopped. He was up front, behind the border guards and their families. He had a clear view of the platform.

Three long horn blasts broke the silence. All eyes turned toward the palace. The thick fog obscured the view, but he heard the gates open and numerous horses coming out. From habit, he got down on one knee like all the others and bowed before Javan as was custom.

Javan was easily spotted in the group that came out. His bright red, bushy hair and full beard splayed against his large chest stood out like a beacon. He rode out on a horse escorted by the palace guards on foot. Tuval followed him. He was much shorter than Javan and wiry, almost old-man-frail looking, but astride a horse, those characteristics didn't show much. The two men were so different in looks but thought so much alike.

Next came the prisoner who wore a black hood over his head with hands tied behind his back. The prisoner was wearing only a thin burlap shirt and a pair of torn trousers. He was shaking from a combination of fear and cold.

The horses stopped in front of the platform surrounded by a platoon of army soldiers. Commander Javan, Tuval, and the soldier who escorted the prisoner ascended the stairs to the top of the platform. The rest of the palace guards left, taking the horses with them and returning to the palace. Most people in the crowd beyond thirty feet could not see the platform because of the fog.

The border guards and their families had a clear view of the platform. They watched the soldier shackle the hands of the one to be executed.

"People of Thanoton, on your feet," commanded Tuval, hearing the thunder of people as they stood up. The fear in their eyes pleased him. "Today, you are here to witness an execution by stoning of a traitor and enabler." The crowd gasped. "But before I read the crime found against this traitor, Commander Javan will speak." Tuval turned and gave Javan a nod.

Javan stroked his red beard and circled the platform while studying the border guards and their families. The silence seemed to last forever. Finally, Javan spoke. "Today, you are going to witness the fate of those that help the cannibals. Cannibals have infiltrated us from our borders. We also have reason to believe, they are living amongst us. They have crossed our borders due to the enablement and incompetence of our border guards." Javan held out his hands to point out the border guards that surrounded the platform. He stared at them and their families, while he circled above.

"Make no mistake," Javan continued. "They look like ordinary people. They could be standing next to you right now." Javan watched as the crowd of people behind the border guards and their families looked at each other with wonder. He also noticed that the border guards and their families did not. They looked like they didn't believe him.

Maximus, along with the others, started to distance themselves from the border guards leaving a gap between them and the crowd. They sensed Javan was directing everything toward them. They could also see the army soldiers, scattered throughout, were moving closer to the border guards.

Javan continued, "The cannibals are here for one thing and one thing only, to snatch people out of the valley of Thanoton for food." Javan heard people gasp in fear. He knew the people of Thanoton were afraid of being taken. So many had come up missing with no clues as to where they went. The people figured it was him and his men that were doing the abducting. Now, they were finding out it wasn't.

Javan let the people think it was he doing the snatching to control them through fear. Now, he was letting everyone know, cannibals were snatching the people.

"Everyone here knows someone that has gone missing," Javan said. He watched the army surround the border guards. He enjoyed the fear he saw in their eyes. "There have been quite a few lately. We also found out that three border guards, the storekeeper, and others were part of this conspiracy to abduct people, and take them out of the valley to Cannibal Land. We know there are others hidden out there working with the cannibals." Javan pulled out his sword and pointed it at the crowd gathered around. "I warn you! You will be caught."

Javan watched as a cart carrying baskets full of big rocks came to a stop next to the stairs leading up to the platform. The border guards feared as the baskets of rocks were passed to the soldiers. "Two months ago, in the process of catching the cannibals, thirty of our soldiers were killed. The intruders fled over the border to the safety of Cannibal Land after they abducted a few of our people. We believe that a small group of intruders fled north. We are searching for them as we speak. If you have any information, you need to come forward." Javan gave Tuval a nod and picked up a rock.

Tuval walked over and stood next to the prisoner, and commanded, "Soldier, take off his hood." The border guards and Maximus watched as the soldier pulled the black hood off the prisoner. They all were surprised. Tuval continued, "Hyrum, the head of the border guards, has been found guilty of helping the cannibals infiltrate the valley of Thanoton. He purposely allowed slack security on the border, making it easier for them."

"Impossible!" "He's innocent!" came several shouts from the border guards.

"Silence!" Javan shouted. He waved his sword as if he was about to jump off the platform and start slaying.

"No!" "He's innocent!" "It's a lie!" "He's not a traitor," roared the border guards getting louder, pushing against the soldiers around the platform.

The market square police quickly blew the horn signaling the army to come and crush the tumult that had started. The army moved in, beating and smashing the border guards, along with any women or children that got in their way. In a matter of a few minutes, the border guards and their families were subdued. There were broken bodies and blood everywhere. Moans and crying rose from the border guards and their families, as some less hurt struggled to help bandage up wounds of the more severely hurt. Then reality set in. Many were dead, including one woman.

Maximus scrambled to his feet after he had fallen. He tried to get away from the soldiers. He had never witnessed evil so up close and personal before. Maximus' resolve was strengthened to do whatever it took to rid Thanoton of this evil.

"I want all of you to watch this execution," Javan said. He flashed his sword covered in a border guard's blood. "Anyone who looks away will be killed."

Maximus watched in horror as Javan, Tuval, and three army soldiers hurled rocks at Hyrum's head. The rocks could be heard cracking his skull and smashing up his face. The blood gushed until he hung there lifeless. They finally stopped throwing the rocks.

All that could be heard was weeping.

Labin could no longer watch. He kneeled down with his arm around Asa, who wept, worried for his son, Ezra.

CHAPTER 34

"Yah!" commanded Lot. He snapped the reins that controlled the horses pulling his supply wagon. The horses worked hard to drag the heavy supplies through the snow. If Lot had known it was going to snow like this, he would never have loaded this many supplies onto the wagon.

Good thing I don't have to deliver the supplies till tomorrow, he sighed. *That is if we don't get snowed in.*

He turned onto the road that led to his house, close to the eastern border of the valley of Thanoton. Right away, Lot was excited to see a branch lying across the road. "Whoa," said Lot, bringing the horses to a stop. *Someone wants a little chat, eh?* He hopped down and grabbed the branch, throwing it back into the woods. Lot pulled the wagon toward the barn and noticed Kern as he got closer. He was opening the barn door for him. Lot pulled in and brought the horses to a stop. He climbed down.

"Kern, good to see you. It's been a long time," Lot said, as he gave him a bear hug. "What brings you to the east side of the valley, instead of the west side where you belong?" Lot's whole body shook with laughter.

Kern laughed, and said, "It's really good to see you too." He slapped Lot on the back. "We can talk later. There is someone in the back room that needs to talk to you. I will take care of the horses."

"Thanks," Lot said. He headed to a small supply room at the rear of the barn. *Kern is all business,* thought Lot. *Whenever we meet, it always is. But then he has farther to travel being from the west side running supplies and carrying messages.*

Lot opened the door to the back room. "Zesha! You? I thought we should never meet! It's too much of a risk," Lot stood frozen, stunned by his presence.

"So much has gone wrong," Zesha said. He stood up to shake Lot's hand. "Things aren't working out as planned, and we are without our key people. We had to regroup and come up with a different strategy, to get ready for spring."

Lot slowly closed the door behind him. He could not believe that Zesha, the chief investigator of Thanoton and one of Javan's twelve, trusted council members, was standing in front of him. Zesha was a

Seeker, just like Lot. He'd been able to infiltrate Javan's evil regime without them knowing and become a trusted advisor. Zesha's position helped facilitate and protect the Seekers by passing information of the doings of Javan's council. He sent information to elders living in a northern city outside the valley of Thanoton. He was also good at delivering misinformation to Javan, to help facilitate the Seekers' missions.

Both men were very different. Lot was a loud, friendly, joyous man that everyone loved. People always relaxed around him because he genuinely cared for them. He was a working man with a short stature but was broad like a tree trunk. Now with age, he was supporting a belly. No one ever suspected Lot as being a Seeker and a worshipper of the Light of the Word, or that he was involved in smuggling people out of the valley. That's what made him so good.

Zesha on the other hand was wiry with a serious look on his face. He was a little bit taller than Lot but was small in stature. Standing next to Lot, he looked petite. He was bald with a pointed beard and a permanent scowl on his face. All this combined to give him a mysterious air. He hardly smiled and rarely laughed. No one suspected him. He was the person in charge of investigating the intruders and missing people. Outwardly, he seemed like one of Javan's close advisors.

They both lived a double-life with one purpose, to deliver this valley from the grip of Darkness to the freedom found in the Light. They both were descendants of the Children of Light and dedicated to the Light of the Word.

Lot turned a bucket upside down and sat. "This must be important if you are willing to risk coming here. Our paths would never cross under normal circumstances. You know how paranoid Javan is. If anyone finds out, it will raise suspicion."

"It is worth the risk," Zesha responded. "We have some urgent business."

"We should be communicating through messages," Lot pointed out, still uncomfortable with Zesha's visit.

"Ian is gone," Zesha added, referring to the only one they used to pass messages to each other. "Since he is not coming back to the valley until spring, I had no choice but to contact you personally. Don't worry. No one will be suspicious of us meeting. I'm up here on official business to talk to everyone who lives by the eastern cut. So, I'm supposed to be here. It would be more suspicious if I skipped you."

Zesha rubbed his hands together to stay warm. "Kern has someone in mind we can use as a go-between until Ian comes back. He also lives in the town of Pistio. He's not fully trained, but I guess he catches on fast. I realize the Elders told us to lay low and not do anything until spring." Zesha paused to put his gloves back on. "We were to wait until Sanctuary's headquarters operations moved from its current eastern location outside the valley to inside the western border, to the town of Pistio. But things changed. Not everything worked out as planned."

"I never expected our people to be compromised," added Lot, shaking his head. "Only Ian and the three witnesses were to go to the city. Now Caleb and Neptali are in the city, and we can't use them. Myka escaped, I thank the Light of the Word for that. Then, she will also leave the valley and go to the city. They cannot come back or be killed for sure."

"Actually, Myka was not compromised."

"What?" Lot blurted out.

"Javan's men never heard her name. They only heard Neptali and Caleb's names. They think she was abducted like the Three Witnesses. I've made sure it's stayed that way."

"She thinks she's compromised," Lot said. "I have to get her back," he said, all excited. "She is so vital to this operation."

"We'll have to wait till spring thaw," Zesha added. "There is no way we can get up to the northern mountains now."

"Okay, so what is so vital that we have to change our plans?" Lot asked. He sat back down on the bucket.

"You saw the devastation in the marketplace a few days ago," said Zesha, still disgusted by it. He pulled out a brown leather notebook. "Javan is intent on evil for the border guards and their families. He has told Dakar, who is now in charge of the border, to torture the border guards for information. He is to do whatever it takes to find out who is helping the cannibals. Dakar has orders to kill anyone he suspects. I'm afraid for the hundred border guards and their families. We need to get them out of the valley."

"How? It's winter." Lot snorted, "They won't believe us."

"I think they're afraid and desperate enough to believe us," Zesha said. He gave an unnatural smile. "I have really good evidence one of the leaders of the border guards is a secret believer and a worshipper of the

Light of the Word. I also have proof that there are many more. I've purposely kept this a secret to protect them."

"You mean they have passed down the faith for a thousand years?" Lot responded. He watched Zesha and thought how odd he looked when he tried to smile.

"That's exactly what I am saying. Just like we did. Although, I don't think they have a complete understanding. But they secretly worship."

"Do they have the *Book of Prophesies*?" Lot asked.

"No, I don't think so. They have memorized stories and passages they have passed down." Zesha tore a page out of his notebook and handed it to Lot. "Do you know Marcus, a border guard leader?"

"Yes, of course," Lot answered. "He's a good man. He's a secret believer?"

Zesha nodded his head. "I want you to make contact with Marcus, and tell him all about us. Give him a complete history of the Children of Light, the Light of the Word, and our northern city outside of this valley. All the border guards know this city exists. They can see it from their most northern point so they will believe you. They also know cannibals do not exist. I think it will be quite easy to persuade them."

"Can we trust him?" Lot asked.

"Yes, I believe so. Otherwise, I wouldn't have you make contact with him," Zesha answered.

"You want me to prepare them to leave in the spring?"

"We can't wait that long. I am afraid Dakar will kill them all by then. I want you to coordinate for all of them to flee the eastern border. They can occupy Sanctuary holding up there until spring. Then in spring, they can go north to the city."

Zesha paused to stand up and stretch his back. He continued, "Since they have moved Sanctuary operations, that whole town is abandoned. There is still a stockpile of food and plenty of water. We kept it that way, just in case we needed it. They will have to cram into the houses and barns to fit, but at least they will be safe. I don't care how you do it. Their life depends on it. Use your discretion when you make contact with Marcus. Make sure it goes off without a hitch. At least, they will be safe. Sanctuary is only two valleys over, so they shouldn't have any problems making it in one night, even in the snow. All Dakar will see in the morning is a bunch of tracks. Javan won't want Dakar to pursue after them into Cannibal Land. Anyway, I'll make sure that does not happen."

Lot smiled. "Won't that be great if all the border guards and their families left? That would help us get a jump on next year's operations."

"Indeed," Zesha agreed. "Of course, we need to be in agreement with this. We have to conduct this without the Elders' consent. We have no way of communicating with them until spring."

Lot held out his hand to shake. "I'm in agreement."

"Good," Zesha said. He shook his hand. "Hopefully, this is the last time we meet in person until we establish the Kingdom. From now on we will pass messages through Maximus, the boy Kern recruited." Zesha stopped in the doorway, turned back to Lot, and pointed. "If anything happens to me, you need to continue with the plan, no matter what! Agreed?"

"Of course," Lot answered, unnerved by his penetrating eyes and anger. Lot watched Zesha leave and wondered.

CHAPTER 35

The next day, Kern visited Maximus at Calvin's house. It was located close to the market square in the city of Thanoton. Maximus had moved from the town of Pistio a couple hours away. He lived with an older retired couple, Calvin, a key player in the Seekers network, and his wife.

"Remember what I told you, Maximus. Just act natural," Kern said. He put his arm around Maximus and walked him to the front door.

"I will," Maximus responded. He took a deep breath while reaching to take his coat off the hook. Today was his first day of work at the palace. Maximus tried hard to conceal his nervousness.

"Everything's cleared. You shouldn't have any problems. Calvin and his wife are good people and well respected in Thanoton. They love having a boy living with them again. I mean," Kern corrected, "young man." He smiled at the look on young Maximus' face. "Calvin has lined up this job. You're in a key position to help us communicate from the inside. Keep your ears open for any information that might help us."

"Who's the believer on the inside?" Maximus asked as he buttoned up his coat.

"I'm not going to tell you right now."

"Why not? Wouldn't it be better if I knew?" he said with a surprised look.

"It's best if you don't know who this person is. We don't want you to treat anyone differently by watching them too much, or worse be tempted to talk to them. Sometimes, we can unconsciously give someone away by our mannerisms. The people at the palace are paranoid and suspicious of everyone, including each other. The person that is on the inside is a professional, never fear. He will treat you like everyone else, and you will never suspect him. He has infiltrated Javan's regime because he does not compromise his position, ever. This is the opportunity you wanted, Maximus," said Kern, while he opened the front door. "So, do exactly as I have taught you and go about your daily business as normal."

Kern watched as Maximus left Calvin's house and headed for the palace. He felt a little apprehensive sending him at such a young age. Maximus was thirteen years old, or as he would always say, almost fourteen. However, they really needed him. He would be in a perfect position to courier messages and overhear vital information. Overcast skies and thick fog swallowed him after twenty feet down the path. Kern closed the door.

Young Maximus walked up to the front gate of Javan's palace. The large metal gate was thirty feet wide and opened in the center. Four palace guards stood behind the metal gate. Guard towers on both sides of the gate held guards ready to shoot arrows at any unauthorized person who tried to gain entrance.

"Hey! This gate is only for horses and wagons," said a palace guard. He pointed to the left. "The walk-in gate is over there."

Maximus spied the small metal gate built into the rock wall, ten feet from the main gate.

"What do you want, boy?" said a large palace guard, standing behind the metal gate. He looked down at him with contempt.

"Sir, I'm here to see the head steward."

"What about, boy?" The guard eyed him skeptically.

"About a job," answered Maximus sternly. He started to get mad at this fat guard that looked like he was about to burst out of his metal body armor. He was tired of being called a boy.

"What's your name, boy?"

"Maximus!"

The guard pointed his finger. "Don't get smart with me, boy. How old are you?" he asked. He ran his finger down a roster of names.

"I'm almost fourteen, sir."

"Well, well, I guess you are allowed to come in. Those doors and straight down the hallway until you run into a staircase. Wait there for the head steward."

Maximus walked into the palace and was instantly amazed at how beautiful it was on the inside. The floors were polished marble with white rock walls and tall ceilings. All the highly polished doors were made out of mahogany. Lamps and candles spread bright light in the palace. He was mesmerized by all the paintings on the wall. The light took some getting used to, compared with everywhere else in the valley where it was always grim and dark.

The border around the valley of Thanoton is bright like this, thought Maximus. *Of course, that's real light from the sun, not candles and lamps.*

The head steward watched him noting his inquisitive, light blue eyes as they studied and enjoyed the paintings on the walls. The boy had short brownish hair with some freckles on his cheeks and nose. *He looks about thirteen*, thought the head steward. *Skinny and lanky*, *probably going through a growth spurt. He'll be tall someday when he stops growing.*

"Hello, young man," said the head steward startled young Maximus out of his adventure.

"Ahh! Hello, sir." He thrust out his hand.

"You must be Maximus!" he said, giving him a smile. "You come highly recommended by Calvin. Did you know I used to work for him?"

"Nossir, I didn't," answered Maximus, returning his smile. He immediately felt relaxed around the head steward.

"Yes. When he retired, I was given his position," said the steward. He was pleased Maximus was there. "You have to tell Calvin to stop by. We miss him around here."

"I will, sir."

"How's his health doing?"

"When he's outside, the cold and rain cause his joints to hurt, making it hard for him to walk. If he warms up in front of the fire, he feels much better," Maximus answered. He nodded at the people that walked past.

The steward gestured with his hand. "Come with me down to my office, and we'll get started."

Maximus followed the head steward down the steps. He never thought his day would start out like this. He liked the steward who displayed a contagious youthful energy even though the steward was old. He followed him into his office.

Maximus watched as the steward pointed to a large board. "This is the master board that shows where everyone is assigned. You're new so you will start out as a floater. You will work wherever is needed. That is why this board is so important to you. Next to your name, I will give you your assignment for the day and specific tasks to accomplish. I update this board periodically, so you must check it throughout the day for changes." He admired how intently Maximus studied the board.

The head steward continued, "You don't have to know everyone else's schedule, young man, just your own. Now, let me show you around the palace. I will introduce you to each steward in charge of a floor. That person you will report to if you are assigned to that floor.

They will show and teach you what needs to be done. Do you have any questions so far?"

"Yes, sir," answered Maximus, not taking his eyes off the board. "How many floors are there?"

"There is one floor below ground where our office is. It's where the supplies are kept. All shipments for the palace come in and out of here. There are numerous supply ramps, leading down to this floor from the outside. All food is prepared in the kitchen, and delivered throughout the castle from this floor. You will have to help with that, along with many other things."

"I smelled the food. It smells good."

The head steward patted Maximus on the back and chuckled. "That is one of the many perks you will have here—good food. We eat after everyone else eats." The head steward could sense Maximus was excited. "There are five aboveground floors. The top floor is where Commander Javan and some of the council members live. That floor is where the conference room is and all the planning is done. Fourth floor is off-limits, and you will never enter that floor. The doors are locked, and they are heavily guarded."

"What's on that floor?" Maximus asked innocently. The head steward grabbed his arm and pulled him close. Maximus immediately tried to back away.

"Don't ever ask or inquire about the fourth floor to anyone ever again! Do you understand?" The head steward gripped Maximus' arm harder, scaring him.

"Y—yes, sir."

The head steward released Maximus' arm and changed back to his usual self. "While we're at it, let me give you some rules that will help you here. There are many difficult people that live and work in the palace."

I know that, thought Maximus, as he rubbed his arm.

"You are a servant here. Don't address anyone other than fellow workers, unless they address you. Do not be offended if people yell at you or treat you badly. Those people treat everyone badly, even each other. Don't be scared of them. Ignore it. Be respectful, and do what they ask."

"Yes, sir," Maximus answered. He was still shaken from the head steward's outburst.

There is another whole side to the head steward, thought Maximus. *I surely don't want to get on his bad side.* He remembered what Calvin and Kern had told him. "Don't trust anyone."

CHAPTER 36

"Get down from the wagon," said one of Dakar's soldiers. He pointed at Lot with one hand and had a sword in the other. "Stand off to the side, while we search you and your wagon."

"He's all right. He delivers all of our supplies," a border guard pointed out.

"He lives on the border with us."

"Everyone gets searched," said the soldier. "That's the orders. No wonder the intruders were able to come in and snatch people without getting caught. You border guards are lazy."

"Keep it up, and you will come up missing," added another soldier to the border guards. He caused the rest of the soldiers to laugh.

"Go on, old man," said a soldier to Lot. "Let me warn you. If you try to smuggle anything through this border, I will slit your throat." He touched the point of his knife against Lot's throat.

"Not to worry. I only bring supplies," Lot smiled at all of them, his jovial attitude undaunted.

As Lot drove the horses away, the soldiers could tell Lot wasn't the least bit scared or worried.

Upon arrival at the eastern cut headquarters, Lot noticed that Dakar's soldiers were everywhere. It looked like there were more than two platoons of soldiers. *This is going to be tough*, he thought.

"Where is Marcus today?" Lot asked one of the border guards that came out to help unload.

"He's in his office. Go ahead; we'll unload the supplies."

"Well, thank you, kind sir," Lot bowed his head.

He walked into the headquarters building and saw Marcus was alone in his office. He reached inside his coat and found the small rip that had a message hidden in the inner lining. He quickly pulled out the message. It was folded several times into a small square. He held it in the palm of his right hand.

"Hello, Marcus my good friend," Lot said. He reached out his hand to shake. He noticed how haggard Marcus looked. *I wonder how long it's been since he's had a good night's sleep*, thought Lot. He marveled how Marcus waited patiently for him to say something. He was a great leader, rising up from the ranks to become Hyrum's second-in-command at a young age. Not only was Marcus a strong leader, but he was physically strong. He trained all the border guards, and his men respected him as an excellent warrior. He was an expert hunter and tracker. Marcus looked bigger because he was muscular, but he was of average height with black hair, brown eyes, and dark skin.

Marcus stood up from his desk and managed to smile. "Good to see you Lot." He shook his hand.

Lot gripped Marcus' hand and made direct eye contact with him. He kept a hold of Marcus' hand to make sure he felt the message against his hand. After he gave him an intense look, he knew Marcus understood. He watched as Marcus naturally put his hand into his pocket, depositing the message.

"I was worried you wouldn't be able to drop the supplies off this week due to the snow," Marcus said. He pointed to a chair for Lot to sit down.

"No thanks. I can't stay," Lot said. He gave Marcus a wink. "I will be back tomorrow to pick up your supply request." He made sure he said it loud enough for the soldiers to hear. It would give him a legitimate reason to come back the next day.

"Good. That will give me time to see what supplies came in today and what we might need next week."

"It might be good to stock up this winter. It looks like it might be a rough one," Lot said as he shook Marcus' hand.

"If last week is any indication of how the rest of the winter will be, you're probably right," Marcus responded. He watched Lot leave and sat back down. *What was that all about?* he thought as he fingered the paper. It was clear he'd have to wait to read it.

Lot pulled past the checkpoint where he was searched earlier. "See you all tomorrow," he said, giving them a smile and wave.

"Thanks for the supplies."

"Have a safe trip home," said another border guard.

"I will," Lot answered. "Yah," he commanded, snapping the reins of the horses to pick up the pace. He would eventually head home, but first, he needed to go to Thanoton to deliver another message. A message he still needed to write. He would find an isolated spot along the way to draft it.

~*~

"I'm going up top to the observation post. I will come back down the ridgeline trail," Marcus said to one of the border guards. He hoped none of Dakar's soldiers would follow him today. Marcus walked up the steep, rocky trail and periodically glanced over his shoulder, *No one following*, Marcus noticed.

It didn't surprise him that eventually the soldiers would stop following him. They were lazy and out of shape. The soldiers were not used to the cold and high altitudes of the mountains. They were motivated at first, but they quickly stopped going up to the observation posts. The soldiers stayed at the checkpoints or walked the ridgeline trail, which was two hundred feet below the rock crest. The observation posts were at the top of the rock crest with many trails that crisscrossed from the posts. The crest had nooks, crannies, and caves everywhere.

Marcus turned off the trail halfway up to the observation post. He weaved his way through the rocks and bushes until he found a good spot hidden from view, and sat down. He pulled out the message and read.

M,

"You and your border guards, along with your families, are in grave danger. I have a solution that will keep you all safe. We need to talk privately. The best way for us to get together without suspicion, or be caught in the wrong place, is for you to invite my wife and me for dinner. When I come to pick up the supply list tomorrow morning, suggest the fourth night of the week. If this does not work, slip me a message in the same manner as I did to you.

Destroy this message after reading.

L

Marcus took out a match and lit the message on fire. *Maybe this is the answer to prayer that I've been waiting for*, thought Marcus. He sat there for a few minutes and looked down at the dark valley of Thanoton. The border area high up in the mountains and beyond were sunny and beautiful, but down in the valley, it looked like a thick blanket of darkness. The black clouds were so thick, it gave the illusion you could almost walk on it.

Marcus bowed his head and prayed silently, "Light of the Word, please deliver us from this evil set on destroying us." He got up and headed back to the trail, and on to the observation post.

CHAPTER 37

After breakfast, Maximus gathered all the ashes from the fireplace dumping them in the trash bin outside, his daily morning chore. *I'm so glad I'm living with Calvin and his wife,* he thought. *They really motivate me to give all for the Light of the Word, as they have.* Maximus knew he was going to learn a lot from them. He remembered the night before, how they talked about the Light of the Word, and he studied the *Book of Prophesies* with them. Maximus didn't want it to end.

He repeated to himself the passage from the Book of Prophesies Calvin had told him to memorize. *For of him, and through him, and to him, are all things: to whom be glory forever.*

Maximus went out the backdoor into a small yard enclosed by a wooden fence. In the back, a wooden gate led to a trash bin. After dumping the garbage in the bin, he came back through the gate. Before he closed the gate, he removed the message wedged in between the hinge and the wood. The slot was just big enough to hold a message. For someone that didn't know, they would never notice a message there.

Maximus knew he had a message this morning. The signal was a certain board in the fence was crooked, If it was straight up and down, it meant he had no message. The garbage bin blocked the view of the wooden beam from any passerby. It could only be seen from the backdoor.

Maximus dumped the garbage everyday to check for messages or to deposit one. If he left one, he would also make one of the board crooked. Someone checked it every night. A straightened board signaled message received. Lot and Kern were busy, so Maximus assumed they probably passed the responsibility off to someone else.

"P" meant he needed to deliver the message to the palace. If it was addressed to "H," it went to Calvin. Maximus was tempted to read the message he had to deliver. But Calvin had made him promise not to read any messages that were not addressed to himself. Calvin had harped so much about it, and the need for obedience, Maximus felt guilty for even thinking about it.

He arrived at the palace and entered the head steward's office filled with workers, checking the board for their assignments.

"Good morning, Maximus," said the head steward. He glanced over his shoulder pausing in the middle of writing assignments.

"Good morning, sir," Maximus tried to see around the head steward for his assignment.

"You're working on the fifth floor today," he said. He continued to write on the board. "They're having a big meeting so be respectful, and don't let them scare you. You will be serving Javan and his council."

Maximus suddenly didn't feel good, his stomach a bit queasy. "Should I go now?"

"Yes. After you put your coat and stuff away, report to the steward in charge of the fifth floor," He finished the assignments, and turned catching Maximus before he left. "Oh, I almost forgot to tell you to grab a clean dust rag every day."

Maximus headed up the steps made of marble and wound clockwise going up to the top. One side was a marble wall with lamps every five feet. The other side had gold, metal supports with polished, wood handrails. The steps were eight feet wide, and every step echoed up and down the stairwell. If you leaned over the railing and looked up, you could see a large crystal chandelier with hundreds of candles hanging from the ceiling.

At the third floor corner, Maximus leaned over the railing making sure no one was close then continued up the stairs towards the fourth floor. At a blind spot, he pulled the message out of a hidden pocket in his trousers and looked for a certain lamp with tiny markings too small to notice. He twisted the base, and quickly deposited the message inside the base then twisted it closed. He turned the lamp's globe to signal there was a message inside. Suddenly, he heard footsteps below, and stepping lightly, he rapidly went up the stairs.

"Excuse me, sir. Could you tell me where to find the head steward of the fifth floor?"

"You must be the new fellow," a steward studied Maximus. "Aren't you kind of young?"

"Yeah, I'm new," Maximus blurted out. He was angry with this guy for treating him like a kid. He didn't seem much older.

"Hey, relax. I'm just joking. My name is Anwar," he said as he held out his hand.

"My name is Maximus." He shook his hand and relaxed a bit.

"There he is," Anwar said. He pointed to the supervisor of the fifth floor. "He's the tall, old man with glasses over there. We just call him the Fifth. The other floors do the same. They call their head steward by the floor number. That way, they don't get confused with the head steward over everyone."

Maximus noticed right away how noisy it was on the fifth floor. Everyone was busy, from those that worked in the Command Center to the stewards that served them. No one seemed to notice he was there, compared to the other floors he had been on. He felt more relaxed and remembered what his mission was, to keep his ears open. *Somehow I have to get permanently assigned to this floor,'* he thought. *This is where Javan does all his planning.*

"Sir? Excuse me, sir?" He didn't get the Fifth's attention, so he spoke louder, "Sir?"

"What is it you want, boy? Can't you see I'm busy?"

There's that word boy *again,* thought Maximus. "I'm assigned to work here today." Maximus followed the Fifth down the hall and noticed he walked with a limp.

"Grab that pitcher of water, boy."

"My name is Max-i-mus! Not boy."

The Fifth stopped and gave Maximus an odd look. "Right. Grab that pitcher Max-i-mus and follow me."

Maximus followed the Fifth through the Command Center into another room. He stopped at the doorway, frozen with fear. Javan was only ten feet away.

"Don't just stand there, boy. I'm thirsty," Javan said, holding out his mug.

Maximus felt all eyes on him as he went around the conference room, filling up the mugs. He could tell they were all waiting for them to leave so they could continue with their business.

"What's wrong with you, boy? Your hands are shaking," said a council member.

There's that word boy *again,* thought Maximus. His anger overrode the fear of being in the presence of Javan and the council—his enemies.

"My name is not "boy,"' Maximus barely spoke above a whisper.

"What did you say?" Tuval asked. He set his pen down and looked up.

"M—M—"

"Speak up, boy," commanded Zesha, the chief investigator.

He glanced at the Fifth who was motioning with his hands for him to speak. He felt the nudge and gathered up the strength to say, "My name is Maximus, not *boy*, Sir." Maximus looked around the table and expected to be yelled at, but one by one, they all started to laugh, beginning with Commander Javan.

"Well, Maximus it is," Javan said, as he roared with laughter. "Fifth tell the head steward we want Maximus to be permanently assigned to serve us."

"Yes, Sir," the Fifth said, nodding his head.

"Now, leave us alone," Javan said. He waved them away with his hand. "We've had enough distractions."

Good job Maximus thought Zesha. *Four ears are better than one.*

"From now on, you stay right here at this table outside of the conference room. If they need anything, bring it to them. Do not go in unless they call you. On the table, there is food, tea, and water." The Fifth smiled and placed his hand on Maximus' shoulder. "I will periodically check on you throughout the day to see if you need anything. The kitchen staff will keep your table stocked. Do you have any questions?"

"No," Maximus answered. He studied the table to see what was on it.

I can't wait to tell Kern, thought Maximus. *He will be so proud of me.*

Maximus sat down next to the table, but couldn't hear what was being said in the conference room. He moved his chair just close enough to the doorway to hear.

"What do you think?" Javan asked. His attention was directed toward Tuval, his second-in-command.

"I think we're all in agreement then," Tuval answered. "In two weeks we will move in and round up all the border guards and their families. We'll relocate them down to the southern part of the valley to work in the coal mines."

"They won't like it," said one of the council members. "They'll put up a resistance."

"Let them try," Javan said, as he slammed his fist down on the table. Everyone in the room grabbed their mugs. Maximus was startled, and quickly slid away from the door, closer to the table.

I better send a message on what I just heard, thought Maximus.

Later that day, Zesha opened the message he had retrieved from the lamp. In the safety of his office, he read.

P,

I've made preliminary contact with *****. We are meeting for dinner at his house tomorrow night. Pray that everything goes well. At first, I thought I would ease into telling him about us, but I think he's desperate. I'll get straight to the point and tell him everything. The border guards and their families are miserable. They are under Dakar's complete control. They can decide how and when they execute their escape. I will let you know what happens in the meeting tomorrow.

Seek Him!

L

Zesha threw the message into the fire and watched it burn. He contemplated his next move. It was too late to get a message out to Lot before his meeting with Marcus the next night. The only way Lot would hear about Javan's plan to move the border guards and their families forcibly to the coal mines before his meeting with Marcus is if Maximus overheard and passed it on. *I hope he did*, thought Zesha.

CHAPTER 38

Marcus turned over two wooden crates and placed them facing each other. He motioned with his hand to Lot. "Go ahead; have a seat. We can talk freely here in the shed without being heard or interrupted."

"Thanks for inviting us to dinner tonight," Lot said. He wrapped his scarf around his neck to ward off the cold. "You have a beautiful family."

"It's seems to me you're the one that invited yourself for dinner tonight," Marcus smiled at Lot and turned up the kerosene lamp.

"Yes," he laughed. Lot paused for a moment, not knowing how to get the conversation started.

Marcus sensed this and said, "Look, just tell me what's on your mind. Whatever you say to me will be confidential, just between you and me. Believe me, I won't go tell Dakar. That's for sure. We border people have to stick together."

Lot knew if he and Zesha were wrong about Marcus, it could totally expose the Children of Light's operation and jeopardize the final push in the spring to liberate the valley. But if he didn't try to change the situation, the border guards were in grave danger. Dakar would gain even more power over the people. Lot knew he had not only to trust what Zesha had found out about Marcus but to follow his own gut instincts.

"Sorry about what happened to Hyrum," Lot said, finally breaking the silence.

"Yeah, it was awful how they murdered him," Marcus agreed. His countenance changed. "I know you didn't come here to talk about Hyrum. Just spit it out."

"It does kind of go along with Hyrum being killed," Lot said. His hands moved as he talked. "I received a message this morning. In two weeks Javan and his men are planning to round up all the border guards and their families. He will relocate them to the southern part of the valley to work in the coal mines."

"He's what?"

"He's turning the border guards and their families into his slaves," Lot answered.

"How do you know this information?" Marcus asked.

"I'm a worshiper of the Light of the Word." Lot noticed Marcus' surprised look. "We have secret believers living throughout the valley, and have infiltrated Javan's evil empire. We also have knowledge you are a worshiper of the Light of the Word. Is that true?"

"Is this some kind of trick to get me to confess?" Marcus stood up and backed away. "Are you trying to get me killed?"

Lot motioned with his hands. "Relax, relax. Sit back down. You don't have to say anything. Just sit back down and listen. I'm not trying to kill you or set you up. I will start from the beginning, and bring you up to date, so you know who we are. You might know a lot of this already." Lot stood up and took a quick glance outside the shed. He wanted to double check they were alone.

Lot sat back down and told Marcus everything about the Children of Light, the Prophecy, and the Three Witnesses' escape.

"So, that's how it all happened," Marcus said, looking like a light just switched on in his head.

Lot smiled and relaxed. "This leads me to what I came for," Lot took off his scarf. The coal bucket was doing a good job heating up the shed.

"We have a small town named Sanctuary two valleys east of here that cannot be seen from the eastern border. We used it to conduct missions into the valley of Thanoton. We have since abandoned Sanctuary and relocated the operation to another city. In Sanctuary, there are houses, barns, wells, and storage for food. There might be enough food for all the border guards and their families to make it through the winter as long, as you hunt for your meat. It's not enough housing for all the families unless you double up and use the barns to live in."

"Are you suggesting we move there?" Marcus said, not able to hold back any longer.

"Yes, that's what I'm suggesting. Organize all the border guards and their families and flee to Sanctuary. We leave it up to you how and when you execute your escape. You can easily get there in one night. The way the valleys wind around, you don't have to go over any mountains to get there. It's quite easy to get to.

"Who is we that you keep talking about?" asked Marcus, excited.

"I can't say," Lot answered. "We strongly suggest you sneak out quietly," Lot said. He noticed that Marcus gave him an odd look, and said nothing. Lot continued. "In the springtime, some representatives of the Elders will make contact with you and tell you more about our communities. They will also spend some time teaching out of the *Book of Prophesies*. There are copies in Sanctuary."

"Great!" responded Marcus, all excited. They only had parts of the *Book of Prophesies*, passed-down hand written copies.

"Those that believe in the Light of the Word and want to live in the city up north can. Only those that believe are allowed to live there. It's a community of believers. Some that believe might choose to stay in Sanctuary, help build the community, and lead others to the Light of the Word. Either way, you will be part of a larger community that looks out for each other. We are all the descendants of the Children of Light, whether we admit it or not."

Marcus scooted his crate away from the bucket; he had started to sweat. He felt refreshed by the cooler air. "I knew there was a city up north, but I had no idea there was one out east."

"The terrain masks the town perfectly. It's in a perfect spot," added Lot, getting a little too warm himself. "Are a lot of the border guards believers?"

Marcus thought about the question, while he shrugged his shoulders. "There is a mixture. We have a lot of real believers that seek the Light of the Word. Then we have those that say they are but truly aren't. They're the most frustrating. Then there are those that do not want to hear about the Light of the Word because they are afraid."

"We hope you convince all the border guards to flee."

"I don't think I'll have a problem convincing them to leave, considering all that has happened. Even the fearful, I think, will be willing to take the risk."

"Of course, they don't have much of a choice," Lot added. "Freedom or slavery, it will be up to them. I'm always surprised when people choose slavery, but we see it all the time."

"It'll be difficult to coordinate because we have border guards at different points around the valley," Marcus added. "But the majority of border guards and their families are right here at the eastern cut," Marcus said.

"Yes, easier for you. We will take care of the border guards out west. You only have to worry about the few border guards up north and down south in their outlying posts."

Lot stood up and stretched out his hand. "Again, we leave all the details to you. The less we know, the better. The only thing we ask is that you execute it quickly and quietly."

Marcus shook Lot's hand and thought about what he had just said. In his mind, Marcus was thinking something else. *We have been waiting for this opportunity for a long time. We definitely won't go quietly. They will regret the day they meddled with the border guards.*

CHAPTER 39

Calvin watched as Maximus came in from dumping the morning trash. He motioned with his hand for Maximus to come over. "Sit with me by the fireplace. I'd like to have a talk with you."

"I'll be right there sir after I wash the grime off my hands from the garbage," Maximus answered.

Calvin checked his pocket watch. "It's still early; we have some time before you have to go to work." He waited for Maximus to sit down. He and his wife truly enjoyed having a boy around again. *Maximus brings life and excitement into our lives*, thought Calvin. "Did you retrieve a message today to deliver to the palace?"

"Yes, I did," Maximus answered. He reached in and double-checked to see if he had stuck the message into the hidden pocket within his main pants pocket. He had.

"We are really proud of you," Calvin said. He struggled to talk, his breathing heavy. "Kern and I thought it would be best if one of us told you personally, how important and timely your message was. If it wasn't for your message and the information you provided, Lot would not have been able to pass on Javan's plan to enslave and relocate the border guards down south before his meeting. We would've had to risk arranging another meeting. But you saved us from having to do that by keeping your eyes and ears open. Most importantly, you passed the information on. Keep up the good work." He could tell Maximus was proud of himself. He could barely contain his smile, his blue eyes gleaming with joy.

"Sir, what is it you're writing all the time?" Maximus asked. He felt guilty for making Calvin talk because he looked so weak and frail from old age. "I see you writing into the late hours of the night and studying different books."

Calvin laughed. "That's what makes you special, Maximus. You're always so curious. You don't miss a thing." He coughed a few times. "I'm working on a few projects we plan on printing for everyone to read in the future."

"What's it about?" Maximus said, all excited. "Can I read some now?"

Calvin adjusted the blanket over his legs to keep warm. He said, "It's not ready to read yet. Plus, the environment in Thanoton is not prepared to receive it."

"Is that why you hide all the papers in a secret spot?" Maximus asked. He immediately regretted what he had said, as soon as he said it.

"Well, well. I guess I'm not as sneaky as I once was," Calvin said. "Old age will do that to you." He thanked the Light of the Word in his heart for the privilege of being a part of Maximus' life.

"I'm sorry for snooping," Maximus said, embarrassed.

Calvin raised his boney arm to stop Maximus from saying anything more. "I'm glad you're that way. We need you to be that way. Maximus, I was going to bring this up later, as we got to know each other, but you've already found out on your own," he said, in between laughing and coughing.

"You want me to get you some water?" asked Maximus.

"No, no. It feels good."

"The coughing does?"

"No, it feels good to laugh," Calvin responded. "You make me laugh. Listen, I'm pretty old and in bad health; I could die anytime. Kern also knows where the secret spot is. Make sure he gets all my writings and books when that time comes." Calvin took a deep breath and continued in a raspy voice. "Don't let anyone else know it's there. If for some reason Kern can't pick the writings up because something has happened to him, you need to find a way to deliver it to the printer in the town of Pistio. I'm sure you know him." Calvin watched as Maximus nodded his head, speechless. "Be careful. These writings are very important. If it gets into the wrong hands, it could get you killed. They will burn all the writings, and no one will be able to read it." Calvin shifted his gaze on Maximus. "What I have written is worth dying to preserve. Do you understand Maximus?"

"Yes, sir. I won't disappoint you," Maximus responded.

I hope he doesn't die, Maximus thought. *My grandparents had died before I was born. My parents died in a fire when I was young. I'm tired of the people I love dying and leaving me all alone.* Maximus prayed in his heart. *Please don't let anything happen to Kern and keep Calvin alive.*

Maximus entered the palace, and after checking the board, he headed up the staircase to his new assignment on the fifth floor. At the blind spot, he pulled the message out and quickly deposited the message inside the base. Then quickly went up to the fifth floor.

"Good morning, Maximus," Anwar said.

"Good morning."

Anwar crouched down a little and whispered, "The council is already in the conference room arguing about something. I'm glad I don't have your job," Anwar immediately resumed sweeping after he saw the Fifth watching him.

Maximus peeked into the conference room just long enough for a council member to notice. "Hey, b—Maximus bring us some tea."

As he moved around and filled each teacup, Maximus thought, *He almost said boy didn't he?* He noticed how freely they talked today, not bothered by his presence.

"That's what I'm saying," said one of the council members. "Dakar, the captain of the army, requested two more fifty-man platoons to be sent to the eastern cut to help with the upcoming operation."

"How come Dakar isn't here?" said a frustrated Tuval. "He's got over one hundred men up there. Is he so vitally needed he can't come to this meeting?"

"He's busy planning the upcoming mission," answered the council member. "He's also preparing to send some soldiers to capture the border guards in the most northern and southern points. He planned on leaving some soldiers at those points to guard the border. The rest will come back with the captured border guards the day he moves everyone down south."

The conference room got quiet suddenly. Everyone noticed Supreme Commander Javan standing in the doorway.

"Commander Javan," Tuval said. He snapped at attention, along with everyone else in the room.

Maximus quickly stood at attention and glanced out the corner of his eye to see how the others were standing. He was worried he might be doing it wrong.

Javan motioned for everyone to get back to work. He looked at the council member who was talking to Tuval, his second-in-command. "Go tell Dakar he better get to this meeting. Otherwise, I will find another commander for my army. The eastern cut is only a good thirty-minute horse ride away. There's no excuse."

"Yes, Commander Javan," said the council member, about to leave the room to dispatch a soldier to get Dakar.

"Wait a minute," Javan said. He stopped the council member. "I hope he hasn't sent soldiers out to capture the northern and southern border guards yet. If he hasn't, tell him to kill them and not take them, prisoner. We won't use any soldiers guarding them. Now go!"

"What about Dakar's request for two more platoons?" Tuval, asked as he studied the board that showed where all the army troops were located.

"Grant the request," Javan answered. He held out his teacup for Maximus to fill. Javan walked up to the board and stood next to Tuval. "We needed additional troops down south anyway, so we will permanently assign them down south after Dakar is done."

"That only leaves us two companies of four platoons left in the city of Thanoton," Tuval said, pointing at the board. "Of course, when we're done moving the border guards, we will only need one platoon at the border. We can bring the other one back."

"Replacing the border guards and the need for more southern troops has stretched our troop levels," Javan agreed. "What do we have out west?"

"We have one platoon in the small town of Pistio about two hours away and one platoon on the western border."

Javan scratched his red beard and asked, "It's about thirty minutes to the western border from Pistio, isn't it?"

"In the spring and summer, it is," Tuval answered. He walked over to the area map on the wall. "This time of year, it's about double."

Javan turned around and addressed everyone in the room. "I need everyone to get out for a few minutes. I will call when I want you back. Bring me some more tea first, Maximus."

"Yes, Sir," responded Maximus. He brought the pitcher of tea and then went out of the conference room.

Javan waited until everyone left and then spoke, "We need to send more troops out west to recon the situation. We rarely hear from them because they are so far away."

"I was thinking the same thing," Tuval said. He sat down next to Javan. "The west is almost too quiet. Just like it was on the eastern border until everything came to light."

"Exactly," added Javan, pleased with Tuval's insight. "I don't trust the two platoons we have out west or anyone out west for that matter. They act differently. We will replace the border guards out there."

"We definitely will have to do something soon to maintain control out west," Tuval continued. He felt Javan's green eyes pierce straight through him. "The population out west continues to grow as more people choose to live out there."

Javan stood up and motioned for Tuval to join him at the area map. He whispered, "Let's keep this between you and me. I don't want the two platoons and the border guards out west to find out this information. Next spring, we will push out west. We'll switch out the two platoons that are there for the two working down south through the winter. The border guards and the platoons out west are used to not getting any information all winter so they won't be suspicious. We will command Dakar to kill any prisoners that try to escape, so they can't warn the western border guards."

"Dakar needs to make sure none of the soldiers leak this information about relocating the eastern border guards," Tuval added. "The west will find out eventually, but if we can keep it quiet for two months until the snow starts to melt, we'll already be there."

"We'll make sure Dakar is clear on all this when he shows up," Javan said. He turned around and yelled, "You can come back now."

Maximus quickly moved away from the opening of the door, hearing only bits and pieces of their private conversation.

Zesha locked the door to his office and sat down. He started to read the message he had just retrieved from the lamp.

P,

"I passed all the information we talked about to *****. He's a believer in the Light of the Word, and he is not alone. There are many strong believers among their ranks. He also said there are a lot of nonbelievers and those that say they believe, but truly don't. If given any kind of pressure, they would deny their faith, their comfort, and security coming first. We will pass this information on to the Elders. They can watch out for those in the group that profess faith only when it's safe and convenient. That way they are not fooled and allow them into the northern city.

He didn't know much of the history of the Children of Light. I could tell he was very enlightened by our conversation. They do have some parts of the Book of Prophesies that have been hand-copied and passed down.

Most of the border guards have not studied it. I will pass this information on.

I do have one concern. When talking to *****about our desire for him to quickly and quietly flee to Sanctuary, he never said anything or acknowledged it in any way, even after I mentioned it a second time. It almost seems like he already had a plan he was working on. When I mentioned Sanctuary, it completed his plan. Either way, we will need him and some of his men next spring. When the time comes, I will make contact with him.

I was tempted to tell him there is a strong possibility they will be able to come back to their houses in the future if all our plans are successful. But he knows too much already. I didn't want to risk the information getting leaked out and Javan finding out.

I guess we will wait and see.

L

Zesha sat up and stuck the corner of the message into the candle flame until it started to burn. Just before the flames engulfed the message, he threw it into the empty fireplace and watched it completely disintegrate.

I hope Maximus gets a message to Lot in time for him to deliver, thought Zesha. *We must warn Marcus of Javan's plan to send soldiers to kill the northern and southern border guards.*

CHAPTER 40

The next day, Lot pulled up to the border checkpoint and stopped his horses. He noticed there were no borders guards present, only Dakar's soldiers.

"Hello, gentlemen. I'm here to deliver supplies," Lot said. He waved with one hand while holding the reins with the other.

"No, you aren't," said one of the soldiers. "Turn around, and get out of here."

"I have much-needed supplies to deliver," Lot argued.

"We don't need any more supplies," said the soldier. He walked up and pulled out his sword.

"Can I come back later today?" Lot said, worried he wouldn't have a chance to deliver the message.

"No one is allowed up to the border for the next two weeks by order of Dakar," said the soldier with his sword still drawn. "Now get out of here. I won't tell you again."

Lot turned his horses around. As he drove away, he prayed, "Light of the Word, send the Whisperer to warn the northern and southern border guards."

Up at the guard command center, Marcus whispered to Joel, one of his subordinate leaders, "How did Dakar find out we sent some border guards to the northern and southern points this morning?"

"I have no idea," answered Joel. "I didn't think they were paying attention to where we assigned people."

"They're obviously watching who goes north or south on the ridgeline trail."

"They must have just started. I never noticed before."

Marcus agreed. "Something is going on that has them watching the ridgeline trail. Go get Tiras and meet me on top in two hours."

"Will do," Joel said. He left.

As Joel left, a border guard came in breathing heavy from running up the hill. "Marcus, Dakar is coming up, and he looks furious." The border guard left before Marcus could say a word.

"Who gave you permission to send border guards up to the northern and southern points?" Dakar said, slamming his fist on Marcus desk. He leaned over so closely, he could smell his breath.

"No one," Marcus responded. He stood up and pushed the table back that slid his way when Dakar leaned up against it. "It's our normal routine to send border guards to see how they are doing in our most northern and southern points."

"Didn't I order you to approve everything through me?"

"I didn't think that meant routine operations. You were in Thanoton yesterday when I made arrangements for them to go."

"I don't want you sending out any more border guards," Dakar said looking down at the shorter man. He paused for a minute and contemplated whether to kill Marcus or not. His black, pointed beard bobbed as his jaws muscles worked. Finally, he said, "Every single decision you make, you better get my approval. This is your last warning. Is that clear enough for you?"

"It's clear," Marcus answered. He watched as Dakar left. *It's going to be a pleasure killing you*, thought Marcus.

Two hours later Marcus headed up the steep slope to the observation post.

Just before reaching the top, he turned off the trail and squeezed through the large rocks. He maneuvered to a place where Tiras and Joel were waiting for him. They had posted a guard higher up in the rocks to warn them if one of Dakar's men was coming.

Before Marcus had a chance to greet them, Tiras looked like he was about to burst at the seams. "Did you know Dakar just sent some soldiers out to the northern and southern observation points?"

Marcus made eye contact with them. "Are you serious? When did he do this?"

"About fifteen minutes ago," Joel answered. "We were contemplating whether to risk sending some border guards out to warn them."

"We can't do that," Marcus added. "Dakar is keeping an eye on where everyone is."

"This couldn't have happened at a worse time," Tiras said. "We leave in two nights."

"We will have to trust their instincts, and hope they follow our orders," Marcus said. He eyed a few rocks until he found one that was comfortable enough to sit on.

"We did tell them to get the border guards at those points close to the eastern cut before the night of the operation," Joel said. He rehearsed aloud what he had told them.

"They were told several times to kill any of Dakar's men that got in the way," Marcus agreed. "We have to trust they will." Marcus pulled a small notebook out of his boot and continued, "What is left to prepare for the night we leave?"

"As far as preparing all the people, we're almost done," Tiras answered. "Everyone is eager to leave."

"They know what to bring, right?"

"They know," Tiras nodded, "I've told them to take only what they can carry out quickly. They will secretly stash anything extra they might need in the caves in the upper crest. We'll try to come back for them later."

"It's been easy for us to prepare at night," Joel said. "Everyone has grown up here and knows this area well. Preparing at night has not slowed us down one bit. The people know the trails leading to the caves and have been filling up every single cave they can find the last few nights," Joel laughed. "Dakar's men don't know their way around at night, so they never leave the base camp. They are afraid to venture out at night. They just sit around getting drunk, not paying attention to anything that's going on."

"I think it's going to be easy to kill them," Tiras said.

"I think you're right; they won't know what hit them," Marcus agreed.

"I want you to remind our men that after we kill all the soldiers, we will light the command center on fire. There will be no way anyone will miss that signal. When they see the flames coming from the command center, they are to let all their livestock go, light their barn and house on fire, then come to the eastern cut to cross over and move to Sanctuary," Marcus said. He realized he had rehashed and reminded them a bunch of times. *They are probably sick of hearing the plan*, he thought.

"All the livestock should stay up in the mountains where the grass and sunlight are. Maybe we can come back for them someday," Joel added.

"That would be nice," Tiras agreed.

"Let's go over the plan of attack," said Marcus, reading his notes. "Tiras, tell me what you are doing that night."

"After nightfall, I will stage my men close to the checkpoint. Two hours after the sun goes down, we will sneak up from the side, and kill everyone, making sure all are dead. We won't leave any alive."

"Good, keep going," Marcus said. He smiled.

"Next, we will slowly move up the eastern cut, killing any soldiers that may have escaped your attack. Then, we will lead the way out of the valley. I will send out an advance team to secure Sanctuary, start the fireplaces, and prepare for the families arrival. They will have a checklist to make sure we didn't leave anyone behind. Then, I will mark the route with torches over the eastern crest and all the way to Sanctuary so everyone can see the route. I will also have men stationed throughout the route with torches to help everyone over the rocks and provide security."

Marcus nodded his head, pleased. "Remember this operation only involves the border guards and their families. This does not include the others that live on the border like the farmers and businessmen. This will be a big surprise for them, like it should be. We can't trust them." He turned to Joel and said, "Tell me your part of the plan."

"Two hours after the sun goes down, I will take my men and half of yours and attack and kill every one of the soldiers in both barracks. I will do this while you attack the command center where Dakar and his leaders stay. We will kill everyone in those barracks making sure they are all dead. Then, I will burn it all down, signaling its completion. I will set up a security perimeter with half of my men around the eastern cut while the families are coming through. The other half of my men will go down south, starting with the farthest house, to make sure everyone is out and on their way to the eastern cut." Joel finished and turned to Marcus to hear his part.

"I will kill Dakar, his leaders, and the ten men detailed to guard him," Marcus said. He paused for a few seconds. "Then, I will send half of my men up north starting with the farthest house, to make sure everyone has left and is on their way to the eastern cut."

"You skipped an important part," said Tiras, as he laughed.

"It's my plan. I can't think of any part that I might've missed."

"You did miss a part of your plan," Joel agreed. "What do you always make us repeat over and over?" he said with his hands out as if it was obvious.

"Oh, yes," Marcus said. He took a deep breath. "I will kill Dakar and his soldiers in the command center and make sure they are all dead. Then—then, I will burn down the command center."

"That is the signal you know," said Tiras, laughing.

"Last, but not least, I will be the last one over the eastern cut," Marcus said. He stood up and drew his sword straight out about waist-high. Tiras and Joel did the same, forming a circle. Then all three said in unison, "To the everlasting freedom we fight."

CHAPTER 41

It had been months since she had helped the Three Witnesses—Ezra, Dara, and Jared escape. Myka's quick thinking and skill helped to get them safely through the eastern cut and out of the valley of Thanoton. Her diversion led the soldiers away from going after the Three Witnesses to pursuing her.

Myka's cover had been blown when a border guard had recognized her and yelled out her name for everyone to hear. It made it impossible for Myka to return to the city of Thanoton. She had to escape and evade to the cache sight. She headed to the northern mountains on the border of the valley of Thanoton. It didn't take long for the soldiers to stop pursuing her.

The trip was long and grueling. Myka was tempted more than once to use the ridgeline trail to get to the cave. It would have made her trip so much easier and taken only two days. That way was far too dangerous.

The evasion route was torturous. Myka endured thick snow, storms of ice and freezing rain, and bitter cold with very little food, but the loneliness was worst of all. Myka made in two weeks what would normally take others four.

The only thing that kept Myka going during the trip was her faith in the Light of the Word and the desire to see her friends Jared, Dara, and Ezra again. She longed to see them and wished she could have gone with them out the eastern cut to Sanctuary then on to the city up north. Her mission was to ensure their safety so they could flee to the city up north. They would prepare to fulfill the last prophecy spoken by the prophet, to deliver the people of Thanoton.

She finally found the cave's small, hidden opening. It was so small she had to duck to enter. She was glad the opening was low and protected the cave from the wind but allowed fresh air to come in.

When Myka finally arrived at the cache sight, she was completely spent. Exhaustion, combined with near hypothermia, had drained her of her last energy reserves. The cave was so warm and cozy that she slept the first week, waking up only to eat, drink water, and pile wood on the fire.

The cave opened up into a large area with small caves that went out from it. Packed with supplies the inside was everything one would need to live for a very long time. When Myka first arrived she thought, *This place could hold and feed an army. The Seekers really did a good job finding and preparing this place.*

She wondered if she was the first one to actually use the place. Everything looked untouched. It had lanterns with extra fuel oil, wood for fires, clothes, blankets, bows, arrows, knives, swords, and barrels of water. The food in the cave consisted of all dried goods—meat, fruit, lima beans, and potatoes. A supply of fresh water trickled through the rocks into a small pool that drained slowly somewhere else into the vast cave system. Myka used that small pool to clean herself up. It was cold, but refreshing.

Every day Myka would make a big pot of stew, mixing meat, beans, and potatoes. She would eat it throughout the day. As the weeks went by, she prided herself on how creative her stews turned out. She spent her day reading the *Book of Prophesies* she had found among the books provided. She had taken the opportunity to spend good quality time studying about and praying to the Light of the Word.

Myka was told to never leave the cave and venture out, but as the weeks went by she felt cooped up and was itching to go outside. Besides, why would the white snowsuit be here if not to wear as she scouted a bit? She wanted to feel the sunlight and get some exercise walking around in the snow. She had found snowshoes, donned the snowsuit, and loaded her backpack with everything she might need. She liked the feel of her backpack on her back; it felt like old times.

At first, Myka would only venture out a little. However, as time went on, she hiked for longer periods. She even started to climb farther up the mountain, until she actually went all the way to the top. Myka had found the best route and frequently went to the top to look out over the mountains.

One time, Myka went out at night to the top of the mountains. She hoped to see the lights of the northern city with her scope, and she finally did. Myka had contemplated long and hard about trying to make her way to the city. She was getting lonely with no one to talk to. Myka missed her friends. She thought about Jared every day and could not wait to see him.

Then one day everything changed. As Myka explored further away from the cave, she spied through her scope two border guards. Watching them became a part of her daily routine. It made her feel like she was having some human interaction even though they had no clue she was watching them. Myka wondered how old they were. They didn't seem much older than she was. Watching them became so enjoyable. It made her laugh with their crazy antics. They always played jokes, sneaking up and trying to scare each other.

Myka wanted to say hi to them, but she knew the border guards were probably still looking for her. They didn't seem like they would hurt her, but she couldn't afford to take that chance.

Then one day, Myka spied more border guards coming to the northern observation point. The two guards also noticed them. They were easy to identify with their brown fur coats and hats. The two guards looked as if they wondered why they had visitors. It was funny watching them run around the camp, to straighten things up. Myka decided to move up and get a closer view, using the rocks and snow as her concealment. Myka arrived at a location where she knew she would have a better vantage point. She pulled out her scope and started to watch.

Four border guards had arrived, making a total of six at the northern observation point. They were heavily armed with bows, swords, and plenty of arrows. They all wore snowshoes and carried large backpacks. The two northern border guards along with two guards that had just arrived sat down by the campfire. The other two went out one hundred feet in either direction to pull security. They started to scan the area with their scopes.

Oh no, thought Myka. She ducked down and wondered why they posted security. Myka peeked over her rock cover carefully. The four border guards stood up and started to throw all the extra wood on the fire, along with wooden buckets, furniture, or anything else lying around. *This is very strange*, thought Myka. She took off her mittens to adjust her scope, making it clearer. The two border guards she knew went inside their shelter. The other two outside were still throwing stuff in the fire to burn. Finally, the two northern border guards came out of the shelter with loaded backpacks.

Myka watched one of them grab a burning stick out of the fire, and start the wooden shelter on fire. *They are burning everything down*, mused Myka. *They must be leaving*. The border guards stood around and watched everything burn.

Myka wondered what to do. She sat and contemplated what she had just observed. *Should I investigate, considering what has happened? I wonder why they're leaving. Am I missing something? What happened back in Thanoton that I don't know about? I know there's no need for security on the border other than to keep people in. Do they now know that, too? I have to go follow them and find out what's happening. That's the only way I can get answers to all my questions. Things change, and missions change,* she tried to justify her decision.

Luckily, she had everything she needed with her. It was a habit she had developed over the years, and had saved her on several occasions. Myka thought about the cave. There was no reason she could think of to go back there first before she followed them. She had left one lamp on, but that would safely burn out. She started to follow at a great distance. She noticed they were not concerned at all with security behind them, only forward in the direction they were moving.

I wonder who they're worried about running into? thought Myka. *They sure look like they're ready to fight.*

~*~

Dig, the leader of the six-man patrol, led his men down from the northern observation point. He held up his hand and gave the signal to stop and make a small security perimeter. He waited for everyone to circle up and face out to maintain security before he spoke. "I wanted to get us away from the top of the mountain before I talked to you two some more. That place is too visible. It can be seen for miles." Dig directed his attention to the two border guards they had just picked up from the most northern point.

"More than miles with all that smoke coming from the all we burned," added a border guard.

Dig nodded his head in agreement and continued, "You know why we are leaving the valley of Thanoton. Now, I want to explain our movement to the eastern cut. I will be the point man of this six-man patrol. I want everyone to be in a single file line spread out at a twenty-foot interval, walking on the ridgeline trail. It's always a tendency when patrolling to get bunched up, and not maintain that twenty-foot interval. Resist that temptation."

Dig squinted into the distance, "We can expect a confrontation from Dakar's men, and if we are bunched up, it's easier to ambush and kill us. Spread out, we are less of a target that way. They won't see everyone, and it'll be easier for us to maneuver and conduct a counterattack. If attacked, we need to engage the enemy with everything we have. Do not take prisoners. Kill every one of them. The same goes if we see them first. We need to set up an ambush and kill them all. No survivors."

Dig went down on one knee and continued, "We will make our way to the outskirts of the eastern cut and be there tomorrow night. At two hours after sunset, we will help the border guard families from the farthest house to the closest, move towards the eastern cut. We will direct them to the eastern cut, and help burn everything that is left behind. In the process, we will also link up with more border guards from the eastern cut to help us with what we're doing. Then, we will proceed out of the border as directed. We are to kill any soldier we run into." He stared directly at the two young northern border guards, who already had fear written all over their face. "No prisoners. Is that clear?"

The two northern border guards said, "Clear."

Anyone have any questions?" Dig looked around, surprised no one did. He stood up. "Let's move out. Remember, keep your interval."

~*~

From a distance, Myka watched the six-man team through her scope. She had caught a quick flicker of light, like a reflection, out of the corner of her eye way ahead of the six-man team. Myka studied the area the flash had come from and saw it a second time. It was too far away to tell for sure what it was, but it almost looked like there was movement of some kind. Myka wondered, *People or animal? Which is it?* She continued to study the area while she followed. *Animals don't have anything on their bodies that would reflect like metal does.* Myka caught a glimpse of something again. It looked like an outline of a person. *People* thought Myka.

Oh, no! What do I do? The border guards don't see them. They'll be there within two hours. What should I do? She screwed the scope closer to her eye and tried to see the shape or shapes more clearly. *Should I warn them? Then, they will probably capture me. Should I try to circle around, if that's possible, and ambush the soldiers or whoever is up ahead? Maybe it's nothing. Light of the Word what should I do?* prayed Myka. As she followed, she tried to get ahead of the group, by going around as fast as she could to see for sure. *I hope I can get there in time. I hope it is not what I think it is.*

CHAPTER 42

"Thanks for helping me clean up this mess, Anwar," Maximus said, grateful for his help. He enjoyed the little time he'd spent with Anwar since he'd started working in the palace. Today, Anwar was assigned to help Maximus who was glad he'd get the chance to get to know Anwar better.

"No problem," Anwar responded. "It gives us a chance to talk." Anwar was very funny and made everyone laugh with his crazy antics. He also looked funny. He was tall and lanky with droopy, dark eyes. He had a big nose and ears that stuck out from his thin, straight, black hair. *It needs cutting, or at least combed*, thought Maximus. Anwar was the brunt of everyone's jokes, but he didn't seem to mind. He got away with a lot because he was always in trouble. Everyone expected it.

Maximus went around the table collecting all the scrap pieces of paper strewn on the conference table. He placed them in a basket to burn. He tried to look at every piece he picked up without being noticed. He looked over at Anwar and couldn't help but laugh. Anwar was not even covert about reading the paperwork; he just stood there and read.

"Anwar," Maximus whispered.

"What?" Anwar answered. He glanced up from what he was reading.

"Be careful. Someone might see you reading that " Maximus answered. He moved around the table, picking up as he went. He kept an eye on the door.

"No one is going to come in," Anwar said. He rolled his eyes. "I saw them all leave."

Just then, the Fifth walked in. "Anwar, are you talking or working?"

"Working, sir," Anwar answered. He quickly picked up some trash from the floor.

Full of suspicion, the Fifth stared at Anwar. Not taking his eyes from Anwar, he asked Maximus, "Is Anwar helping, or is he just talking?"

"He's helping, sir," Maximus answered. He coughed to resist the urge to laugh. Maximus purposely did not look at Anwar, afraid he would not be able to hold back his laughter.

The Fifth turned and left.

"It looks like they practically lived here for two days," Anwar said, working harder and faster.

"They must've," Maximus said. He consolidated all the dishes in stacks on the conference table. "When I left late last night they were still here."

Anwar moved closer to Maximus. He acted as if he was up to no good even before he started to speak. Anwar bobbed his head around like a chicken as he looked around to make sure they were alone. "You know what I heard?" he whispered.

If you just acted normally instead of this exaggeration of secrets, you would be better off, Maximus cast him a sideways glance. "What did you hear?" He sensed he would probably regret he asked.

"They have a problem with the armies out west. And in the spring, they plan on getting rid of them."

Maybe I won't regret I asked, thought Maximus. "What do you mean get rid of them?"

"You know, kill them," he whispered.

"Are you sure?" Maximus asked, sounding skeptical. He had heard them talk about the west, but he did not hear anything specific about it. *Should I trust what Anwar heard?* thought Maximus.

"Yes, I'm sure," he said. His eyes bugged out even further.

"Where did you hear this?" asked Maximus, suspicious. "You weren't around the conference center."

"I overheard two council members as they walked down the hallway," Anwar said. He helped pick up some dishes to take down to the kitchen. Anwar could tell Maximus didn't believe him. "Seriously, I was inside a doorway, and they thought they were alone."

Maximus stopped just before the doorway that led out of the conference room, and asked, "What else did you hear about the west?"

"That's all I heard about that," Anwar answered. He followed Maximus out of the door. His tone defensive, he said, "Look, I hear a lot of things working here. I know what's going on in Thanoton."

Throughout the day, Maximus and Anwar made several trips from the fifth floor to the basement. They cleared away dirty dishes, plates, old food and took all the old paperwork out to burn. Maximus marveled that the council left sheets of paper with secret information for someone else to get rid of. He couldn't believe they didn't worry about someone getting this information. During the clean up, Maximus was able to grab and hide a few pieces of paper. When Anwar wasn't looking, he picked the ones he thought were most important. On one of his trips up and down the stairs, Maximus noticed he had a message. The glass on the lamp was turned a certain way. He didn't have a chance to retrieve it with Anwar tagging his heels. He'd have to snatch it on his way out at the end of the day.

As they went back up the steps, Maximus warily watched a loaf of bread balanced precariously atop the basket Anwar was carrying. Maximus came up beside Anwar as they climbed. "You want me to help you with that?" Maximus asked as he was carrying a platter of cheese up the steps. He hoped Anwar would say yes. It was stressful watching that basket of bread wobble. He held his breath when the loaf slid to the side. Anwar was about to spill bread all over the stairs.

"No, thanks. I got it," Anwar answered. He grabbed a bun that almost slid off the top.

Maximus tried to ignore the breadbasket. "Don't you think it's kind of weird they leave important paperwork lying around? Anyone could've seen it."

"No," Anwar answered. He stopped between floors and set the basket down to pull up his pants. "Knowing them, they probably thought someone else would take care of it, and no one did." Anwar picked up the basket and continued, "Not everyone is going to see that stuff. Only certain people like us, are authorized to go up to the fifth floor. It's not like we're spies or anything. Who would we tell?"

"You're right," Maximus agreed. *If he only knew the truth*, Maximus thought. They arrived back at the conference room. Maximus asked Anwar, "What do you think is on the fourth floor?"

"Fourth floor," Anwar answered. He bobbed his head up.

"Shh!" Maximus said. He motioned with his finger over his lips.

"Yeah, right. Sorry," he whispered. He came closer, his stance was exaggeratedly suspicious with his elbows cocked way out, his body bent way forward, and his hand to Maximus' ear. It was almost as if he was an actor sharing a secret on stage somewhere.

"Anwar, just act normal and whisper," Maximus said, while he grabbed Anwar's arm. "When you try *not* to be sneaky, you look *sneakier* than you looked already," said Maximus, as he shook his head and laughed.

"My younger sister Mina works on the fourth floor," Anwar said. "She is the same age as you." His eyes brightened as if a light went off in his head interrupting his thoughts. "You should meet her sometime. You two would get along; she's uptight like you."

"Uptight? I'm not uptight," Maximus said. *If she's anything like Anwar. I don't know if I want to meet this sister, thought Maximus.*

"You are a little."

"What about the fourth floor?"

"Oh, yeah. Half of the fourth floor is where all the printing presses are. They print all of Javan's stuff for the valley of Thanoton. Actually, everything's printed there, including all the material used in Thanoton's schools. Well, you know, it's illegal to print anywhere else in the valley," said Anwar, as he ate a piece of cheese from the platter Maximus carried. He saw the look on Maximus' face and continued, "That's where Mina works—in the print shop. She reads things over to see if it's grammatically correct. She's a good speller."

Maximus slid the platter on a table and waited for Anwar to continue, but he looked like he was finished talking.

"What's in the other half of the fourth floor, the part that's off-limits," Maximus asked. He whispered but showed his frustration.

Anwar gave Maximus a sly look. "She has told me it's some kind of storage of old information. It has shelves of books, written documents. There is also a lot of stuff like a—a history, from different times and people."

"What kind of documents and books?" Maximus asked. He wondered how he was going to fit all this information he was learning in a message, including the paperwork he stole.

"I don't know. She's never been on that side long enough to see much. If they found out she was snooping around, she would be in serious trouble. They guard that place better than anywhere else in Thanoton. She did say there's information about other groups of people living in faraway places. No one keeps up with all that, though. It stays locked up, and no one goes in there unless putting things or papers inside. I guess the chief investigator goes in there once in a while," finished Anwar. He could tell Maximus was pleased with the information he had heard. "See, I told you I knew a lot."

"You do," Maximus responded, while he nodded his head.

"Why are you so interested in the fourth floor anyway?" Anwar asked, his eyes glued to the wall clock. He was ready to leave.

"Just curious," Maximus answered, shrugging his shoulders.

A short time later, Maximus arrived home with a message he had retrieved from the lamp for Calvin. He also had the papers he had stolen, folded up and crammed into his boot.

"Hello, sir." There was a message for you today from the palace."

"Thank you," Calvin said. He opened up and read the message.

H,

Javan and the council are planning on killing everyone in the army out west as soon as spring breaks. They don't want to enslave them to work in the mines down south. They think the soldiers out west are too well trained. They believe the soldiers would eventually escape and get the upper hand. The council has a plan to catch them off guard and kill them, a plan I left out for ***** to find. I hope that he did.

The council thinks the army out west has purposely alienated itself from the rest. It's so obvious that they are. We've been warning them not to, but they still do it anyway. Now, it's going to cost us. Javan, Tuval, and Dakar have had enough, and are paranoid. They want to make sure they have a loyal army that far away. I'm weary of warning the western commander. He didn't heed our warning, so this is the result. Nevertheless, have "K" warn them and give them the plan that "*****" should have. If "*****" didn't get the plan, let me know. I will get it to you so the western commander can prepare.

For His glory alone! Maybe we need to remind everyone in this last hour.

P

Calvin turned to Maximus who was waiting patiently. "Do you have the plans that outline the attack on the army out west?" he asked while he crumpled up the message and threw it into the fire.

"How did you know?" Maximus asked. He pulled the message out of his boot and unraveled it before handing it to Calvin.

"It was in the message that it was left out for you to find."

"I wish you would tell me who it is," commented Maximus. He watched Calvin read by the fireplace. *It has to be a council member,* thought Maximus.

"I can't," he said, as he studied the plan. He didn't look up. "Maximus, you don't have to pass this information on any further. I will personally make sure Kern gets it and passes it on.

"Good," Maximus said, relieved.

Calvin stopped reading and took off his reading glasses. He smiled at Maximus. "You've done a great job today, Maximus. Everyone is so pleased with you. I will make sure the Elders find out all the great things you are doing."

Maximus' face turned red. He didn't know what to say. "I found out some information about the fourth floor."

"Really? Let me hear," Calvin said. He folded up the papers and settled back to listen.

CHAPTER 43

Myka realized she couldn't circle around the group of border guards in time to stop what looked like an ambush by Dakar's soldiers. She had tried hard to get around and ahead of the group without being seen, but the terrain did not cooperate. It was obvious to her why everyone used the ridgeline trail. *I should have known better, after my grueling trip to the cache sight.* Myka was out of breath and wet from sweat. She unbuttoned her snowsuit, to let the heat out and the cool air in.

Myka worked hard, and all she managed to do was get closer to the border guards without being seen. She looked through her scope again, keeping an eye on Dakar's men. They were waiting for the border guards. Now that she was closer, it was obvious they planned to ambush the group. Myka wondered, *But why?* She tucked her wavy, brown hair back under her hood and moved forward. She was as close as she could be to the border guards without compromise. She had to warn them somehow. How could she without becoming a target? Myka noticed farther down the trail, a rock outcropping that gave her an idea.

The trail snaked around the ridgeline, making it hard for the border guards to see what was coming up. Dakar's men were set to catch them off guard as they came around the turn. Myka's plan was to climb up to the top of the rock outcropping directly across the trail from those ready to ambush the border guards. She would only be fifty feet from them. To get to her, they would have to climb down to the ridgeline trail and go over to the rock outcropping and climb up. Dakar's soldiers were positioned forty feet above the trail, ready to rain arrows on the border guards as they walked by.

Myka was strong and agile, quickly scaling straight up the side of the rock outcropping. Any other time she would've enjoyed this challenging climb. Not today. Today she was driven like a mountain lion scaling up the rocks.

Because of the way the ridgeline trail snaked around, Myka had some time to prepare a good fighting position before the border guards reached the last turn. She reached the top quickly and found a concealed fighting position. She could fire arrows from different locations yet be protected by rocks.

Myka looked through her scope and could see ten soldiers. They were all fixated on the trail below. The soldiers were not expecting any opposition from anywhere else. They were all exposed. She took off her gloves and pulled the crossbow out of her backpack along with all the arrows. *I can't waste any arrows. I need to save half of my arrows just in case I need them later.* She replaced half of the arrows.

Myka loaded an arrow in her crossbow and focused on one of the soldiers' legs. Her plan was to wound the soldier, causing him to cry out to warn the border guards below. She needed to shoot quickly before the border guards went around the turn. She firmly held her crossbow, resting her arm on the surface of a rock for stability. Myka closed her left eye and focused on the front sight of her crossbow. She took a deep breath and slowly let it out; she held and fired. The arrow flew with precision through the air until—

"Ahh!" echoed through the mountains. It caused everyone to freeze.

That must've hurt, thought Myka, *just above the right knee.*

"Take cover!" Dig commanded, the leader of the border guards below. "I want a 360-degree security! Anyone hear where that yell came from?"

"It had to come from somewhere above us," said a border guard, looking through his scope.

Myka stayed hidden as she watched Dakar's men trying to figure out where the arrow came from. It was obvious the way the arrow penetrated the leg that it had been shot horizontally from their position. There was no way it could've come from the border guards below. They would've had to practically shoot straight up. So, they studied the area around them with their scopes.

Myka watched as they wrapped a bandage around the soldier's leg. The soldier had a hard time keeping quiet; the pain was unbearable. She felt badly she had caused his pain. She comforted herself with the thought that maybe she would save some lives today.

Oh, no, thought Myka. *Two soldiers watching this direction ready to shoot. They have the wounded soldier propped up to help. The other seven are climbing over the rocks to get closer to the border guards. I can't believe they're going to risk going after the border guards not knowing where I'm at.* She prayed silently, *Light of the Word, stop them from pursuing the border guards.*

Myka watched as a soldier climbed over to the edge and looked down to the ridgeline trail below. He signaled to the others that he could see the border guards' location. *Why can't the border guards see them? It must be the sun's position, casting a glare from the rocks and making it hard to see.* She watched two soldiers load arrows and climb around to get the best foothold on the edge, to fire down at the border guards. Myka quickly aimed. She knew she would have to kill them in order to protect the border guards below. One of the soldiers started to draw back his bow. All of a sudden, he was knocked him off the cliff by an arrow that hit him. He landed forty feet below only a few feet from the border guards on the trail. All the border guards looked up but quickly ducked back down to avoid being hit by another body. It landed almost on top of the other one.

"Over there," pointed one of the border guards. He motioned toward Myka's position. He caused the border guards to start shooting that direction, until an arrow from above hit one of the border guards.

"They're straight above us," Dig said. He pulled the wounded border guard closer to the rocks and out of the soldier's line-of-fire. "Back up and move around the side! We can't stay here. We're sitting ducks. We need to hit them from the side."

"We can't move to that side," said one of the border guards. "We have an enemy position over there. We're pinned down."

"I think they're on our side," said another border guard, watching through his scope. "It's—it's a girl, shooting at the soldiers above us!"

"Let me see that scope," Dig said, as he moved with the group around the side. He saw a girl with brown, wavy, shoulder-length hair in a white snowsuit, firing at the soldiers. She had distracted the soldiers from shooting at them. Dig wondered, *Who is she?*.

Myka exposed herself to the border guards after she saw they understood she was on their side. *I can't believe they fired at me. Good thing I'm surrounded by rocks.* Myka watched as Dig and the other border guards maneuvered their way around, and up the side without being seen. She kept the soldiers' heads focused on her by occasionally exposing herself. She would act as if she was going to fire an arrow at them. Then, they would all react and fire at her. She hoped after the border guards' surprise attack they would give up.

Myka watched the border guards climb over the top and catch the soldiers off guard. They caused two of the soldiers to quickly flee down the other side. *Good*, thought Myka. Two ran off, leaving five with their hands up surrendering. She watched in horror as the border guards killed the unarmed soldiers with their swords.

"Wait! What you are doing?" shouted Myka. "They surrendered, you murderers!"

She heard Dig tell his men, "Go after and kill those two soldiers that got away." Dig turned toward her. He grabbed a border guard, and started down the side he had just gone up.

Oh, no, she thought, *they're coming after me. What's going on? Did Thanoton turn upside down while I was gone? I helped them. Why are they doing this?*

Myka quickly went down the other side of the mountain away from the ridgeline trail, scaling down the steepest location. She knew they were no match for her when it came to climbing around the rocks. Myka found a perfect spot hidden in a crevice, out of view from above. She waited there a few minutes listening to the voices way above.

"Ahh!" someone screamed.

They must've caught one of the soldiers,' thought Myka. Then she heard someone breathing heavy, not too far away. She couldn't resist, so she snuck a peek to see who it was. Myka saw a young soldier, straining to climb down the rocks. He looked scared. He had taken off his body armor to lighten his load, making it easier for him to climb. She noticed how young he looked, his face all red from clutching the rocks. *He sure doesn't look scary with all his armor off*, thought Myka. *He's actually kind of cute with his short, black hair.*

Myka decided to take the risk and help him. She wondered if the soldier would try to kill her once he was safe like the border guards had. She heard voices getting louder from above. Myka grabbed the edge of the crevice and swung out, reaching for a ledge above. She pulled herself far enough up to get the soldier's attention.

Myka saw the look on the soldier's face, and said, "Don't be afraid. Let me help you."

"You were trying to kill us too," the soldier said. He looked around like he didn't know what to do next.

"I tried to stop the killing," Myka pleaded. "If I had known both sides wanted to annihilate each other, I wouldn't have chosen a side. Believe me, I want you to live. Let me help you."

The soldier knew the predicament he was in. He could see the border guards above, making their way down the side of the rocks. He decided to take Myka's help.

Myka helped the soldier over the ledge and into the crevice. She put her finger up to her lips for him to be quiet. They sat there quietly, staring at each other until the border guards gave up their search and left. Myka and the soldier decided to remain there until the morning. They both eventually fell asleep. Myka woke up early and climbed out to look around. She didn't see or hear anyone. She went back and helped the soldier climb up over the ledge.

"I think they're gone," Myka said. Her smile made him smile.

"What's your name?" asked the soldier.

"Myka. What's your name?"

"Zion," he answered. "Hey, you're one of the girls that got abducted by the intruders a couple months back." His eyes lit up with excitement.

"Yeah," Myka said. *That's not exactly what happened*, she thought.

"You must've escaped."

"I did," Myka answered, playing along. She couldn't believe they thought she was abducted and not one of the ones helping the intruders. Myka wondered if Lot knew. She pondered the possibility of her going back to Thanoton.

"They'll be all excited when they find out," Zion said. "Of course, I will be in trouble. I'm the sole survivor. This makes me look like I was a coward, and ran away from the fight."

"You're not a coward," Myka said to reassure him and win his trust. "Were you ordered to kill the border guards?"

"We were sent to kill all of them, by Dakar," answered the soldier. He carefully followed Myka up the rocks to the top.

"Why?" Myka asked. She stopped to look behind her.

"Javan wants to replace all the border guards with Dakar's men."

Myka sat down to take a break on top of the ridgeline, and said, "I think you shouldn't go back to the eastern cut yet. We don't know if the border guards are waiting for you. I—I also think there is something else going on."

"I have to go back to tell Dakar what they did to us," Zion said, agitated.

"I don't think that's a good idea," Myka added. "Maybe we can sneak up to the eastern cut and watch from a distance, to see if the coast is clear for you to go back."

"For you to go back too," Zion added.

Myka wondered if she should head back to the cache sight or risk going back to Thanoton. She watched Zion climb the rest of the way up and sit down next to her.

They think I was abducted, thought Myka. *I can easily play along and act like I escaped.*

CHAPTER 44

Myka had taken off her heavy layer of clothes and strapped it to her backpack before they headed to the eastern cut. She didn't want to overheat and get her clothes soaked with sweat. Myka knew wetness and cold would be a dangerous combination, especially if they were going to sit all night as they planned.

Myka and Zion moved cautiously down the ridgeline trail toward the eastern cut. They used as much concealment as the terrain would allow. They walked, hid, listened, and kept quiet. With every little sound, they would quickly dive and hide behind the rocks or bushes. They made for a good team, using hand signals and reacting in unison. Dig and his murderous border guards were ahead of them. They kept this in mind as they cautiously moved forward.

Myka's plan was for them to get as close to the eastern cut without being seen, to observe and assess the situation. She knew things were out of the ordinary because the army and the border guards were trying to kill each other. Myka had a perfect spot in mind on the eastern border. It was a spot far enough away to escape, if they had to, and yet, close enough to see everything they needed to.

Myka and Zion were near the location to make their ascent off the ridgeline trail when they spotted Dig and his men. They both watched them through their scopes.

"I can't figure out what they're doing," Myka said as she adjusted her scope. It was harder to see, now that the sun had started to go down.

"Looks like they're observing something," Zion responded. He moved around to get a better angle. "I can't see what they're looking at."

"Or waiting for something," added Myka. "We better get moving. It's starting to get dark."

"What about them?" Zion asked, still looking through his scope at the border guards.

"It's better if we go to the top of the crest while we still have some light, so we can observe the entire eastern cut," Myka said. She grabbed Zion's arm. "It's getting dark. We need to move now to go up while we can still see. We'll be able to see the border guards' headquarters and the army barracks; they're always lit up at night."

"I want to follow the border guards," Zion said.

"There is something bigger going on here besides them. If we go to the top, we'll be able to see when it's safe for us to come out."

"You're right, let's go," Zion agreed. "It's just that, I want to kill them so badly for what they have done."

Myka led the way, and Zion followed right behind. They crept down the ridgeline trail until Myka found the path that went straight to the top. They stopped fifty feet up to see if they were followed. They weren't. They climbed until they reached the top of the crest that overlooked the valley to the east and the dark valley of Thanoton to the west. It was almost total darkness.

Out of breath, Myka sat down in a low spot on top of the eastern crest shielded by rocks. She took off her backpack, pointed over her right shoulder, and whispered, "When it gets totally dark, we can crawl over to the edge of the cliff. We'll have a good view of the eastern cut." Zion nodded, still out of breath. Myka continued, "We have to be careful. There are other observation posts around the eastern cut. They don't man the same ones every night. They change."

Myka felt a chill run though her body as she started to cool down. She unstrapped the coat from her backpack and put it on.

He felt the chill and did the same. "Good idea," Zion said.

An hour after the sun went down, they low crawled to the edge of the cliff. Myka couldn't see any observation points that were occupied.

"That's weird," offered Myka, as she scanned with her scope. She was shoulder-to-shoulder with Zion, who was doing the same thing.

"What?"

"I don't see any border guards manning their observation points."

"Maybe we just can't see them," Zion said. He tightened his hood over his head, to shield it from the cold air blowing off the mountain.

"No. We would be able to see them," Myka said. "They always have fires to stay warm. Something's up."

"It looks pretty normal to me down there," Zion said, as he laughed. "The soldiers are drinking by a bonfire outside of the barracks."

"You mean getting drunk," Myka said, with disgust. "How can they be an army ready to fight the enemy when they're drunk?"

"We don't have any enemies."

"That's what you think," Myka said. She turned to Zion and asked, "You didn't get drunk every night, did you?"

"Well, uh—"

"What a waste," Myka said. She shook her head. "True warriors stay strong, sober, and vigilant. Alcohol takes all those things away."

"I'm strong," he said, "and who are you to tell me about being a soldier?"

"I'm the one who saved you, remember?" Myka said. She rolled on her side and faced Zion. "Alcohol is addictive, unhealthy, and causes you to make bad decisions. It definitely lowers your guard, case in point," she motioned to the army soldiers around the bonfire. "They're not ready for anything."

They both sat quietly for a few minutes and observed the border, lit up by the bonfire.

"I think I see some movement in the woods that surround the checkpoint that leads to the eastern cut," Zion said. He leaned farther off the cliff, like that would make him see farther.

Myka grabbed his shoulder, firmly held him, and said, "You need to back up Zion. You're going to slide off."

"Look!" Zion said, pointing at the barracks.

Myka saw dark shadows that looked like men creeping up to the army barracks. "They're also surrounding the border guards' headquarters," she said.

"The soldiers don't even see them," Zion said. He started to get up. "I need to warn them."

"Wait," Myka said. She reached out to grab him.

Suddenly, Myka heard yelling and men's screams coming from below. It was so loud, Zion came rushing back down next to her to see what had happened. They watched in horror as the soldiers below were slaughtered. The ones running away shot in the back.

"It's the border guards," Myka said. She had recognized them in the light of the fire.

"They're even killing the wounded ones," Zion said. His voice trembled as he listened to Myka crying quietly next to him.

"They're making sure everyone is dead," Myka added. She sounded defeated.

"Maybe some soldiers will come from Thanoton and rescue them," Zion responded.

"They won't even see or hear this," Myka said. "The fog is too thick down in the valley."

"I hope Assam, from my platoon, wasn't killed," Zion said, all choked up. "He's my best friend." Zion paused and lifted his head. "Wait, I think he's supposed to have palace duty this week."

"Maybe he wasn't there," Myka said. She put her arm around Zion.

It quieted down on the eastern cut. Myka heard only the border guards as they shouted commands to each other. The border guards' headquarters went up in flames, followed by the barracks. She sat there mesmerized, not saying a word, not knowing what to do next. Myka started to see a large number of people moving down the ridgeline trail, and every single house was going up in flames.

"They're leaving their houses and setting them on fire," Zion said. He stood up to get a better view.

"Leaving to go where?" Myka asked. "Never mind."

They could see a trail of torches leading the way through the eastern cut out of the valley of Thanoton. It was clear out east and was easy to see the column of people that followed the torches.

Looks like they're headed for Sanctuary, thought Myka. *Can't be. How would they know it existed? There's no way the Elders would condone what just happened. It goes against everything we believe. We want to preserve life, not end it. I don't care what the risk is; I need to talk to Lot.*

Myka and Zion waited until morning, and then they climbed down the crest to the ridgeline trail. The people who lived on the border had started to gather around the burnt-out buildings. They didn't know what to do with all the dead bodies. It was silent. No one said a word. The moms kept their kids a safe distance away from the dead. There was an awful smell in the air. Myka smelled it once before. Burnt, human flesh. She felt sick. The people stared at Zion, the only soldier left alive on the border.

"Myka," sounded a voice that came out of the smoke from the other side of the burnt barracks.

It startled her until she saw who it was. "Lot!" she screamed. Myka ran over and jumped into his arms. She wept so hard, she was unable to speak.

"How's my favorite of favorites?" whispered Lot in Myka's ear.

Myka was all choked up, holding him tight. "I'm so glad to see you."

"Who is this?" Lot asked. "Hello," he said as he shook Zion's hand.

Myka released her grip around Lot, and said, "This is Zion." She chuckled. "It's a long story."

"Have a seat and tell me," Lot said. He motioned over to a spot away from everyone. Lot listened to both of their stories, and when they were finished, he said, "Zion, go back and tell your army commanders what happened. We were about to send someone to the palace in Thanoton to let them know. I'm sure Javan will want to come out and see for himself."

"I'll go right away," Zion said, as he stood up. "Are you coming with me?" He looked at Myka. "They'll want to know one of the missing persons was found."

"Well, uh—"

"It's best if Myka stays with me and my wife here at the border," Lot interrupted. "She's been through so much. It would be better for her adjustment. Just tell them she's staying with me. They can stop by and talk to her anytime."

Zion nodded and smiled at Myka, "Thanks for saving my life."

"All I did was help," she said, her face red with embarrassment.

"Hey, can some of you catch one of the loose horses for this young soldier to ride?" Lot said to a group of people gathered around.

Lot and Myka watched as Zion went with them to catch one of the horses.

"It sounds like everyone is convinced you were kidnapped and you escaped," Lot whispered.

"They never heard my name that night we helped the Three Witnesses escape?"

"No, they didn't," Lot answered. "I have sources all the way to the top that say Javan does not suspect you of anything. You're back in business as usual."

"Can I go back to my aunt's house?" she asked, all excited.

"Eventually, yes. First, it's best if you stay with me so we can bring you up to date on everything that's happened."

"You weren't a part of this, were you?" Myka whispered.

"No, of course not. Although, I feel like I'm responsible. I will explain that to you later when we're alone."

"Have you heard from the Three Witnesses?" Myka asked. Her voice trembled, and her eyes were moist. It was obvious she missed them.

"They're being trained and doing well," Lot said. He put his arm around Myka as they walked toward his wagon. "You'll see them soon. Have patience."

"I hate waiting," she said.

"So do I."

CHAPTER 45

"Commander Javan," said a palace guard lieutenant. He had barged into a meeting Javan was having with Tuval.

"Can't you see we're having a private meeting?" Javan said, irritated by the interruption.

"Something bad has happened at the border," responded the lieutenant. He motioned for Zion to come into the room.

"What is it soldier?" Javan said. He studied Zion as he leaned back in his chair.

"Everyone was killed. They killed everyone. I'm the only one left," Zion stumbled around the facts, too excited to talk.

"Slow down and take a deep breath." Tuval slid into a convenient chair. "Maximus," yelled Tuval, "bring this soldier some water."

"Yes, sir," could be heard from outside of the room.

"What's your name?" Javan asked.

"Zion."

"Are you assigned to Dakar?"

"Yes, and I'm the only one left," his eye's huge.

"Who did you say was killed?" Tuval asked. He watched the soldier drink the glass of water Maximus had just handed him.

"All the soldiers," Zion answered. He started to talk fast again. "I'm the only one left."

"Are you sure? Which border?" Tuval said, scrutinizing him.

"Who killed them?" Javan stood up and leaned close, palms flat against the conference table.

"The border guards," Zion answered Javan first. He could tell they didn't believe him. "It's true. They killed them and left the valley of Thanoton over the eastern border."

"Maximus, go get Zesha, the chief investigator," Javan commanded. "And how come you're still alive?" he asked Zion.

"There was this girl," Zion stuttered, not knowing where to start.

"Slow down and start from the beginning," Tuval said. "No," he put up a hand, "let's wait until Zesha gets here." He glanced at Javan, who was uncharacteristically quiet.

The lieutenant rushed into the conference room again. "Commander, we have received more reports verifying the soldier's story. The soldiers are all dead, and the border guards and their families have left. They even burned down their own houses."

"Who are these reports coming from?" Javan shouted. Everyone flinched when he slammed his fist on the table.

"From the border people."

"I want you to take a platoon of men and check out the eastern border," Javan said to the lieutenant in the palace guards. "Stay there and secure the place until I arrive this afternoon. If you encounter any resistance, I want you to come back for orders. We'll go after them with an overwhelming force.

"Yes, Commander," responded the lieutenant.

They both watched him leave as Zesha came into the room followed by Maximus.

"Maximus, close the door and leave us alone," Tuval commanded. "Don't let anyone come in. Is that understood?"

"Yes, sir," Maximus answered. He closed the door behind him.

"What's going on?" asked Zesha to Zion.

"Zion's about to tell us," Tuval said. "Start from the beginning and tell us everything. Don't leave anything out."

All three listened in amazement to Zion's story—from the ambush that backfired, to being saved by a girl named Myka, to the trip they had made to the eastern cut. They listened to the horror of the soldiers being slaughtered and everything burned, to watching the border guards and their families leave the valley to an unknown location.

Maximus wanted to listen, but he could not hear with the door closed. The news of the soldiers' slaughter and the border guards fleeing the valley had already circulated through the palace.

"Maximus, did you hear?" Anwar asked. His head bobbed around like a chicken that looked suspicious.

"I already heard," Maximus answered. "Now get out of here, or you will get us in trouble."

"You already heard about the slaughter on the border?"

"Yes, now please go," Maximus said, giving Anwar a slight shove. "You are not supposed to be here."

"All right, all right, I'll go," Anwar said. "I can't believe you already know. I'm the one telling everyone."

"Go," he whispered, while he motioned with his hands.

"All right. I'm leaving." Anwar shook his head. "You're so jumpy lately."

"Go."

The door to the conference room opened. Maximus heard Javan say, "We'll leave in one hour to go to the eastern cut with Zion. Zesha, you go to Lot's house to interview Myka."

Myka, pondered Maximus, *she was that kidnapped girl. She must have escaped.*

After they all left, Maximus went to work cleaning up the conference room. He neatly straightened the heavy, wooden chairs around the large conference table. With a clean cloth and a little bit of oil, he polished the table, bringing it to a rich dark brown. It revealed the intricate grain patterns of the wood that added to its beauty. He was proud of himself. When he had finished, it was smooth, shiny and he could see his reflection on the surface.

"Maximus," The Fifth called out from outside the conference room.

"In here, sir," Maximus answered. He grabbed his bottle of oil and came out.

"Maximus, this is your lucky day," said the fifth-floor supervisor. "One of the council members told me to send you home the rest of the day. You'll be paid for the whole day of course."

"Really?"

"I'm serious," said the Fifth with a slight smile. "You can go. Just take the dirty dishes down with you."

Maximus gathered up the dishes and headed out. On the way down the stairs, he saw he had a message and quickly retrieved it. *This is strange, no message earlier and suddenly here is one. I wonder if this is the reason I'm going home early. I wish I knew who it was on the inside passing me these messages. They must be on the council or really close to it.*

Maximus walked into the house and retrieved the message out of his hidden pocket. Labeled with an "H" meaning it was for Calvin. He knocked on the wooden trim around the door to Calvin's office. His door was open as usual; he was writing. Maximus peeked in, and said, "I have a message for you."

Calvin glanced up from his desk, "Bring it in. You're home early?"

"They let me leave early," Maximus answered. He sat in a chair next to Calvin's desk and wondered how he found anything. He had paperwork and books scattered everywhere.

"This message must be important," Calvin acknowledged.

"I have other things to tell you after you read the message," Maximus said. He felt a sense of accomplishment. "The message comes first like you told me."

Calvin unfolded the message and read.

H,

"I have horrible news to report. We are verifying what I am about to tell you before we actually see it. We've had several people come from the border to the palace to tell us the same story. So, I believe I'm safe in giving you this information, and how we can turn this tragedy into something good.

Marcus and the border guards killed every single one of the soldiers at the border except one. Zion was rescued by our special girl "M." As always, the Light of the Word has our little warrior gem at the right place and the right time.

She is currently with "L," and I've been tasked to question her. I'm on my way to do that today. I will also explain to "L" the same idea I'm about to tell you.

We know that Javan does not trust the army out west and wants to get rid of them in the spring. To avoid a fight, let's bring the army out west back into good graces with Javan. It would be easy to do right now.

The commander of the western army has been systematically separating himself, and his men, from the rest of the army. Here is an opportunity for him to redeem himself. He really has no choice, and you need to make that clear to him. He needs to come in with his men and volunteer to help Javan in whatever capacity he needs. He needs to exploit this situation to our advantage, show his loyalty to Thanoton, and possibly gain control of the whole army by spring. It's not impossible and could happen, only if he can get his priorities in order. Regardless of what he thinks, he has to do it in order to make our spring push successful. I pray the Whisperer would reveal all this to him. We don't need any more people doing their own thing, not looking out for the good of all.

Remind them we want to preserve and save lives, not destroy. It is written, "For the son of man is come to seek and to save that which is lost." He also said, "For the son of man is not come to destroy men's lives, but to save them." We want to turn everyone, including our enemies, to the Light of the Word. We are not like them, so let us not behave and think like them. Marcus betrayed us and showed his true colors by slaughtering all the soldiers. There's no justification for revenge. The outcome is never good and most of all, it grieves the Light of the Word. There will be many wives and children mourning when they find out their husbands and fathers were slaughtered.

I'm writing this fast. I know you know what needs to be done. We have to salvage all this bad and turn it around for our good. Tell the western commander. <u>NO MORE KILLING</u>!

In Him is life, the Light of the Word, our Lord.

Life is the key word!"

P

Calvin crumpled up the message, struck a match, and burned it in an empty cup on his desk. "Maximus, can you go get Kern in the market square and tell him to come here as soon as possible? I need to talk to him. He's usually selling goods about this time of day." Calvin saw the expression on Maximus' face, and continued, "Then, you can tell me all the other things you learned today."

Maximus left right away and headed for the market square. He could hear the hustle and bustle of the market long before he could see it. The fog was thick. He could only see twenty feet ahead. Maximus knew exactly where Kern would be because he used to go with him.

"Hello, Kern."

"Maximus, good to see you," Kern said. He gave him a bear hug. "Shouldn't you be at work?"

"They gave me the rest of the day off," Maximus said. He checked the area and whispered, "Calvin needs to talk to you right away, it's important."

"He wants to see me right now?"

"Yes, right now!"

"It must be important," Kern agreed. He turned around to look at his wagon, full of potatoes. "Can you stay here and try to sell some potatoes? I don't want to leave them unattended."

"Yeah, I'll watch it, just like old times."

Before Maximus knew it, Kern was lost in the fog and on his way to talk to Calvin.

CHAPTER 46

"Hey, Lot! I hear some horses coming up the driveway," Myka called. She got Lot's attention. He was in the back. She sat in the living room with Lot's wife.

"Stay here. I'll see who it is," Lot said. He went out the front door and closed it behind him. Lot stayed on the front porch and watched Zesha ride up on his horse. He was surrounded by six soldiers on horseback, two in front, one on each side, and two in the rear. It was his security detail.

"Hello, Lot," Zesha said. He stopped near the front porch.

"This is a pleasant surprise," responded Lot in his usual jovial self. He watched Zesha dismount his horse.

Zesha straightened the stiffness out in his back, and he reached out to shake Lots hand.

"What brings you here?" Lot asked. He returned his handshake.

"I would like to talk to you and Myka about what happened at the border."

"Did you just come from there?"

"No, I haven't had a chance to see the devastation," Zesha answered. "I'll see it after I'm finished here."

"Well, come on in," Lot said, while he motioned with his hand.

Zesha turned to the soldiers, "All of you can stay here. I should be done in thirty minutes."

"Sir, one of us should stay with you," said a soldier assigned to protect him.

"That's not necessary," he snapped with a sinister glare. He grabbed his leather satchel and headed up the porch. Over his shoulder, almost as an afterthought, he tossed "It's safe here."

Lot had to laugh at the looks on the soldiers' faces as they watched Zesha walk away.

"Zesha have a seat in the living room. I'll go get Myka, and we'll have some tea." Lot let the kitchen door swing as he called for his wife and Myka.

"Myka, "Zesha, the chief investigator, wants to talk to us." Lot saw how big Myka's eyes got at the news. He grabbed her by the shoulders and looked directly into her eyes. Lot whispered, "Don't be nervous at all. Just give him the answers he would want. He's not suspicious of anything. Trust me."

"Okay," she answered. Myka took a deep breath and regained control of her trembling body.

"I'm going to make some tea for our soldiers outside as well," said Lot's wife. She was happy to have guests. Living out in the country could get lonely at times.

"That's a good idea. I bet they'd love some," Lot said. as he and Myka went into the living room.

"Well, hello, Myka," Zesha said. Bones creaking, he got up from his chair.

Myka wondered why he looked so happy to see her. She returned his smile and said, "Hello."

"Have a seat," Zesha gesturing toward a chair.

Zesha watched as Myka took a seat. She was a cute girl who always had a glow about her. Her brown, wavy hair seemed to have a mind of its own. Her hair seemed to look different every time he saw her. The light freckles on her nose and cheeks grew less pronounced as she got older.

Myka waited patiently as Zesha pulled his notebook out of his satchel.

He stroked his pointed beard and returned Myka's smile. "I talked with Zion, and he told me all that happened. You saved him, and later you both witnessed the slaughter of Dakar and his soldiers." Zesha turned some pages in his notebook, and without looking up said, "I just have a few questions for you. Is it true you escaped your captors, and you have been hiding out in caves until you came out to help the soldiers?

Myka looked over at Lot who was sitting beside Zesha. Lot gave her a nod and a wink. "That is so," she said.

"It was obvious the border guards helped the intruders abduct you, Ezra Jared, and Dara. Is that right, Myka?" Zesha asked.

"Yes," Myka answered.

"Let's talk about the night you were abducted," Zesha said, still reading his notes. "After the fight started on the border, the abductors split into two groups. One group fled over the eastern border, and I assume you do not know where the other group went since you escaped from them."

"No, I don't know where they went," Myka agreed.

Zesha stopped taking notes and studied Myka for a few seconds. "Myka, that's all the questions I have for you. Now if you will excuse us, I need to talk to Lot alone."

Myka smiled back at Zesha the chief investigator. As she left them, she wondered what he was about. He didn't really ask her any questions. He actually answered all the questions he was asking and wanted her to verify the same answers. *Strange*, she thought.

Zesha waited for Myka to leave before he said, "Make sure she sticks to the story that the border guards abducted her. It's more believable after what has happened." Zesha said.

"I will," Lot agreed.

"Her story is she escaped, and hid out in a cave. She could no longer trust the border guards, so she hid and slowly worked her way back to Thanoton. That is when she ran into the soldiers under attack and rescued Zion." Zesha thumbed through his notebook. "How soon will you have her back working? We need her right away. There is a lot that needs to be done before spring."

"I want to keep her here another week or so to rest up. She has been pushed to the limit," Lot advised.

"That's too long," Zesha pointed out.

"I know her Zesha; she really needs it. She's not back to her old self yet."

Zesha nodded. "I trust your judgment."

"Wait till you see the border," Lot said. "Marcus really betrayed us."

"It sounds like he used us to accomplish his murderous ambition. I never thought he would do something like this. Did he give any indication that he planned to do this?" Zesha asked.

"No, he didn't," Lot answered. "I specifically told him we wanted them to leave peacefully."

"I had originally planned on using Marcus and the border guards for the operation in the spring, but he can't be trusted now. The situation is that now we have a group outside the valley that might not fall under the

Light of the Word's authority. If they have any ambitions other than peace, we've got a problem."

"The Elders are not going to like what happened," Lot said.

"No, they won't," Zesha agreed. "We are the Children of Light. We don't want to kill anyone. We want everyone to believe in the Light of the Word and be saved. That is why we cautiously operate to liberate this valley."

Lot nodded his head in agreement. "For decades you and I only communicated through messages, never in person. But the last couple of weeks, we have met twice. Is this how you want to continue to meet?"

"No, definitely not," Zesha answered. "I had no choice about this meeting—uh, investigation. I have a plan that I think will help us turn this tragedy into something good."

"That would be a miracle," Lot stated.

"If my plan works, this tragedy could set us up to be in a better position for our spring operation."

"What's the plan?" Lot asked, all excited to hear.

CHAPTER 47

Kern finally approached the outskirts of the western town of Pistio. It was a long, grueling trip in the deep snow, which made it hard to move at a normal pace. It was tougher to see than usual because it snowed the whole way. His two horses plodded through the many deep snowdrifts. The two-hour trip from the city of Thanoton had turned into three hours, and he was still not there. He thought about what Calvin had told him. He contemplated the best way to approach and convince Gabriel to go along with the plan.

Gabriel was the commander of the armies out west. Gabriel and his soldiers controlled the entire western region. He was also secretly a Seeker and the commander of the ghost team. The exemplary training of the western armies was because of Gabriel's keen skill. He took pride in their expertise and led by example. He handpicked his soldiers and made sure they were all hard-core believers in the Light of the Word.

Out of those soldiers, he had an elite group he led called the Ghost Team. There was no mission too tough for them to accomplish. They did everything from smuggling people in and out of the valley to snatching those that got in the way. Their ghost rides were famous. They abducted a person and took them out of the valley, so secretly no one knew how it happened.

Everyone felt safe. Kern knew Gabriel had his own way of doing things, and might not like Calvin's plan. He would want verification from the Elders, to make sure this is what they wanted. However, there was no way to get that kind of confirmation in time. Gabriel's window of opportunity to get back in Javan's good graces was now. Kern thought about how to approach Gabriel. He decided he would let Gabriel read the message first since Calvin was so well respected. Then, he would further convince Gabriel of the deep need to go to Thanoton and volunteer his help in this tragedy.

Kern arrived in Pistio, his hometown. The town, filled with believers, had grown by significant numbers in the past four years because Sanctuary closed down operations out east and moved to Pistio. A whole group had come from the northern city to resume Sanctuary operations there. The whole town was preparing for the spring push. They eagerly awaited the arrival of the Three Witnesses.

Only one road led in and out of the town of Pistio. The western command center was the first building all travelers had to pass in order to enter the town. In front of the command center was a permanent checkpoint the soldiers manned. No one could take the main road out west or go to the city of Thanoton without first stopping at this checkpoint.

Kern pulled around to the back of the command center to tie up his horses. He brushed as much snow off as he could then entered the back door heading directly for Gabriel's office. Gabriel was alone and got excited when he saw Kern.

"Kern, come on in," Gabriel said. "I hope you have a mission for me."

"I do, actually," Kern answered.

"Good, let me hear about it," Gabriel responded. "Have a seat. Have some tea." Gabriel dragged a chair close to the fire.

"If you don't mind, I'd like to stand," Kern said, while he closed the office door. "I've been sitting for the last couple hours, and my feet are half-frozen." He moved close to the fire. The snow on his fur cape quickly melted, dripped, and sizzled on the hearth.

"It looks like you brought all the snow in with you," Gabriel pointed out.

Kern had to laugh, along with Gabriel, after he saw the puddles forming around his boots from the melting snow. Kern knew even though Gabriel was laughing, deep down inside, he couldn't wait to clean up the mess. He liked things tidy and in order.

Gabriel had a chiseled face and was much older than he actually looked. He kept in tip-top shape. He had short, brown hair that never seemed to grow. He had deep-set grayish, blue eyes. They always gave the impression he was thinking about something else, while engaged in conversation.

Gabriel never seemed to miss a thing and could read people like a book. Whenever anyone talked with Gabriel, the person always had the sense he was sizing him up to understand his character.

"So, what is it?" Gabriel asked.

"Here. Read this message from Calvin first," Kern said, as he handed it to him, then he turned his back to the fire and lifted his coat so the warmth would get to his nether region.

Gabriel unfolded the message and read.

G,

So much has happened in the last forty-eight hours. We are forced to change many of our plans. We need you to act immediately on what we are asking you to do. This is urgent, and there is no way we will be able to get approval in time from the Elders for this. However, we believe they would agree to what we are asking you to do.

We had an operation out east you did not know about that completely failed. We think, with your help, we can turn this situation to our advantage.

We received word from our insiders that Javan planned to enslave the border guards and their families. He wanted to relocate them down south to work in the coal mines with the other slaves. We sent "L" to convince Marcus, the head of the border guards of Javan's intentions and to win his trust. They were to flee the valley peacefully with their families and occupy the abandoned town of Sanctuary. We thought they were on our side. We had no indication they were going to do what they did.

Instead of fleeing, they killed Dakar, the head of Javan's army, and all his soldiers at the border. Then they set fire to the eastern command center and their own houses. There are only a few border people left. All the border guards along with their families are gone. Currently, the captain of the palace guards and a platoon of his men are in control of the eastern border.

You know Javan does not trust you. He is planning to destroy the western armies this spring, killing every soldier. We are well aware you are itching at the chance to go against him. You are almost too eager, and that concerns us. We do not need another incident like we just had. We want to redeem people, not destroy them.

We need you to humble yourself, come in immediately, and offer Javan your help. Remember, you are one of Javan's commanders. Leave a few men to maintain security out west and bring the rest with you.

We believe this will be an excellent way for you to get back in good graces with Javan. This will also put you in a strategic advantage come spring. Who knows? Maybe you can gain control of the whole army, peacefully."

H

Gabriel crumpled up the message and leaned back in his chair. He stared at the ceiling. "Who is the Seeker on the inside who is working closely with Javan?"

"You know I can't tell you that yet," Kern answered. "You do know Maximus though. He works in the command center."

"I heard he was," Gabriel commented. "He did a good job of infiltrating his way to the top."

"He did," Kern agreed. "This would be a great opportunity for you to work your way into the inner circle."

"Wouldn't it be great if I could gain control of the whole army?" Gabriel said.

"That would be great."

CHAPTER 48

Maximus headed down to the basement floor to check in with the head steward. He needed to see if the head steward had anything for him before he went up to the fifth floor for the day. When he entered the main room, workers greeted Maximus as they hung up their coats and prepared for the day's work. He hung his coat on his assigned hook and went into the office area.

"Maximus," the head steward called. "I need you to go to the kitchen, and help carry food to the conference room on your way up. There will be a lot of meetings and people up there all day. Once you get up there, stay, organize, and serve. I will have a number of people assigned to you to help. Use them to shuttle stuff up and down from the basement."

"I will be helping you today," Anwar interrupted.

"Anwar, what are you doing here? I already gave you your assignment. You're supposed to be taking food up to the fifth floor," said the head steward.

"I did. I'm on my way to get another load," Anwar said, as he backed out of the doorway.

"Then go!" shouted the head steward. He shook his head. "I lost my train of thought."

"You were saying you had a number of people assigned to help me," Maximus reminded him.

"Oh, yeah. If you need anything, tell them to go get it. You know what to do, Maximus." He pointed at Maximus. "Let me know if Anwar is causing you any problems. I am so sick and tired of him."

"I will," Maximus answered, as he backed up.

"Go ahead and get started."

Maximus lifted a platter of sliced cheeses and headed up to the fifth floor. He started to see why everyone was mad at Anwar all the time. Anwar always seemed to say things at the wrong time no matter who was around. Maximus was tired of Anwar embarrassing him. He was not looking forward to having Anwar work with him all day. He did like Anwar, but he was a liability. Maximus was worried that Anwar would say something he shouldn't and make everyone suspicious. Maximus was in a perfect position to help the Seekers. He didn't want anything or anyone to ruin it. Maybe he could get the fifth-floor supervisor to reassign Anwar.

With no one around, Maximus stopped between the third and fourth floor. He set the platter down and quickly deposited a message. There was no message for him.

The Fifth met Maximus at the top of the stairs. "Good morning, Maximus."

"Good morning, sir."

"Did the head steward fill you in on today's activities?" asked the Fifth.

"He did. He said he has people assigned to help me."

"That's right. There are meetings scheduled all day."

"Who with?" Maximus asked.

"There are meetings with the council, government officials, and police and army leaders. They have scheduled meetings with store owners and representatives from the border and neighboring towns." The Fifth set his hand on Maximus' shoulder. "Do you have any questions?"

"Yes, I do," Maximus said as he looked around. "Is it possible you could reassign Anwar to work somewhere else for the day?" Maximus waited until the Fifth was done laughing.

"Yes, it's possible," answered the Fifth, as he tried to contain his laughter. "Once we are done with setting everything up, I will put him to work at another location. We just need him this morning to get started."

"Thank you, sir."

Maximus entered the main room outside of the conference room and immediately went to work. He grabbed a pitcher of hot tea and entered the open door of the conference room to see what was needed.

"Good morning, Maximus," Zesha said. Immediately, he got up and headed for the door.

"Good morning, sir." Would you like some tea?"

"I will when I get back," Zesha answered.

"I'll take some," Tuval said. "Do you want some tea, Javan?" He nodded and Tuval handed Maximus both cups.

Maximus finished filling the cups and went out of the conference room. He stopped, awestruck at the beautiful girl that was straightening up the serving table. The girl had long, shiny, black hair that went past her shoulders. She had beautiful dark brown eyes. *Mysterious eyes,* he thought. They stood out against her olive-colored skin. He wondered who she was, but was too shy and intimidated to ask.

Mina felt like someone was staring at her. She turned and noticed as Maximus slowly approached the serving table. His face turned red as she smiled at him.

"Hi, you must be Maximus. I'm Mina. I'm here to help you today."

"Oh, good," Maximus said, not knowing what else to say. He watched as Mina went back to work.

"Hey, are you going to stare at my sister all day or work?" Anwar said, loud enough for everyone to hear, while he slapped Maximus on the back.

Maximus was stunned. "Keep your voice down. Why do you always do that?" He was no longer embarrassed but angry.

"What?" Anwar responded, with his arms out. "What did I say?"

"You opened your big mouth again, that's what," Mina added. She had a fierce look on her face.

"Maximus, this is my sister I told you about," Anwar said.

"Oh great, what did he tell you?" Mina asked Maximus.

"I didn't say anything Mina. Just that you two would get along. Both of you are—"

"Are what?" Mina asked, with her hands on her hips.

"No fun!"

"Anwar! Are you causing problems already?" the Fifth asked.

"He is," Maximus said.

"Some friend you are," Anwar said, too loud.

"That's it Anwar. You're working in the kitchen the rest of the day," said the Fifth pointing to the door.

Anwar leaned over in his exaggerated sharing-a-secret stance, and whispered a little too loudly, "If you want to know about the fourth floor, she's your girl."

Maximus shoved Anwar away and said, "Go! I don't care about that."

"What did he just say?" the Fifth asked, as he watched Anwar leave the room.

"I don't know what he said," Maximus answered. "Can you keep him permanently off this floor?"

"You don't have to worry about him," the Fifth said. "The head steward has permanently assigned him to the kitchen. If you need anything, let me know," he said on his way out.

Maximus hoped no one else heard when Anwar talked about the fourth floor. He knew Mina had. Somehow, he had to let her know he was not interested. When he told Calvin what he had found out about the fourth floor, the man didn't want to know any more about it. Calvin told him not to waste time investigating it. Maximus thought it rather strange that Calvin didn't care about the fourth floor, yet he thought it best to leave it alone.

Maximus could not believe that someone so beautiful was related to Anwar. When she first introduced herself, it did not register that she was Anwar's sister. She didn't look or act like him.

"Mina?"

"Yes," she smiled.

"About what Anwar said concerning the fourth floor—" Maximus whispered.

"Yes?" she said. Maximus caught a wary look in her eyes.

"I don't want to know anything about it. I could care less what happens on the fourth floor. I don't know where he got all that stuff from."

"Don't worry about it," Mina assured. "My brother never thinks before he talks."

He recognized suspicion when he saw it. From that point on, she seemed standoffish. She kept her distance the rest of the day.

~*~

Zesha closed the door to his office. He unfolded the message he had just retrieved and read.

P,

K delivered the message to "G" yesterday. We should hear from "K" today or tomorrow on what "G" said. It depends on how badly the snowstorm affected the roads out west. Hopefully, "G" will submit and come in to render Javan help. I have prayed hard, as I know you have, that the Whisperer will convince him his need to do this for the glory of the Light of the Word.

"K" also delivered the last of my written material to the printer. He has assured me he will be able to print enough booklets to distribute to every household by spring. I told him we want him to print enough booklets to go down south before he starts on the other books. Then, he can start printing the books the Children of Darkness tried to destroy. I know the southern regions are not part of the spring push, but I want to be prepared if everything goes as planned. It will give us a jump on things when the time comes.

I will talk to "L" about using our little warrior, to make contact with the leader of the Watchers. It's time we bring them out of hiding and into our mission. They have a lot of people and resources we need here in Thanoton. They would be quite useful.

Tell your girl she's doing an excellent job smuggling the books I have requested. She has been invaluable as you all have.

Seek Him!"

H

Zesha lit the message and watched the flames devour the paper.

We're almost there, he told himself.

CHAPTER 49

"Captain Arton, Captain Arton!" shouted a platoon leader, storming into the large tent that housed the temporary eastern cut command center.

"What is it?" asked Arton, the head of the palace guards temporarily assigned to the eastern border along with a platoon of his guards.

"This morning, while we scouted around to get to know the eastern border, we came across several caves on our way to the observation points were filled with food and other household goods."

"Take me to them," Arton interrupted, as he got up from his makeshift table.

"That's only half of it," said the platoon leader. "At one of the caves, we found fresh footprints. We estimate four to five people came and removed supplies."

"Where did the footprints come from?" Arton asked. He held his hand above his eyes and squinted to adjust to the light as he stepped outside of the tent.

"From outside of the valley," said the platoon leader over his shoulder. He picked up the pace. "There are foot trails all over that area going up and down both sides of the border. The border guards didn't just stay on this side of the valley."

They both walked as fast as they could up the trail. It was so hard to breathe in the high altitude no one talked the rest of the way.

Arton had fallen in love with the border in the short span of his assignment. It was sunny and beautiful. The guards were in their own world away from the city of Thanoton. All the palace guards took their jobs seriously hoping among themselves this would turn into a permanent assignment. They dreamed of building houses and moving their families out to the eastern border. No secret that he wanted to be in charge of the border, this was a good opportunity for Arton, their leader. He took it as a sign when Javan sent him out there, that his time had finally arrived.

The platoon leader stopped and pointed at a row of caves that were near the top of the crest, not visible from the ridgeline trail two hundred meters below. "Over there. Do you see the caves?"

"Oh yeah, I do see them. They are hardly visible unless you know where they are."

"That's why we missed them the first couple times we came up here," the platoon leader agreed. "Over here is where the tracks in the snow were found."

Captain Arton studied the footprints and followed them until they started to go down the other side. He sat down on top of the ridgeline and thought about how he should handle all of this. He didn't want to go into Thanoton, but this was the kind of news Javan would love to here. It would help to permanently establish him and his men on the eastern cut.

"This is what I want you to do," Arton said to the platoon leader. "I want you to pull all your men off the ridgeline. We don't want to scare anyone away with all our activity. Next, set up good surveillance positions on these caves before nightfall. I hope it snows like it has the last few nights to cover all our fresh footprints. I want you to ambush and kill anyone that tries to come into the caves from outside of the valley. It's too risky to try to capture them alive."

"Good, we were hoping that's what you would want to do," the platoon leader said. "It would make us look good if we killed some of the border guards coming back."

"It would," Arton agreed. "From the looks of it, they planned on coming back to retrieve all their supplies and equipment. It's only a matter of time before we have the opportunity to kill them. In the mean time, I am going to Thanoton to report this information while you set up the ambush. Also, Lot will stop by later this afternoon for a food order. He will have a carpenter with him. The carpenter will survey this area and look over our plans to rebuild. He will estimate how much material we will need to rebuild the command center and bunkhouse. Javan wants this done right away, so we should have the people and resources to get it done quickly.

"Captain Arton, come on in," Javan said, as he motioned with his hands for him to come into the conference room. "We were just talking about rebuilding the eastern cut command center."

"Good, I just passed the carpenter on the way here to the palace," Arton said. "He said he should have the estimate of everything we need to you by the end of the day."

"This is a top priority," Tuval said, to the builders and store owners present at the meeting. "As soon as the carpenter gives us the figures, we need you to fill the order immediately."

"And get every available man to help rebuild," Javan added. "How are things at the border?"

"Actually Commander Javan, could I speak to you and Tuval alone," Arton asked.

"Clear the room," Javan commanded. "This meeting's done anyway."

They all waited for the room to clear, and Arton closed the door behind them.

"Commander Javan, we have discovered a number of caves located throughout the upper crest of the eastern border filled with supplies."

"What kind of supplies?" Javan interrupted.

"Food and household items that we believe the border guards stashed to retrieve later," Arton answered. He watched Javan and Tuval look at each other with amazement. "What's even better, this morning my men found fresh tracks that came from outside of the valley to one of the caves. It looked like four to five men entered and took supplies out of the cave and went back over the border."

"It's the border guards!" Javan shouted. He pounded his fist on the table.

"I have set up surveillance on the caves. My men are ready to ambush anyone that comes near from the other side of the border," Arton said.

"Try to capture one of them if you can," Tuval added. "It would be great to know where they are living outside of the valley."

"We do need to find that out," Javan agreed.

Someone knocked on the door.

"What is it?" Javan shouted. He hated interruptions.

A palace guard opened the door and stuck his head in. "Sir, the captain of the western army, is here to see you."

"Gabriel?"

"Yes, Gabriel," answered the palace guard.

"Give us five more minutes. Then, send him in," Javan ordered. He made eye contact with Arton and said, "I don't want you to mention to anyone what we just talked about. Keep all this between us and make sure your men keep this quiet. We think we have a mole in our ranks."

"I'll make sure," Arton said. "I guess I'll head back to the border unless you need me for something."

"Not yet," Javan said. "I want you to stay while we talk to Gabriel."

"Watch your back with him," Tuval added. He made eye contact with Arton. "Do not tell him anything regarding the border."

"Send him in," Javan shouted.

"Captain Gabriel reporting for duty, Sir," he said. Gabriel stood at attention, while his right hand gripped the handle of his sword, the traditional address to a commanding officer. It caught Javan off guard because he was not used to such formality. They were more casual at the palace.

"At ease," Javan said. He motioned for Gabriel to sit down. "What are you doing here?"

"Commander Javan, I heard about what happened at the border with Dakar and his men. What a huge dent the border guards caused in one night, the loss of the head of the army and two platoons of soldiers! When I heard, I came as soon as I could with a platoon-and-a-half of my men to offer my help wherever you need us."

"What about the security of the western region?" Javan asked.

"I still have half a platoon on the western border, along with a platoon of new recruits in Pistio with an experienced leader."

"Who gave you the authorization to add another platoon?" Tuval argued while he stood up.

"I didn't add another platoon," Gabriel answered, not the least bit intimidated. "As per your directive, we are allowed to recruit to make up for those who choose to leave the army after their obligation is done."

"Don't play games with us Gabriel," Javan added. He motioned for Tuval to sit down. "You are to train a few to make up for the losses, not a platoon at a time."

"We have reports that you are training every eligible boy to fight in the western regions," Tuval said.

"That's an exaggeration," Gabriel said to purposely antagonize. "I don't know how the boys I recruit will do unless I put them through some rigorous training. I need a pool to choose from."

Javan had enough. He stuck the point of his sword right on the captain's neck and pressed so hard, he had to lean back. "You take orders from us. You don't make any decisions on your own, is that clear?" Javan commanded. He marveled that Gabriel did not appear the least bit afraid or intimidated by him.

"It's clear," Gabriel answered. He waited for Javan to pull back the sword and then rubbed his neck. "So, where do you need me and my men?" Gabriel said, as if nothing happened. "I could take over the eastern border."

"No," Javan said. "We've got that covered. Half of your men will work as palace guards under the direction of Arton. The rest, including you, will fall under the market square police."

"They're my men. I command them," Gabriel said, his deep-set eyes penetrating Javan's.

"Not anymore," Javan laughed. "You will take your directions from the head of the market square police."

"Maybe, now you will learn how to follow orders," Tuval added. "Guard!"

A guard opened the door and stepped in. "Yes, sir."

"Go get the head of the market square police. We need to talk to him."

CHAPTER 50

Myka left her aunt's house and headed for work. It felt like old times, almost as if she had never left. Out of habit, she checked the fence post to see if there was a message for her. There wasn't. No stick was leaning against the post. Lot had wanted her to stay another week at his house to rest up. But she had told him she was fine and wanted to get back to work—her work as a Seeker, that is. Truth was, she needed more rest. However, she knew everyone was excited for her to get started again. She was impatient to get things moving and ready for spring. Lot had already told Samuel, the assistant storekeeper, she would be at work today. Samuel was excited when he heard the news. She would have to use that to her advantage.

Myka cut across the market square and headed for the storefront. She immediately noticed all over the market square the soldiers with the western insignia, a cobra etched into their breastplate. Lot had told her that Gabriel was demoted. He now worked under the head of the market square police. It was hard to believe he would submit to that kind of treatment unless he had a plan. Lot also shared the rumor that the head of the market square police loved having Gabriel, and had made him second-in-command.

Gabriel was in the perfect position to facilitate things, Myka thought. She, too, had heard he was quickly winning over the hearts and minds of the people, fellow soldiers, and police. In just a few days, the people trusted him.

Both she and Gabriel were told to act as if they didn't know each other. That went for anyone in the western army that might know her. They were to look the other way, no matter what she did. Myka knew it would be hard to ignore Gabriel since she had received most of her training from him. He helped develop and choose her for the mission she had now. She felt safe with Gabriel so close.

Store workers swamped Myka with warm greetings as she entered the store.

"Welcome back," Samuel said, giving her a big hug. "I'm so glad to see you."

"I'm so glad to be back," She said. "I missed all of you." She looked around the store and commented, "Everything looks about the same as when I left."

"Pretty much everything is as when you left," Samuel said. "The storekeeper has not shown back up, so I've been running things." With a somewhat surprised look on his face, he said, "It seems to be running smoothly without him."

"Smoother," someone else said. It caused the group to laugh.

"I bet," she said, as she laughed along with them.

Samuel's face turned red. "Myka, I need to talk to you alone. Why don't you come back with me to the storeroom?"

"I need to talk to you too," she added.

Samuel closed the door behind them. "I'm so glad you're back. I was the only Watcher working in the store while you were gone."

"What's going on with the Watchers? What are we up to?"

"Nothing really," Samuel answered. He took a seat and offered Myka an apple. "With the Three Witnesses abducted, we really don't have a mission. Most of our key Watchers are missing. Only you have come back. Not to mention we had two traitors, Caleb and Neptali, working for the enemy. Who knows what they told them? Everyone is scared and paranoid. So, we are to remain underground, until we figure out what to do next."

"No one is doing anything?" She crunched on the apple.

"The market square Watchers are keeping an eye on the vegetable cart to see if it's under surveillance. The vegetable cart is still used to secretly signal which entrance to take to the inner chamber. They also watch the hidden entrances. So far, they have not identified anyone even remotely interested. Nevertheless, Shobal has not summoned anyone down to his chamber for months. He's suspicious of everyone." Samuel handed Myka a towel when she wiped her sticky fingers on her skirt.

Myka smiled, "Thanks. I want to go talk to Shobal."

"You can't."

"And why not?"

"You have to be summoned," Samuel said. He could tell she didn't like the answer. To be nice, he said, "I can send a message that you want to talk to him. Maybe he will summon you."

Samuel knew Shobal would never agree to see her. He wouldn't take the risk. Samuel could hear him now, "What useful thing could that little girl possibly have to tell me?" It was no secret. Shobal did not want any women in the Watchers' organization. He finally agreed because women watching were less suspicious in certain settings. It added to their resources. Although, Myka was the only female Watcher recruited, and they were always reluctant to use her.

"What if I just go," Myka continued. "I think I remember the different entrances and passages to take. I will just take a look at the vegetable cart to see."

"No, you can't do that," Samuel pointed out. "What's gotten into you?"

"Why can't I do that?" Myka asked.

"That's not the way it's done," Samuel answered. "You know that. They might not let you in, or worse yet—kill you."

"Do you really think they would kill me?" said Myka, scrutinizing him.

"They might."

Myka stood up and got in Samuels' face. "I have been through a lot and have important information that only I can give him. He needs to get over himself and see me. Put that into a message and give it to him."

There was a knock on the door. "Who is it?" Samuel responded.

"Lot is here and would like to say hi to Myka."

"Tell him we'll be right out."

Samuel stood up. "I'll send a message to Shobal. We should hear back today."

Myka nodded her head. "Can you tell Lot to give me a few minutes while I put my stuff up?"

"I will," he said and closed the door behind him.

Myka pulled a notebook out of her backpack and drafted a quick message for Lot. She had to tell herself to calm down. She needed to be back to her confident, laid-back, sweet self. She could tell she was less patient and was getting tired of people treating her as less than. Myka finished the message and folded it several times, praying. "Light of the Word, give me strength to persevere to the end."

"There's my favorite of favorites," Lot said, as he gave Myka a big hug.

Myka slipped a message into his pocket and squeezed his arm as they released, signaling he had to read the message right away.

"Sorry. I don't know what is wrong with me," Myka said, as she wiped tears from her eyes. She felt embarrassed and could tell both Lot, and Samuel looked concerned. Maybe, it was seeing Lot or the hug that prompted it.

"W-Well, I'll see you a little later," Lot said. "In an hour or so, I need to finalize an order."

"I'll be here," Myka said. She tried hard to regain control of her emotions.

"Are you all right?" Samuel asked.

"I'm fine," Myka answered. "I'm sorry I yelled at you, Samuel."

"If you need to go home—"

"I don't," interrupted Myka. She gave Samuel a hug and whispered, "Please tell them I need to talk to Shobal. It's urgent."

"Right," Samuel said. "I'm going right now."

Lot walked to a house one block west of the store and knocked on the front door.

The door opened. "Hello, Lot. About time you showed up." Calvin was happy to see Lot.

"Yeah, I thought I would stop by to say hello," he said, as he looked around.

Calvin closed the door and said, "We're alone; it's just us here. Why is it you only stop by when we have business?"

"It seems like that's all we have time for."

"That's true," Calvin agreed. He offered Lot a seat and poured him a cup of hot tea.

"Actually, I just received an urgent message from Myka, and I needed a secure location to read it. So, I figured I would come here since it probably concerns you."

Lot unfolded the message and read out loud:

L,

Samuel tells me Shobal has not summoned anyone down to the inner chamber in months. They describe him as very paranoid, and he does not trust anyone in his organization. I convinced Samuel to send a message to Shobal about my need to talk to him personally. Samuel was nice to me and will pass the message on, but I could tell he knew that Shobal would never agree to it. You know how he feels toward me—a girl.

I don't want to just give this message I have for Shobal to Samuel to pass. It's too risky because I know he would read it before he passed it. Then he would know about us.

There are three options from what I see. Let them stay underground and don't bring them on board. I go down to the inner chamber, anyway and try to talk to him. Or, I lead the Ghost Team down to the inner chamber, since they are here in the market square and we ghost ride him. The last option would be my recommendation.

Your fellow soldier,"

M,

"For of him, and through him, and to him, are all things: to whom be glory forever."

Lot finished and handed the message to Calvin. "Do you want to look at this some more?"

"No, go ahead and burn it," Calvin said. He watched Lot throw it into the fireplace. "I think we should wait to see how Shobal responds to the request. In the meantime, tell Myka to wait. We will consult Zesha and see what he thinks we should do, if Shobal does not allow Myka to see him."

"I don't like the ghost ride option," Lot added. "It's true we have Gabriel and his Ghost Team here, but I don't think it will be that easy to get him out of the inner chamber. The inner chamber guards live in their own world. Their one purpose and mission is to protect Shobal at all costs. They will do whatever it takes. I don't think it will be that easy. Even if we did ghost ride Shobal, there is no way we could rally the Watchers after that. Their whole organization is focused around him. It's almost cult-like. Not like our organization that is focused around the Light of the Word."

"That was one of our worries about the Watchers. It's turned out to be true," Calvin said. "They espouse to be believers, but in reality their loyalty is to Shobal and their organization first. As you know loyalty to the Light of the Word needs to come first in a believer's life. Everything else then falls into divine order."

"So, should we tell Myka to wait?" Lot asked.

"Yes. Tell her to wait and act indifferent toward her request. If Samuel comes back and says Shobal won't see her, tell her to do what she is good at. Play it off as just a teenage whim. She needs to act like it really wasn't that important."

Both Lot and Calvin settled down to write a message. When Lot had finished, he folded the message down into a small square. Then he hid it into a small tear in the stitching of his coat lining. He then said goodbye and headed back to the storefront next to the market square.

CHAPTER 51

Myka was busy the rest of the day because most of the workers had to help in the storehouse out back. They had multiple wood and supply shipments that came up from the south. The shipments had to be transferred to the eastern border. The rebuilding of the eastern cut command center and barracks had turned out to be very lucrative for the store. Samuel enjoyed the added business, even if it was turning into a logistics nightmare.

Myka couldn't wait to hear back from Shobal and kept an eye out for Samuel to come and tell her. She hoped he was not too busy in the storehouse, and forgot to check. Myka wanted to ask Samuel if there was an answer yet, but she knew she couldn't. She would comply with the earlier message from Lot and be nonchalant about the whole affair. No matter what the response might be.

Myka watched Samuel walk through the store and glance over at her on his way out the front. She figured he was going to check. Myka waited a few minutes and, sure enough, Samuel came back and headed for her.

"Myka, can I talk to you over here a minute?" Samuel said as he led her over to an isolated corner.

"Yeah sure," Myka said.

"We did get a response from Shobal. He said he doesn't want to see you."

"Really?" Myka shrugged. "Well, no big deal. It's not that important anyway." She saw the relief on Samuel's face. "Is that all you wanted to tell me?"

"They didn't want me to tell you this part, but I don't want to keep any secrets between us Myka. You are too good of a friend," Samuel whispered. "Shobal doesn't want you involved anymore in our operation. We are to keep you out of the loop and watch your activities. He doesn't trust you."

"Who cares?" she said. "Let them watch. I'm tired of all the useless Watcher secrets anyway."

So am I, thought Samuel.

"Can I work in the storehouse my last hour of work?" Myka asked. She needed to try to catch Lot to tell him what she had found out.

"I will send someone to replace you. I'm headed back there now."

Myka waited for him to leave and quickly went to the back room and drafted a message.

She wrote.

L,

Shobal does not want to see me. He told the other Watchers to keep me out of the information loop and future operations. They are to keep an eye on me.

M

She folded the message and went out to the storefront. As soon as she saw her replacement, she headed back to the storehouse. There were people everywhere loading and unloading. She spotted Lot, tying his load down to the hooks on the side of the wagon.

"Oh, I'm sorry," Myka said, accidently bumping into Lot. No one saw her put a message into his pocket and squeeze his arm, signaling he had a message to read right away.

"No problem," he laughed. "We're so busy back here. We are stepping all over each other."

~*~

Several hours later as the sun was going down, one of the palace guards at the eastern border spotted someone watching.

"Over to your right more," said the guard to the platoon leader. "You will see some bushes, then a rock outcropping. Just to the right of the largest rock you should see him."

"Oh, yeah, I see him now," said the platoon leader. "He's easy to see, now that I know where he is. Are you sure he has not spotted you?"

"I'm almost positive he hasn't," said the guard. "He looks through his scope periodically in the direction of the caves. He hasn't once looked this way."

"How long has he been there?"

"I have no idea," answered the guard. "I only spotted him an hour ago."

"Keep a watch on him, and I will check back with you later," said the platoon leader. "Hopefully, this means they will try to go to the caves tonight. I need to tell Captain Arton what you have found."

The platoon leader was all excited as he came off the ridgeline. It would be great if they killed one of the old border guards coming to retrieve some of their stuff. They needed this to solidify their place at the border. As he approached the eastern cut area below it was busy with activity. Loads and loads of wood and supplies were being offloaded. The builders had started to stake out where the new command center and barracks would stand. The platoon leader spotted Arton directing in the midst of the chaos.

"Captain Arton, I have some information I would like to discuss with you, in private," said the platoon leader. He hadn't seen Arton this happy in years.

"Certainly, Let's go for a walk,' Arton said. He smiled from ear to ear.

When the platoon leader was satisfied they were a safe distance away, he got straight to the point. "Sir, one of the guards, has spotted a lookout on the next ridgeline over, watching the cave area. We think this might be the night they come to the caves."

"Good," Arton said, as he looked around. "It will be total darkness in half an hour, and all these workers are about to leave. I want all our resources focused on the caves. I also want a squad ready to circle around and catch them in the valley, if they escape our trap."

"I'll go get everyone ready," the platoon leader said, as he started to walk away.

"Wait," interrupted Arton. "Tell the men if they can, to catch one of them alive. Supreme Commander Javan would love to have a prisoner to interrogate."

The platoon leader laughed. "I'll tell them."

It was dark. Arton's guards, hidden strategically around the caves behind cover, purposefully stayed away from any approach or trail the intruders might use to come to the caves. The guards wanted them to show up, so they set up an ambush line, half-moon shaped, around the front of the caves. The caves were facing the valley of Thanoton. Behind the guards, the usual thick, black fog hung over the valley, like a blanket. It was clear to the front, and stars hung in the sky. The guards would have the distinct advantage of being able to see the intruders as they came over the ridgeline. The moonlight would illuminate them. The intruders would not see them hidden behind the rocks and shrubs in the pitch black. The plan was for the guards to capture or kill them before they ran back down the other side into the valley. They had a contingency plan for intruders trying to escape, too.

Down the ridge, there was a hidden squad just on the other side of the ridgeline watching the valley. The squad leader spotted three silhouettes cutting across the ridgeline. It was easy to pick them out with the moon so bright. The squad leader wished he could signal the ambush team that the intruders were on their way, but Arton had ordered them to take no chances of scaring them off. Either way, the squad would risk going into the valley, circle around, and cut them off if they escaped the ambush.

The platoon leader marveled how quietly his men were in their hidden ambush positions. He could faintly hear Captain Arton breathing next to him. They were ready, and everyone expected the intruders to come. Therefore, the sound of crushed rocks echoing in the valley was no surprise. As the sound came closer, they waited. The platoon leader was ready to shoot the first arrow, initiating the attack.

The plan was to kill one of the intruders. Then some of the guards, with their swords drawn, would quickly close the half-moon around them killing all who resisted. The rest of the guards were in two groups. Group one, with their bows drawn, was to provide security for the guards closing in to capture the intruders. Group two, was to provide three sixty-degree security around the whole operation, extending over the other side of the ridge. They were there in case the intruders had more men lurking to try a counterattack. All the moving parts were to spring the trap quickly when the platoon leader initiated the kill signal.

The platoon leader watched the three silhouettes crest over the ridgeline. They cautiously worked their way down to the caves and came around the front. The platoon leader took a deep breath and drew his bow back farther. He took aim. He slowly let out his breath and aimed for the middle of the back of the first man that entered the cave. He released the arrow, heard a thud, and a gargled yell. The platoon leader realized he had sat there a little too long; he found himself all alone. As planned, his men had immediately sprung up and executed their parts of the mission. He got up and joined the rest at the cave opening.

"There you are!" Captain Arton said to the platoon leader. "We captured one. The other one had to be killed; he put up a fight. Two killed, one captured, and none of us hurt. That is what I call a perfect mission."

"It did go perfectly," agreed the platoon leader. "Now, what do you want us to do with the prisoner and the dead? Are you going to take the prisoner to Thanoton tonight?"

"No, we'll keep the prisoner here for now," Arton said. "Javan did not want anyone to know about this operation. I will talk to him early tomorrow morning, and see what he wants me to do. The bodies he might want to look at—to identify. Keep security tight; we don't want any retaliation."

"Yeah, I wonder what the old border guards' reactions will be when these three don't return?" said the platoon leader.

"We need to be prepared for that," Arton responded. Fear of consequences quickly overshadowed the joy he had from the night's work.

CHAPTER 52

Maximus spied Kern selling vegetables from the back of his wagon at the usual spot. He knew Kern liked to set up at the same place, every day in the market square. That is why he was there early. Usually, he was one of the first ones to set up. It was quite a feat, considering how far away Kern had to travel every day.

Maximus had a message to pass to Kern. The message was actually for Gabriel, but Maximus was not allowed to pass it directly to him. He wondered what the message was about. He had retrieved it from the fence behind the house when he took out the garbage. Calvin read it and quickly gave him a message to pass. When Maximus asked Calvin what it said, he replied, "It does not concern you." This morning, Maximus realized he was only one of many different players in this vast network. He wondered, *Who was it that delivered the message to their back fence? It must be someone on the inside of the palace. And why didn't they use the same message drop I use?* He had many questions, and maybe someday he would get answers.

"Hello, Maximus," Kern greeted.

"Hi," Maximus said. He shook Kerns' hand and passed the message.

"Are you on your way to work?"

"I am," Maximus said. "I just wanted to stop by and say hello."

"Well, have a good day at work," Kern said.

"I will," said Maximus as he walked away. He couldn't resist looking around to see if—Ah, he spotted Gabriel smiling at him. Maximus smiled back. He hoped Gabriel had heard all the great and brave stuff he was doing for the Light of the Word.

Maximus started up the stairs after dropping off his coat. As he rounded the second floor, he could hear Zesha and Mina's voices. They were coming down the steps.

"Good morning, Maximus," Zesha said. He stopped.

"Good morning, sir," Maximus responded. He tried to smile at Mina, but she quickly looked away and said nothing.

"It looks like it might be another busy day for you again," Zesha said as he walked away.

"I'm ready for it, sir," Maximus said. He knew he sounded too confident, and caught Mina rolling her eyes. Maximus wished he never would've said anything about the fourth floor. They were getting along great until Anwar opened his big mouth.

Between the third and fourth floor, he saw he had a message. He retrieved it and deposited one. The conference room door was shut, but the small space outside it was packed with people talking and waiting to go inside.

Maximus had brought up a fresh pot of tea. He decided after seeing Gabriel earlier, to be bolder—braver. The people waiting outside of the conference room were eyeing the pot. *What if they drank all of it, and there was none left for Javan?* he thought. He went up to the door and knocked.

"Who is it?" Javan commanded. All the voices around him stopped. It was completely quiet.

"It's Maximus. I have some fresh tea for you."

"Come in!"

Maximus entered and poured a cup of tea for Javan, Tuval, and Arton, the only three in the room. On his way out Javan said, "Maximus, tell everyone out there, the rest of the meetings are cancelled for the day."

"You want me to tell them?"

"Yes, you," Javan answered. "Do you have a problem with that?"

"No, sir."

"Then do it!" Javan commanded. "And go downstairs and tell them we want lunch early, like right now. Not breakfast. We started early."

Maximus closed the door behind him. "Listen up! All the meetings are cancelled for the rest of the day." Maximus couldn't help notice how some of the council members looked at him with contempt, and he supposed it was because of his age.

~*~

"Your prisoner, this boy, won't say anything?" Javan asked Arton.

"Nothing. He won't even tell us his name. We have tried different methods."

"Hopefully, some of the border people will be able to identify the bodies today," Tuval added.

229

"That would help," Arton agreed. "We think one of them was his father. At least, they look alike."

"After we eat our lunch, I'll go to the eastern cut with you to interrogate the prisoner," Javan said to Arton. "I'll get him to talk."

"It might be hard. The boy is angry," Arton added. "He probably feels he has nothing to lose, if it was his father that was killed."

"We'll see how he will handle pain," Tuval laughed. He caused Javan to laugh.

"From now on Captain Arton, you are the head of the border guards. You and your men are permanently assigned to the border as border guards, no longer palace guards. Eventually, we will get everything back up and running. Then, we will be able to move your families out there as well."

"Thank you, Sir!" Arton said. "My men will love that."

"You are the border guards," Tuval added. "No longer call the old border guards by that name. Call them what they are—traitors. They are the enemy."

~*~

Gabriel sat down on one of the many benches located throughout the market square. He got out his notebook and thumbed through it as if he was looking over his notes. Earlier, he had unfolded the message and slipped it into his notebook. Gabriel figured no one would suspect him of reading a secret message, in the middle of the market square with people all around. The less suspicious he looked, the less suspicious they would be. He turned to the message and read.

G,

"We have an immediate problem that demands your attention. Last night, the guards assigned to the border killed two and captured one entering the border. They were the old border guards, coming to retrieve some items they had stashed in a cave. The prisoner is a boy. There is no doubt the boy will be interrogated, most likely by Javan, later on, today. We hope he does not give him any information that could hurt us. We don't think he knows that much, but he will probably give up where they're located.

This is what we want you to do. Free the boy and send him back to Sanctuary. Do this with the least amount of violence as you can. We know this will be difficult because he is heavily guarded. Do not take him to Sanctuary. We don't trust what they will do to you if you show up with him. *Send him over the border on his own. We know at this point, they are watching the border. They will see when he is dropped off on the other side. They will come out and meet him.*

In regards to the last message, we are waiting for a response. We need secure locations around the city of Thanoton to store the booklets until the day we mass distribute them. Everyone is waiting to see if we can get the Watchers' assistance since they have the secure locations. It does not look promising. Either way, we have some time. We do need to spread the booklets around for security sake. The printer has boxes full of the booklets, piling up in one location. If that is compromised, we're in trouble.

We want you to quit asking about the south. We know you hate slavery. We do too, but they are not part of our spring operation. We do not want to overextend ourselves. Once we secure Thanoton and the surrounding areas, then we will push further south. For now, forget about them. Cordon that area off when we take over the city.

May the Light of the Word and His power go with you!"

H

Gabriel closed his notebook and stood up. He walked over to one of the western soldiers and said in a low voice, "The ghost team has a mission tonight." He had to smile at the excitement he saw in the soldier's face. "Listen, we can't meet as a group to plan this mission. It would look too suspicious. So, I want to talk to everyone on the team individually, as I walk around the market square. Then everyone will know exactly what to do tonight. As soon as the sun goes down, we execute the mission."

CHAPTER 53

Gabriel and the Ghost Team moved up close. They hid in the woodline with a clear view of the border guard's makeshift camp. It was well lit, and the team had taken off all their metal body armor for speed and stealth of movement. They all wore black with smudged coal on their faces. This would eliminate any reflective shine if light flickered in their direction. They were on their stomachs, watching and assessing the situation.

The majority of border guards focused on watching the east along the border. That would be an advantage for Gabriel and his team to get the prisoner, but a disadvantage when trying to get him over the border. There was a large campfire in front of the command tent where the off-duty border guards were. There were three other tents, two with no activity. Gabriel determined they were probably full of supplies. Next to the supply tents, were stacks of wood and other supplies for the planned construction projects. The third tent, one hundred feet away from the others, was heavily guarded. There were two guards posted front and back and a roving patrol of three men that walked around the whole area. Gabriel wasn't worried about that.

The problem was the border. There were many border guards watching who were alert, and expected something to happen. Gabriel knew they would have to cause a diversion to get the prisoner out. Adding to the problems, they heard through an informant that Javan had tortured the boy so badly he might not be able to walk. If that were the case, Gabriel would have no choice but to take the risk and deliver him to Sanctuary himself.

Gabriel passed down the commands and assignments using hand signals. The team knew it was all or nothing. This was going to be harder than they originally thought. After everyone had received an assignment, each moved into position to execute his part of the plan.

Gabriel waited for the groups to move and get settled. He couldn't see if his team was ready because it was pitch black, so he gave them a time hack. In ten minutes, they would wait until the roving guards were at the farthest point south of the command tent and the other guards. Then one team would take them out, which would signal everyone else to move. Next, a team would go get the prisoner, first taking out the guards. At the same time, another team would start the wood and supplies on fire, causing a diversion. The last team would wait to see how the guards on the border reacted to the diversion and clear the best possible path over the border.

Ten minutes passed, and Gabriel watched as the roving patrol worked their way south of the camp. He knew one of his teams was hidden in the tree line ready to shoot arrows, killing the three rovers instantly. Gabriel and his little group were ready to rescue the prisoner. They also had their bows ready waiting for the signal.

Gabriel saw the three rovers at the southern end of the camp drop dead, killed instantly and silently, unknown to the other guards. In unison, they let their arrows go, and all four guards around the prisoner's tent went down. One guard struggled to get to his feet, but Gabriel quickly swished his sword, and he lay dead.

"Hey, hey—are you all right?" Gabriel whispered to the young boy. "We're here to help get you out." Gabriel could hear him breathe, and felt the boy's heartbeat. He knew the boy was still alive but barely. He quickly untied the boy's hands and feet. Gabriel could see by the firelight all the dried blood around his face and eyes, which was swollen beyond recognition. He knew if the boy did not get medical attention soon, he could die. He scooped him up deciding to carry him to Sanctuary.

Gabriel quickly headed out into the tree line. The diversion worked, and everyone started to head to the big bonfire the supplies produced. Gabriel skirted around the camp, his little group growing larger as the other teams slipped into place for security. The last group had cleared a path over the border and killed the border guards that came too close. Gabriel carried the prisoner over the border and told one of his men, "I'm going to take the boy to Sanctuary myself. Go back, and I will find a way back over."

"Wait," said one of the team members. "I see a group coming this way in the valley. You won't have to go all the way to Sanctuary."

Gabriel could see a large group coming up the valley. "It must be Marcus and his men. I will leave the boy at the base on the other side of the eastern border, where they can see me and find him. It should take me about five minutes."

"We'll wait for you."

Gabriel worked his way down the other side of the ridgeline and set the boy down where they would find him. He laid his hands on the boy and prayed, "Light of the Word, please keep him alive, and heal him completely. I pray Marcus and his men not to retaliate this night's work."

Gabriel headed back up to his men. They worried about being seen now that the blaze from the diversion lit up the whole area. As soon as Gabriel joined them, they quickly slipped into the darkness of the woods and left. They were grateful no one was injured or killed on their team. However, it did not turn out as they thought it would. The Ghost Team ended up killing many of the new border guards.

Marcus was the first one to approach the body they had seen dropped off. "It's Shue," he said. "Shue, can you hear me? He's hurt badly. Make a stretcher."

One of the men from Sanctuary asked, "Do you want me to send some men back with him, while we go get the others?"

"We're all going back," he said, as he watched the flames shooting over the ridgeline from the other side. He could hear the shouts and commotion that came from the border. "There's something else going on there. We'll have to find out what it is. Hopefully, Shue will be able to tell us."

Marcus and the men carried the boy back to Sanctuary wondering what had happened at the border.

CHAPTER 54

Myka prayed as she walked along the dirt path that led from her aunt's farm. She loved the peaceful time in the morning when she would walk to work. Myka was in no hurry, taking her time. She reached the end of the dirt path that connected to one of the main roads that led to Thanoton. Myka looked to see if there was a signal. There was.

Myka went over to the fence post and kicked the stick, flat on the ground. She then walked down the road fifty feet to a large tree on the side. Satisfied no one was lurking, she went into the woods another twenty feet. Kneeling, she picked up a certain small rock with a message in it, and read in silence.

M,

Through much prayer and consultation, we have decided we want you to deliver a message to Shobal, the head of the Watchers. The message is to be delivered covertly this morning. "L" will let Samuel know you will be late for work. He will tell him you had to take care of some business. Other Watchers in the city probably will see you. We chose this morning because there is a lot of distraction today with the chaos that happened at the border last night. We'll use that to our advantage.

Destroy the message we gave you earlier to give to Shobal. We have a new message for you to deliver. It is in the market square drop. You can retrieve it when you find out which route to take to the secret chamber. "G" and his men will be watching you in the market square. They do not know the signals on the vegetable cart so they will need to follow you to see what entrance you take. Two of his men are going with you. Also, "G" does not know who all the Watchers are. You will have to point out which one is watching the entrance to the secret passage so he can distract him.

You are the only one in our group that knows the entrances and routes. We need you to give "G" an estimate how long it should take. Use all our standard hand signals to communicate.

Put the message somewhere Shobal will find it—by the door, under the door.

Fight the good fight of faith!

H

Myka walked ten feet away, lit a match, and burned the message along with the old message she had for Shobal.

Myka entered the market square and looked for the vegetable cart. The secret passage that morning was LA4. *Oh, great,* she thought. Myka sat down on a bench. She was slumped over, as she dug through her backpack in front of her. No one saw her retrieve the message stuck underneath the bench, and put it into her backpack. Myka fiddled around a little more, then closed her backpack. She stood up and rubbed two fingers against her face, signaling Gabriel it would take twenty minutes.

Myka made her way through the market square and down a street that circled around the outside of the palace where houses butted up against its stone wall fence. The only exceptions were the front of the palace and specific locations with stairs that led down to the aqueduct under the city. There also was a large service entrance to the back, where all the supplies came in and out of the palace.

Myka walked slowly to the first stairway that led down to the aqueduct checking every so often that she was not followed by anyone other than Gabriel and his men. She also wanted to identify which Watcher was watching. Myka could only see twenty feet in front of her, because of the thick fog. She moved cautiously. She saw the Watcher and slipped back around the corner of a house. She signaled to Gabriel where the Watcher was by pointing with her nose.

To her surprise, the Watcher was immediately jumped, gagged, and hooded. Then, he was taken down the steps to the aqueduct. She wondered what Gabriel and his men were up to, but didn't question it when she saw the smile on Gabriel's face. She went down the stairs and led the way to the entrance. The two men that went with her were dressed like common farmers. It was obvious they had planned on taking the captured Watcher to the secret chamber with them. *Good intimidation factor,* she thought. Everything just seemed so funny. Myka had a hard time trying not to laugh.

Myka skirted along the edge of the aqueduct, which was only one foot wide. The prisoner figured it out right away when they let him slip off and quickly caught him. He became very compliant after that. Pitch black straight ahead, but a sliver of light came from the stairwell behind. Myka could hear as they followed behind her. She shuffled her way around the first corner and started to feel for the drainage pipes that came out of the wall.

The drainage pipes were four feet square wide enough to drain water from the storm drains around the city into the aqueduct. She could hear the water flowing out of them as she counted. *Good thing it isn't raining,* she thought. It would have been nearly impossible to get up the pipes if the water was flowing full force. *We'll get wet, though.* The pipes had water sluicing through, but it wasn't enough to slow them down.

Myka grabbed one of the men by the arm and pulled him close. It was too dark to see. She found his hand and placed it on the edge of the pipe, so he knew where it was. She pulled him into the pipe and made sure he knew to follow. When Myka was confident they were following, she slowly worked her way up the pipe slanting at a forty-five-degree angle. She was small enough where she could ascend on all fours, allowing the water to flow between her legs without getting soaked. The others weren't so lucky and got drenched.

Myka felt overhead for a manhole cover while she ascended the pipe. As soon as she found the metal plate, she pushed up and slid it away revealing some light. She climbed up and reached down to make sure they knew where to get out. It had been ten minutes already; they needed to hurry up. They made their way through a large tunnel toward a light. At the end was a large room with an oil lamp in it. Several hallways led from the room. She thought hard and remembered it was the hallway east of the lamp. No matter what position, the lamp was always north. The easterly hallway from the room led to the inner chamber. The hallway changed daily.

They took the hallway to the east and came to the inner chamber door. She quickly set the message by the door and pointed at her pocket watch. The two men smiled at each other, knocked on the door, and grabbed Myka to run. They just left the prisoner standing by the door, gagged and hooded. It seemed funny as they ran. They could not contain their laughter as they flew into the room with the lamp and headed down the tunnel. They quickly went down the manhole and slid down the pipe, finding the edge. They skirted around the corner to the staircase. It went a lot faster this time.

Gabriel had waited for everyone at the bottom of the stairs. He cast them a weird, inquiring look when he saw them. They tried hard to contain their laughter. They separated as soon as they left the stairwell. Myka took her time as she headed back to the store, laughing the whole way. For some reason, the whole episode was so funny, and the laughter from the other Seekers that came along for security didn't help. She still couldn't believe they knocked on the door and took off running. It was obvious why the Watchers never got anything productive done. They spent all their energy being secretive.

~*~

The guard to the inner chamber looked out the peephole of the thickly wooden door. All he could see was a hooded man.

"Who is it?" Shobal yelled. He came up from his back office.

"They didn't identify themselves," the guard said. "I see—a hooded man outside the door."

"This could be a trap," Shobal whispered. He motioned to the other guards in the inner chamber to get ready to confront whatever lay beyond the door. He sent some guards out another secret entrance to circle around to the front. That team would make contact with the enemy first and yell if they needed help. Shobal did not want to take the risk of compromising the inner chamber by opening the front door.

"Who is it?" the inner chamber guard asked. He responded to the Watchers' special knock.

"Hey, it's us," said one of the guards that had circled around.

"What do you have?" Shobal asked.

"It's a tied-up Watcher and an envelope."

Shobal motioned for the inner chamber guard to open the door. A guard handed Shobal the envelope. It was addressed to him. He watched as his guards took the gag off and untied the Watcher.

"Let me know what he has to say," Shobal said. "I'm going back to my office to read this letter. I'm sure this will answer a lot of our questions."

"I hope so," said the Watcher, now able to talk. "I have no idea what just happened. "

"Stay here for now, until I figure this out," Shobal said on his way back to his office.

Shobal entered and closed the door behind him. He took a seat at his desk, opened the letter, and read.

To Shobal, the head of the Watchers:

We know who you are, where you are, and why you exist. We are a secret organization like yours. We have always known of your existence, and have used that to our advantage. You have some great resources we need. You did not know of our existence. Now you do, and we are asking for your cooperation.

Our group works around and through every organization within Thanoton, just like yours. We are a secret organization hidden out in the open. We will not reveal our leadership or the name of our organization until we trust you. We have even infiltrated your organization. We do not hide under rocks, waiting for something to happen, and do nothing like your organization does. You all sit around and wait instead of being actively engaged. We make it happen because we have been directed by the Light of the Word to liberate this valley. That is exactly what we are doing.

Our job is to prepare this valley for the Three Witnesses' return this spring. We exist to make it the best environment, the most fertile ground to receive the Truth. They will come reap the harvest that all of us and you have helped to prepare. We have a big task ahead of us and need your help. We know you probably have more questions than answers. Those questions will be answered in time.

We have enclosed a booklet we plan on distributing to every family in the valley of Thanoton, except the southern region. This little book should further answer a lot of your questions. The title of the book The History of the Children of Light with excerpts from the Book of Prophecies is self-explanatory. It's a brief history of key doctrines to live by. We need your help hiding numerous boxes of these booklets all over the city. The boxes will be delivered from the west. Then, we will need your help to distribute them all over the city and surrounding towns. We will give you more information later regarding the distribution. We would appreciate it if you did not tell your people about us, yet. Let them think these booklets, and hiding them all over the city, is a Watcher-generated mission. The less they know, the better, as you like to say. Don't worry, we will be with you all the way. We have soldiers and government officials in our organization. The booklets will help to prepare the people for the Three Witnesses.

Like it or not, Myka will be your contact for our organization. Set up some way she can get a message to you, without someone reading it or her going to the inner chamber. Vice versa, you need to be able to get a message to her, without someone else reading it. We know you Watchers like to read each other's messages before they are delivered. We can't afford to have her compromised.

We wait for your response and help with the booklets as soon as possible.

The Light of the Word needs you. We need you—the Children of Light.

Shobal set the message and booklet down and headed out of his office.

"I want you to forget this ever happened and go back to work," Shobal said to the Watcher that had been abducted and gagged. "Do not tell anyone about this."

"I won't," the Watcher said, somewhat surprised.

"That goes for the rest of you too," Shobal said. "This never happened."

"We weren't compromised?" questioned a chamber guard.

"It was just a test," Shobal answered, downplaying it. "You all did a great job; now, get back to work. I don't want to hear another word about this. Am I clear?"

"You're clear," everyone responded.

CHAPTER 55

Maximus hurried to close the gap to the employee's entrance where Mina stood in line. She glanced back and noticed him hurrying towards her, but quickly turned away and acted as if she did not see him.

Maximus mustered up some courage, "Mina."

"Oh, hi," she said quickly, glancing back. Mina went back to fiddling with her large handbag. She was pretending she was getting it ready to be searched when she got up to the gate. It was obvious she was trying to avoid him.

All of a sudden, everything stopped. The main gate opened and a large element of soldiers, along with Javan and some palace guards, rode out.

"I wonder what that was about," Maximus asked.

"You haven't heard?" she asked, walking through the gate. She waited for him.

"No," he said again. "I haven't heard anything."

"The eastern border was attacked last night by the old border guards," Mina said. "A bunch of the new border guards got killed."

"I guess Javan will be gone most of the day."

"That should make your job easier," Mina said as she walked faster. "Well, I have to go."

"Wait," Maximus called.

"Your face is all red. What's wrong?" Mina asked.

"Where do you eat lunch or take a break?"

Mina studied Maximus and said, "It depends on the day, and what's going on, where I take a lunch break. That is if I do. I will let you know when and where I'm going to eat lunch. That is if I want you to know." She smiled and walked away.

Maximus walked slowly up the steps and deposited a message on his way up to the fifth floor.

"Good morning, Maximus," the Fifth said.

"Good morning, sir," Maximus said, looking all around. "It's busy today." He could hear them arguing in the conference room. "I thought with Javan gone there would be no one here."

241

"Tuval is in the conference room with most of the council," the Fifth said. "He leaned over and whispered, "Tread lightly. Everyone is in a bad mood and suspicious of each other."

Maximus stepped to the open door of the conference room. One of the council members held out his mug.

"That is what the prisoner told Javan," Tuval exclaimed. "He said he lives in the city of Sanctuary, two valleys over. And he also said there were secret believers in Thanoton, even in the government."

"Gentlemen, gentlemen, we have to keep in mind he was severely tortured when he said this," Zesha said, as he stroked his pointed beard. "We all know how good Javan is at torturing." He laughed along with the others. "I myself would say anything to get Javan to stop."

"He's right," Tuval agreed. "Javan himself said the boy kept rambling on."

"That is why we need to stay unified and not be so suspicious of each other," Zesha said. "Nothing good will come out of disunity."

"Let's just wait to see what happens and keep our eyes and ears open for secret believers' activity," Tuval agreed.

"Everyone is already talking about it in and around Thanoton," said the head of the market square police. "They are saying there are those that believe in the Li—well, you know."

"No one is to ever say that name," Tuval shouted. "Anyone that does must be arrested."

Zesha motioned with his hand. "We need to be careful we arrest the right people, not someone repeating a rumor. This might be a tactic by the enemy to get us to overreact, which is the same thing I told Javan this morning."

"This meeting is over. Now, go find these outlaws," Tuval spouted out. "Maximus, go tell the Fifth I need to see him. And clean these boards off."

~*~

Zesha sat down in his office and opened up the message he had just retrieved from the lamp.

P,

About the time you read this, we will have already delivered a message to our friend Shobal. As soon as we hear from him, we will get started bringing the booklets here. I'm sure you heard what happened at the border. I will not get into detail on our part. "G" did the best he could in that situation and the prisoner delivered.

The boy, Shue is his name, talked. He told Javan the exact location of Sanctuary. At this point, it does not matter that they know. This old guard distraction helped spread Javan's army thin, and will work to our advantage. Although, I do worry that after we take control of Thanoton, Sanctuary will cause us problems in the future.

Shue also told Javan there are believers everywhere in Thanoton, even in the government. Everyone is talking about it all over the city. I am astonished how it spread like wildfire. I believe the Whisperer is turning everyone's heart and mind to think about the Light of the Word and the Book of Prophecies. I pray their hunger and curiosity grows. The Light of the Word is setting us up perfectly to distribute these booklets. First step, is getting them here. I hope we hear from Shobal soon, so we can get things moving in the right direction. I will keep you informed.

He that wins souls is wise.

H

Zesha leaned back in his chair and smiled.

~*~

Maximus was so glad the day was over. Tuval had ordered him around all afternoon with odd, make-work jobs. It seemed like Tuval was taking his frustrations out on the staff. Maximus did not look forward to the next few days. He had heard Javan would be at the border for several days, in the hopes the enemy would attack again. That meant Maximus was stuck with Tuval in charge.

Maximus exited the employee gate in front of the palace and immediately noticed Mina. She was looking right at him.

"Your face is all red again," she said.

Embarrassed, he asked. "Are you waiting for Anwar?"

"No, I'm actually waiting for you."

"You are?"

"Yeah, I couldn't get away for lunch," Mina said. "Anyway, I heard you were run ragged up on the fifth floor."

"We were," Maximus agreed. He started to relax around her.

"I have to do some shopping around the market square and wondered if you wanted to join me."

"I would love that," Maximus said. His voice cracked with excitement. He did have a message to deliver to Calvin, but at this point, he didn't care. He thought she was the most beautiful girl he had ever seen, with her big brown eyes, pitch black, shiny, smooth hair and her dark olive skin. He looked pale compared to her. *Delivering the message can wait*, he thought. He ignored Gabriel's eyes boring into the back of his neck as they walked through the market.

"You know Anwar is really mad at you," Mina said, jokingly. "He tells everyone it's your fault he's working in the kitchen."

"I know," Maximus said. "He has other people believing that too. I actually feel guilty because I know I did have a part in getting him sent there."

"Don't feel guilty," Mina said. "He was on his last straw with the head steward. You just happened to be there. I've been warning him to keep his mouth shut. He doesn't think before he speaks."

An awkward silence filled the air as they walked around.

"So, what does your father do?" Mina asked.

"My parents are dead," Maximus answered.

"Oh, sorry."

"Don't be. It was a long time ago. I live with an older couple, Calvin and his wife."

"Calvin?" she asked, with a surprised look on her face.

"You know him?"

"N—no."

"Is something wrong?" Maximus asked.

"Oh, no. I was just thinking about something else," Mina said, as she glanced around the market square.

Maximus noticed she was trying to act preoccupied. "What about your father? Where does he work?"

"Maximus I need to go," Mina said. "I will see you later."

"Wait. What's wrong?"

"Maximus, I need to go. Now leave me alone."

"Mina, did I say something wrong?"

Mina turned around, grabbed Maximus by the arm, and whispered, "My parents are missing. I don't want to ever talk about what we just talked about again. We need to stay away from each other. It's best for our safety." Mina let go and left.

Maximus could not believe it. Mina was a Seeker.

CHAPTER 56

"Good morning, Myka," Samuel waited in front of the store for her.

"Good morning, Samuel, is everything all right?"

"I need to talk to you in the back room right away."

"Okay," she said. Myka wondered what this was all about. Samuel walked as fast as he could to the back.

He closed the door behind her. "I got a message from Shobal this morning with information. You are to pass it on to some people he assumes you know. Also, there is a sealed message from him to you."

"For me?" she asked, acting all surprised. "I thought I was out of the picture, and Shobal didn't trust me."

"Apparently, that has all changed," he said. "Here. Read the message yourself, and here is the sealed envelope." Samuel sat down.

Myka opened up the message and read.

S,

"Activate all the Watchers. We have a vital mission that involves everyone. We are going to cache boxes of booklets, from the west. I have written down different, secret locations on the second page. This will all be done to later distribute them to every household in Thanoton. From the first shipment, I want every Watcher to get a booklet. Read it and hide it.

Give "M" the list of drop-off locations with the instructions for each particular place. There are verbal, as well as visual signals to know if it is safe to drop off and receive. She knows who the list goes to, and no other Watcher needs to know who she gives it to. She can tell them the drop-off locations will be ready, starting tonight. "S," make sure that happens.

There is a wax-sealed envelope for "M." No one is to open that but her. Anyone else that opens it will come up missing. She is to read it when no one else is around.

Read the booklet.

Now faith is the substance of things hoped for, the evidence of things not seen.

SH

Myka smiled and looked at the second page with the list of drop-off locations and instructions. She had a warm, happy feeling. The liberation of the valley was close. Soon, she would get to see her friends Jared, Dara, and Ezra.

"Do you have a copy of this list?" Myka said while she held up the second page.

"I do," Samuel nodded. "He sent two copies with the message. How do you know who to give the list to?"

Myka shrugged her shoulders. "I don't remember how I know exactly, but I think from a past mission with Storekeeper."

Samuel looked satisfied with the answer and got up to go. "Well, I better get started setting this up," he said. He folded up the list and shoved it into his boot. "Let me know if you need anything."

"I will," Myka said. She waited for Samuel to close the door. She broke the seal and pulled the message out.

M,

This is how you, your superiors, and I can communicate with each other. This will avoid messengers or you coming to me.

On the west side of the market square, next to the palace wall, are three benches that are spread out. The second bench straddles an iron grate. The bench sits centered over the grate. When you have a message, simply drop it down the grate. I have a wire net a foot below, to catch it before it hits the bottom of the drainage pipe. If I have a message for you, the bench will not be centered over the grate. It will be offset a little. It will be easy for you to see at a distance because you will be looking for it. The message will be wedged underneath. It will be in between the frame and the wood, on the left-hand side.

Everything is set up for the cache of the boxes, starting tonight. I await further instructions on their distribution. I do have a good idea on how to distribute them quickly and efficiently, assuming you have people that will help also. Let me know if you would like to hear my plan.

SH

Myka was surprised how fast Shobal came around and was convinced they were all on the same side. He must have waited and prayed for the Light of the Word to show him what to do next. Then, this all came about. Myka was a little jealous he read the booklet before she did. She knew how Calvin wrote. He was a scholar, bringing out scriptural Truth in such a practical way. He only wrote Truth that came from the *Book of Prophesies* and not from any human invention. She couldn't wait to read it.

Myka folded all the messages up, along with the list of drop-off sites, and placed them in her pocket to pass. *There is no need for me to write out another message. These two say it all.* Myka only had to wait an hour before she heard Lot stop his wagon out front.

"Whoa, whoa," Lot commanded. He stepped down and came into the store. "Hello, my friends. How is everyone today?"

"Good," Samuel answered. "Here to pick up supplies?"

"I sure am." He pulled out a list.

"What's going on at the border?" Samuel asked.

"They are fortifying the defensive positions. I guess they're getting ready for an attack," Lot said, as he shrugged his shoulders. "They just need a bunch of food supplies. Eventually, they will want to replace all the building materials that got burned up."

"Well let me know, so I have time to coordinate it."

"I certainly will," Lot said. "There's my favorite of favorites."

"Hello, Lot," Myka said. She walked up and gave him a big hug. She was unable to pass the message off with Samuel so close. She couldn't help but notice how interested Samuel was in what she was doing after they received the message from Shobal. Lot sensed her hesitation.

"Will you help me fill this order, my favorite of favorites?"

"Of course, let's go," she said. Myka took the list from Lot, hooked her arm around his, and headed to the other side of the store.

Myka gathered the supplies into a basket and waited until no one was around before she slipped Lot the message. She squeezed his arm. They loaded the supplies, and Lot left.

Samuel came up to Myka and whispered, "Everything should be set for tonight. All the Watchers are eager to do something. Are you set on your end of things?"

"Oh, yeah. I took care of it right away," she said, in a way Samuel knew not to ask any more questions.

~*~

Lot sat across from Calvin in his house. He waited for him to finish reading the messages. Myka had just passed them to him less than a half-hour ago.

"Good," Calvin said. He looked up and took off his reading glasses. "I want you to give this to Kern right away."

"I will," Lot agreed. "If he leaves the market square now, he can be in Pistio before nightfall. That should be enough time to get all the transporters and the boxes ready to ship."

"We could get a lot of booklets here tonight," Calvin said.

"This would be the perfect night to deliver as many wagonloads as we can, with the army preoccupied at the border. I will let Gabriel know the drop-off locations, so he'll have his men stationed in the area and not Javan's."

"Speaking of Gabriel," Calvin said, changing his tone, "tell him no, on his last request. Absolutely not!"

"What was his request?" Lot asked, somewhat surprised by Calvin's anger.

"He requested permission to take his Ghost Team and attack the eastern cut again. This time he wants to kill Javan and Arton, making it look like the rogue border guards from Sanctuary. He wanted to do it tonight since Javan and his guards are there right now. Neither I nor Zesha, want him to do that. Gabriel seems to think our mission is to take over Thanoton militarily by eliminating the leadership."

Lot thought about it for a minute, and said, "The thing is, we have come down to the wire. What are we going do with Javan? Do you think he will voluntarily step down, and let Ezra take his place?"

"We don't know how we will handle that yet," Calvin calmly said. "Our next priority is getting the booklets here. That is where we need to concentrate. You need to get going. We're wasting time."

CHAPTER 57

The next morning, Maximus headed down to the basement to hang up his coat and heard Anwar screaming below.

"Let go of me," Anwar yelled. "You're hurting me."

"What's going on?" Maximus asked as he got to the bottom of the stairs. The palace guards had Anwar face down on the floor trussing his hands behind his back.

"This does not concern you, boy," said a guard.

"Who are you calling boy?" Maximus spouted out, which surprised everyone, including himself.

The guard shoved Maximus to the ground. The head steward quickly grabbed Maximus as he stood back up before he did anything else stupid.

"Maximus, stay out of this," the head steward said. "This does not concern you."

Maximus heard Anwar, as he was dragged up the stairs by the palace guards, "What have you done with Mina? Where is she?"

"Mina," Maximus asked. "What's going on?"

"Apparently last night, Mina tried to smuggle, some forbidden material out of the palace," said the head steward. "They have her locked up on the west wing of the third floor. She's been there all night. They are probably arresting Anwar to see what he knows."

"Wh—what are they going to do to her?" asked Maximus, barely able to talk. He trembled from the weight of fear that gripped him. The horror of what could happen to Mina. He felt like life had ended. He had known this dread once before when his parents were killed. Maximus determined at that moment, he would not lose anyone else he cared for. He had had enough.

"I don't know what they are going to do," said the head steward, patting Maximus' shoulder. "We know it won't be good. They went to get Javan so he can interrogate her. They won't even let us bring food to her."

"Let me try."

"No, I won't let you," the head steward said. "You need to head up to the fifth floor where you are assigned and forget about this."

On his way up, Maximus could see a group of guards down the west wing on the third floor. They were guarding a room at the end of the hall. He couldn't just sit back and do nothing. He had to try to get her out, or else he would regret the rest of his life that he never tried. Maximus swallowed hard. When Javan tortured someone, it was usually to death.

"Didn't I tell you to stay away?" shouted the guard that had shoved him earlier.

"I want to see Mina," Maximus commanded.

They all laughed. One of the guards stuck the tip of his sword on Maximus chest, and said, "The only thing you are going to see is my sword."

"Where do you work, boy?" said another guard.

"I work directly for Javan on the fifth floor," Maximus answered.

"Sure," one said, as the others laughed.

"I will be back with permission to bring her food," Maximus said. He shoved the sword away. "I'll be back, Mina!" he shouted, hoping she would hear. He headed back upstairs, and as soon as he entered the outer room, he heard Zesha and Tuval in a shouting match.

"Quit trying to cover for her," Tuval shouted. "She had forbidden material."

"I told her to bring me that material," Zesha pleaded. "She just forgot it was in her bag. It's my fault. She was following my orders."

"That's not what she told us," Tuval countered. "She said she acted alone. She just wanted to take it home and read it."

"She is just trying to protect me," Zesha said. "You need to release her now!"

"Who do you think you're talking to Zesha?" I'm second-in-command under Javan. He will determine if she acted alone or if there was some sort of conspiracy. We know she's like a daughter to you. She obviously used that to her advantage, to pull the wool over your eyes and get access to the forbidden material."

"You're wrong."

"That's enough," Tuval said. "I'm warning you."

"Or what?" Zesha said as he leaned into Tuval's face.

"Guard," Tuval shouted out. "Escort the chief investigator out of the room. I don't want you back up here, until Javan talks to you. You are not allowed to visit her."

"Sir, can I take some food to Mina?" Maximus said as he stood in the doorway.

"What has gotten into everyone?" Tuval shouted. "What's so special about this girl?" As Zesha was escorted out, Tuval made eye contact with him then he said, "All right Maximus, you have permission to bring her food. Only you can. No one else."

Maximus gathered up some food at his serving table. In a basket, he put bread, cheese, and fruit. He contemplated whether to hide one of the many knives he had on the table for cutting meat, cheese, and bread into the basket. He hid one of the knives in the small of his back, wedged inside his belt. He determined this trip would be to investigate, to see the best way to get her out. He needed Gabriel's help.

"You're back again," said one of the guards.

"I told you I would be," Maximus said.

"He has permission to bring her food from Tuval," said a guard that had escorted him from the fifth floor.

Maximus laughed at the looks on their faces. He rubbed it in. "Now, let me in."

"It doesn't matter to me if the traitor dies with a full or empty stomach," said a guard. All the other guards laughed.

Maximus ignored them and went in. A candle by the door cast a ray of light into the room. He could barely see Mina's feet in the light; the rest of her body was covered in a dark shadow. She sat on the floor in the corner of the room with her back against the wall.

"Mina—Mina, its Maximus," he said, as he knelt down beside her. He heard the door close, so he got the candle and brought it over. His heart sank as he saw her face, wet from endless crying, and her left eye swollen shut. She had bruises on her arms, and her wrists were bleeding from the tight restraints.

"Maximus, is that you?" she said, barely audible.

"Yes, it's me. I brought you some food and water." He held up a cup of water to her lips, and she choked to get as much as she could down her throat. He refilled it, and let her suck down more. She became more alert as the water refreshed the life in her. She slowed down in her drinking but didn't want Maximus to stop with the water.

Maximus leaned over, and whispered, "I'm going to get you out of here. I have a plan."

"Maximus, don't do anything stupid," she gasped. "Don't compromise the mission. We are so close."

"I'm going to get you out."

"Maximus, you have to tell Anwar to leave," Mina said.

"I will," Maximus answered. He didn't have the heart to tell her he was also detained.

"Promise me, you will make him go to Pistio or out of the valley?" she begged. She studied Maximus with her one good eye, to make sure of him.

"I promise," he answered. He broke her gaze and grabbed the basket. He set it next to her, along with the pitcher of water. "You need to eat and get your strength up."

The door opened, and a guard stuck his head in. "What's taking so long? She can feed herself. Now, get out of here and put the candle back."

"I'll be back later," Maximus said to Mina.

A slight smile lifted the non-swollen side of her face. Maximus left. He could not believe someone would do this to her. Only the worst and weakest kind of man would ever hit a woman. There was never a justifiable reason. That was never tolerated where he came from and was severely punished. They were the worst kind of men; men that were morally weak. His lips thinned in resolve; they needed to pay.

Maximus marched down to the basement to find the head steward. He entered his office.

"What can I do for you, Maximus?" the head steward questioned, startled by how Maximus barged into his office without knocking.

"I need to go home early," Maximus stated. And before the head steward could say another word, he said, "I am going home early."

The head steward sensed this was not up for debate. He could tell Maximus was not in his usual state of mind, so he said, "Fine, go ahead. I will send someone up to replace you." He would deal with Maximus another day.

Maximus grabbed his coat and left the palace. He searched around the market square until he found the person he was looking for.

"Gabriel, I need to talk to you right now," Maximus said.

"What? No hello or greeting?" Gabriel grinned. After seeing the young man's expression, he realized something was seriously wrong. "Follow me. We'll find a private place to talk." They went to the opposite side of the square where no venders and people were.

"What's wrong?"

"Mina, this girl that works in the palace, is locked up by Javan's men. She's been beaten badly. Javan is on his way back to torture her. He will kill her. Did you know she was one of us?"

"Yes, I know," Gabriel, answered. "I heard about it."

"What are you going to do about it?"

"Nothing," Gabriel said. He was ashamed at his response and the disappointment he saw in Maximus' face.

"Nothing?" Maximus repeated. "She was obviously smuggling out that material for Calvin. I always wondered how he got it."

"Look, Maximus," Gabriel said, while he grabbed his shoulders. "When I heard she was caught, I wanted to go in right away and rescue her. I still want to. I feel obligated; I trained her. But, Calvin and the top Seeker on the inside forbade me to do it."

"Who is this Seeker?" Maximus asked.

"I have no idea," Gabriel answered. "He must be on the council. He is probably trying to get her released."

"You have to help me," Maximus pleaded.

"They are afraid if we do this, it will look like we took over Thanoton militarily like we planned a coup. The Elders want the people to influence the change from the lowest level. This is as it should be, not influenced from the top down."

"We are only talking about getting her out, not taking over the government."

"Maximus, in an operation like this, we would end up killing a lot of the guards. They can't know who we are. If they see us, we have to kill them. Otherwise, they will identify us later. It's a big risk. Should we sacrifice one life or many lives? Everyone knows Mina won't talk. She can't be broken.

"What about Anwar, her brother?"

"He doesn't know a thing," Gabriel said. "She never told him any of this."

"I'm going anyway," Maximus said. He pushed himself away from Gabriel.

"You better not," Gabriel said. "I will stop you if you try."

"How?" Maximus said. "I'll be in the palace working."

"Wait."

"I have to get back to work," Maximus said as he walked away.

Maximus reentered the palace and went down to the basement to check in with the head steward.

"Maximus, you're back," said the head steward. He ran into him at the bottom of the steps.

"Sorry, sir. I just needed some fresh air. I feel better now. Can I go back to work?"

"Sure," said the head steward. "Go ahead and send your replacement back down."

CHAPTER 58

Myka glanced up and noticed Gabriel watching her as she worked in the front of the store. He stood out front and motioned with his head for her to follow him. Then, he disappeared into the fog.

Myka found Samuel in the back. "Is it all right if I take a break? I feel like taking a walk." She would go anyway, but she asked to be polite. Myka knew Samuel could never say no to her.

"Sure, go ahead," he glanced at her; a slightly suspicious expression creased his forehead.

"Good. I won't be that long," Myka said. She headed out front to catch up to Gabriel.

When they saw each other, Gabriel kept ahead, and Myka followed. They walked to the other side of the market square, where he had been with Maximus earlier. There were no venders or people around. Myka noticed right away there were numerous western army soldiers there for security. *Probably, members of the ghost team*, she thought.

"I thought we were never to meet out in the open like this," Myka said, as she sat on the bench.

Gabriel looked around and sat next to her. "We aren't supposed to meet. This needs to stay between us."

"This isn't sanctioned?"

"No. Our leaders don't know about this," he said. "I need your help."

"I don't know about this," Myka said. "I don't like to break protocol. I'm only allowed to get my orders from Lot. That's how I know if a mission is legitimate or not. It's my authentication." Myka started to get up.

"Wait," Gabriel said, as he grabbed her arm. Just hear me out first, before you make your decision. If you don't want to do it after I explain it to you, then fine. We will be able to accomplish it without you."

"Okay what is it?" she asked.

"Promise me first, before I tell you, no matter what, you will not mention this conversation ever again."

"Oh, great. Another secret," Myka commented. "I promise."

"I have two Seekers that I trained working in the palace. A girl named Mina and a boy named Maximus."

"The girl that got caught with the forbidden books?" Myka inquired.

"That's right," Gabriel responded.

"I figured she was a Seeker after I heard about it."

"All three of you were selected and trained in different locations so you would not know each other. It keeps everything compartmentalized and less risk. You got placed in Thanoton first. Then, shortly after, Mina did. She and Maximus are a few years younger than you. Maximus just started, and he has done a good job, up until now I'm afraid."

"I didn't think Maximus was quite ready emotionally and tactically for his present assignment. His fighting skills are not where they should be. But we needed him after we lost some of our Seekers, so he was thrown into the lion's den. He actually has done a great job, regardless of his incomplete training. Anyway, somehow Mina and Maximus found out each other were Seekers."

"How?" Myka asked.

"I have no idea," Gabriel answered. "They also like each other."

"Like boyfriend, girlfriend?"

"Yeah, Maximus loves her," Gabriel said. "I can tell."

"That might cause some problems," Myka said.

"It already has," Gabriel agreed. "He is not a mission-first person, like you. All he cares about right now is freeing Mina. He was here earlier trying to solicit my help."

"So, you told him you would?" Myka questioned, surprised.

"No, I didn't," Gabriel said. "I told him no. I don't want him involved in what I'm about to do. His emotions and instability would get him killed. I want to ghost ride Mina, without anyone finding out—not even Maximus so he can complete the mission without distraction. If I don't free her, I'm afraid Maximus will try. He'll probably get killed in the process."

"What about the Seeker that's supposedly in a high position in the palace? What's he doing?" Myka asked.

"I have no idea," Gabriel answered. "I don't know who it is."

"Oh, I thought you knew."

"I wish I did."

"So what's the plan?" Myka asked, giving him a smile. She knew Maximus was probably a lot like Gabriel. He would do anything for the people he loved.

"Right now the palace security is at a minimum, due to all that has happened at the border, and so many soldiers and guards killed lately. They are stretched thin. They no longer man the east and west wall, only the south and front entrances. They do have a patrol that sporadically checks the grounds in between the wall and the palace."

"How many?" Myka asked.

"It's usually two to three men," Gabriel answered. "Some nights it has been only one roving guard."

Myka nodded.

"Since my team is soldiers assigned to the market square police, we can legitimately enter the palace. That is what we plan to do tonight. We are going to wait till it is night. Most of the workers have gone home by then. We will enter in at different times, so as not to be too suspicious. I will place my men at strategic points for security, and a couple of us will kill the guards that are watching Mina and get her out."

"What do you need me for?"

"The problem with the plan is getting her out of the castle without someone finding out," Gabriel said. "At the end of the west wing where Mina is being held, is a window enclosed by shutters, locked from the outside. Obviously, they were made that way, to keep prisoners from escaping. The window is right next to the holding area. We need someone with expert climbing ability to scale the outer wall of the palace. Then, unlatch that shutter so we can open the window. If we broke the window, it would leave too much evidence. We want to leave no trace, to slow them down in their investigation later. You're probably the only one I know that could make a climb like that. It's a rock wall with very little foot and finger holds, all the way up to the window."

"You're going to lower her out the window?" Myka asked.

"That's the plan. We will lower her when we get a clear signal from you. You will also have one of my men with you to provide security and help. He will stay hidden until needed. Then we want both of you to take her, along with the rope, to the far end of the west wall and hoist her over. The soldier with you will take her to a wagon around the corner, heading west. You will be done after you climb over the west wall. Go straight home."

"What time do you want me to do all of this?" Myka asked.

"One hour after pitch black, you will meet the soldier at the far west wall. Then both of you can proceed and unlock the shutter. We will give you thirty minutes to accomplish it. Just unlatch it. Don't open. Climb back down and hide. Then, when you see us open the window, come out where we can see you. Give us the signal when it's clear to lower her. Once she's lowered and you have control, we will close everything up, lock the dead guards in the room, and go out the rear supply entrance in the basement." Gabriel paused for a moment. "So, will you do it?"

"I guess I will," she answered.

"Again, you can't tell anyone, and you have to kill any enemy soldier that sees you. We can't be compromised."

She grabbed his arm. "Gabriel, you know what this means, don't you? I mean if we kill soldiers in the palace?"

"I know," he jerked a nod, "but it can't be helped."

"I understand," Myka agreed. "I know the drill."

"Good," Gabriel said, getting up. "I will see you tonight."

CHAPTER 59

Maximus heard a guard enter the conference room and tell Tuval that Javan was back.

"Good. Where is he?" Tuval asked.

"He wants you to meet him on the third floor," the guard said. "He wants to interrogate the prisoner right away."

"Let's go," Tuval responded and left with the guard.

Maximus didn't know what to do. He was hoping Javan wouldn't be back until later that night. It was the end of the day, and most of the workers were still there. He decided he would try to interrupt the interrogation by bringing her food. Maximus wasn't sure that would actually do anything, but he had to do something. He wished he would have tried to get Mina out earlier.

While Maximus loaded a basket of food, a brilliant idea came to him. If he got into the room and killed Javan, he could then overpower Tuval and take him prisoner. Tuval was a little, frail, old man. Maximus was confident he could easily take control of him. The guards would not try to stop him for fear he would slit Tuval's throat. Once out of the palace, he would steal a wagon and head out west. Then, the Seekers would be forced to ghost ride him and Mina.

Maximus hid a large knife used to slice cheese in the bottom of the basket. The thick blade was twelve inches long and super sharp. It was heavy with a large wooden handle. Maximus still had the other knife concealed in the small of his back. He left to go to the third floor with a basket in one hand and a pitcher in the other.

Maximus' anger grew, as he could hear Mina screaming and Javan yelling. He couldn't take it anymore. It had to stop.

"What are you doing here again?" a guard asked.

"I'm here to bring food," Maximus answered.

"Look, Javan and Tuval are interrogating the prisoner. Can't you hear?" The guard laughed and said, "I'm sure they do not want to stop to let the prisoner eat."

"They do," Maximus lied. "They asked me to bring some food," he said shrugging his shoulders.

"They never said anything," a guard said, as he opened the door.

Javan stopped and growled, "What is it?"

Maximus dropped the basket when he saw Mina curled up on the floor. She was nothing but cuts, blood, and torn clothes from a leather whip Javan was using. Her very life breathed out agony. Mina groaned out in the deepest of pain. She was bleeding to death.

"What is this?" Tuval said, grabbing the pitcher out of Maximus' hand before he dropped it too.

"I—I brought some food for you," Maximus said, as he felt himself step beyond this realm to a peace that passes all understanding. He had a moment of clarity and saw things as they really were. This was it for him, and that was okay.

"Put the food over there and leave," Javan said. He raised the whip up and struck Mina as hard as he could. The whip cut into her hands, protecting her face.

Maximus set the basket down on the table, dug out the knife, and turned around. Both Javan and Tuval stood with their backs toward him, looking down at Mina. He lunged quickly closing the gap to Javan. Maximus thrust the knife into Javan's side between the front and back plate of his metal armor. Javan reacted out of instinct and spun around. He grabbed Maximus by the throat, pulling his own sword out. He thrust it as hard as he could into Maximus' body. Javan had stuck him so hard, the sword protruded out his back.

Maximus gasped for air he couldn't breathe in. His eyes widened as if he was looking at something beyond. Then, he fell to the floor dead.

"Guards!" Tuval yelled. "Get the doctor, and bring me a stretcher to carry Javan up to his quarters," he said, as he tried to help balance Javan.

Javan was still in unbelief over what had just happened. He stumbled, wondering what to do next. "Pull the knife out of my side," he sputtered. Tuval grabbed and yanked. Javan fell over. The guards came in and rolled Javan onto the stretcher.

Javan took a deep breath, and commanded Tuval, "I want you to put extra security up here and around the palace. I have a feeling others will try to break this girl and Maximus out if they think they are still alive. Don't tell anyone they're dead. Set a trap and keep the extra security hidden. It's obvious we have infiltrators right under our noses."

"The girl is still breathing slightly. Do you want me to finish her off?" a guard asked.

"No," Tuval answered. "She can suffer the last few minutes of her life."

The door closed. Mina, with every bit of strength she could muster, slowly reached over and touched Maximus. She could feel his warm blood as it seeped around her arm. "Light of the Word, forgive them, for they do not know what they are doing. We give you our spirits, oh, Lord," said Mina. She felt herself leaving. The pain stopped. The peace came, and she drifted off into eternal rest.

~*~

Gabriel and his men had entered the palace at different times. They waited the last few minutes to make sure Myka would have enough time to unlatch the outer shutter. Gabriel noticed security around the palace seemed to be abnormal. Only one guard was posted outside of the prisoner room. He finally found a guard he had befriended in the last week, and asked him, "Is something going on?"

"Didn't you hear?" the guard said.

"No, I didn't."

"The prisoner is dead and so is Maximus," the guard said. "He was one of them. Maximus wounded Javan pretty badly, but I guess Javan will recover. The knife went into the meaty part of his back, missing the vitals. He is in his quarters."

"Oh, no," Gabriel said. "Not Maximus."

"They are setting a trap, hoping the enemy will come and try to break them out. I'll see you later."

Even though Gabriel knew this whole thing was a trap, he must warn Myka. At this point, she was waiting for them to open the window.

They decided to go down to the west wing and kill the guard outside the door and the ones waiting in the room. Then, they would quickly open the window to warn Myka, close it back up, and leave. Gabriel and his men would have a distinct advantage because the guards didn't suspect fellow soldiers.

Suddenly, they heard shouting outside the palace, as they approached the guard at the end of the hallway.

"There, over there!"

"We got them!"

The guard by the door smiled at Gabriel, went over and opened up the window, and pushed open the shutter. He turned to Gabriel. "One of the guards outside recently noticed the shutter was unlatched, so they have been searching the grounds."

Gabriel stuck his head out and could see soldiers with torches searching the whole area. He searched until he spotted one of his men lying there full of arrows, Myka's security.

Below he heard, "Keep searching."

Gabriel searched some more until his heart sank. Myka was laying flat on her stomach, not moving with three arrows in her back. He turned around, and his men could tell what had happened. By this time, four guards had left the room where Mina and Maximus were laying dead. The guards were all staring at the action below the window.

Gabriel motioned to his men, and they killed all the guards by the window. They closed it back up. Gabriel stopped by the doorway but didn't enter. He watched as one of his men checked to see if Maximus or Mina had a pulse. The soldier shook his head. Gabriel wiped a tear from his eye and said to his men, "Tonight we take Thanoton." They headed up to the fifth floor.

CHAPTER 60

Zesha sat in his office, tormented that Mina was being tortured by Javan. He knew how evil Javan could be when he tortured. By now, Mina was either dead or wished she was. He felt helpless, unable to convince them to release her.

Javan and Tuval figured Zesha would say anything to save her, thinking he was deceived and manipulated by Mina. Never having a family and kids was his weakness, they agreed. "He actually thinks Mina is like a daughter to him," Tuval told Javan. They both laughed, and Javan said, "She'll be a dead daughter."

It was true. Zesha was very old, and he had never married. He was a Seeker that had worked his way up through the ranks to become a trusted advisor. He had dedicated his life to preparing for the Children of Light to regain the valley of Thanoton for the Light of the Word. And for this, it had cost him a lot of luxuries others took for granted, like a family. So, when Mina became his helper, she was like a daughter to him. He enjoyed having her around in the dreariness of serving Javan. Killing Mina was like killing a part of him.

Zesha heard a knock at the door. He wiped the tears from his eyes, "What is it?"

"I have the information you requested," a guard said.

"Come in," Zesha responded.

"The prisoner is dead, along with Maximus who tried to save her," the guard said.

"Maximus?" Zesha inquired.

"Yes, the Maximus that serves in the conference room, that Maximus. He severely wounded Javan with a butcher knife. I guess Javan will recover from the knife wound, but he will be bedridden for a long time."

Zesha sat there, stunned for a minute in unbelief.

"Investigator Zesha?" said the guard to get Zesha's attention. When he saw that Zesha was paying attention to him, he repeated his question. "Is that it, or do you need me for something else?"

"One more thing," Zesha said as he stood up. "Tell Gabriel the western commander, to take both of their bodies to Pistio. He'll know what to do, and then you can go."

Zesha waited for the door to close. He opened the top drawer to the desk and took out his dagger. It had a thin eight-inch blade that looked more like an ice pick. He shoved the dagger in between his belt and pants on his right side. His coat went over the top to conceal its location. He headed down the hall to Javans' quarters. He entered the outer room and passed the guards stationed in the hallway.

"I came right away when I heard the terrible news," Zesha said to Tuval outside of Javan's room.

"It was terrible," Tuval said, shaking his head. "That boy almost killed Javan. Although, Javan got the last laugh and killed him."

"I need to tell you something," Zesha said. He whispered and motioned that he did not want the guards out in the hallway to hear what he wanted to tell him.

Tuval came in close. "What is it?" he whispered.

Zesha immediately grabbed Tuval by the back of the neck and pulled, while he thrust the eight-inch blade as far as he could puncturing his spleen. Zesha stared into Tuval's widened eyes, the eyes of someone that knew he was dead. He said, "This is for Mina, and the rest of the Seekers that are taking back this kingdom." He lowered him to the floor and hid him behind some furniture. Zesha hid his dagger again and entered Javan's room, closing the door behind him.

When Zesha approached Javan, his eyes opened slightly as he awakened out of sleep. A slight smile entered his face when he saw Zesha standing next to his bed. The smile quickly changed to fear when Zesha, in one motion, grabbed Javan by the throat while he shoved the dagger into Javan's eyeball. The blade entered his brain, killing him instantly. Zesha stood there holding the dagger, mesmerized. He was awakened out of his daze by the fighting he heard in the hallway. Zesha felt someone enter the room behind him. He turned around and saw Gabriel standing there with his sword drawn. The blade dripped with blood.

~*~

"Keep searching," commanded the soldier in charge of the squad patrolling the grounds around the palace. "There are more out there. Don't worry about them; they're already dead."

Zion ran past one of the bodies on his way to the west wall. He recognized the outline of the backpack lying next to one of the intruders. He went to take a closer look because it was pitch black. He kneeled down and checked out the backpack. *It's Myka's*, he thought. He felt the body and took a closer look. *Oh no. It is Myka.* Her body was warm, and she moved slightly. *She's alive!*

"Myka, can you hear me?" Zion whispered.

Barely audible, she said, "Zion, is that you?"

"Yes, it's me," he said. "I have to get you out of here fast, before the other soldiers come back."

"Help me," she gasped.

Zion picked Myka up and threw her over his shoulder, holding her with his right arm. He was careful not to bump the three arrows still in her back. With his left hand, he grabbed her backpack and took off running for the western wall. At the wall, they hid and waited for some soldiers to pass before Zion scaled the wall with Myka.

"Zion."

"What?"

"On the other side of this wall, there are three benches. The middle one has a drainage grate underneath it. I want you to stick me down in it, cover it back up, and forget about me."

"Stick you down in the sewer?" Zion protested. "You need a doctor."

"Trust me, Zion," she said, leaning her face up against his chest. "Just do it! Promise me."

"Okay. Let's go," he said and picked her back up.

Myka felt herself drifting off, as she dangled over Zion's shoulder. She fought the urge not to pass out; she started to feel comfortable. The pain distanced as her mind drifted to her three friends Jared, Dara, and Ezra. Soon Ezra would be the next king of Thanoton, and that thought brought her a smile. She felt herself floating through the northern city toward a warm light. It energized her love for the Light of the Word.

"Myka, Myka," Zion whispered, trying to get her attention. He could hear soldiers around the corner, coming his way. He quickly removed the grate and slid Myka down in the dark tunnel, along with her backpack. He covered the grate and scaled back over the western wall. Zion was terrified. He didn't know if Myka was alive or dead. He didn't have time to check.

Zion sat down on the other side of the wall and thought about what he should do for Myka. He decided the next night, he would slip down in the tunnel and try to help her, if she was still alive.

I wish there was a god, he thought. *If there is a god out there, please, please, I beg you. Save Myka!*

Myka struggled to take a deep breath, and called out, "Help! Shobal, help!

"Who's there?" she heard in the distance, then the pattering of footsteps.

PART THREE

CHAPTER 61

"Zion, there you are," said Assam as he ran by. He stopped and went back to Zion. Assam had been looking for Zion ever since they were parted in the chaos. "What are you doing sitting down? Are you hurt?"

"No, I'm not hurt," Zion answered, still distraught that Myka might be dead.

"Hey, relax! What's wrong?" Assam asked. "Where did you go? I've been looking all over for you."

"I'll tell you later," Zion answered, frustrated by all the questions.

Assam crouched down in the shadows when he heard voices. He saw the light reflected off the torches as they came near. He whispered, "We have to get out of here. The intruders have killed Javan and taken over the palace. A lot of the soldiers have defected to their side."

"Really?"

"It's hard to tell who is on what side," Assam whispered. "The soldiers are fighting against each other. What should we do?"

Assam always looked to Zion to guide him, ever since they were drafted into the army together. Zion was only one month older, but he reacted better under pressure. Zion's quick thinking and blind luck had gotten them out of many tough situations. Assam always thought something or someone was protecting Zion.

They both were sixteen, the youngest soldiers in their platoon. Zion and Assam stuck together and became the best of friends. They worked well together. Assam was taller, stronger, and more athletic with a contagious smile, but he needed to be pushed. Zion would always push Assam because he thought Assam was lazy. Zion was aggressive and took it upon himself to motivate Assam. They both sported the same military haircut. Zion's hair was black, and Assam's was brown.

"We need to go east toward the swamp. We can hide out in the thick woods until this is all sorted out," Zion said, regaining his confidence. "Then we'll join whoever is in charge."

"Good idea," Assam agreed, leaning closer.

"If we get split up, let's link up at the southwest intersection of the eastern route," Zion added. They both knew that meant for them to hide in the woods two hundred feet from the southwest corner of the intersection, not visible from the road. If for some reason it was not a safe place to hide, they would rotate clockwise to another corner until they found a good spot. If the southwest corner was compromised, they would go on to the northwest corner. This way they would have a safe place, easy for both of them to find. It was a quick contingency plan, just in case they had to split up.

"Okay," Assam said. "But let's try to stay together." He did not want to split up again.

Zion stood up and looked around to see if the coast was clear. "Follow me," he whispered.

Zion climbed just far enough to clear the top of the wall, so as to see if it was safe to go over. He could see to his left a bunch of soldiers with torches at the front gate two hundred feet away. Down on the other end of the market square, he heard shouts and swords clanking. They needed to cut in between them, to get to the woods on the other side.

Zion knew there were many objects that would provide good cover as they bounded across. There were stands and wagons used for selling goods, all closed up for the night. He couldn't see them because of the dark, but he would use all of it to his advantage to make it across, without being detected.

Zion motioned for Assam to follow, and slide down on the other side. He waited for Assam to join him. When Zion felt the squeeze on his arm, he knew Assam was ready to go. They had learned how to communicate without talking in the army. Zion moved out setting a good pace, making sure Assam stayed close. They maneuvered around some carts located in the middle of the square and froze when they heard some noise. To the front was an outline of a person leaning up against the side of a wagon. They crouched behind and waited. Satisfied that no one had heard them, they backed out and maneuvered around.

"I got you!" shouted a soldier that grabbed Zion from the side.

Zion immediately swept his arm underneath the soldier's left arm, twisting it over. The soldier lost his grip. Zion heard a crack in the solder's arm as he drove him to the ground. Assam hit the soldier in the back of the head with the blunt, metal handle of his sword, which knocked him out. Another soldier came at them and thrust his sword at Assam, missing. Assam spun out of the way, grabbed the soldier, and threw him against the wagon. He toppled to the ground. They heard soldiers coming their way.

"Go as fast as you can to the link-up," whispered Zion, breaking the silence. "I'll meet you there."

Assam ran as fast as he could, zigzagging through the market square to get to the woodline. On his way, he knocked a soldier over. This made a lot of noise, alerting the pursuers.

Zion could hear a group of soldiers chasing after Assam. He was in trouble, and Zion knew he wasn't close enough to help. He had gone a different direction when they split up. Zion had to think fast. He tripped a soldier running by and kicked him in the stomach, knocking the wind out of him. Zion took the soldiers torch. He started the stands and wagons on fire as the soldier struggled to catch his breath. When the flames of the fire started to grow, he took off for the woodline before the soldier regained his breath.

Zion crashed through the brush as he entered the woods. He put his left hand up to protect his face from the snapping branches, limbs, and vines, while he chopped with his sword with the other. Zion distanced himself as far as possible from the market square. All he could think about was Assam. He hoped the diversion had worked.

Zion would find out at the link-up sight if Assam had escaped.

CHAPTER 62

"Wait, stop. Take a deep breath," Shobal said to one of his messengers. "You're not making any sense. Tell me again. What happened up top?"

"From what I could gather, a group of intruders infiltrated the palace and have tried to take it over," answered the messenger. He wiped his sweat with his sleeve.

"Who?" Shobal asked.

"I don't know," he admitted. "I came underground to let you know right away. It seemed like they had help on the inside."

"Why do you think that?" Shobal questioned.

"The soldiers were fighting against each other," the messenger answered. He heard a knock and turned around to face the office door.

"What is it?" Shobal yelled, annoyed by the pounding. He hated interruptions.

"Sir, we need you to come right away,"

"For what?" Shobal repeated. "Come in!"

The door flew open as one of the secret chamber guards came through. "Shobal, we discovered a wounded girl down in one of the sewer tunnels."

"How bad is she?" Shobal asked.

"It's hard to tell down in the tunnel," said the guard. "But it looks like she has three arrows stuck in her back. She's barely conscious."

"Where is she now?" Shobal asked.

"Still down in the bench tunnel," said the guard. He saw the look on Shobal's face and spoke up. "We wanted to wait for your instruction before we moved her."

"Quickly, bring her here to the secret chamber," Shobal ordered. He watched as the guards left to get the wounded girl. *Who could it be?* he wondered. *Could it be Myka? She's the only girl who knew about the loose grate.*

Shobal fretted. *What is going on up top in the palace?* Strange things were happening. Was it a revolt? Or is someone trying to take over? Were the Seekers involved?

Down in the chamber, Shobal was cut off from the outside world. He never ventured out. He commanded the Watchers from underneath the palace in his secret chamber. He only communicated to those above, through messages or messengers. He was paranoid and had a right to be. He was a descendent of the Children of Light. It would be certain death if Javan found out. He prided himself on the fact that the evil Supreme Commander Javan, the head of Thanoton, never did.

"Bring her in and lay her on the table," Shobal ordered, as he finished clearing it off. He had the medical kit out, ready to treat her.

"It's Myka," a guard said. "Myka, Myka." He tried to get her attention.

"I thought it might be her," Shobal agreed. "I was praying it wasn't. This presents another problem."

"What do you mean?" a guard asked, while he pealed the blood-soaked, linen shirt from Myka's back. Shobal cut it away from the wound. He knew Shobal always thought about the mission first.

"Nothing," Shobal said. "It's not important right now." He acted like it wasn't important, but in reality, it was. He didn't want them to know what he meant. Myka was his only link to the Seekers. The Seekers needed the Watchers' help to store some forbidden material to distribute to the people in the valley when the time came. With Myka incapacitated, how would he communicate with them?

Shobal figured he would let the information out to the Watchers that Myka was injured and unconscious. The Seekers would find out and come up with another way to communicate with him.

"I can't work with all of you crowding around me," Shobal grumbled. "Who's guarding the secret chamber with all of you here? Go do your job. I need only one of you to stay and help. He glanced at the messenger, "I need you to deliver a message to Samuel."

"What is it, Shobal?" the messenger asked, after a long pause. He watched as Shobal dug out the first arrow.

"Guard, hold the clamp shut, while I sew up the incision," Shobal ordered. "I want you to go tell Samuel what happened to Myka. Tell him she is unconscious, and we don't know if she will make it, yet. We need everyone to pray."

"I'll let him know."

"Wait!" Shobal shouted, bringing the messenger back in the room. "I almost forgot. Find out what is going on in the palace as fast as you can and get back to me."

"I will," the messenger responded, itching to leave and find out.

CHAPTER 63

Zesha stood over Supreme Commander Javan's dead body. His hand still gripped the dagger he had used to kill him. Zesha was surprised how easy he was to kill. He had seized upon the opportunity that presented itself.

"I am a Seeker," Zesha said. He could tell Gabriel had come to kill Javan by the way he looked at him.

"That's obvious," Gabriel said. "You did what I came here to do, kill Javan and his second-in-command, Tuval." He turned to his men, "You know what to do. Go do it."

"Javan killed Mina and Maximus," muttered Zesha, barely audible. He leaned against the bed, unable to contain his sorrow.

"It gets worse," Gabriel said. He waited for Zesha to regain himself and look at him. "Myka and one on my team were killed tonight, trying to rescue Mina."

"Who gave you permission to conduct that mission?" Zesha said, back to his stern self.

"No one," Gabriel answered. "I knew Maximus was going to try, no matter what I said. I wanted to save Maximus and Mina. So, I thought it would be an easy mission for the ghost team."

"Instead, you roped Myka into your unsanctioned mission and got her killed," Zesha added.

"What about you?" Gabriel said. "This definitely wasn't sanctioned by the Elders."

"It was what I had to do."

"Exactly," Gabriel agreed.

"Commander Gabriel," called Elam, his second-in-command, as he came into the room. "I can see you both have been busy," he said looking around.

"What is it?" Gabriel responded.

"We have secured the castle and won the allegiance of most of the guards. They are happy Javan is dead. The captain of the police is also on our side. He has secured the market square area, and he is awaiting further orders. We had many soldiers and guards that fled. We don't know where they went."

"Hold on!" Zesha interrupted. "Leave us alone for a minute," he said to Elam. Zesha waited for Elam to leave the room. "What do you think you are doing?"

"Securing Thanoton," Gabriel answered. "What? You didn't think that you could kill Javan, and the army would immediately swear allegiance to the Children of Light, did you? I have to do my job and protect our interest. I'm really working with you, not against you, as you think."

"You're right," Zesha agreed, while he sat down. "Things are a lot different now. We have no choice but to take over Thanoton. You are the new commander of the army. I will be interim leader until we can establish Ezra as the King. Then, I will be one of his advisors, along with the other Two Witnesses. I want you to at least make sure the palace and the market square area is totally secure. Cordon it off and search everyone coming in or out. If they have no reason to be there, then don't let them in until we get a handle on things. Do you think you will have enough men to accomplish that? I should have asked that first."

"I think we'll have enough men," Gabriel answered, while he paced around the room. "We have most of the palace guards and all but a few market square police on our side. I sent a soldier to activate the three platoons of men I have been secretly training for this day. They should be here by daybreak."

"Yes, the three platoons," Zesha said. "All that preparation paid off. What about your regular platoon out west?"

"I thought I would keep them out there, securing the west," Gabriel answered. "At least we know the town of Pistio and the western region belongs to the Children of Light."

"Hopefully, in a few days we can push out from here and secure more of Thanoton and the surrounding areas," Zesha added. "Tomorrow if you think we are secure enough, contact Lot, Kern, Calvin, and Shobal. Have them come here for a meeting. They will be my new council."

"Shobal?" Gabriel asked. "He's not one of us."

"He is now," Zesha shrugged. "He has followers all over Thanoton and is a believer in the Light of the Word. So that makes him one of us."

"It might be hard to get him out of hiding," Gabriel chuckled.

Zesha laughed along with him. "Tell him it's time for both our secret organizations to come out in the open. We are no longer secret. We need to lead this valley back to the Light of the Word."

"What about the palace workers in the morning?" Gabriel asked.

"I want you to send the head steward and each floor steward for a meeting with me first thing in the morning. Don't allow anyone else into the palace until I talk to them. By then, I should have a list of workers that will not present a problem. I have worked here my whole life, and I know the workers very well. Do not let any of the old council members back in. They are finished. They can learn how to be moral, upright citizens first. Then, maybe they can become leaders. I will leave the military leaders up to you if you want to promote or demote some of them."

Zesha stood up and made eye contact with Gabriel. He raised his boney finger and pointed, "Remember, we want to restore people to the Light of the Word. We are not here for political gain or power. We are here for the people, to set them free—free to worship the Light of the Word. Our highest purpose is to glorify Him."

"I understand that," Gabriel nodded, but didn't like being scrutinized.

"We can't expect this place, or the people, to be perfect until our Lord returns and ushers in a final deliverance from all evil. We want to make this place the best we can. This will be a haven to glorify the Lord, an environment free of all restraint and obstructions to worship. We will learn and teach out of the *Book of Prophecies*. This place is a long way off from becoming a city like Alethia. It won't be like that overnight. It has to be cultivated. There are many young plants in the city of Thanoton. We need to make sure we nurture them, not trample them."

"Zesha, I clearly understand our purpose," Gabriel said. "What about the booklets that are being hidden around the city tonight?"

"Oh, I completely forgot that was tonight," Zesha responded. "We never planned for all this to happen."

"Yes, unintentionally overthrowing Thanoton did overshadow it," Gabriel added. "It's probably happening as we speak."

"What do you think we should do?"

Gabriel was surprised Zesha had asked for his advice. "I think we should bring all the booklets to the market square. Start handing them out to the people, beginning with the soldiers. Since the western route is secure, we can bring the rest of the material here to the palace to distribute.

"That is a good idea," Zesha added. "We need to—"

"Commander Gabriel," Elam called.

"What is it?" Gabriel answered, putting his hand on Elam's shoulder. Gabriel liked having Elam as his second-in-command. He reminded him of himself. He was an aggressive leader, who quickly got things done. They thought alike. Some even thought they looked alike. Elam was about the same height, six feet. They both had short brown hair that never seemed to grow, with a chiseled face. Gabriel was much older than Elam and looked it. Elam's eyes had more blue in them than Gabriel's, which were slightly grey. From a distance, people got them confused because they both had an aggressive walk.

"We decided to collect the bodies of our people to take them back to Pistio for a proper burial. But—" Elam paused.

"But what?" Gabriel asked.

"We couldn't find Myka's body," Elam answered. He hesitated and spoke, "Are you sure you saw Myka dead?"

Gabriel was perplexed. "When I looked out the window, I saw her lying on the ground with several arrows in her back. She was not moving. I figured she was dead because the soldiers just ran past her. If she wasn't, they would have made sure she was."

"We can't find her body."

"Take what you have to Pistio and keep searching for her," Gabriel said. "Wait," he stopped Elam who was eager to move on to the next task. "Divert all the shipments of the booklets to the market square. Start handing them out to the soldiers, the people—everyone. No more being secretive."

"Will do," Elam said. He was unable to contain his joy. He pointed to Javan, "What do you want us to do with the rest of the bodies?"

"Find a good spot on the palace grounds and bury the rest of the dead there," Gabriel said, "Mark the graves for the family members." He looked over to Zesha for approval.

Zesha nodded and waited for Elam to leave again. "Your men have gotten a lot done in a short amount of time. I'm amazed."

"We have waited, prepared, and trained for this night our whole lives. We pretty much knew who would be loyal to us before this all happened. They were prepared to help us when the time came."

"Let us set the precedence, and pray together before we further establish the Kingdom. It says in the *Book of Prophesies*: Be careful for nothing; but in everything by prayer and supplication with thanksgiving make your request known unto God."

"It also says," Gabriel added. "But seek ye first the kingdom of God, and his righteousness; and all these things shall be added unto you."

Zesha nodded in agreement, and said, "Let's pray."

CHAPTER 64

Gabriel spent that night fortifying the palace and the market square area. He personally talked to every guard, soldier, and police, to make a smooth transition. He marveled that there seemed to be a different spirit in the air. A great weight of evil had been lifted with Javan's death. Everyone felt it. There was an excitement in the air.

Many soldiers that initially fled the palace in opposition to Gabriel changed their minds and trickled back in throughout the night. They reported that Javan's army had re-formed, and was hiding in the swamp by Green Lake.

Arton led the enemy force. Throughout the night, soldiers fled from the eastern cut and gathered with Arton to hide out and re-form for a counter attack. His plan was to attack the palace at night in a few days to take it back, Arton also had the support of the soldiers on the eastern cut. They had abandoned the border and joined with Arton. With this information, Gabriel had come up with a good plan. He would ambush Arton's army, long before they reached the outskirts of the city of Thanoton. He couldn't wait to implement the plan.

Gabriel sent out a recon element to locate the enemy force, observe, and report on their activities. They would report when it looked like the enemy was prepared to move out for the attack. Gabriel wanted to ambush them when they were the most vulnerable, on his terms.

Elam, with the help of Ashur, the head of the market square police, worked all night consolidating all the booklets. They rerouted the wagonloads to deliver the booklets to the center of the market square. They were glad the booklets were not in the market square when the enemy set the fire. The fire spread so rapidly. By the time they had extinguished it, there were very few stands, carts, and wagons left untouched. Elam made sure the booklets were heavily guarded so the enemy couldn't destroy them. He had his men start passing them out. The western passage was clear so they had them making multiple trips to bring more booklets.

Gabriel spotted Lot and Kern heading toward him in the market square. He had been so busy, he didn't notice that it was a lot easier to see. Lot and Kern were more than a hundred feet away, and he could almost see them clearly. It was early morning, and a dim light was shining through the fog. Gabriel looked up because others were gazing up at the outline of the sun. It was something no one had seen from the city of

Thanoton for over a thousand years. He marveled how odd it looked. He watched the people. They were smiling.

"Good morning, Lot. Kern," Gabriel extended his hand.

"Morning," they did not accept his handshake.

"You and Zesha have been quite busy," Lot added sarcastically. "Elam filled us in."

"We had no choice."

"No choice? You both did your—" Lot stopped and lowered his voice so others around would not hear. "You both did your own thing and got Myka killed," he said, all choked up. "Getting killed for a sanctioned mission is one thing, but killed because you want to do things your own way is another."

"And Maximus," Kern added.

"I was trying to rescue Maximus," Gabriel defended.

"This is going to devastate my wife when she hears," Lot said, as he wiped his eyes.

"I'm truly sorry," Gabriel said, and he truly was. He had never seen Lot this angry or upset before. Lot was always gentle, jolly, and friendly to everyone. He understood by the look in their eyes they no longer trusted him, and it hurt.

"Sorry?" Kern repeated, shaking his head.

"So what's next?" Lot asked. "Since we're all doing our own thing without the Elders' guidance."

"Zesha wants to have a meeting around noon with you two, Calvin, and Shobal."

"Good luck trying to get Shobal out of his hole," Lot said.

"How do I get a message to Shobal or talk to him?" Gabriel asked. "Without M—," he stopped and caught himself before he said Myka. "I don't know how to communicate with the Watchers."

Lot let what Gabriel almost said slide. He took a deep breath and looked around. He had to admit, the world around them had changed rapidly. What they had planned for all those years was upon them. New life was beginning. He needed to set aside his emotions and get on with completing the mission. Lot broke the awkward silence, and said, "Samuel, the storekeeper is the head of the market square Watchers. He can get a message to Shobal. Tell him who is going to be at the meeting, especially Calvin. That might help. Calvin, Zesha, and Shobal knew each other when they were young men. I'm almost certain he will not come to the meeting today. He is very paranoid and might think it's a trap. He'll want to test the waters first."

"Have you told Calvin yet?" Kern asked.

"No, not yet," Gabriel answered.

"I will go tell him," Kern responded. "He will need some help getting to the palace. He's in poor health."

"I'll go with you," Lot added.

"Thanks," Gabriel said. "I'll see you both in the meeting. Pray that I can get Samuel to convince Shobal to come to the meeting."

"Yes, praying is what we all should be doing," Lot said, with a stern look as he and Kern walked away.

Gabriel headed to the store and Samuel. In his heart, he prayed the Light of the Word would give him favor with Samuel. He was frustrated he had let everyone down. Gabriel hated to live in a world of what-ifs. What if he would have done this, or what if he would have done that? It might have turned out differently. He knew that kind of thinking held people back. He needed to make the best of the current situation for the glory of the Light of the Word. He needed to stabilize and secure Thanoton for the return of the Three Witnesses and to establish Ezra as the king.

Truly the Whisperer was with them, thought Gabriel. *In everything that happened—good or bad, planned or mistakes, it worked out for the benefit of establishing the kingdom. Everything fell into divine order, despite our failed plans.* Gabriel encouraged himself as he walked. The fact was, the Light of the Word was the one in control. He chose to use people to accomplish His will. Even though they sometimes fail, He uses even their failures to accomplish His purpose.

Gabriel headed toward the front of the store where Samuel stood, admiring the outline of the sun.

"Hello, Samuel," Gabriel said, with a smile. "I'm Gabriel, we've met briefly before."

"Yes, I remember," Samuel's voice cracked from being nervous. He cleared his throat and spoke, "Your, Commander Gabriel now, aren't you?

"I'm officially the commander of the armies of Thanoton, but you can just call me Gabriel. I prefer it."

"The weather this morning is strange, isn't it? The light, I mean," Samuel said. He felt awkward talking to Gabriel, not knowing what else to say. Samuel always talked too much when he was nervous.

"It is different," Gabriel said, as he studied the sun.

"It must be the end of the world," Samuel said, half-joking and half-serious.

"Actually, it's the start of a whole new world, which is why I am here. Is there some place private we can talk?"

"Sure," he answered, even more, nervous now. "We have a room in the back of the store where we can talk privately."

"Good," Gabriel said, as he followed.

CHAPTER 65

"Ezra, the Elders, are ready to see you now," said a woman, out of the conference room through the double doors.

"Dara and Jared are coming in with me," Ezra said to the woman.

"Of course," she said as if it was expected. "Please." She held the door open for them.

"Ezra, come on in and have a seat," said Zadoc, the head Elder.

Ezra noticed they had three chairs set up, facing the Elders' table. In the past, their meetings were less formal and more informational. But lately, the meetings had become heated—heated for the city of Alethia that is. It was more like a disagreement among the Elders, each with the highest purpose in mind. It would be the three of them facing the twelve Elders.

Ezra took the middle seat, with Dara on his right side and Jared on his left. His two friends would help him rule Thanoton. They were in complete agreement with Ezra's petition.

Ezra stood up and looked into the eyes of Zadoc, the head Elder. "I had another dream last night. It was the same recurring dream I have had the last couple of weeks."

"I thought we already discussed this Ezra," Zadoc said, clasping his hands together.

"In the dream, the people of Thanoton were begging for me to come," Ezra pleaded.

"We know about the dreams," Zadoc responded.

"The Whisperer woke me up again and told me to go."

Zadoc stood up and looked at the Elders assembled at the table and back to the Three Witnesses. "I know I speak for everyone here," Zadoc said, referring to the Elders at the table, "when I say that we interpret these dreams, and what the Whisperer is saying to you, as part of the preparation to motivate you to go. The fact you are eager to go is a great sign. Nevertheless, the plan is for you three to go to Thanoton in the spring. It is only eight weeks away, and that is the plan they are preparing for in Thanoton. That is soon in our estimation. It doesn't go against what the Whisperer is telling you."

"We believe it does go against what the Whisperer is telling us," Ezra said. He noticed Dara and Jared stood up with him. "There is urgency in the dreams. The Whisperer is commanding me to go. Now."

Zadoc's heart leapt as he heard the Three Witnesses plead their case. They had grown leaps and bounds in their faith and knowledge of the Light of the Word. Though they were young, they had matured greatly. The Three Witnesses were confident and bold in their calling. They knew their purpose and were ready to fulfill it.

Ezra, Jared, and Dara had changed significantly since coming to Alethia, and everyone knew it. They devoured the *Book of Prophesies* in their studies. They couldn't get enough of learning about the Light of the Word.

Ezra couldn't wait to proclaim the Truth, and spoke to anyone who would listen. His hair was still brown and wavy, but his body had filled out more. He had become more muscular in Alethia. Ezra had a presence about him that radiated a King. He was a leader, which was obvious to all.

Jared was no longer timid and shy. The *Book of Prophesies* had revealed to him how much the Light of the Word valued and loved him. Jared knew he was made for a special purpose that he alone could fulfill. He wasn't self-conscious of his glasses or his freckles anymore. Jared didn't care what people thought. He had lost his fear of man and vowed to live only to please the Light of the Word, no matter what the cost. He also looked a lot healthier than when he had arrived. That was because of the good, healthy choices of food in Alethia, and working out in the sunshine. That was something they did not have in Thanoton.

Dara had become bolder and more confident than she already was. She still was a jokester but was unafraid to speak up for the oppressed. She had a compassion for those in need that was convicting. Dara had become even more beautiful with the Light of the Word radiating through her. She stood out with her flowing, blond hair that went to the middle of her back and her shiny, bright blue eyes. Her smooth skin sported a slight tan from working outside. Dara's hair and eyes sparkled in the sunshine.

"You said yourself that you have not heard from the Seekers in Thanoton for a long time," Dara said.

"That's right. We haven't heard from them since we closed down Sanctuary on the eastern border," Zadoc answered. "The Seekers are no longer allowed to use the eastern route to deliver messages. The western route can't be used when the snow comes. There is too much snow in the mountains to pass."

"That was part of the plan," said another Elder. "We knew we wouldn't be able to communicate with them until after the snow melted. By then, you three would be on your way. We planned for that. They know to hold you up at the western border if there is a delay in the plan."

"We know all of that," Jared added. "The point is you don't know if they need us to come now." He looked at Ezra and Dara, "Although, we know they do. We believe the Whisperer is commanding us to go immediately."

Both Ezra and Dara nodded their head in agreement. They were impressed with Jared's boldness. They waited while the Elders whispered among themselves.

The Elders were good men. They looked more like farmers than rulers did, because they worked alongside the people in the fields. Everyone in Alethia was expected to pitch in and help, no matter who they were. The Elders were approachable and accessible. They made a point to know personally everyone in their community to serve them better. They served the people, not themselves.

That is why the Three Witnesses would never think of going against the council. They might not agree with them, but they trusted their wisdom. They were appointed by the Light of the Word and had His best interest at heart. To go against them, would disrupt the blessing and unity of spirit they all felt as the Children of Light. Nothing good would come out of them doing their own thing. That is why they needed to convince the Elders to let them go. All Three Witnesses prayed silently for the Whisperer to convince them.

"May I add something?" Ezra interrupted. "We have heard rumors that some of you have sensed the urgency we feel." He watched as a few of the Elders shifted in their chairs. "We know the Whisperer has probably put on all your hearts that something is going on in Thanoton. It needs our immediate attention. None of us knows what that is. We understand all of you are united. We know you want to lean on the side of caution, until you have been shown something specific. We are that sign. The urgency in us is the answer."

Zadoc stood up again and rubbed his tan, leathery face. "We were just discussing this among ourselves. Even if you left now, it would take a month to get to the western border. Then you would still have to wait for the snow to melt. At the most, you might get there three weeks earlier than what was planned."

"You couldn't do anything immediately if you wanted to," another Elder added.

"I have a different plan," Ezra said. "If we use the eastern cut we could be there in three days or less. We can leave now and ride on through."

Zadoc shook his head, "Absolutely not. The town of Sanctuary is abandoned. We closed it down and moved its operations to Pistio. This is where you are supposed to go first. Hold up there until it is safe to go on to the city of Thanoton. Plus, the border guards are looking for us to come through there, after all the ruckus we caused getting you three out of Thanoton, that area is compromised."

"It would save us time," Ezra added. "The eastern cut is only thirty minutes away from the city of Thanoton."

"That's if you don't get caught at the border or Javan's army doesn't get you," Zadoc added.

"Ian seems to think—"

"Ian?" Zadok interrupted. He now was leaning up against the front of the Elders' table with his arms folded, close to Ezra.

"He thinks he can easily sneak in and out of the valley of Thanoton, while we wait in Sanctuary. He can find out what is going on and let the Seekers know where we are. If they are ready for us to come, we'll find a way," Ezra said. "And," he hesitated, "if the Seekers in the valley tell us to stick with the plan, we will come back and wait."

"We don't doubt Ian can sneak in and out of there without being caught," Zadoc said with a chuckle. Just the mention of Ian and the word sneaky brought smiles to everyone in the room. "That's what he's good at and loves to do. He is our messenger."

Ian was a proven expert at infiltrating impenetrable places. He knew how to use the terrain to his advantage. He would change disguises to match the environment and people around him. He was the Elders' messenger. Ian delivered messages and people in and out of Thanoton through the eastern border, as his father and grandfather had. He had started young and learned from the best.

Ian was a lot younger than he looked. He was tall and thin and looked rugged. Only his gentle, light blue eyes revealed his youthfulness. He was also one of the many trainers that instructed the Three Witnesses on various military, combat, and survival skills, skills they needed to be effective leaders. The training boosted confidence and military understanding to lead the army.

Ian taught them to survive and live off the land. They learned how to stay hidden, by using the terrain and foliage to camouflage and conceal themselves. They were taught how to navigate through the woods in all different environments, quietly, without being detected. Ian's training techniques were good, and the Three Witnesses enjoyed Ian's instruction, but it was obvious he'd rather be doing than teaching.

"Ezra, just so we're clear," Zadoc said as he paced around, "we are not trying to sneak you in. We could have easily done that. We are waiting for the right environment in Thanoton to bring you three in. You will have two platoons of guards with you at all times for your protection. At Pistio, other platoons will join to escort you to the palace. It will not be a stable environment at first to go without guards. You will not go anywhere without them. It will be nearly impossible to sneak all of them across the border without being detected."

"I understand all that," Ezra said. "All we're asking is to go to Sanctuary—with our two platoons and wait there until Ian does a thorough recon. He will find out quickly if the Seekers are ready for us to come in or not. If they are, then obviously it will be safe enough for us to go in with our two platoons. If not we will return here. Either way, we will know for sure."

Zadoc sat back down and took a deep breath. He looked to the Elders on his right and left then directed attention back to the Three Witnesses. "We will pray about this and give you a decision after lunch. That decision will be final. Do not bring this subject up again. We are weary of it. If we grant you favor, then you can go today. If not, we will stick with the plan in place."

CHAPTER 66

Zesha marveled how clearly he saw the market square from the fifth floor balcony of the palace. It had been years since they could see glimpses through the thick fog. The last year, it was too dark to see anything, including the torches down below. Today, Zesha could see the marketplace filled with people, talking to one another and reading the booklet. Zesha caught himself smiling throughout the morning. He was excited and could not contain his joy.

He prayed the booklet, *The History of the Children of Light with excerpts from the Book of Prophecies* would open their eyes to believe. It certainly would unify the people of Thanoton and bring Truth and understanding to their existence.

"There you are," Gabriel said, as he walked up and leaned over the balcony.

"The light has come," Zesha answered.

"It sure has," Gabriel responded. He had to laugh at the way Zesha squinted when he looked up at the outline of the sun through the clouds. It was brighter making it almost impossible to look directly at it. "We're ready to start the meeting."

"Were you able to assemble everyone?" Zesha asked, while he followed Gabriel to the conference room.

"Everyone except for Shobal," Gabriel said, over his shoulder. "I sent Elam to bring an alternate to sit in his place. Maybe that will bring him out of his hole."

"Alternate?" Zesha said, but he quickly changed the subject when he saw Calvin. "Calvin, it has been a lifetime," Zesha said, embracing him with a hug.

"It has been a long time," added Calvin. "I never dreamed I would see—ahh—ahh." He was overcome by emotion.

They both wept tears of joy. They had been childhood friends. Infiltrating the palace, their roles changed. They could no longer be close friends. Their social distance made a relationship impossible. Therefore, if one were caught, the other wouldn't be given away. They only communicated through messages for years never seeing each other. They had relied on Mina to deliver messages back and forth. For safety, Calvin never met Mina, but he knew she delivered and retrieved messages at the secret drop behind his house.

"I'm sorry for what happened to Maximus," Zesha added, as he wiped tears from his eyes. "It's my fault Mina and Maximus are dead. If only I was satisfied with the forbidden material I already had smuggled out. I shouldn't have pushed to get more out."

"It's just as much my fault," Calvin added. "I was in agreement to send Maximus in before he had completed his training. I was too eager to keep things moving."

"And no one anticipated Mina and Maximus would like each other and find out they were Seekers. I wish—"

"Zesha and Calvin, we need to get this meeting started," interrupted Gabriel. He needed to redirect them from dwelling on the past. "We need to press on with the future."

"He's right," Zesha agreed. "We are here today for one purpose, to re-establish the Kingdom for the Light of the Word. This is the direct result of many sacrifices by the Children of Light. I invited all of you here today to form a new cabinet. I will be the interim leader until we can establish Ezra as King."

Zesha paused and glanced around the room at Calvin, Lot, Kern and Gabriel. He said, "The rest of you will be my advisors, each with a specific assignment to help re-establish the new government. Before we discuss our next phase, Gabriel why don't you brief us on the current security situation in Thanoton."

Gabriel felt uneasy. The looks he received from the others lacked the respect he once had. *He would have to work to change that*, he thought.

"Look, no one's going to hurt you," Elam's voice rang from outside the conference room. Everyone turned toward the door to watch him and two soldiers bringing in Samuel.

"Good, our alternate," Gabriel said.

"You let go of him right now," Lot said, standing up. "Are we taking prisoners now?" He gestured toward Samuel as he glared at Zesha.

"Uh—it was the only way I could get Samuel here," Elam said. He felt stupid as soon as he said it.

"We couldn't get Shobal to come out of his hole," Gabriel added, trying to take the heat off Elam, his second-in-command. "So I decided to bring an alternate, to sit in his place."

"Zesha! This is a meeting about restoring the Kingdom for the Light of the Word, right?" Lot interjected.

"Gentleman, gentleman, let's settle down," Zesha said. "Everyone, sit down please, including you, Gabriel. Elam, you and your soldiers may leave. You have done enough already." He gave Elam, then Gabriel, a piercing look.

"Come over here and sit down next to me," Lot said, as he pulled a chair out for Samuel. "I'm so sorry this happened."

"Are you a prisoner too?" Samuel asked Lot. He had whispered, but everyone heard.

Lot put his arm around Samuel. "No, I'm not a prisoner," he said, while making eye contact with everyone around the conference table. He stopped and stared at Gabriel.

"Samuel, do you know why you are here?" asked Calvin.

"No," Samuel spouted. "I was minding my own business, and the next thing I know I was being chased, and then dragged here."

It remained quiet for a bit before Zesha sat down, and said, "We really need to pray. We all have started out on the wrong foot." He saw the surprised look on Samuel's face. Zesha directed his attention to him, and said, "Yes, we are the descendants of the Children of Light, like you. Although, we certainly have not been acting like it. Everything will be explained to you, but first, we really need to pray."

Zesha bowed his head, "Lord, we come to you in desperate need. First, we thank you so much for delivering this valley from its evil grip. We thank you for making everything work out right, in spite of our disobedience and self-directed plans. Unite us all in this room and all over this valley for one purpose, to do your perfect will. We pray that you would awaken people's hearts to believe in you as they read the booklet. We pray that the fighting stops and the Children of Darkness surrender, not just to us—but to you—and become Children of Light. Last of all, we remember those that died recently in the fight to help make this all happen. We thank you for Myka, Maximus, and Mina. We take comfort in knowing they are with you, Light of the Word—their first and last love. We bring this all to you, Lord. You are the one and only, the first and last, that sacrificed everything for us. Empower us to do the same. Amen."

When Zesha had finished the prayer, the advisors noticed Samuel stood up and had a puzzled look.

"What is it?" Zesha asked.

"Well, it's just that—" Samuel paused.

"What?"

"Myka is alive."

"She's alive? Where?" asked Lot.

"She was severely wounded and came down through a secret entrance for Shobal's help. He has mended her wounds, but she is still in a bad state. Shobal says she will make it."

"Take me to her now," Lot commanded, all excited. He turned to Zesha, "I will fill Shobal in on everything. I really need to see her now." He wiped the tears from his eyes.

"You're not allowed down there," Samuel said.

"We really need to talk to Shobal about restoring the valley of Thanoton back to the Children of Light. We must prepare for the Three Witnesses' return in the spring. Although, I wish they were here now," Zesha added.

"You seem to know everything about us," Samuel said. He saw the nod of agreement from Gabriel. "This also explains a lot, knowing that Myka was a Seeker in your organization and a Watcher in ours."

"We are all on the same side," roared Lot. He was back to his own self. "Now, let's get going, young man."

Gabriel thanked the Light of the Word for Myka being alive. He so much wanted to see Myka too, but he thought it best to let Lot go by himself. It was great to see Lot smiling and excited, as he usually was.

CHAPTER 67

Later that night, Zion slowly lifted his eyes up over the ravine where he and Assam were hiding. He surveyed the woods around them for movement. They had narrowly escaped the marketplace square the night before and were successful in their link-up. There were many groups of soldiers on foot headed toward Green Lake. Some were coming from escaping the palace area, and some came from the eastern cut. If they were the enemy or friendly, Zion didn't know.

Zion and Assam stayed concealed with sticks and grass they gathered as a covering for camouflage in the ravine. They lay on the side of the ravine with only a little bit of space to look out.

"It's finally starting to get dark," Zion said. "What a weird day."

"Yeah, I know," Assam agreed. "I can't believe how light it is outside. It makes everything look so different."

"It makes it hard to hide, that's for sure," Zion agreed, while he shifted around. "I thought we would be able to sneak up close to the palace today. I wanted to watch an opportunity to go down the sewer, and look for Myka. But with so much light, it was too risky."

"I can't believe you still plan on going through with this," Assam said.

"Of course, I am," Zion answered while pushing a pile of brush off of him because it had gotten darker. "Why do you think I have been talking about this all day?"

"I was hoping you would have changed your mind by now," Assam answered.

"Like I said earlier, you don't have to go with me. You can either stay here or wait for me in the woods. It's up to you."

"I'm going with you," Assam said, hesitantly, "at least to the market square. I need to find some food."

"Me too," Zion agreed. "That's our first priority, to find some food. Are you ready to move out?"

"It still doesn't seem that dark out," Assam answered, as he rolled over on his back. "Like that big round light in the sky, is that the sun?"

"I don't know what that is," Zion answered. "Everything is so strange lately."

"And nothing makes sense."

"I think this is as dark as it's going to get," Zion said. "Let's move out."

Zion crawled up out of the ravine, and Assam followed. They moved out cautiously taking great care not to step on any dry sticks or leaves. They knew sound traveled farther in the woods, and they could not afford to be caught. Periodically, they stopped to look and listen for danger. Zion motioned with a clenched fist over his right shoulder for Assam to freeze. At a great distance away, they could see the light from fires in the direction of the market square.

Zion and Assam continued toward the market square. They used the thick vegetation and stands of trees to mask their approach. Zion was already worried about crossing the market square to get to the benches on the west side. The peoples' voices grew louder, and the area got brighter as they moved closer.

They low-crawled the last three hundred feet creeping under bushes and trees until they found a thick patch of bushes. It was close enough, out of line of sight of the market square. They knew they had found a good spot. They squeezed their way through the thick bushes until they could see out the other side.

"This is going to be harder than I thought," Zion said, stating the obvious. The soldiers and market square police had formed a perimeter one hundred feet into the wood line around the market square. They had elaborate fighting positions spread out throughout. One fighting position, built up with burlap bags filled with dirt, was directly one hundred feet to their front.

"See, I told you," Assam whispered. "Do you still want to go through with it?"

"Of course. We just have to figure out another way," Zion answered. "Do you recognize any of the people or soldiers in the market square?" He was searching the market square area with his single lens scope. With the fires in and around the market square area, it was easy to see.

"I recognize some of the locals and market square police, but none of the soldiers," Assam answered. "Our platoon must have gone to Green Lake, along with all the other soldiers that escaped."

Zion grabbed Assam by the arm with one hand and covered his mouth with the other. *Crack, crunch, snap.* They both heard it coming from behind. They froze, while a patrol slowly made their way from behind, around the bushes and headed to the market square. Zion watched as the patrol stopped at the fighting position and gave some kind of signal or verbal authenticator to pass. The soldiers at the fighting position waved them by.

Five minutes later, another roving patrol left out near the fighting position to their front and walked past them.

"What luck," Zion whispered. "It looks like they have roving patrols coming and leaving from this fighting position."

"I don't see how that makes us lucky," Assam said.

"Did you see how they moved through the woods?" Zion questioned.

"I don't know," Assam answered.

"Think."

"I guess they weren't that smooth," Assam said, "like our squad is."

"Exactly," Zion said. "They look like they have not worked together. Some soldiers stayed to help overthrow the palace, and the others escaped to Green Lake to regroup. So, they had to re-form into new platoons."

"I still don't see how this makes us lucky," Assam said. "I think we should go to Green Lake and link back up with our platoon. We can report what we have seen."

"You can go back if you want," Zion said. "I'm getting sick and tired of you trying to talk me out of this. I have to try to save Myka."

"You said yourself she might have been dead when you stuck her down the sewer," Assam said.

"You don't know her," Zion said. "She would do the same for me. Actually, she did do the same for me."

"She's the enemy," Assam insisted.

"Not my enemy. Shh!" whispered Zion, as he covered Assam's mouth with his hand. *Crack, crunch!* They heard many footsteps coming from behind their position. Zion leaned close to Assam's ear, and whispered, "This is our chance. I'm going. You can follow if you want."

Zion slipped out of the bushes and fell into the patrol, as they made their way around the bushes. The patrol was spread out, making it easy to become a part of. It was dark and hard to see against the glare radiating from the market square. Zion was surprised to see that Assam was following close behind. He had to pick the right time to slip away from the patrol before they got to the fighting position. Zion knew the patrol leader would stop at the perimeter and count the members of his patrol, to make sure he had everyone. A few extra bodies would cause an alert.

Zion waited for the patrol to slow down as it came up to the fighting position. He heard some talking up front and figured it was the best time to go around the fighting position. He grabbed Assam, and they slowly made their way around the right side of the position. They snuck twenty feet away before they cut in between two fighting positions to enter the perimeter. The patrol was now moving again, masking their noise and keeping attention away from them.

Zion smiled at Assam, as they walked into the busy market square.

"Where are you soldiers going?"

Zion was startled. He turned around to see a market square police with his hands on his hips. Zion recognized him but did not know him.

"What did you say?" Zion said, with boldness. He didn't want to give the illusion he was nervous.

"What are you two doing in the market square? Shouldn't you be with your patrol on the perimeter or at the assembly area?"

"Actually, we work on the western perimeter and came in to get some food," Zion said. He could tell he surprised Assam with his quick thinking. They needed food and to get to the western side of the market square.

The market square police laughed. "You two are lost. This is the eastern side of the market square. You need to go over there," he said as he pointed to the assembly area. "That's where the food is being served."

"Oh, great," Zion said. "Thank you." He walked away toward the assembly area, not looking back. Zion hoped the market square police wouldn't stop him.

"There it is," Assam said, all excited. "There's the line for the food." Assam passed Zion and led the way to the food line.

Zion followed Assam and made a quick glance behind to see if the market square policeman was still watching. He wasn't.

Zion was relieved to see no one was paying attention to them going through the line. There was plenty of food. Zion had to contain his laughter at how much food Assam was trying to pack on his plate. Every centimeter was filled and piled high. He had roasted chicken, turkey, potatoes, carrots, cheese, and a half-loaf of bread tucked under his arm.

"Don't take too much food," Zion whispered. "You're going to draw unnecessary attention to yourself."

"I can't help it," Assam said. "Look at all this good food. Look around. Everyone is feasting. The community has pitched in and provided food for everyone." He really wanted to say enemy but was afraid he would be heard.

Zion looked around and nodded. Assam was right. Everyone was enjoying the big dinner and toasting one another to freedom. They sat down and ate, without raising suspicion.

CHAPTER 68

Myka's eyes fluttered, and her eyes barely opened. All she could see were gray blurry shapes of lights and figures moving around the room.

"Myka's opening her eyes!" she heard an echo at a distance.

She saw a shape come closer, and it leaned toward her. "Myka, Myka, can you hear me?"

Myka blinked a few times and started to see the shapes more clearly. Her mouth was dry, and she was unable to speak. Slowly the many shapes became clearer. *They must be people*, she thought still groggy. She closed her eyes and went back to sleep.

"Everyone needs to stand back and give her some room," Shobal barked. "We don't want to startle her when she comes to."

"Thank the Lord," Lot said. He had been by her side all day, praying she would become conscious.

"Yes, thank the Lord," Shobal agreed. "This is a very good sign she is recovering." Myka looked like she was trying to talk. "The sedatives have really dried her out." Shobal put his hand on Lot's shoulder, and said, "Keep moistening her lips with the sponge, and see if she will start to drink, now that she is conscious."

Lot filled the sponge and pressed it to her lips. "That's my girl," roared Lot. He was pleased to see her drinking the slow trickle of water he was giving her. "Keep drinking, Myka. Everything is going to be all right," he said, rubbing his hand on the side of her head.

~*~

Zion and Assam hid behind a few rain barrels around the corner of a building. The building was at the edge of the market square with a clear view of the middle bench. After they had finished eating, they quickly found this place to hide. They waited for the right opportunity to sneak down the drain.

"Follow me," Zion whispered. He was surprised when Assam put up no resistance and followed. Activity in the market place had died down, and they had not seen anyone for over a half-hour. Zion decided this would be the best time to go.

They both stayed on their hands and knees alongside the building, to avoid the lights flickering from the palace and the market square above. They stayed hidden in the shadows beneath. Zion's plan was to crawl to the corner of the building and, when no one was looking, bound across to the palace wall. At the wall, they would low-crawl to the second bench, remove the grate, and slip in.

Zion waited at the corner and listened. He looked both ways and bounded across. He lay next to the wall, in the shadows.

"Hey you!" Zion heard. A sudden fear came over him as he saw Assam dive back to the corner of the building. *Oh, no! We've been caught,* he thought. Zion pulled out his sword, ready to fight, and waited.

"There you are," a voice came from the front of the building. "Are you ready to go home?"

"I'm waiting on you," the other called.

Zion heard footsteps on the cobblestone road between the building and the palace wall. His heart was pounding so loudly, he hoped they could not hear it. The two walked by. Zion stayed frozen and waited, afraid to make a sound.

Pat, pat, pat, shuffle, shuffle, slide, crunch, Zion turned in the direction of the sound, but before he realized it, Assam had landed on his legs.

"That was a close call," Assam whispered. "Sorry about your legs."

"Not that sorry," Zion said, as he tried to move. "You can get off me now." He thought about reminding Assam he was to wait for the signal to cross over. Zion decided to let it slide. He was happy Assam had decided to come along. He made Zion promise they would link up with their old platoon at Green Lake after they found Myka, and Zion reluctantly promised.

Zion low-crawled to the first bench and froze. He got as close to the ground as he possibly could to avoid the periodic flicker of lights coming from the market square. When the lights scattered away, he continued to move. Zion was annoyed at Assam's constantly bumping into his feet.

He squeezed behind the second bench and the wall and waited. Satisfied no one was near or watching, he grabbed the grate with both hands and lifted it up. Sliding it would have made too much noise. Bracing his elbows on the ground, he picked it straight up, pivoted the grate, and gently lowered it.

"Fine, I'll go first," Zion whispered after Assam shook his head no. Zion slid down the opening and realized the sewer pipe was bigger than he imagined. He grabbed the edge of the opening and slid through slowly until his feet touched the floor. The pipe was not wide enough to stand upright. In a crouch, Zion pushed to the side Assam's legs sliding through the opening, before he landed on his head. "Whatever happened to waiting for my signal?"

"I got tired of waiting," Assam replied.

Zion thought about Myka as he reached up to replace the grate. She must have landed on her head when he slid her down the drain. Zion could see a light way at the other end of the tunnel. There was no other way to go but toward the light. He drew his sword. "Follow me."

Zion moved slowly down the tunnel with Assam so close he could hear his heavy breathing. He signaled Assam to freeze when they got to the end of the tunnel. A quick look, and then he came back and motioned for Assam to back up. When they were far enough back, he grabbed Assam, "That's good," he whispered.

Assam sat down, "What's in there?"

"It's a room with several passages branching off from it. It's lit by candles in a candelabrum on top of a table."

"Did you hear any voices or anything that would show us what direction to go?" Assam rubbed his tummy, which hurt from eating too much.

"No, nothing," Zion answered. "All the tunnels are dark. There is no way of telling which way to go. We will just have to take a guess until we can figure out the tunnel that leads to Myka."

"She's probably heavily guarded," Assam said.

"We need to kill anyone that gets in our way," Zion said with resolve. "Let's get her, and get out. I will mark the end of the tunnel with a scrape at the top of the opening, so we know which tunnel to go down when we escape. If we split up for some reason, get out, and I will meet you back at the intersection."

Zion motioned for Assam to follow. They crept up to the opening and entered the room. Zion etched a small line on the lip of the tunnel at the top. When Assam had seen the etching, Zion moved around the room looking down each pipe. He decided to take the tunnel straight ahead.

"Code red! Code red! Code red!" a chamber guard shouted, as he entered the chamber.

"Go see what he needs!" Shobal commanded. "You two guards stay here and lock everything down." Shobal left the back room to head up front. A guard was locking the front chamber door behind the guards that had just left. "What's going on?"

"A guard reported two intruders went down one of our false passages," he answered.

"Maybe it is one of our Watchers," Shobal said, "that did not get the word to go through Samuel. He has the route assignments since the vegetable stand burnt down."

"I doubt it," answered the chamber guard. "The guards said they were soldiers with their swords drawn."

"They must be intruders then," Shobal agreed. "I hope they take them alive so we can find out more."

"Who is it?" the chamber guard asked, responding to the pounding at the door. He looked out the peephole and saw a guard.

"Cascade," responded the guard with the password. A chamber guard opened the door and let him in. He immediately locked the door behind the guard.

"Did you catch them?" Shobal inquired.

"Yes, we caught two young soldiers—teens," the guard answered. "They will not tell us a thing. We have them bound in our holding area."

"Let them sit and stew for a few hours," Shobal said, as he stroked his beard. He caught himself staring at the wall in deep thought then shrugged, "Maybe they will talk later."

"They sliced one of our guards with a sword," a guard said. "It was nothing to serious, so we treated him ourselves."

"Let me know if you want me to take a look at it," Shobal said. The guard nodded his head, then left.

Shobal went back to the room to find Myka's eyes opened, and Lot talking to her.

Lot turned. "What's going on?" he asked.

"The chamber guards caught two young soldiers going down one of the passages," Shobal answered. He smiled at Myka. "Of all the entrances that an intruder would come into, that's the last one I would suspect. Only a few people know about the grate underneath the bench. I'm wondering how those two young soldiers knew about it and what they're looking for."

Myka's eyes brightened. She coughed as she tried to sit up.

"What is it, Myka?" Lot held his ear close to her mouth.

Tears flooded her eyes. "Zion," she said, with a scratchy and barely-audible voice. "My soldier." She coughed some more.

Lot returned her smile, chuckled, and stood up. "Shobal, take me to the two young soldiers. I have a feeling that I know one of them and why they are here."

Lot and Shobal followed a guard out of the secret chamber. The guard turned the corner and was immediately thrown to the ground. Shobal startled and jumped back. They were surrounded by swords.

"Gabriel put down your swords!" Lot said sharply, stepping to the front. "What are you doing?" He watched as Gabriel and his men hesitantly put down their swords.

"We were told two soldiers infiltrated," Gabriel glanced around, then back at Lot. His gaze and tone softened, "We came to help."

"Yes," Shobal answered, as he regained his breath. "We did catch two intruders."

"Where are they?" Gabriel asked.

"Don't you worry about them," Lot answered. "I'm on my way to talk to them right now," his chin jutted out, "by myself. Guards take them to Myka. It will cheer her up to see you, Gabriel," Lot admitted.

The chamber guards that had recently joined them because of the tumult looked over at Shobal. They weren't going to take orders from anyone other than him. Shobal shrugged. He didn't understand the tension between Lot and Gabriel. *Everything has turned upside down*, he thought.

"Guards, they're on our side," Shobal said as he motioned for them to put down their swords. "Escort them to Myka. Lot, let's go talk to the two young soldiers."

Gabriel knelt down and kissed Myka on the forehead. He watched as she opened her eyes and smiled.

She croaked, "Hi," then winced at her throat's dryness.

A guard brought over a glass of water for her.

"You need to drink some water," Gabriel said. "We have all the time in the world to talk." Gabriel lifted her up, almost to a sitting position to drink easier. "Don't try to talk Myka," he said again. It was obvious she had something on her mind. He continued, "I don't know if anyone has told you yet, but the Children of Light are in control of the city of Thanoton. Soon we will control everything but the south."

"G-Gab-riel!" Myka forced out. She was mad and pushed away the water glass.

Oh no, Gabriel thought chagrin all over his face. *Myka's angry with me too.* "What is it?" He leaned in close to her.

Her voice was scratchy, "A soldier named Zion saved me and helped me down here. Find him and make sure he is safe."

"Zion, you said? I will find him."

"No need to look for him," Lot chuckled. "He found us."

"Myka," Zion said, as he kneeled next to her bed.

"Zion, my soldier," Myka said with a burst of energy. She grabbed around his neck and held on as tight as she could. She wept a deep cry that came from her inner soul. Tears of joy gushed from her eyes as she thanked the Light of the Word, overcome by the Lord's great deliverance. "My Soldier, my soldier," she kept repeating.

CHAPTER 69

It was the third day on horseback since the Three Witnesses left Alethia. Caleb, the head of the protection detail, refused to allow Ian to forge ahead of the group. Ian had requested several times to go on ahead, but the Elders' orders were specific. He knew the area well, and he had helped the Three Witnesses escape over the border the first time.

The trip had been slow with two platoons of guards, one in front, and one behind the group. Ezra was itching to get to Sanctuary so Ian could be dispatched right away to find out what was happening in Thanoton.

Ezra didn't complain about Caleb's refusal, and he supported Caleb's obedience. Nor would he disobey the Elders. Ezra wanted the Light of the Word's blessing and was grateful the Elders had decided to let them go. The Elders were adamant; they wanted everyone to travel together as a group for safety. Then once at Sanctuary, they could dispatch Ian to find out if the Children of Light were ready for Ezra to come. In the course of their training, the Elders revealed who all the key players of the Children of Light were.

Ezra put his face toward Thanoton, and the Light of the Word's will for him. Although he loved it at Alethia; living with his mom, spending time with her every day, it was like a dream come true. He knew in his heart of hearts he would not stay. As a Chosen, Ezra was committed to the restoration of Thanoton. He was impatient to fulfill his divine purpose.

Ezra could tell by the tenderness in his mother's eyes that Eva hated her son's leaving. However, she stressed first and foremost her deep desire for him to serve the Light of the Word. She made Ezra promise to send for her as soon as the city of Thanoton was stable. Eva told Ezra she was eager to reunite with his father, Asa.

Ezra had thought a lot about his father his grandfather, Labin. He prayed throughout the trip that they, along with everyone else in the valley of Thanoton, would put their faith and trust in the Light of the Word.

As the group entered the valley of Sanctuary, they could see the city just ahead. They were all eager to get there and finish the journey. The pace quickened; no one talked. All the horses galloped along in rhythm.

They headed down in the valley toward Sanctuary. To their right, off in the distance, they could see the eastern edge of the valley of Thanoton. Ezra's stomach turned. The jagged rock peaks hemmed in the valley of Thanoton giving it a caged in appearance. Ezra knew it was not just caged in physically but spiritually also. The whole valley was oppressed by the enemy, bent on keeping the Truth of the Light of the Word out.

"Whoa! Stop! Everyone stop!" shouted Caleb to his two platoons of guards. His horse slid to a stop.

"What is it?" Ezra asked. He rode up to the front where Caleb had stopped. Caleb was now looking through his scope all around.

"Look for yourself," he said, handing Ezra the scope.

Ezra looked through the scope at the direction the leader was pointing. On top of the ridgeline, a good distance away, they were being watched. Ezra could make out two heads, peering over a rock at them.

"I wonder who they are," Ezra asked. He turned to the head of the security detail.

"Ezra, Ezra!" shouted Dara, as she rode up from the back. "Look!" She pointed.

"What is it?"

"Look!" She pointed again.

Ezra looked through his scope. He could see a large number of horses, coming from Sanctuary. They were headed straight toward them. "Turn around," Ezra commanded. "Let's get out of here."

"There is nowhere to go," Jared shouted. "We are surrounded."

Ezra could now see a group riding up from behind. They split up to form a circle around them. He couldn't see any place to take cover. They were completely vulnerable in the open. "Circle up and form a tight perimeter," Ezra commanded.

The guards immediately formed two tight circles around the Three Witnesses. In the inner circle, the guards stayed on their horses, with swords drawn. In the outer circle, the guards dismounted and kneeled five feet in front of the inner circle, with a ready bow. The extra horses were bunched in the middle.

Ezra watched as the riders from all direction drew closer to them. He was weighing what he should do in his mind. Ezra could tell that the archers were ready and standing by for his command to fire.

"They have such an advantage, and they are a large force," Dara said, while looking through her scope. "Are we going to try to fight them?"

"We surely can't let them capture us," Jared said.

"They're border guards," Caleb said.

They were close enough for Ezra to see their uniforms. "What are the border guards doing past the border?" Ezra waited for an answer, and when he did not get one, he put down his scope. Dara, Jared and Ian were waiting for him to give direction. He was a king. He needed to take charge and act like a king.

"Guards, I don't want you to shoot, until you hear a command from me," he shouted, as he rode around the inner circle. He gained more confidence as he rode. He thought about his situation, and the Whisperer made it very clear for him. *The Light of the Word has promised to restore the Valley of Thanoton to the Children of Light. I am chosen by the Light of the Word and commissioned by the Elders to be King. As King, I am to help the Whisperer turn the people's hearts of the valley to the Light of the Word. The Light of the Word, my Lord, has never failed me,* he thought. *His promises never fail, no matter what the situation looks like.*

He prayed, "Light of the Word, give me favor with this group. I pray you fulfill your promises of restoring your Kingdom and destroy anything that stands in its way. Give me boldness, wisdom, and discernment to be the King over your people."

Ezra remained silent and ignored the various looks he was getting from the guard force, Dara, and Jared. He watched the border guards close in on all sides and stop four hundred feet away. They halted their horses and waited.

"Stay here," commanded Ezra, to his security detail. "I'm going out there to talk to their leader."

"You must not go out there, King Ezra," Caleb said. "I will go out with some of my men and talk to them. You stay here."

"No," King Ezra commanded, with a force that demanded everyone's attention. He noticed they were now addressing him as King. He was no longer in training. Somewhere along the trip, the farther they got away from Alethia, he had transitioned to King in everyone's mind—in his, too. *I am a King,* he told himself. *Act like one.* "My two aides and I will go talk to their leader." Ezra motioned with his head for Dara and Jared to follow him. Dara and Jared said nothing. They exchanged a glance of surprise and followed.

Marcus could not believe when his scouts returned with news that a group was heading their way. He was told the group was two days out. Marcus had just recently started sending small patrols out to explore the land, to see what was around. It had taken several months to get established in Sanctuary after fleeing the border. He knew that Alethia was three days out. Marcus purposefully did not send any patrols more than two days in that direction.

He was told he was not to go there. Lot had said the Elders from the city of Alethia would make contact with them later on in the summer. The Elders would not even know they occupied Sanctuary until late spring.

Marcus wondered what was going on. He never expected they were going to send representatives so soon. They had only been there a few months. It wasn't even spring.

"It looks like three riders are coming out of there security perimeter," Joel observed.

"One of them is a girl," Tiras added.

"Let me see the scope," Marcus said. He held out his hand for Tiras to hand it to him. Marcus looked and sure enough, there were three teenagers—two boys and one girl. "Listen up! Everyone hold in place, and no one does anything unless I command you." Marcus addressed Joel and Tiras. He said, "Let's go out to meet them."

Marcus rode past the frontline, along with Joel and Tiras to meet them.

"Let's stop here," said King Ezra. He had observed the three riders headed their way to meet them. "We don't want to get too far away from our security perimeter."

"Are you going to tell them who we are?" Dara asked.

"I am not sure what I'm going to tell them," Ezra answered. He started to laugh. Ezra was unable to contain it. Dara and Jared started to laugh along with him. It was a nervous laugh that helped them relieve the stress they all felt.

"I think you should just tell them you are the King of Thanoton," Jared said in between laughs. He continued, "and—and, they need to step aside."

"Yeah. Tell them to prepare a place for you and your assistants to stay," Dara said, jokingly. She and Jared knew he was not that kind of a

King. He was to be a servant to the people. He was to be a leader, not a dictator. It was fun to joke around, though. It took the edge off.

The Three Witnesses watched as three riders slowly approached. Their horses were walking toward them. Ezra could see through the scope that the riders wore border guard uniforms. *The one in the center is the obvious leader*, thought Ezra. He wore captain's insignia on his uniform.

Ezra put away his scope as they got closer. The captain had an intense, wondering look on his face. It was not an angry, challenging look like Ezra was expecting. Ezra still was not sure what he was going to say. They did have them completely surrounded. *Give me the words to say*, Ezra prayed.

The captain sat rigid in his saddle as Ezra approached. He was very muscular with dark skin. His hair was cut as short as possible. There was just the shadow of black hair on his head.

"Who are you?" asked Captain Marcus.

"I'm Ezra, King of Thanoton," Ezra claimed boldly. Ezra was as surprised as everyone else that heard it. It just came out. It was a time for truth. He didn't know if they knew anything about the Three Witnesses. Ezra sensed the Whisperer prodding him to be straightforward.

Captain Marcus turned his head quickly to Tiras and Joel, his subordinate leaders. He was about to say something when—.

"We're here to take back the Valley of Thanoton for the Children of Light," Jared said. He had moved closer to Marcus as he spoke, giving his words emphasis.

Dara, who felt like she needed to say something next said, "We need you and your men to escort us to Sanctuary. We will stay there until we find out what is going on in the valley."

Marcus was taken aback and said nothing. He just stared at them with wonder.

"Is there something wrong?" King Ezra asked. "Is there something you do not understand?"

"We understand, King Ezra," Marcus finally said. "Lot told us about you Three but—"

"But what?" questioned King Ezra.

"We weren't expecting you, King Ezra. Lot made it sound like the Children of Light were no longer going to use the eastern cut. He told us representatives from the Elders of Alethia would come later this summer."

Ezra stole a glance at Dara and Jared. He was thinking probably what they were thinking. *This Marcus and his border guards know all about them. They know about the Children of Light and Alethia. Things in Thanoton must have progressed quickly since they had left.*

"The plans have since changed," Ezra said. "We'll fill you in on why we're here. Why aren't you guarding the border?"

"You haven't heard?" Marcus asked. "Why we fled the border?"

"No."

"That's a long story and better told back in Sanctuary. We can sit down and talk," Marcus answered.

"Yes," King Ezra agreed. "We need to hear everything you know about recent activities in Thanoton."

"King Ezra, we are at your service," Marcus said. "Please, you and your men follow me."

Marcus turned his horse around, and Ezra rode up next to him. Ezra watched as Marcus gave some hand-signals for his men to lead the way. He turned around and saw Jared had done the same for their two platoons to follow. King Ezra thanked the Light of the Word for preparing a way ahead of time.

CHAPTER 70

Gabriel and his small team followed Zion through the woods to the culvert where Zion had stayed two nights before. They were on a reconnaissance mission to locate Arton and the reorganized renegade army. Gabriel planned to strike them before they attacked.

The enemy had consolidated in the Green Lake area. They planned on taking back the palace and control of the city. The soldiers guarding the eastern border had left their positions to join forces with Arton. There was no longer anyone guarding the border.

The night before in the secret chamber, Zion and Myka shared with Gabriel how they met, and all they had done for each other. Gabriel took stock of Zion and convinced him to show him the area where Arton and his men were hiding. Zion knew the general area because he had heard and seen many soldiers heading in that direction when he and Assam were hiding in the culvert.

Gabriel crouched next to Zion and leaned in close to whisper, "We're almost at the intersection."

It was the east to the west road that went from the eastern border past the city of Thanoton, and out to the western border. The southern road intersected with it, forming a "T" intersection. The southern road wound around Green Lake to the southern regions naturally closed off by the Silver Rock Ridge Line.

There was only one route passable through the Silver Rock Ridge, and that spot was heavily guarded. It was called the Southern Gate. It took an hour to get there by horseback from the intersection on the southern road. Gabriel was afraid some of Javan's army had already fled to the southern area of the valley of Thanoton and warned them. He hoped the southern army would not find out about the overthrow, giving him time to stabilize the city, and then bring them in without a struggle.

"Over there is the culvert we stayed in the other night," Zion said. He pointed in the direction. It was nighttime, but he could easily see with the clear sky and the bright moon. *The moon seems so low*, he thought.

It was unusual for the nights in Thanoton to be so clear and bright. No one in the patrol was used to this much light at night. They were spoiled. Sneaking around in the pitch black was so much easier. This night required some thought and skill, using the shadows and thick vegetation to mask their movements.

"Which way did they go?" Gabriel asked.

"They were in the woodline on the other side of the road, heading south. They stayed in the woodline and used the road to their right as a guide. We could see and hear them as they continued south."

"You still think they are in the swamp? They might have gone through the southern gate," Gabriel said. His voice sounded skeptical.

"Yes, I'm sure they went into the swamp," Zion answered. He quickly lowered his voice, realizing he had gotten louder. "Look how light it is."

"The swamp is two miles away," Gabriel added.

"We could hear them as they moved through the woods as far as Green Lake. Then later on in the night, we could see the flicker of a fire coming from the swamp. Who else would it be?"

"Okay, we'll take a look," Gabriel said.

"Commander Gabriel, I'm sure the southern armies already know what happened here in Thanoton. I'm willing to bet a number of soldiers escaped down south. That was our plan, to go south if Assam and I were unable to link up with our old platoon. That is, of course, until you showed me what is truly going on."

Gabriel signaled for one of his men to come forward. "Go back and have the assault force get ready. Bring them to this location, and wait till we return from reconnaissance. Take an extra man with you, and I will leave four men here to secure the area. I will take six men with me to find them."

Zion waited for Gabriel to give the final instructions to the four soldiers who were to stay behind. He was surprised when Gabriel came back, signaling him to lead. He wished Assam could be here to see him. Zion would have to tell him about it when he got back. Assam had chosen not to go. Zion slowly approached the road. He looked all around and listened. When he thought it was clear, he sprinted across the road into the wood line. He crouched down on one knee and signaled the rest to follow.

Gabriel and his men were all across before Zion started to move down south, skirting the road to the right. Zion was nervous. He was intently focused on making sure he moved quietly and cautiously. Zion wasn't nervous about running into the enemy. He didn't want to look bad in the eyes of Commander Gabriel. Gabriel had given him the honor of leading the patrol, and he did not want to mess that up. He also wanted to impress Myka when they told her all about it. He wanted to show her how brave and good a soldier he was.

As they approached the Green Lake area, Zion noticed movement up ahead on the road. He gave the hand signal for the patrol to freeze. He waited and studied the area up ahead. He could hear their muffled voices, but they were too far away to understand anything said. He analyzed the situation until he figured out the enemy was building a roadblock out of trees. Zion signaled Gabriel to kneel down next to him. He pointed in the direction of the roadblock.

Zion leaned in close and whispered, "They're building a roadblock."

Gabriel signaled for two men to move in closer and pull security, while the rest maneuvered around. Again, Gabriel motioned for Zion to lead them deeper into the woods, to go around the roadblock. Zion set out and immediately understood why the enemy had put a roadblock there. They had run into the lake. There was only a small patch in which to maneuver through, and there were enemy soldiers close-by. He raised his right fist eye level, signaling for the patrol to freeze once again.

Zion shook his head as Gabriel looked at him. Gabriel could see the problem right away. They would not be able to go around the roadblock in that direction. If they crossed the road and tried the other way around, they would be seen for sure. The vegetation was very sparse.

Crunch crunch, Zion heard. They all froze.

A soldier headed straight toward them. Zion was not sure what he should do. Should he run or stay there? He hoped the enemy soldier would not run into them. Yet, the soldier kept heading their way. Out of the corner of his eye, he spied Gabriel shifting to the side with a knife in hand. As the enemy soldier got closer, it was obvious what Gabriel was about to do.

Crunch, crunch. Gabriel sprung up, grabbed the soldier around the mouth, and stuck the knife into his back, penetrating the spleen. Another soldier slipped past Zion and assisted Gabriel by quietly lowering the dead enemy soldier to the ground.

Zion immediately felt jealous. *Why did I just sit there?* he scolded himself. He was right there. *I should have jumped up and helped Gabriel with the enemy soldier.*

Gabriel motioned for Zion to back out and lead the patrol back the way they had come. A few of the soldiers took turns carrying the dead soldier until they could hide the body. They found a small depression with a lot of fallen debris from trees on the ground. They stuck him down in the depression and laid a pile of debris over him. It was temporary, but it would buy them some time. A dead body with a knife wound would cause Arton and his army to heighten security. Then Gabriel and his assault force would lose the best advantage, the element of surprise. They needed that and the violence of action to be successful. By the time the enemy figured out what had happened, it would be too late.

When they were a safe distance away from the roadblock, Gabriel stopped the patrol. He briefed and placed two soldiers behind a rock outcropping to watch for any enemy that might head their way. Gabriel took the rest back to the patrol base. They would plan the attack with the assault force, using the knowledge they had received from the recon.

One hour later, the assault force left the patrol base. Once again, Gabriel had Zion lead the way. Because of the terrain and moonlight, the two platoons walked single file to where Gabriel left the two soldiers. The assault force spread out. They waited for the platoons to form two lines behind the rock outcropping and account for everyone.

First, platoon headed out. They edged away from the road to the lake skirting around it until they were close. They stayed a safe distance away from the small area between the roadblock and the lake. The platoon neared the area where they had killed the enemy soldier. After the second platoon initiated an attack on the roadblock, they would assault through this small area.

Fear began to creep into Zion's chest as they waited for the second platoon. No one knew what to expect after they assaulted past the roadblock. Zion hoped his old platoon was not there. They weren't really his enemies. How could he kill them, really? It was more personal for him than Gabriel's men.

Zion did sense Gabriel really didn't want to cause more deaths. He really only wanted to secure Thanoton and prevent a counterattack. He kept repeating to the assault force to try to capture as many as possible. The other soldiers had started to question Gabriel's tactics. Capturing was harder and you were more vulnerable than killing the enemy. Zion knew Gabriel had received pressure from Zesha and his Cabinet to stop the killing.

Gabriel's plan involved specially made arrows to light on fire and shoot through the air. The day prior, they had made thousands of them for this attack. Both platoons had them out, ready to light and fire on command. They hid behind trees shrubs or anything they could find until they initiated the attack. Men were scattered throughout the two platoons with torches to light the arrows. Each torch was pre-made,

313

wrapped in kerosene dipped-rags. The men assigned would strike flint and steel together sparking the torches ablaze.

Both platoons would move into position, and then hold position for fifteen minutes while on the alert for anything they might have missed, like another defensive position close by. If there was no change, second platoon would light the torches and fire into the roadblock, causing a blaze of fire. The roadblock was now a huge pile of tree trunks across the road. Second platoon would shoot anyone running away from that position.

First platoon would wait until the roadblock became a raging fire, illuminating the whole area. They would engage targets within their range, using regular arrows. Once the area was lit up, first platoon would move up, looking for secondary targets and defensive positions. These would be set on fire with their fire-tipped arrows. Burning, wagons, tents, and supplies would light the whole area.

After the enemy was neutralized, the second platoon would assault across the road and around the burning roadblock. As they crossed, they would engage any targets until finding a good covered and concealed position. They would take out immediate threats and signal with a loud blast from a ram's horn for the first platoon to attack. Several soldiers scattered throughout first and second platoon were specially trained in blowing the horns. After the initial blast, they would all blow their horns causing a fearsome, psychological fear in the enemy. Finally, the first platoon would assault through the objective with the second platoon covering.

The second platoon waited for Gabriel's signal to initiate the attack. It had been over fifteen minutes. They all wondered what he was waiting for.

Gabriel leaned in close and whispered, "Something is wrong. I don't hear any movement, and there are no fires like there were a few hours ago."

It was obvious to Zion now after Gabriel had said it. He hadn't heard or seen anything either, a direct contrast from the last time they had been there. He had been too scared and his heart beating too loudly to notice.

Just then, they all heard a soft, bird whistle at a distance behind then. It was a ghost team signal. A friendly patrol was in the area, approaching their position. Gabriel responded back with the same bird whistle. It resonated in the quiet of the night.

A few minutes later, Zion could hear the small patrol as it worked its way to the front. That was the only noise he could hear. No noise came from the enemy's direction. Zion secretly hoped the enemy had escaped to the southern territory.

Zion moved over, as a soldier kneeled next to Gabriel. "Elam, what are you doing here?" Gabriel said to his second-in-command.

"I came to warn you," Elam said. He gave a quick glance to Zion and then gestured for Gabriel to come with him to talk privately.

Zion watched as they moved ten feet away. He wondered why Elam's glance held suspicion. They glanced several times in his direction as they talked.

"How could this have happened?" Gabriel responded. "Assam was with Shobal and the guards in the secret chamber."

"They all thought he was on our side, so they stopped guarding him," Elam added. "It didn't help that Lot did not want the chamber guards to treat him like a prisoner. Then when Zion volunteered to help, all suspicion went out the window." Elam watched as Gabriel studied Zion.

"I'm surprised you were unable to catch him," Gabriel said, as he took a deep breath. He was frustrated.

"Assam had a good hour head start on us. About the time they figured out he was missing and alerted us up top, we had to play catch-up. It took some time initially to find his tracks, but once we did, he was easy to follow. He was moving as fast as he could most of the way. He did not care about trampling down shrubs and knocking down tree limbs. He wanted to get to this area as fast as he could."

"You sure he made it to the enemy camp?" Gabriel whispered. He already knew the answer. He didn't even know why he asked the question.

"Assam made it to the camp. The tracks cut through the open area on the other side of the roadblock," Elam answered. "We never encountered any enemy nor did we see anything on the other side of the roadblock. We went as far as we could, without risking compromise."

Gabriel tapped on his left shoulder, signaling all the leaders to come to where he was. He leaned over and whispered to Elam to secure Zion. Gabriel watched as Elam pretended to pass Zion. As soon as he was close, Elam pounced on Zion. Others came from the shadows and quickly gagged, tied, and hooded him before he knew what had happened.

Gabriel waited until he had all the leaders assembled. "We have good reason to believe the enemy has been warned that we were coming. When we did our recon earlier, we could see and hear movement. There were campfires scattered throughout, on the other side of the roadblock. Right now, we see and hear nothing. So, they have either left the area or are preparing for a counterattack. If they were warned, they have the advantage.

"I have come up with a new plan," Gabriel said. "I want both platoons to pull back to the rock outcropping we staged at earlier. It will provide a good defensive position. I will give you thirty minutes to get there and set up a perimeter. Elam, you take charge of that and the prisoner."

"I will keep six men with me," Gabriel proceeded. "In thirty minutes, we will set the roadblock on fire and anything else we can to illuminate the area. If we do draw the enemy out, we will do so beyond your position. You can ambush them from the flank. If there is no activity, we will wait all night until sun up." Gabriel stopped for a second. He could not remember when or if he had ever used that term. "We will wait till sun up," he repeated. "Then, we will sweep the area and look for tracks to find out where they have gone. Any questions?"

"If none, let's go," Gabriel commanded. "Oh wait! Leave half of the fire arrows and one torch to light them. Take the rest with you." Gabriel and his men lined up the arrows ready to light, while they waited for the two platoons to get set. They planned to shoot as many as they could in a short time.

Gabriel waited thirty minutes, and then he lit the torch to ignite the arrows.

CHAPTER 71

The Three Witnesses spent the rest of the day exchanging stories with the border guards and their families. They didn't even consider resting from their long trip. Ezra, Dara, and Jared were eager to get started.

Ezra took the opportunity to talk to the people about the Light of the Word and to read out of the *Book of Prophesies*. The families of Sanctuary were hungry to hear about the Light of the Word and to learn about the history of the Children of Light. He filled in the blanks and answered many questions they had. They were eager to be a part of the restoration of Thanoton. They felt compelled by the Light of the Word to do so.

Ezra was amazed when he heard the border guard's story of how they ended up in Sanctuary. He learned what Lot had told Marcus about the Three Witnesses and the Children of Light. They said Lot had warned them to leave.

Ezra was surprised to hear there were so many secret believers—Children of Light—that had remained hidden within the border guards. They had secretly passed the truth down for a thousand years.

The most amazing news was the many strange occurrences that had happened lately in the valley of Thanoton.

"So, we all have decided to go up to the border tonight?" Dara asked as she admired the moon and the stars. They seemed so close. Dara was tired. The adrenaline and excitement of the day had taken its toll.

"Just to see Ian off," Ezra reminded Dara. He said it loud enough for the others to hear, "and to look into the valley."

"Wait a minute!" blurted Caleb, the head of Ezra's security detail. "All due respect King Ezra, the Elders gave explicit instructions not to go to the valley until Ian finds out if they are ready for you."

"Caleb, we're just going to go up to the border to look in," King Ezra explained. "Marcus has had men watching the border. Two nights ago his men reported that all the soldiers had left the border." He turned to Marcus who had just walked up to them, "Isn't that right?"

"I have men up there right now," Marcus added. "They have reported no enemy activity. It will be easy for Ian to enter into the valley of Thanoton. If you want, you can send some of your men ahead to secure the area before King Ezra goes up. Caleb, it would be good for King Ezra to see the valley. It's no longer—" he hesitated.

Jared was the first to ask, "No longer what?" eager for Marcus to finish his sentence.

"You must see for yourself," Marcus said. "I don't want to spoil the surprise."

The Three Witnesses gave each other an excited look. Ezra could tell Jared and Dara could not wait to find out what Marcus was keeping from them. "What do you say, Caleb?"

"I guess it will be all right just to go up to the border," Caleb agreed. He was curious himself. "I will send some of my men immediately to look around. We will leave in an hour," he commanded. He realized he said it a little too loud. Caleb wanted to be a worthy leader, and not be pushed into any mistakes. He was surprised when no one objected to the hour wait. Still, the Elders' mandate weighed heavy on his shoulders.

"Good," Ezra agreed. "We will wait an hour before we go." Ezra saw that Ian was disappointed he had to wait another hour. He said nothing. He just sat down and waited.

An hour later, Ezra was climbing up the side of the eastern cut to the top of the ridgeline that surrounded the valley of Thanoton. As Ezra approached the top, the guards that had gone ahead were bunched up. They looked toward the south, and he could hear the chatter of their voices. Ezra was surprised how easy they were to see. They reflected the light from the valley.

"What's going on?" Ezra asked when he approached the top.

"There is a large fire on the south road." Marcus pointed, even though he really didn't need to. The flames from the fire were easy to see.

"It looks like the fire is around Green Lake by the swamp," Ezra added. He heard Dara say, "Look, you can see the city of Thanoton."

"I wonder what the fire is all about," Marcus said.

"I will find out, King Ezra," Ian said. He started down the other side.

"Hold on a second," Ezra said. He had everyone's attention now. They all stopped, watched, and waited for what he would say next. He really didn't know why he stopped Ian. "Look at the valley. It's all lit up by lights."

"That's the surprise I wanted you to see," Marcus said.

"The houses in the city of Thanoton are all lit up, the market square and the Palace. Most of all look how easy it is to see with the moon so bright. Unbelievable!"

They all waited quietly. Finally, Jared spoke up, "King Ezra, are you surprised the prophecies are actually being fulfilled?"

"This is what's supposed to happen," Dara added, as she slipped her arm under his and gazed at the valley.

"You're right," Ezra said, as he regained his composure. "I'm always surprised when promises are fulfilled. I don't know why, but I am."

"Me too, King Ezra," Ian said. "Can I go now? I'm ready to see what else our Lord has done, since we've been gone."

"Yes, go find out," Ezra answered. "Don't worry about the fire Ian. Find out if they are ready for me to come. Talk to Lot. Marcus, I want you to send a small recon element south and find out what that fire was all about."

King Ezra, Dara, and Jared sat down next to each other and watched as Ian climbed down the other side and disappeared into the woods. They sat there quietly admiring the valley. They were exhausted but excited at the same time. They needed sleep but could not wait to find out if the Seekers were ready for them in the valley.

"The valley is actually beautiful, now that it's no longer overcast," Dara said. She was lying on her back.

"The physical light has come and dispelled the darkness," Jared said. "Now it is time for the Thanoton people to receive the true Light of the Word, and for the light to expose the lies and darkness in their hearts."

"We've been prepared and empowered by the Light of the Word to do it," King Ezra said. "We're ready!" He stood up next to Jared, who was bouncing around with excitement.

"We are the Children of Light," Dara added. They looked down at her stretched out, the picture of ease, and they laughed.

"What?" she said, much too comfortable to get up. "With this nice breeze, I could quickly fall asleep up here."

. "We better go back to Sanctuary to get some rest. I think we're going to need it," King Ezra laughed as he stretched out his hand to help Dara to her feet. Jared laughed at Ezra and Dara as they resisted and pulled each other until she was up and in his arms. Jared could not help but think about how much he missed Myka. *She must still be in the cache site*, he thought.

"Caleb, we're ready to go back," Ezra said. He followed Caleb and paused for a few seconds to watch the recon patrol disappear in the woods.

It was daybreak. Gabriel and his six men were concealed in some thick bushes around a clump of trees. They waited and watched all night for the sunrise. The sun had peeked over the ridgeline in the east. The barricade they torched the night before still smoldered. All that remained was the charred fragments and ashes where the roadblock had been. Gabriel had not seen any enemy activity all night. He stuck to his plan. They would sweep through the area and look for tracks and clues to where they might have gone.

Gabriel suspected Assam had warned them in time to flee. He hoped they did not go past the Southern Gate. That was as far as he was allowed to go, according to the Elders. If they went to the southern part of the valley, then they were out of his reach. It would create a problem later. Gabriel wondered what Myka would think about Zion's betrayal.

"Let's go," Gabriel mouthed, without a sound. He signaled with his head for the rest to follow. Gabriel, with his sword drawn, moved as stealthy as he could. He gave the signal for his men to fan out and work their way around the roadblock. It was as Gabriel had suspected. The base camp was deserted. All that was left were remnants of a hasty escape by the enemy troops. Campfires still smoldered and pots were full of burned food from where the water had boiled out. Clothing articles, blankets, canteens scattered about. They left in a hurry. Gabriel now knew for sure that Assam had warned them in time to escape.

"I want you two to go back, and tell Elam to send me one platoon to pursue the enemy. Have them bring enough provisions to last a week. I have a feeling they went through the southern gate," Gabriel said. He motioned with his sword at the tracks made by the hooves of the horses and all the footprints. They led straight toward the southern gate.

"I'm sure they did," agreed a soldier. "That's the only safe place left for them."

Gabriel nodded. "We'll verify if they did. Regardless, we will leave the platoon that Elam sends to block the southern gateway. They cannot come back, and no more can escape. Tell Elam to stay in place with the rest. I will link up with him later today so we can return to the palace. I've been gone too long."

Later that morning, Gabriel along with the platoon of soldiers, followed the enemy's tracks toward the southern border. The border was distinct, a natural rock wall that split the valley of Thanoton in two parts. The rock wall stood over a hundred feet and had no gaps all the way across. It wasn't always one solid wall. Over the years, they had filled in the gaps to the natural wall, leaving only one opening, the southern gate.

The rock wall was dangerously steep and difficult to climb. Even if you could climb to the top, you would be seen from any of the many observation posts peaked on top. All traffic went in and out through the southern Gate. It was heavily guarded and tightly controlled. The rock wall kept the slaves and prisoners from escaping. They were used to work the coalmines and timber mills in the southern region.

The surface was rocky and inclined upward toward the southern border. There were large boulders that helped conceal Gabriel and his men as they made their approach. Close to the southern gate, he had second thoughts that his plan would work. He needed to block the southern gate but didn't want an armed conflict either. Gabriel and his men hid behind the last great boulder, forty feet tall and thirty feet wide. The boulder stood just before the southern gate.

Blocking the southern gate would be difficult without taking out the observation points. Gabriel knew this would have to wait until later. He had too small of a force to take the southern border properly. His first priority was to stabilize Thanoton up to the southern regions. Even if he was able to take the southern gate, they would have to deal with the large military base that it opened up into. The southern road ran straight through the military base on the other side. Their best bet was to take over the checkpoint prior to the southern gate and control it from there.

Gabriel glanced over at his men and waited to give them enough time to get in position. They would wait for his signal then attack the checkpoint that led to the southern gate. Half of the platoon would provide security while the other half took over the checkpoint. From there, they would occupy the area, and block the southern route.

Gabriel planned to leave the platoon behind at the checkpoint. It would not be enough men to repel a full-blown attack from the southern army, but he gambled that the enemy would not be foolhardy and run out into the open. They did not know how many of his men would be there. The enemy would probably wait, watch, and analyze the situation before they acted. At least, that's what Gabriel would do given the same situation. He planned to deceive the enemy by sporadically changing the numbers at the checkpoint. Periodically, he would bring large amounts of troops up to the border on routine patrols. Gabriel would make it difficult for them to determine how many men were stationed there.

Securing this checkpoint was vital for Gabriel. Once secured, he could push out from the market square area and set up roadblocks farther east towards the eastern cut. The west was already secure.

Gabriel slid all the way to the ground. He low-crawled around the base of the rock to observe. It was just as he suspected. There was an unusual amount of soldiers at the checkpoint, eighteen and heavily armed. They were quiet and waiting. Gabriel calculated they were two hundred feet away. He wondered how close the other half of the platoon across the road was able to get to the checkpoint. Gabriel shifted his scope farther from the checkpoint. One hundred and fifty feet farther, the southern border was barricaded with soldiers ready to defend.

Gabriel gave the signal for his men to follow. The plan was to low-crawl as far as they could get without being seen. Then they would initiate the attack. They would distract the enemy, giving the other group the time to sneak up and attack from the opposite direction. Gabriel was as low as he could get to the ground. Using forearms and the sides of his legs to propel forward, he shielded his movement with rocks and vegetation.

With keen calculation, Gabriel neared the precise distance with the most protective cover to initiate the attack. He signaled for his men to get in line and prepare to attack with arrows. His soldiers used hand and arm signals to pick out which enemy soldier they were going to shoot making sure to hit as many as they could, if not all. He didn't want them wasting their arrows on one target.

They identified their target and were ready and waiting for Gabriel to initiate the attack. Gabriel shot, followed by a volley of arrows from his men.

"Ahh!"

"Take cover," Gabriel heard. Half were dead, and the rest wounded. He watched as his team from the other direction moved in and killed a few enemy soldiers as they tried to run to the southern border gate. Gabriel signaled his men to close in and kill the rest.

Gabriel was pleased. They had taken the checkpoint over. Just as he had predicted, the enemy soldiers at the southern gate did not come to the checkpoint's aid. Instead, they fortified their positions expecting an attack. Gabriel would use that to his advantage.

CHAPTER 72

Ian had spent the entire night trying to stay hidden. It was much more difficult with the moon illuminating the night. His usual routes and observation points were no longer good. He felt vulnerable and naked with all the light. Ian was spoiled. He depended on the pitch black to conceal his movements. Now that it was day, he was stuck. He was at the edge of the market square in a clump of bushes, unable to move without being seen. Things were much different in the market square.

Ian had snuck past small groups of soldiers to get to his hiding spot. The soldiers were distracted as they worked to push the security perimeter out. The market square was bustling with activity. People were talking, laughing, and enjoying each other's company. Ian noticed right away that the soldiers were not scrutinizing and watching the people as before. The soldiers were actually protecting them. Ian wondered if he would be less conspicuous if he just simply got up and walked around as normal. He needed to get to Calvin's house.

"Don't move," Ian heard. The soldier that approached from behind startled him.

Ian was so preoccupied with the noise and people of the market square, he hadn't heard the soldier sneaking up.

"I want you to stand up with your hands over your head," the soldier commanded.

"What do you have over there?" another soldier shouted as he ran toward them.

"I caught someone spying on the market square," he shouted back.

Ian watched as other soldiers came over to help.

"Tie his hands up. I've got him covered," said the soldier that caught him. He had his eye fixed on his arrow, ready to shoot.

"What do we have here?" asked the sergeant that approached.

"I found this man hidden in the bushes watching the market square."

"Who you working for?" commanded the sergeant.

"W-Working for?" questioned Ian. "No one. I don't know what you are talking about."

"Don't get smart with me," the sergeant shouted as he struck Ian in the stomach with his fist. Ian doubled over and fell down.

"Ohh! I've done nothing wrong," Ian groaned, clutching his stomach.

"Spying on us for the enemy," said the sergeant.

"No! I'm—"

"Shut up! We'll get the truth out of you," the sergeant said. "Take him to the palace. Commander Gabriel will want to interrogate him."

"Gabriel?" Ian repeated.

"Don't play dumb with me," the sergeant said, "Gabriel, the commander of the Army of the Children of Light."

"The Children of Light," Ian perked up.

"Ha, ha," the Sergeant laughed. "The Children of Light have taken back the valley of Thanoton from your evil regime."

"I am of the Children of Light," Ian said, all excited.

"Sure you are," the sergeant said. "Gag him!"

Ian could not believe what had happened since he left. The Children of Light had taken back the kingdom from the Children of Darkness, and he was now their prisoner. He felt self-conscious as he was led through the market square to the palace. All eyes were on him. *Don't they know? I'm the intruder that helped make this happen. I brought the messages from Alethia to the Seekers. I helped smuggle King Ezra and the other two Witnesses out of the Valley*, he thought.

The crowd parted as Ian was brought through the front gate of the palace. Ian always wanted to see what the palace looked like on the inside. He never thought it would be under these circumstances. They entered the main palace entrance, and Ian couldn't help admiring the beauty. The shiny marble walls, high ceilings with hanging candle chandeliers, and murals on the walls throughout were beautiful. They were pictures of Thanoton's past when the Children of Light ruled the valley.

We must never get complacent and allow the Children of Darkness to gain a foothold into our society again, Ian said to himself. He looked up to see a group of people descend the staircase in the middle of the palace. "Wait, I—Hey!" he said all muffled. His eyes met Lot's.

"Ian!" Lot shouted as he came down the steps. "Untie him, sergeant."

"But we caught him spying on us," the sergeant protested.

"He's our spy. Now let him go," Lot said.

"Release him," the sergeant said, reluctantly.

"Lot," Ian said, as soon as his gag came off. He returned the hug. "I need to talk to you," he whispered in his ear.

"Let's go upstairs," Lot said. Calvin and I were just talking about you.

"Calvin?"

"Yeah, Calvin is upstairs," Lot answered. He saw Ian's look. "Oh, you don't know, do you? We've taken back the Kingdom."

"So I've heard.

"Yeah, Zesha is running the Kingdom and we're part of the interim council until King Ezra arrives. You probably don't know, but Zesha was our insider on the council. He actually killed Javan."

"Javan is dead?"

"He sure is. What brings you here?" Lot asked, as they reached the door to the conference room.

"I'm here to see if you're ready for the Three Witnesses," Ian said, entering the room."

"We're ready for King Ezra to come," Calvin said, getting up from his seat to shake Ian's hand.

"I can't believe all that has happened," Ian said.

"Where is King Ezra now?" Zesha asked, walking over from the head of the table.

"King Ezra, Jared, and Dara are in Sanctuary, waiting with his security detail," Ian answered.

"Sanctuary? How?" Zesha asked.

"What about Marcus?" Lot asked.

"Marcus is on our side," Ian answered, overwhelmed by the questions that were fired at him.

"Hold on! Quiet," Calvin commanded, gesturing with his hands to calm everyone down. "It seems that we all have questions. Why don't we sit down and bring each other up to date on what has happened on both sides."

"Calvin is right," Zesha said. He laughed at the excitement everyone was showing. "We have time. Gabriel is due back this afternoon from pursuing the enemy. He can give us a better idea of the security situation."

Ian told the council about the training the Three Witnesses had gone through in Alethia. He shared how the Whisperer spoke to Ezra to come immediately to Thanoton. Ian told about Ezra, Jared, and Dara petitioning the Elders to come early and see if all was ready. He listened as Zesha, Lot, and Calvin gave the details of how Javan's evil empire was overthrown by the Children of Light. They all glorified the God above for orchestrating everything into such divine order. The good and bad He used to accomplish His purpose.

"So are you ready to go see Myka?" Lot asked Ian.

"I can't wait," Ian answered. "It's a miracle she's alive, after all, she has been through."

"Shobal has taken great care of her," Lot added. "Come this way." He gestured to Ian to follow down a small staircase that led below the palace. "We recently convinced Shobal to give us an easier access to his chamber. Now we can get to him from the basement of the palace."

"Does he ever leave his underground complex?" Ian asked as they reached the doorway that led to the inner chamber.

"No, we haven't convinced him of that yet," Lot answered. "It's Lot and Ian here to see Myka," he said to the chamber guard.

"Ian!" Myka screamed. She had her arms, out ready to give Ian a hug. She was sitting up now and feeling much better.

"I heard all that has happened," Ian said. "You've been through a lot."

"I had a lot of help," she said. A fleeting thought of Zion made her angry for a moment. She suddenly directed her attention to Lot. "I heard that Gabriel had Zion arrested. Lot, there is no way he could be a traitor. Gabriel is wrong. You need to get him released."

"Gabriel is convinced that Assam and Zion sabotaged their surprise attack on the enemy. It was Assam that warned the enemy that Gabriel and his men were coming."

"I know Zion. He would never betray us like that," Myka pleaded.

"I'll have a talk with Gabriel when he gets back," Lot assured her. "Ian has some good news that will cheer you up," Lot said.

"Myka, you will never guess who is in Sanctuary right now?" Ian said.

"Who?" she asked with a skeptical look.

"King Ezra, Dara, and—Jared," Ian said. He was surprised by the look on Myka's face.

"Jared," she said, laying back down on the bed. Myka hadn't thought about Jared for a long time. Myka had been too preoccupied with thinking about Zion, ever since he saved her.

Ian looked perplexed. Lot shrugged his shoulders, and said, "Isn't that great news?"

"We're planning to talk to Gabriel this afternoon and coordinate a time to bring King Ezra here tomorrow. We will officially anoint him as the King of Thanoton before the people."

Lot laughed. "That's the plan anyway if the security conditions are right. Everyone is in a hurry to make it happen. The people are ready. They have been devouring the booklet we passed out, *The History of the Children of Light with excerpts from the Book of Prophesies.* They too are waiting for King Ezra to arrive."

"I can't wait to go back tonight to tell them the Kingdom is ready and waiting for their arrival," Ian said. "They will be happy to hear you are all right. You *are* okay, right?"

"Actually, I'm not!" Myka said, sitting back up. "I want Zion released now!"

"I'll talk to Zesha and see if I can get Zion released," Lot said, holding out his hands for Myka to calm down. He wondered what had gotten into her. "Why don't you tell Myka what you told us upstairs? Tell her how the Three Witnesses came to be in Sanctuary."

Myka could see the worried look they both were giving her. "I'm sorry. I just want him released," she said, crying. Ian put his arm around her causing her to cry even harder. She listened to Ian talk about the Three Witnesses, but all she could think of was Zion. She didn't realize until now, but she had fallen in love with Zion. It wasn't a crush like she had with Jared. She and Zion were knitted together. They had been through a lot. He had saved her life.

CHAPTER 73

Zesha glanced around the conference table. Calvin, Lot, and Ian had waited for Gabriel to return from the south before they made any decision. "So, Gabriel," he paused, "now that you have heard from Ian, what do you think? Is it safe for us to bring Ezra tomorrow and officially anoint him King in front of the people?"

"I see no problem bringing him in tomorrow," Gabriel said. "All of Thanoton is safe and under our control, except for the southern border. I will send extra troops to monitor the southern checkpoint. The rest will provide security around the palace and the route in. I will personally escort the King from the eastern cut tomorrow."

"I'm really eager to tell them," Ian responded. "Can I go?"

"Yes, you can go," Zesha said.

"I'm going with you," Lot added.

"I'm sending some security with you also," Gabriel said as they walked to the conference door. "Elam," he called out to his second-in-command waiting outside the door.

"Yes, Commander?"

"I want you to get a security detail ready to go with Ian and Lot to the eastern cut immediately. I will be down to brief them before they go."

"Taken care of," Elam said as he left.

Gabriel turned back to the council members his expression serious. "It's interesting how you asked for my input on this matter, but you totally undermine my authority by releasing Zion, the soldier!"

"Myka—" Zesha was cut off.

"Myka—" said Gabriel, angry now. "She is making a decision out of emotions. Myka has been through so much; she's not thinking straight. He's my prisoner, not hers. Because of Assam, Zion's friend, the enemy was warned and had a chance to escape to the south. He just made our job harder in the future."

"Zion assured us he is not a part of what Assam did," Calvin said. "And we believe him."

"You need to accept our decision," Zesha added. He watched as Gabriel left the room without saying another word.

~*~

"Zion, they released you," Myka said, all excited. She was trying to stand up at the edge of bed.

"Thanks to you," Zion responded. "Don't get up." He gestured with his hands and then grabbed her under her arms to steady her. He felt awkward so close to her. He slowly put his arms around her and felt her do the same. He heard her as she wept quietly. "What's wrong?"

"I'm just happy they released you," Myka lied unable to share the real reason she was emotional. She regained her composure and dropped her arms from Zion's shoulders. "I still can't believe Gabriel arrested you."

"I didn't know Assam was planning to escape and warn the enemy," Zion said. "Gabriel thinks I was in on it."

"Who cares what he thinks?" Myka added. "You're free now. That's all that matters."

"You have to be excited. All you have worked for your whole life is happening tomorrow. The Children of Light have taken back the Kingdom, and King Ezra will be established as its ruler."

"I am," Myka said. "The Light of the Word was faithful. He fulfilled all His promises."

"There's the smile I love to see," Zion said. He sat next to her with his arm around her. She leaned against his shoulder, nervous but excited about the reunion the next day.

~*~

Lot was the last to reach the top of the eastern cut. Doubled over with his hands on his knees, he took a deep breath. He looked up to see Dara and Jared smiling at him.

"Are you all right?" Dara asked. She tried to contain her laughter.

"I'm fine. Ha, ha," Lot answered. He walked over and stood next to Ezra, whose mind was somewhere else as he looked over the valley of Thanoton.

"Are you ready King Ezra?" Lot asked. He was happy to finally meet the Three Witnesses. In the short time they had been together, they had become fast friends.

"I'm ready," Ezra answered. "I'm just thinking about what I will say to the people this afternoon."

"I'm sure the Whisperer will give you the right words when it comes time to speak, Ezra. I mean, King Ezra," Jared said. He had to switch gears from Ezra being his best friend to his king.

"Here comes Gabriel and a platoon of men," said Marcus, as he looked out his scope.

"Just think, Jared," Dara said all excited, "within an hour, you will see pretty Myka."

"I can't wait," Jared said, almost to himself. He ignored Dara's look.

"Remember everyone the order in which we travel to Thanoton. First, it will be Gabriel and his platoon in the lead, followed by King Ezra, Jared, and Dara, surrounded by his security detail. Marcus and his men will bring up the rear. When we get there, Ezra will mount the stage placed in the market square, and the inauguration will begin. Does anyone have any questions?"

"None," Lot heard from several people.

"Gabriel is waving us down," Marcus said. He put away his scope.

"Let's go," said the King

The group led their way down the eastern cut to link up with Gabriel, then on to the palace. As Ezra rode, he thought back to all that everyone had been through to make this happen—the sacrifices and lives lost. It had been a thousand years since the Children of Light ruled Thanoton.

Ezra knew it was still incomplete with the Children of Darkness in control of the south. For now, they had regained control of Thanoton. Again, the Light of the Word would be openly proclaimed and worshipped. It would be only a matter of time before they would overthrow the south and rid it of evil. Setting the slaves in the south free would be Ezra's highest priority. He resolved in prayer not to rest content until all of Thanoton unified in their commitment to the Light of the Word.

Ezra could see and hear the people cheering, long before he reached the city. They were lined up on both sides of the road. He marveled how different the city looked in the bright sunshine. He had never seen Thanoton in the light. His whole life, it had been pitch black and overcast.

"King-King-King," Ezra heard as they approached the platform in the center of the market square, surrounded by an excited crowd. The market square was packed. They had to squeeze through to get to the platform.

"King Ezra, Dara, and Jared," Gabriel called out over the noise. "Zesha wants you up on the platform."

"King Ezra," Zesha greeted. He spoke as loud as he could. "I will speak first, and then give you the platform to speak. That is if they will give us a chance."

Ezra laughed and relaxed. He felt the joy all the people were expressing that day.

"Myka!" Jared shouted. He ran over to greet her as she was lifted up to the platform in a chair. No longer shy, he kneeled down and gave her a hug. "I've dreamt of this day."

"Jared, I never thought this day would come either," Myka replied. She immediately felt guilty and decided the truth would be best. "I really need to talk to you alone, Jared."

"Sure," Jared answered. "It looks like the ceremony is about to start." He gave her another hug and a kiss on the cheek. She was self-conscious and looked around to find Zion. He had watched the whole thing. Zion looked hurt.

Myka slightly pushed herself away from Jared, and he released her but held on to her hand. Myka tried to let go, but he smiled and grabbed it again. She found Zion and tried to gesture that things weren't like it seemed. He shook his head, turned around, and walked away. She lost him in the crowd.

"People of Thanoton," Zesha shouted. He stood behind the podium with his arms out to gain their attention. He waited for the crowd to quiet down. "Today we officially establish the Kingdom for the Light of the Word. It was a thousand years ago when the Children of Darkness overthrew the Children of Light and banned the *Book of Prophesies*. During that time, all Truth was lost, and darkness crept in until there was no light. All this happened because we grew complacent in our personal lives and society. We allowed things in that destroyed our faith. In spite of our disobedience, the Light of the Word had people and organizations working to regain the Kingdom for the Children of Light." Zesha paused to look behind him at the Three Witnesses.

Zesha continued, "'One thousand years ago, the last prophet, prophesied before he was martyred. *The whisperer will come and empower three witnesses that will make manifest the works of darkness and destroy it, and deliver my people from the grip of darkness to the freedom found in the light.* Today we anoint King Ezra and his two advisors, Dara and Jared,"' he said. Turning around, he presented them, "The Three Witnesses!"

Ezra approached the podium. He motioned with his head for Jared and Dara to join him. He waited for the crowd to quiet. Ezra studied the people until he found his father, Asa and his grandfather, Labin. He waved and fought back the tears in his own eyes, as he watched his father wipe his own. It was quiet, and all eyes were on him.

Woosh! Suddenly, a breeze rushed through the crowd. People gasped as they felt the presence of the Whisperer and the reality of the Light of the Word. Joy and peace filled their souls. They directed their attention back to Ezra.

Ezra smiled at Dara and Jared. "The Elders in Alethia trained and commissioned us to be your leaders. We are not like the leaders you are accustomed to, but leaders submitted to the Light of the Word. We will faithfully carry out His perfect will by being a servant to all. As King, along with my two advisors Dara and Jared, we promise to be faithful to the *Book of Prophesies* as we carry out our duties. One of our priorities is to teach what is written in the *Book of Prophesies* and make sure every institution in Thanoton is guided by it. We are not finished. We must remember this. As long as the enemy controls the southern areas where slavery is condoned, we must not rest day or night until they, too, are set free. What we have begun here is just a start. I will outline the steps we must take as a people to establish Thanoton as a place that glorifies our Lord. First, let us begin with prayer. Corporate prayer will unite us by faith in the Light of the Word. Let's bow our heads and kneel. We need to humble ourselves before our true King—our Lord and Savior, the Light of the Word."

Myka's mind wandered as Ezra prayed. With her head bowed, she tried scanning the crowd to find Zion. She prayed Zion would not do anything rash like he was prone to do. Myka hoped she would have the chance to explain to Zion and Jared what was in her heart.

~*~

An enemy soldier at an observation point on the southern border spotted someone. He was trying to sneak past the checkpoint occupied by the Children of Light to get to the border. "There is a soldier trying to escape and get to us," he cried down to the southern gate."

"Cover him when he gets out in the open," the guard said below. "We'll be ready to open the gate for him to come in."

The soldier watched from above as this soldier ran, without opposition, to the southern gate. "Open the gate," he yelled down.

"I'm Zion," the soldier called out, as he approached the southern gate. He had his hands up. "I was a prisoner of our enemy, and now I have escaped. Let me in."

"Come on in, Zion," they said, slapping him on the back and welcoming him.

––––––––––––––

"Go ye therefore, and teach all nations, baptizing them in the name of the Father, and of the Son, and of the Holy Ghost: Teaching them to observe all things whatsoever I have commanded you: and, lo, I am with you always, even unto the end of the world. Amen." Matthew 28:19-20

Then spake Jesus again unto them, saying, "I am the light of the world: he that followeth me shall not walk in darkness, but shall have the light of life." John 8:12